*Acclaim for* Smith, *"a superb performance by one of Canada's great story tellers"*

"Undoubtedly, this is one of the finest pieces of Canadian fiction ever written! . . . It somehow grasps the very soul of Canada."
*St. Catharines Standard*

". . . wonderful stories by a master story-teller . . . [they] live in your mind long after the book has been put down."
*London Free Press*

"Paul St. Pierre relays these stories beautifully, in the language of the people and places he describes, the kind of vivid language that provides literature the nourishment it needs."
*New York Times Book Review*

"Paul St. Pierre is one of Canada's great story tellers . . . There are so few masters of true humor that [he] deserves a special award for giving us so much pleasure. I laughed out loud when I wasn't crying."
Edith Iglauer, writer for *The New Yorker*

". . . some of the most spirited characters found in Canadian literature."
*Ottawa Citizen*

"Picking a favorite is hard when so many of these warm, unsentimental tales leave you laughing out loud."
*Publishers Weekly*

# SMITH AND OTHER EVENTS

# SMITH
# AND OTHER
# EVENTS
TALES of the CHILCOTIN

## PAUL ST. PIERRE

University of Oklahoma Press : Norman

ISBN 0-8061-2677-9

Oklahoma Paperbacks edition published 1994 by the University
of Oklahoma Press, Norman, Publishing Division of the
University, by special arrangement with Douglas & McIntyre,
1615 Venables Street, Vancouver, British Columbia V5L 2Hl.
First published in 1983 by Doubleday Canada Limited,
Toronto, Ontario. Copyright © 1983, 1985 by Paul St. Pierre.

1 2 3 4 5 6 7 8 9 10

Design by Irene Carefoot
Typeset by Type Master Graphics
Printed and bound in Canada by D. W. Friesen & Sons Ltd.

This book is dedicated to my wife, Melanie.

# PREFACE

A CURRENT ISSUE of the twice-weekly *Tribune of Williams Lake* carries the headline: RANCHERS END GROUP AS FENCE PROTEST. I regret not attending that meeting. It must have been a dandy.

Forestry Department, which controls grazing on Crown lands, had apparently determined to build a new drift fence to control cattle on the range near Riske Creek. The District Forester and other government men had addressed the Riske Creek Stockbreeder's Association and had produced many large studies and statistics. The audience was unmoved. The ranchers' position was that the drift fence was a waste of the British Columbia taxpayers' money, that it was being built of the wrong materials in the wrong place for the wrong reasons and that finally, and above all, the last thing in this world they needed was help from their goddamed government. Seeking some way to register their displeasure, they chose to disband Riske Creek Stockbreeders' Association. The *Tribune* reporter calls the discussions heated.

At first glance, a familiar account of the usual. At second glance, however, one catches the date of that final meeting of the Riske Creek Stockbreeders' Association. May 17, 1938. The story was one of a series of reports taken from the newspaper's back files which were being run to mark the Silver Jubilee of the incorporation of Williams Lake.

This has reassured me about this book. The stories told here are set in the late forties and fifties. One cannot write about those days without a nagging fear that the material is too dated for readers of the eighties. The Chilcotin country itself has changed since then. In some areas the oil and gas lamps of the fifties have been replaced by B.C. Hydro lines and monthly billings. Many of the roads are now passable to ordinary cars, even when it rains. Also, by the eighties, debasement of the currency has proceeded so far that figures from the less diluted currency of the fifties seem absurd. Who can now remember when a ten-dollar bill was a yard long? Is there anything here which is current?

I think so because, reading of the wrathy meeting at Riske Creek in 1938, I recognize that this will be duplicated sometime during the eighties at another such meeting. The roads and the dollar values may have changed, but the people haven't.

I am reminded also that wherever I have met him — in Chilcotin, in the Kamloops country, on the Canadian prairies, in the American West or on the highlands of Chihuahua in Mexico — the rancher is always recognizable for the same attitudes, the same mannerisms, the same virtues and the same damned old foolishness. Neither do these people appear any differently in accounts of them written from the last century. However one may catalogue their faults, there is one of which they are not guilty. They have never been trendy. Consistently, they have marched to the beat of a different drum. A lot of the time they won't march at all.

As for the Indians, among whom the changes since the fifties have been much more profound, I recognize that their greatest stories are yet to be told by themselves. I have done no more than try to see them as they were seen by the whites of those years.

It may be that some residents of Chilcotin and Cariboo will think they recognize events or people in these stories. I would be ashamed of myself if they didn't. But let it be clearly said that however much may be drawn from real life, all the characters in these pages are fictitious. Except for one or two historic personages, there is no attempt to portray real persons, living or dead.

I have exercised the prerogative of the fiction writer, which is to try to tell the truth with a lot of lies. For instance, it is true that there is a Lakeview Hotel. It is not true that the owner/manager, during the fifties, threatened to evict a guest who declined to join a drinking party. That was Benny Abbott of the Maple Leaf Hotel.

There is no place called Namko. That name is fictional. Almost all the other place names are real, for the reason that the real names are so much better than imagination can produce, but they are names borrowed from all over the map.

Half of the stories here appeared originally on the Canadian Broadcasting Corporation national television series, "Cariboo Country." It could have been called "Chilcotin Country," but in those days the name Chilcotin was so little known that some people might have thought it was something to eat. To Phil Keatley, the producer of most of the "Cariboo Country" series, to the actors and to the technicians, I express belated thanks. Their equipment was crude and their budget comically low, but they gave a far truer rendering than Hollywood did later.

This book was written for the very best of reasons—to make money—but there is also some admiration and, I guess, love in it too. If it rings untrue the blame is mine, not that of many people who gave me advice. So I do not name any of those helpers but I say to them, here, thank you. In any case, to name some would be to miss others and I would not want to do that.

However, there was one encouragement which came from a stranger, that must be acknowledged. He was a Chilcotin of the older generation. He and I were occupying a fence rail at a jackpot rodeo. English was a second language for this man. His formal education—no fault of his—was barely adequate for life in the twenties.

"I read that book you got 'Smith's Quarter Horse,'" he said. I waited, apprehensive. He took plenty of time. Finally he said, "You come pretty close."

If this one comes pretty close, I am gratified.

# CONTENTS

# SMITH AND OTHER EVENTS

# OL ANTOINE'S
# WOODEN OVERCOAT

THE NEWS OF OL ANTOINE'S death came to the Namko Country at the end of a soft summer day and interrupted the celebration of a famous victory by Namko's Cattlemen's Association. Death and glory commonly come together, the one factual, the other no more than an exhalation of the human spirit and intangible as the breath of God. But in Namko a familiar epic of mankind could be played out in a fashion not known elsewhere. In Namko, death and the glory were dissociated, one from the other. They began as no more than coincidence. They became enmeshed only because nature so often imitates art.

As for the glorious victory, it was, by global standards, a small one, suitable to the rural poor. It involved a new federal/provincial program for public uplift called the Agricultural and Rural Development Act. Here and there across the land, it had succeeded in draining a swamp or two.

In that year Namko's entire economy was a swamp. The winter had been cold beyond any where the memory of man runs. Spring had come one step forward two steps back, so that for much of it the country was glazed in ice. Neither cows nor horses could rustle through the crust and those that had exhausted the hay stacks starved. Even the moose, weakened by hunger and cold, began dying during that long and reluctant spring. The new sun nourished only the ticks in their fur. When Smith moved his horses to his Spring Turnout, a valley bottom where the new grass first appeared each year, he took five days for a two-day drive because they were too weak for more than a lank, slow shuffle and some kept falling. ''It wasn't a drive,'' he said. ''It was more like escorting some old ladies across a street. To the hospital.''

In that year the price of beef fell, the price of furs fell and taxes, as ever, rose.

Hunger, despair and death were shared by all, men and animals. The story of their collective miseries coursed back and forth across the wide plateau.

In a valley not far from the Namko ranges, one of Chilcotin's better men did not winter in that year. He was a quiet, gentle soul who, ranching two hundred head of breeding stock, had been able for five years to pay board for a mongoloid daughter in a Vancouver nursing home. In that winter, broke, he had to bring her home. By Christmas, he was no longer able to endure what he perceived to be the reproach of her pale and vacant eyes, so he poked his 30-30 into his mouth and blew his head away.

Some echo of this anguish reached the great world outside the realms of the cattlemen and there was a vague public sentiment that help should be rendered them. The help, naturally enough, did not materialize until the following summer.

By that time there was lots of grass, lots of hay and more than one rancher had forgotten how cold and hungry he had been a few months before. However when help did come it was of a spectacular nature, so much so that a special summer meeting of the Cattlemen's Association was invoked to hear an announcement by the government men.

There, without preliminary discussion, without time to consider and without having asked for anything, they were informed that Namko was to become an ARDA district. There would be a major range improvement program, the draining of wet meadows and the irrigation of dry ones by damming creeks. They would be employed by their governments to do this work, on their own lands, at staggering hourly rates of pay. Being unblessed by any form of local government, they would be required to make no contribution of any kind to the great project. The entire capital cost, half a million dollars no less, would be borne by the federal and provincial governments.

This boon was purveyed to them by a bureaucrat of the mandarin class. It was his misfortune to enjoy a good salary, lifetime tenure and the prospect of a pension larger than he could hope to spend. He therefore had very little understanding of such things as cold, hunger and other troubles of the vulgar sort, and when he rose to speak before the assembled ranchers his manner was that of God letting the fish have water.

He and the clutch of officials who had accompanied him experienced a sudden education. The ranchers responded gravely, softly, even courteously but in a manner totally unexpected. In less than an hour they had publicly debated, found themselves to be of a common mind and voted. They voted an absolute and unequivocal rejection of the offer on the principle that governments knew bugger-all about ranching and were best kept far away from where anything worthwhile was to be done.

"The wages and the investment and the range improvements sound nice," as Larsen put it, "but if we once let government start messing around with our business we will never get rid of the bastards."

To men of the nation's new ruling class, the churlishness of such peasants was beyond comprehension. They tried, politely as they thought, to suggest that such ingratitude was unseemly, but the ranchers retreated into a glassy silence. Despairing, the government men fled in their rented four-wheel drive station wagons, the sleek and shiny vehicles glinting in the sun as they rustled over the narrow, twisting and humped little Namko trail, flying like a wisp of teal which had been shot at and narrowly missed.

The ranchers remained, deeply satisfied with whatever it was they had accomplished. The whole matter had come to them unbidden and had been disposed of by instinct rather than by rational thought, but they were conscious, nevertheless, that they had nailed a flag to a mast while the cannon shot flew thickly about their ears.

Suffused in the rich brew of righteousness, which was further enriched in that their wives were berating them for their decision, they decided to tarry a day at the centre of Namko. Abandoning all the duties of riding, haying and fence building they threw up a little tent city beside the small river. The women found food and fry pans, the men found whisky, both familiar miracles at such times. The women raised tents, sent their children for water and cooked. The men sat around, drank whisky and talked about things that really mattered. Darkness pooled in the bottom of the shallow valley, filled it and crept up over the hills to overwhelm the red fire of a long sunset as the stars, one by one, came out to watch over the campfires. It was at times like these that they knew they were blessed among all men.

There was nothing in the manner of Young Alexander's arrival in the camp which gave warning of the news about Ol Antoine. Young Alexander, who was old enough that most men had forgotten who the Old Alexander was, was a frequent visitor at the ranch houses. He had cowboyed across most of the country for twenty years or more and still hired out occasionally in the pleasanter months of summer and autumn. He lived apart from the Reserve, keeping a tent and a couple of horses on the Behind Meadow most of the year and retreating to the cabin of one or another relative on the Reserve only in the bitterest weather of winter.

The men at the fire heard the tap of his horse's feet on the dirt road, looked into the black shadows under the pines and watched the shape of the horse emerge from among the trees. When the rider was close enough that they could hear the creak of his saddle, Young Alexander spoke. "Hello this place."

"It's Young Alexander, en't it?" said Larsen.

Young Alexander did not answer.

He dismounted at a tree fifteen feet from the fire, dallied the lines loosely on the saddle horn, tied a halter rope long enough to allow the animal to feed at its feet and walked over to where the three men sat on a deadfall log.

"We just ate, but there's more," said Larsen. Although the Indian did not answer his silence was consent. "Got some more grub, Margaret?"

Margaret Larsen emerged from the lean-to and began to rustle meat for frying and a pan to do it in.

"Here, Alec," said Morton, producing a bottle, "something that will make a better rancher out of you."

Morton and Alec had a drink together the odd time.

They had developed a ritual for this, and in that country rituals were cherished, particularly homemade ones. Morton would pass the bottle, holding it at the heel and Alec would grasp it with an exaggerated firmness—a recognition that Morton had been in the country long enough to have become familiar with the ancient Indian style of saying thank you.

Instead of grasping the bottle in the usual style, Young Alexander held his hand out, palm forward.

"What's got into you," said Morton.

Young Alexander sat on the log, crossed his arms on his knees and looked at the flames.

"Well have some coffee while you're waiting for grub," said Larsen. He poured a cup from the billycan.

The man took it and drank. He would, they knew, talk when he was ready. It he did not, it meant that he had nothing to say, and that, too, should be a man's privilege.

He spoke just before the other three were about to pick up the thread of a conversation they had dropped.

"I guess you don't hear about that thing on the Reserve," he said.

"Ain't none of us been over there today, I don't think," said Larsen.

"Not so good," said Young Alexander.

He rolled a cigarette and lit it.

"Peoples feel bad," he said. He paused again. "Ol Antoine, he's dead in that place Williams Lek."

"Well I'll be a go to hell," said Larsen.

"You maybe got it wrong," said Smith. "Ol Antoine wasn't sick. He just went to hospital to have them look at his eyes. New glasses or something."

"That's all it is," said the Indian. "But he gets in that place and he dies."

"I'll be damned," said Smith. "You know, he had talked about dying for so long I figured he was never gonna do it, that he was gonna talk it out instead."

"Same like us," said Young Alexander. "We figure there's always gonna be an Ol Antoine this place. We all got to think that way."

"The closest thing to a national monument we ever had in Namko I guess," said Morton. He produced a bottle again. "Come on. Let's all have a drink to him. He was a good old man."

This time Young Alexander joined as they drank, passing the bottle hand to hand.

"Well look at it this way," said Larsen. "There is no reason people should feel bad. He lived a long time and I guess he went quick and easy. People don't have to feel bad about that, Alec."

"It's not same thing. The peoples feel bad because they bury Ol Antoine at Williams Lek."

"He's buried already!"

"No. Not now. Little time, pretty soon, they bury him at Williams Lek."

Through Margaret, who had been standing within earshot, the news spread around the half dozen camps on the flat beside the river and others came up to the fire. There was general discussion which was slow and often confusing. Young Alexander was known as a man who said very little in Chilcotin and English came a poor second, devoid of tense and sometimes of sense. The story was slow in taking final shape, as had been the Indian and his horse emerging from the darkness, but in time it fleshed out and was tangible and clear. Ol Antoine was to go to a pauper's grave in Williams Lake Cemetery.

The story delivered, Young Alexander departed with his horse, carrying his message to others of the Namko band who, this night, would be camped on meadows where they were cutting hay on contract.

"Potters' field for that old man," said Morton. "What do you think of that?"

"I don't know that it makes much difference once you're dead," said Smith. "But of course I have never been much for funerals. Your funeral is just where people who never knew you give you a bunch of flowers that you can't smell."

"But it does make a difference," said Frenchie, who had now joined them. "I guess the band would feel bad. I'd feel bad."

"Damn right," said Larsen. "He should be buried here on the Reserve."

"Yes," said his wife, "along with all the others. Two sticks nailed together for a cross and his name written in pencil on the wood."

"You got that tone in your voice," said Larsen to her.

"When were any of you last in that graveyard?" she said. "There's a pine box a few feet down in the gravel and on top there's just what I said. Sticks with pencil writing on them and the marks bleach out in the sun and soon the only identification of who lies down there is in the mind of somebody who's still alive up here."

"That ain't our fault," he said.

"It's somebody's fault," she said. "When some people have so much in this world and some have so little."

"Alright then," said Smith. "Why can't the Cattlemen's Association bring him back to be buried here?"

"Yes, and get him a good coffin too," said Morton.

The electricity of that heady afternoon meeting had not left them. Instinctively, like a school of fish, they turned to face in a single direction and swam with the purpose lent by powerful instinct. It had always been their style. When they chose not to do something, neither glory, gold nor choirs of angels could move them, either singly or collectively. But on the rare occasion when they were seized with a common purpose they would go through the fire and ice of Norwegian hell to achieve it.

There ensued a series of abrupt command decisions of considerable tactical skill.

Stettler, who was known as a good tracker, was sent to trail Young Alexander through the pines and retrieve him to the camp.

Two men were dispatched to the Namko Hotel and Store and told to summon Arch MacGregor, Honorary Treasurer of the Cattlemen's Association. He was a man often hard to shift but they were instructed to use force if necessary.

Some other Indians from the Reserve had now made their way into the camp and when Larsen declared a formal session of the Cattlemen's Association to be in session they were tacitly included as members pro tem.

Larsen, standing on the tailgate of his pickup truck, presided over the second meeting of that day and it was, like the first, extraordinary for the speed with which it was conducted and the lack of talk involved.

It was moved, seconded and approved by vote that Smith, in company with Young Alexander, would drive Larsen's truck to Williams Lake for the body of Ol Antoine, leaving before the dawn.

Another motion required that Herb, the sometime local mechanic, be snatched from his bed and taken to his log garage near the hotel, there to install by the light of gas lanterns a needed oil gasket in Larsen's truck. It was recognized that force would be needed in this case to overcome Herb's natural misanthropy and laziness but the posse was told not to use it excessively. "Break his arm and he'll be no good for monkey wrenching anyhow," as Morton observed.

There would be a wake for Ol Antoine, and the community's single phone line, if it could be roused from its silence, would be used by a phone committee to alert the rest of Chilcotin to this event.

Since the salmon were running in the big river twenty miles

distant, the main fare would be Chilcotin turkey. Three men were to be dispatched at dawn to dipnet them, two to use the net and one to stand on a nearby hill and watch for a game warden. The Indians would barbecue the turkeys.

Norah and Margaret were to cook bread and dried apricot pies and other foods.

Henry James was to ride, leading a spare saddle horse, across the mountain to fetch the Oblate priest, Father Fitzjames, who was known to be visiting an off-road reserve there.

There were to be drums, dancing and a LaHelle game at the wake and children were to be detailed to collect masses of wild roses to lay upon the grave.

"As for the price of the coffin, we will use the Cattlemen's Association surplus for it. So moved? Moved. Seconded? Seconded. All in favor? Motion passed. We do have enough, do we Arch?"

"Hell yes," said Arch.

"How much is it?"

Arch pulled a paper from his shirt and read from it. "The surplus as of today is one thousand, two hundred and forty-seven dollars and fifty-three cents."

Larsen almost lost his balance on the tailgate.

"Did you say twelve hundred? Twelve hundred dollars!"

Arch read the figures again.

"Impossible," said Smith.

"I thought it was about three hundred dollars," said Larsen.

"You forget," said Arch, "you guys were your own bootleggers at this year's Stampede. You brought a bunch of booze in on the stage and I sold it to you a bottle at a time."

"But that was to be at cost," said Larsen.

"At cost plus one percent for handling," said Arch.

"And at one percent it amounted to a thousand dollars?"

"One percent profit," said Arch. "Buy for one dollar, sell for two dollars. One percent."

Silence overtook them all. Men scratched their back hair, peered at their boots, clutched their belt buckles. It had indeed been a day of shock and surprise. Finally all the faces, the white and the brown, turned toward Larsen. They did not speak to him. They looked at him. They granted him the lonely weight of command.

He may have remembered the rift in the ranks of the association a few years previously when an entire afternoon had been spent debating the unauthorized spending of twenty-five dollars on a new gate at the stampede grounds, a bitter battle which had ended in Frenchie resigning the presidency. But the past is not master of the present and Larsen trusted to instinct, which prompted him well.

"Well that's good," he said. "Smith, you got enough to buy a good one."

"That's what we voted," said Morton.

"If necessary, spend it all," said Larsen. "Just be sure you get one with some style."

"Something that measures up to the dignity of the Namko Cattlemen's Association," said Smith.

"Agreed," they all said.

Later, the meeting ending and the crowd dispersing, Morton drew Larsen aside and said, "Imagine, the government offering us money when we had all that of our own."

"There is no understanding governments," Larsen said.

By dawn, Herb had infused some new life and vigor into Larsen's truck, although it still spit clear blue smoke from the exhaust. Also the shocks had given up, the engine sounded like a bagful of hammers and steering it, as Smith said, was like leading a poodle on a leash.

With a dedication unusual of him he ground steadily east into Williams Lake, pausing not to visit and stopping not to talk for he knew that it was in such practices that the gods stole time from mankind. When sleepiness overtook him near the Sheep Creek Hill switchbacks, he rolled the truck into the pines and he and Young Alexander slept a few hours, crouched in the cab.

They rumbled into the Lake at 3 A.M. Smith left Young Alexander at the Holding Grounds above the town. He might sleep some more there and in the morning, make his way into the town and begin, even if not complete, the process of claiming Ol Antoine's body.

Smith drove north to Prince George, a town which served as bellybutton for the province of British Columbia. Prince had been no more than a fur-trade post for most of its life, but the Pacific Great Eastern Railway had now, after more than a quarter of a century of political convulsions, crept into the place and met the

Canadian National Railway line. Lumber and pulp mills were being built and the main street had stores with large plate-glass windows and such exotic stock as lawn mowers, plate-glass coffee tables, wall-to-wall carpeting—all the stuff of the new prosperity in the great national suburbia. Smith was unshaven, the crotch of his jeans was torn and he was dirtier than six pet coons. As so often in these places, he felt alien and unwanted.

Having ten dollars of his own, he decided to spend five of them on a new shirt. It might, he felt, offset the torn jeans. The first clothing store he encountered was a new one, built to look like an old English one, and the clerk, who aspired to old English ways, enquired, ''What is your pleasure, sir?''

''Fucking and shooting pheasants,'' said Smith. ''But what I came here for was to buy a shirt.''

The conversation was all downhill from that point, but Smith walked out wearing a new shirt. He sensed, however, that it wasn't doing much for him. He was still dirty, and had enough smell under his armpits to knock a dog off a gutwagon.

Matters went no better at the undertaking parlor. There were, Smith observed, a lot of soft-handed people with expensive clothes in this country now.

''An Indian?'' said the salesman. ''You don't have to buy coffins for Indians. The Indian Department supplies them.''

Smith had been doing his best to try to forget that fact, so it enraged him to hear it from a stranger. He did not, however, let that emotion out where it could be seen and shot at, but spoke mildly. ''In our country we take care of our own people,'' he said.

He was wandering through the display and paused beside a box of shining oak and satin. ''What's this one?''

''It's excellent. One of the best.''

''I mean, how much?''

''It's five hundred dollars.''

This, by coincidence, was what Smith had paid two years before to buy a hay meadow. He had borrowed from the bank for it and had been two years in the repayment.

He fingered the satin.

"I dunno," he said, "there's something kind of sleazy about it."

He moved on, tapping wood, fingering bronze handles and expressing vague dissatisfaction until he reached the one which he had spotted the first moment he entered the showroom. "Now that," he said, "is as good a wooden overcoat as I've seen in your place."

"It's twelve hundred dollars."

"Well now, it just might be worth that. Silver handles?"

"Silver handles, Philippine mahogany and pure silk. I'm sorry sir, it's taken."

"Taken, you say. Now that's a pity."

"You may have heard that Arvid Green has passed on."

"I have heard of Arvid Green," said Smith. All the country had heard of Mr. Green. When middle-aged, he had made a million dollars in real estate speculation during the Grand Trunk construction boom. He had devoted the rest of his life to preventing fellow citizens from taking a nickel of it away from him. "He's rich, ain't he?" said Smith.

"He was very well-to-do. I'm expecting the family this morning."

"Expecting them? I thought they had already bought it."

"They will buy it, you can be assured."

"You mean, there is nothing signed? No down payment?"

"No. There is, as you put it, no down payment from the estate."

"Then as I understand the law, it is for sale," said Smith. He reached into his hip pocket. He had been supplied the association's surplus in cash, from Arch MacGregor's tin strongbox, a thick mound of twenties and an occasional fifty. "We'll take it," he said.

"Is this some kind of joke?"

Smith kept counting, licking his fingers to separate old bills that stuck. "The guy who died didn't think so. Here, you can count it. Twelve hundred. I'll come around for it in an hour and rope it on the back of the pickup."

He left the mound of money on the stand where the king of all wooden overcoats stood. He started to the door, pausing only to turn and say, in the gentlest of tones, ''When Arvid Green's people come in, you can tell them that this coffin was bought by the Namko Cattlemen's Association. The Namko Cattlemen's Association. Tell them we had an old Indian we needed to bury.''

If the others, Smith thought, were doing their jobs as well as he was, there was going to be a first-class funeral in Namko.

Oddly enough, others were. Frequently in Namko elaborate community plans were erected which collapsed almost as quickly. People forgot their tasks or did the wrong ones twice, or the participants began to bicker among themselves. In the funeral of Ol Antoine, there was to be none of that disarray.

By the evening of the day following Smith's departure the grave had been dug by Indians at the Reserve and a sturdy wooden cross made with Ol Antoine's name carved deep in the yellow pine, so deep that wind, sun and weather might not erase it for a century or more.

The catching of the salmon was proceeding. Henry James had shot a small doe deer and this meat was being given a fast, hard smoke at Frenchie's smokehouse. Mountains of bread and cakes were being baked. There would be food for all.

On the Reserve, where poverty had been general and complete for years, the people were making the same discovery—that there are always riches to be found when giving is required. Stocks of smoked trout emerged. So did many gallon jars of sopallillie, which would give a touch of grandeur to the eating. Sopallillie, made from berries, was a dark, frothy concoction, nonalcoholic, astringent and unique. As with blue cheese, oolichan oil and sometimes sex, people had to acquire a taste for sopallillie, but to those who had—most of the Indians and a few of the old-timers among the whites—it occupied a reserved space in the territory of heaven.

Father Fitzjames had been found in the remote camp to the north and was riding back to Namko across the mountains.

''At this rate,'' said Arch MacGregor, ''not only is the funeral going to be held on the day we said, it is going to go off at the hour we said.''

''Do not speak well of the day until the sun has set,'' said Frenchie's Wife.

"What could go wrong?" said Frenchie.

She did not answer.

What could go wrong went wrong twenty thousand feet above their heads.

As happened from time to time during Chilcotin summers, there had been a pooling of hot, moist air on the land behind the Coast Range. It made for a sticky heat, but pleasant scenery. For days, each noon saw small and innocent puffs of cumulus clouds forming to give some pattern to a sky which would otherwise have been a solid stretch of uninteresting blue.

On the third day, all this was in convulsions. Out of the Pacific, impelled by the whimsical forces which meteorologists can never fully comprehend, a flow of cold air from the Alaskan Coast turned sharply east and drove across the crests of the Coast Range. So rapidly did it move that the cold air rode over the top of the warm, moist air in Chilcotin. Just east of the range, the system stalled. The result was a cauldron. Cold, heavy air plunged earthward; moist, warm air burst upward. The sky turned black. Fierce and erratic winds broke trees and flattened haystacks. Thunderhead clouds rose twenty-five and thirty thousand feet into the far skies. Hail as large as hens' eggs pounded the ground and then rains came, an inch an hour and more, such rain as the land had not seen for a year, five years, maybe more. Morton Dilloughboy was to later testify that in that rain he had to hold his pipe in his mouth upside down that he did not drown.

The single phone line to Williams Lake went down, a full half mile of it, together with the score of trees to which it was nailed. This did not much matter, since the lines had been dead for days from causes unknown. It did, however, ensure that days more would elapse before Namko might again speak to an uncaring world outside.

By noon on the day set for the funeral, when Smith had been expected to arrive, all creeks had risen dangerously and one a few miles from Namko, called the Lettergo Gallagher, was tearing at the foundations of its bridge.

Alarmed by reports that the one bridge on the road might go out, Larsen led a party of men to it. If there was one place where Smith might be stopped by such a storm, the Lettergo it seemed to be.

The storm was leaving and making its way eastward as they

arrived. The hammer of the rain stopped beating, the winds turned playful. But the Lettergo continued to rise.

The bridge, a few stout logs bound by cables and crossed by thick planks, stood well above the boil of the water but each end rested on only a flimsy fretwork of log cribbing. When they arrived, the cribbing had begun to break loose. Within half an hour it was gone and so was the gravel bank and the end of the little bridge dropped into the creek which frothed white against it and, plank by plank, ate it for breakfast. Sodden, their clothes now steaming in the rapidly drying air, the little band solemnly watched it go.

"We could of saved it if we had a tractor," said Frenchie.

"And if we'd packed a ham sandwich, we could call it a picnic," said Morton. "What the hell's the use of talking about tractors."

"All is well," said Larsen, whose lips and hands were blue and body shivering. "We will ferry Smith and the coffin across it."

"A boat will go half a mile downstream in that current," said Morton.

"So will we, to meet it," said Larsen.

"I don't think Smith he likes water much," said Jim Dan.

"He will have to learn to like it today, fast," said Larsen.

Jim Dan was given a truck and sent back to the Reserve for a rowboat. The ferry party waited, warming themselves at a bonfire and speculating on how many fallen trees might lie on the Chilcotin road beyond their vision, trees which Smith would have to beavertail his way through with the dull axe stowed in the Larsen truck.

Jim Dan came back without the boat.

"He ain't here, Smith," said Jim.

"We know goddam well he ain't here," said Larsen. "Where is the boat?"

"I said he ain't here," said the Indian.

"Shut up a minute, Ken," said Morton. "Jim. Where is he? Smith."

Jim pointed to a meadow they could not see through the trees. "My kid, he's riding saddle horse, he finds Smith on Wild Horse Meadow. He's stuck that place."

"He's taken Old Road," said Larsen. "Why in hell would he go that way?"

"Why would he come this way," said Morton, "to a washed-out bridge."

"How could he know it was washed out?"

"Let's go see him. We can ask."

Larsen swore again and kicked the fire with his boots, driving sparks and flames about them.

"If he's on the Wild Horse, he must of forded the creek before she boiled up," said Morton.

When Larsen did not reply he continued, "Ken, don't get sore because you can't have your own particular kind of rescue operation. You just got your mind too set on this ferry boat operation. We will get him out of Wild Horse instead of fishing him and the coffin out of this creek. One way is as good as another."

"I s'pose you're right. Okay. We will hike it, cross-country, and push him out."

"Might be best s'pose we take this truck," said Jim.

"And stick two trucks instead of one? There is hardly anything left of Old Road and what there is will be all blowdowns today." Larsen, resuming the command he had almost relinquished, spoke with the firmness natural to generals. "We walk it, I say, and push him. Jim here could push him out all by himself if he had to. The rest of us could just stand and watch him."

Jim smiled. "Hiyu push, I think maybe," he said. He was a big man, two yards high, two hundred and twenty-five pounds of steely bones and rippling muscles. People in the Namko Country were grateful that he had been born good-natured.

"Hiyu walk," said Morton.

They walked to Old Road. Old Road had been cut by the storekeeper who preceded Arch at Namko. In 1935, claiming the distinction of the first man to drive a gas powered vehicle to Namko, he had cut a strange trail through the meadows and forests of the western plateau. Traveling by winter, when swamps were frozen, he had brought the machine through by following a series of meadows and hacking out trees in the intervening arms of forest. For several years, he and other men of Namko had tried to make this an all year truck road, but they could never be more than mildly successful because most of the meadows were soft ground. In the forties Old Road had been abandoned to horses, wagons and cattle drives and they had cut the present road along the jack-pine ridges where the base was rocky.

The party made its way slowly, unwillingly, through the pines. None of them were men who fancied walking, holding firm to the belief that walking had been unnecessary since the taming of horses some centuries before. Walking was a low pursuit, fitted only to trappers, prospectors and Englishmen.

The sun broke through as they reached the Wild Horse Meadow and illuminated the steaming yellow grass, the truck and the figure of Smith, who was sitting on the tailgate, smoking a cigarette. A deceptively placid scene, it worsened as the rescue party drew nearer. The truck sat low, its belly to the grass. Two lines of grey mud, hubcap deep, were traced behind the wheels but to the front there was none. Smith was in the loonshit.

Loonshit was a gumbo; it was undetectable when dry but when thoroughly soaked in water a patch of it took on the character of molasses mixed with glue. All men encountered loonshit sooner or later in that country and all but the strongest wept when they did.

So came the six of them to the silent Smith, the battered, dirty old truck and the grey slime. They stood silently beside it. Frenchie was the first to speak.

"Beautiful," he said. "Absolutely beautiful."

"It is a dandy," said Morton.

And Larsen agreed that Smith could not have done better. They were looking at the coffin, wedged and bound between two bales of hay.

"Philippine mahogany," said Smith. "The heartwood. That's why it's so red. The old man is gonna go in style."

"You couldn't have done better," said Larsen.

"The handles," said Smith, "you can't see them, but the handles are solid silver."

It was some time before their thoughts turned to the matter of saving the truck.

"How did you get her in a mess like that Smith?" said Larsen.

"To hell with you and the horse you rode in on," said Smith amiably.

"What I want to know is, why did you try this road?"

"I told you," said Morton, "he knew the bridge was out. He's got a sixth sense, Smith."

"That's right," said Smith.

"BS," said Larsen. "You never knew the bridge was out. Why this way?"

"Young Alexander's camp is just up that way. He wanted to get a change of clothes and his horse."

"You're a lunatic," said Larsen.

"I forded the creek, didn't I?"

"Alright. Alright. We will get her out. Although how we pick our way into Namko God only knows."

Smith rose and stretched. "All is well," he said.

"All is not well," said Larsen. "The funeral is pretty soon. What time is it, anyway?"

Nobody had brought a watch. They studied the sun and guessed. They guessed they would be late.

"Hell of a note," said Larsen. "Everybody waiting on us."

"Don't worry," said Smith, "only thing a man has got to worry about in this world is does he go to heaven or does he go to hell."

"Right," shouted Morton, who knew and liked the story. "If he goes to heaven he's got nothing to worry about and if he goes to hell he is so busy snatching sparks out of his ass and shaking hands with all his old friends he ain't got time to worry."

For an hour, they did not have time to worry.

They first rocked the truck, Smith playing gears from forward to reverse with six men pushing. The truck settled deeper and Smith pronounced her firmly high centred and maybe there for the winter. Larsen berated him as defeatist.

They dragged deadfall from the edge of the meadow, jacked the truck high and stuffed the slim logs beneath the wheels. The truck slipped off and spun its wheels again in the loonshit.

All except Smith, who retained his position as truck driver, were caked in mud from elbow to breakfast time. Tempers shortened. At one point Henry James suggested that they remove the coffin to dry grass, lest it be dirtied, and climbed to the back of the truck to loosen ropes. Frenchie leapt like a hungry trout and struck down his arms. "Get your filthy hands off that coffin," he shouted.

"That right, Henry," said Smith. "Clean your hands first."

"I got nothing to clean them in but the loonshit."

"Take off your shirt and use it for mitts," said Larsen.

Henry and others removed their shirts, used them for mitts and the coffin was transferred, more or less unmuddied, to a nearby knoll.

Many theories of leverage were exchanged.

A Spanish Windlass was a project debated at length. It was a crude machine, which could be constructed of jack-pine poles and rope and gave leverage such as could shift large buildings or overturn railway trains, but although everybody knew some other man who had used a Spanish Windlass, none among this company, it seemed, had done so.

They jacked up the truck and packed in twigs, they jacked it up again and applied larger logs and finally, chewing away jack pines with the dull axe, they built a corduroy road beneath it. On each occasion, Larsen insisted that Smith was not spirited in his use of the gas and each time Smith warned, mildly, that the oil in that ancient engine was low and that the faint tick of the loose bearing was plain to his ear.

It culminated in the corduroy road stage of the operation when Larsen, enraged, shouted, "Smith, pour the coal to her. She'll move. Give her gas."

Smith spoke though the open window, gently. "The bearings are gonna go."

"Shut up and put your foot on the floor."

Smith put his foot on the floor. The tick became a pound. The main bearing seized. A piston went, driving out through the engine block. In the quiet hiss of the steam from a dead engine six men put Ol Antoine's wooden overcoat on their muddy shoulders and began packing it down to the funeral at the Stampede Grounds.

"I will call time for you," said Smith. "It helps. Hup. One. Two. Three. Hup. One. Two. Three.

"He was just a little stick of a man. How can he be so heavy?" said Morton.

"Its Philippine mahogany heartwood, that's why it's heavy," said Smith. "Come on you guys, pick it up," he chanted. "LEFT. LEFT. My father got drunk and he LEFT. LEFT. LEFT."

Half way to their destination, two men from the Reserve met them with a half Percheron pack horse. They roped the coffin on a Visalia pack saddle, but nearing the Stampede Grounds, where the ranchers' camps were at one side, the Indian graveyard at the other, they smelt the smoke of barbecue fires and they could sense the anticipation of the people. Somehow it didn't seem right to bring the old man in on a pack horse, so they unlashed the coffin and brought it out of the trees on their shoulders again. They were caked in mud and so weary they staggered, but they, and those who waited for them, knew the glory.

There was time in the day to spare for the burying so, for the time, all rested, content with accomplishments, gratified to find among the growing crowd faces from far places, faces they had not seen for months or years. What rain was to grass, a funeral was to the society of the Chilcotin plateau.

Smith circled the crowd on the Stampede Grounds, exchanging the occasional greeting, abstractedly accepting congratulations on his splendid ride and his taste in the matter of selecting coffins. His thoughts, it was clear, were in some other place.

He found Norah, busiest of all the women, setting up tables in the community hall.

"I thought I'd go over to our camp and clean up," he said.

"Go ahead, she said, "but seems to me you are the only clean one in the bunch. Why ain't you covered in loonshit like the others?"

"I was a driver. A driver is not a swamper. Why don't you come over with me?"

"Come over why? I gotta set up tables."

"Come on. There's lots of people to set up tables."

"What for?"

"Just come on."

He did not lead her to their tent but instead they went up the sidehill which rose at the edge of the grounds.

"Sit down," he said.

She sat.

"I brought us a mickey. Have a pull."

"You know I can't drink that stuff without water."

"Have a pull, I said."

She put the bottle to pursed lips and blew a bubble into it. He took it and drank richly.

"What are you up to Smith?"

"I am having a drink. With my wife."

"There is something funny about this."

He pushed the bottle toward her. She pushed it back.

"There is something funny about you, Smith."

He gestured to the crowd below them with the little bottle. "Ain't that a pretty sight, Norah? You know, whatever is good about people in Chilacootin, a funeral will bring it out."

It was a pretty sight. Blue smoke rose from the salmon barbecue fires. Small Indian children, doubled up on bareback horses, rode proudly over the stampede grounds. Pickup truck engines muttered politely and in the cabs old friends passed bottles clad in the original brown paper wrappings. Somewhere a guitar played the melody of "Red River Valley," a string at a time. The sun, now turned on to full, shone on Ol Antoine's coffin which stood on a trestle table, guarded by gentle Jim Dan that it might not be smudged by the fingerprints of those who would want to touch it.

"Who is in that coffin, Smith?"

He gave a short sigh. "Rocks," he said.

"Rocks. I see. There is rocks in it."

"I know, you are gonna chew out my ass and bark at the hole. Go ahead."

To spite him, she didn't utter a word.

So he walked her around the subject some more, hoping to take some of the kink out of her backbone.

"You know how it is, Norah. Moccasin telegraph is never right. Ol Antoine just had something done for his eyes at the Lake. When I got back from Prince there he was, cheerful as a sparrow with a mouthful of horseshit, waiting for a ride home."

"I see."

"So I come in by Old Road and they went up to Young Alexander's place and pretty soon they'll come down here. I said they wouldn't want to miss the party and they're comin' down soon."

"That was thoughtful of you Smith, to invite them."

"Of course, s'pose I'd had a gun, I could have shot Ol Antoine when I found him. That way everything could have gone according to plan. Is that what I should have done? Stuck to the plan?"

"You crazy little turd. Can't you see what you have done? You have smashed Larsen's truck ..."

"He smashed it last month. I did it this month. We are just even."

"You have brought Father Fitzjames riding all night over the mountain ..."

"There is plenty of baptisms and marriages for him here. His time ain't wasted."

"Shut up. The big thing you have done, your real big accomplishment Smith, you have broke the Namko Cattlemen's Association. Broke them flat, flat, flat."

He waved a hand toward the crowd. "It just didn't seem right to disappoint all them people."

"You could have returned the coffin and got our money back!"

"No, Norah. That is one thing I could not do. It would take too long to explain. Just take my word for it. Nobody in this country would ever have forgiven me if I asked for our money back on that coffin."

She called him a double yoked asshole but, from the way she said it, he could sense that she was just about bucked out for the day.

"Norah," he said. "You and me, we will just sit here a while on this sidehill and watch while Ol Antoine comes down for his funeral. I tell you straight this has the makings of a large and fine day."

She called him a turd again, but this time she was laughing. She took the mickey from his hand and, for the first time, took a good pull of whisky straight.

# DRY STORM

THE DRY STORM came down upon Stettler while he was riding a half-broke, half-crazy half-thoroughbred to Frenchie Bernard's place. It bothered him. More, it frightened him, although he was the only man in the world who knew that. No other man in the Chilcotin Country could have wrapped his mind around the idea of a blow of wind frightening Jack Stettler. They might have been gratified, had they known of that weakness, but above all, they would have been amazed. Stettler was a man who was respected but not liked. He preferred it that way.

His appearance was a provocation to other men. He was built like a lady's wrist watch. He was light boned, slender, with delicate hands and small neat feet. His hair, tight curled, lay close on a small fine head and his features, by some wild toss of genetic dice, were almost a duplicate of those of Alexander of Macedon. Much of the time the face was as immobile as a stone bust of Alexander and the grey eyes as expressionless. When he chose, he could arrange those features into some semblance of ordinary human expression, but it was a bloodless exercise. Morton Dilloughboy once remarked that Stettler's smile reminded him of January moonlight shining on a coffin handle.

He passed among other men as one wary wolf among yapping, frolicsome domestic dogs, vaguely contemptuous but generally indifferent to them, provided they did not step too near. Some men who cannot be broken by long years in prison come out with that quality, a stillness strangely menacing.

When he arrived in the country, cowboys, given to simple thoughts, found him mysterious and therefore disturbing. As with other things of this life which puzzled them, their reaction was to tease. He would not, it seemed, provoke and at first men were amused that Stettler didn't know how to get into a fight. When he did fight they were frightened, because they learned that he didn't know how to end one.

In the tradition of the country, fights were common and casual.

A few blows. A recognition that one man was better than another, today at least. A handshake.

When Stettler fought, as he did three times, the fights were unconscionably long. His first blow would be laid not with a fist but a finger, with which he would mark the spot he intended to hit. Then he would box, remorselessly tapping, tapping at that spot with the tiny hands until a nose would be forever wrecked or an eye blinded. Even in the last agony of a Stettler fight, he would not hit hard enough to knock his man down, that he might walk away. "You could never see from his eyes when he was goin' to hit," said one of the men who was marked for life by Stettler.

Women, too, feared him, for reasons they could not define. Even the whores of Vancouver, to whom he paid occasional visits, came to fear him and wanted their pimps in the room next door while they serviced him.

He was an excellent rancher. His fences were strong, his gates well hung, his water control on the meadows precise to the needs of the grass. He had taken up land a full twenty miles from the Namko post office and built it up largely by himself. The help did not stay long with him. There were few visitors. Indians would not let the sun set upon them on Stettler land. It was reported that older Indians claimed that Stettler turned into a salamander at sundown. This story, however, could never be confirmed by whites for it involved a matter of religion and in that area of man's affairs the Indians followed a simple formula—every sensible man understands religion and no sensible man tries to explain it.

On the day he was to encounter his dry storm, Stettler had wakened uneasy in his lonely cabin. Twice while he was preparing breakfast—rice and two strips of sidemeat—he had walked to the cabin door, opened it and looked over his long home meadow, anticipating that a rider was approaching, not knowing why he should expect that.

Turning to work, which was what he did best, he began to fix his mower but mislaid his tools, turned to mending harness and spiked his hand with the awl. Half a dozen times he scanned the meadow, north and south and found nothing on which to focus his eyes. The morning and early afternoon had passed in dreams half-remembered, in voices not quite heard. There was an ache in his forehead, between and just over his slate grey eyes. He tried to remember if he had awakened with the ache that morning or if it had developed during the day; he found he could not. Failing to add up the simple sum of such a bodily function he uttered his first word of the day. ''Shit,'' he said.

Then and there he decided to ride across to Frenchie's and pick up one of his stray horses. A strange decision, for it was a job that did not need doing that day; stranger still because he was deciding too late, leaving too late and choosing to ride a horse he did not like.

It had taken him half an hour to catch the tall bay gelding and he had then been obliged to longline him in the corral for twenty minutes before he could snub him to the rail and throw the saddle over him. Had he waited ten minutes the horse might have stood for him. Had he saddled and then done no more than turn the horse around once or twice it would have accepted him. Stettler knew this but he did as always, darting into the saddle without a preliminary word or gesture, and then letting the animal unwind beneath him.

The thoroughbred bucked six ways across the yard and toppled one log from the corral fence as it tried to wipe the rider off. It almost somersaulted as it ran through the creek. It cut a foreleg thrashing through the woodpile.

''Bleed you son of a bitch,'' said Stettler, and turned its head west. The horse trembled, sighed and moved off at a jagged trot, and they passed into the dark trees at the meadow's edge on a joyless journey that would, he noted, not end until almost midnight. The day had almost stolen away from him before he had noticed.

The beaten trail led from Stettler's to Smith's. From there another led to the Bernard place. Stettler chose not to use the familiar route. Looking at the fading sun and the line of the high ridge which rose between him and the other ranches, he set the compass of his mind on a direct course to Frenchie's. It might not be quicker but it would work the thoroughbred harder. He was of a mind to work that thoroughbred hard.

When the moon hung fat and yellow over the man and horse the dry storm engulfed them with its irrational anger. The lodgepole pines shifted, stirred, bent and flung off thin dead branches from their black trunks. Standing trees, caught and held upright in the arms of those that were living, moaned and shrieked as they sawed like long fiddle bows on the green timber. The swales of grass patched through the forest were tossed in riptides and, on alkali flats, the dust blew.

Dry storm was Stettler's own name for these winds. To those who had always lived among the mountains they were merely winds. There was nothing strange in them, they being no more than the play of air masses moving rapidly among mountains. They were often gentle, like the katabatic winds which drifted down mountain slopes on summer evenings, bringing cold air from the high country to displace the warmer air in the valley bottoms. Sometimes they were warm, compression having heated the air mass as it was forced through narrow mountain passes. Sometimes, as on this occasion, a front of cold air from the north, commonly called the Arctic front, slashed southward in such a sudden and fitful burst. To Stettler, who had lived on the Atlantic coast and on the prairies, they were unnatural and alarming. Thunder and lightning made storms such as these. There should be pelting rain or snow thick as a Hudson's Bay blanket. Such winds, as he perceived them, contained only half the essential elements, and they were only half-believable.

He had never been able to adapt the process of his reasoning to the storms which blew in this motionless ocean of mountains, storms in which no rain fell, no snow blew and often, as on this night, no black clouds formed. The moon shone amiably through the screaming winds, and stars big as a man's hat were warm and yellow.

Stettler spurred the horse. It jumped as the rowels of the spurs struck and then began to run. The thoroughbred was not a horse built for rough country. Its gallop was a clatter. Often it stumbled. When it broke stride Stettler swore and spurred harder. Both of the horse's legs were bleeding when they came out of the trees into a long flat where the alkali patches shone white as old bones. The horse, startled by some vagrant shadow which the wind was chasing across the grass, turned, almost toppled the rider and began to buck. Stettler lashed both flanks with the long reins, spurred some more and, when the horse seemed almost bucked out, took off his hat and slashed at the ears, back and forth. When it was exhausted he drove it again, headlong, and as he spurred the horse began to sob. One of the ordinary range horses would have sooner or later dropped to a canter, a trot, a walk and in the extreme, stood like a mule, bearing any abuse but refusing to move. But this was a hot-blooded horse. It ran until it broke stride and fell, sending Stettler rolling across the grass.

The man hit the ground on his feet as cats do. He ran back and slashed the horse's face with his hat. The nostrils were large as two moons and blood red. The foam of sweat slid down the shoulders and the flanks. Gasping still, the gelding came to its feet, and instantly Stettler was in the saddle and spurring.

Man and horse moved, batlike, in an erratic pattern through the trees and across moon-washed meadows, the wind shrieking, the horse grunting. Stettler's face was white, his teeth were bared. An apocalyptic horseman of no purpose, he fled from nothing, rode to nowhere, and the demons from deep hell came up to cheer them as man and horse went by.

Twice more the thoroughbred fell. Each time Stettler stepped out of the saddle as the horse went down and came back at it in the flameless fury of a white rage, beating it about the face until it staggered to its feet. Remorselessly he spurred, and thoughtlessly, for it knew no better, the hot-blooded horse ran its heart out.

The last time it fell it went down differently, the two front legs folding as in prayer, then the chest and the long neck and head slamming the ground before the final somersault. The horse was dead, and Stettler, although he had pulled his feet from the stirrups, had not been able to jump free. He lay there in the softening wind with his left leg beneath the thoroughbred's shoulder and said, "Damn it all anyway." His passion and the wind both faded as suddenly as they had arisen.

His left collar bone was broken. There was pain enough to tell him that. The leg was numbed by the weight of the sixteen-hand horse. He would find out whether it was broken after he pulled it free.

With the good arm and hand he reached a saddle string on the opposite side of the carcass. He pulled the string over, held it in his teeth, and pulled his broken shoulder from the ground. With the right knee pushing in the saddle, the man tried to drag himself from under the horse but the leg was held firmly. He lay back on the cold ground, looked at the moon and made a painstaking study of his condition. Having rated it as bad, which didn't take long, he devoted his intellect to solving his problem. While he thought, he rested. Energy, he knew, was something he would be needing. There was none for wasting.

His plan finally turned to shape on the lathe of his mind. He pulled his clasp knife from the sheath, opened it with his teeth and placed it on the ground beside him. By experiment he determined that the radius of his right arm was enough for him to cut the saddle loose. This might make it easier to draw himself free. On the other hand, it was only by holding the saddle string in his teeth that he could draw himself off the ground; to support his body on the left elbow ground the broken ends of his collar bone together—he was sure of this because he tested such a system, just once, and the pain had quickly made him faint.

By further slow, cautious and painful examination, he determined that a clump of sod was pressed directly above his left hip bone. It was this which trapped the left leg under the horse. Having so decided, Stettler again pulled his body up with teeth and saddle strings and began to cut away the clump of sod with his knife. It was slower than shoveling gravel with a teaspoon, but, as in all things, Stettler paced himself. His teeth would hold the saddle strings long enough for him to dig with the knife while he counted to twenty-five. At the count of twenty-five he would set the knife on the ground, reach his right hand to the saddle horn for a hold and slowly let his body slip back to the earth without jarring the broken bones. After one hour he had dug a hole beneath his left hip and found that he could move the leg an inch or so. Bracing his knee again he tried to push himself free of the horse but became aware that he was soaked with sweat. Sweat means wet and wet means cold, a danger when a man is alone and far from home. So, he rested once more. To ensure that he would rest long enough, he started to count to a thousand. At around eight hundred he fell asleep.

Awakened about twenty minutes later by his own shivering, Stettler flung his right arm and leg back and forth to restore circulation. It was another hour and two more periods of digging with the clasp knife before he drew free of the horse. He felt the foot and leg carefully, inch by inch, and could detect no broken bones, so he began to slap the numbness from the leg with his hands. Having found that he could stand, he next tried walking. He could do that too.

That the leg was not broken nor so much as sprained was a piece of remarkably good luck. The shoulder was broken, true, but a man didn't walk with his shoulders. Under normal circumstances, a man lost and injured in that country lit a fire and sat beside it until somebody tracked him down. Ordinary men, however, had wives, children and friends who marked their comings and goings. Stettler's absence might go unnoticed for a week or a month. Being permitted to starve to death alone in the bush was what you bought with the right of privacy. He had no objections to that.

His thoughts turned immediately to matters practical and he set out to light a fire. Broken-winged, and limping on the numbed leg, Stettler moved to a fallen pine, snatched up some dry red pine needles and a few tiny twigs and set the clump upon the ground.

He kneeled over the pile, slowly, clumsily, like a broken gate being dragged open. He was now very cold. He struck the heads off three matches before he realized that he was being impulsive, and not noticeably smart.

He had sweated while trying to free himself from the horse and the Eddy Strike-Anywhere matches in his shirt pocket were soaked.

He spread them on the dry ground and counted them. There were eleven left and all the heads were soft.

He rocked back on his ass, sat with his feet spread before him and slowly passed a match back and forth through his curly hair to dry it. He stroked one match twenty times, tapped the head with a fingernail, judged it to be yet soft and stroked one hundred times again.

Judging the match head to be firm enough, he proceeded to dry out three more. These he laid on a rock and covered with a piece of tinfoil from his package of Players.

On his feet again, the man walked among the trees until he found a pine that was scarred and had bled some pitch. The pitch he chipped out carefully with his knife. Next he collected some dry pine needles and some very light and small dead twigs. Small as the twigs were, he split each two-inch long section with his knife to bare the wood. Moisture in dead sticks tended to accumulate against the bark.

Stettler put the slivers of pitchwood on the grey rock. Next it he placed a pile of needles, next that a pile of twigs. He surveyed this accumulation but, resisting the temptation to light it, hobbled away and brought back some larger dead sticks with which he made a fourth pile.

There was no wind now but, wind not being his friend, he prepared for it anyway. He took off his hat and, with a couple of stouter sticks, made a shelter above the rock where he planned to start the fire.

Now, kneeling again, he was ready to try the first match. It was a trifle late. He had begun to shake. The human body has marvellous mechanisms for preservation and shivering is one. It occurs at an early stage of hypothermia, when blood begins to collect in the abdomen while abandoning other parts of the frame. The shivering stimulates a renewed flow of blood throughout the body. Unfortunately, Nature or God had not calculated the natural defense mechanism to a nicety — a man with the shakes is in no condition to scrape a damp match head across a rock.

Stettler knew this and, seeing the match vibrating with his thumb and forefinger, did not try to touch the match head to the rock. He put the match down. He extended his arm, the fingers spread, and ordered them to stop shaking. Nothing changed. His teeth began to chatter. Long shudders ran up and down his spine.

He spoke, for the fourth time that day. "God damn stupid," he said.

Fortunately for him, he had observed other people's stupidity in his lifetime and had learned from it. Among the experiences which had nourished his intellect were those on Vancouver's Skid Road where he had watched rumdums of a morning, frantic for their first alchohol of the day, but shaking too badly to carry the glass to their lips. Remembering them, Stettler worked a large handkerchief out of his pocket and made a sling of it, the two ends in his teeth, the wrist pushing against the pocket end of the sling. So locked, the right hand held firm. He leaned over, head and arm together, picked up the first match, moved it gently across the rock and lit it. The head fizzed, sputtered, but in the end made a point of flame which began to eat backward along the white wood of the match-stick. Head and slinged arm locked still, he transferred that tiny flame into the wigwam of pitchslivers and left it there.

The frail bud of yellow flame crawled along the match stem. There came a slender line of smoke above the pitch, thin and black as a pencil mark. It thickened. A new flame, redder than that of the match, formed, flickered and slowly increased within the pile of pitch.

He waited until the flame was as large as his little fingernail and reached for the pine needles, keeping the stress on his right wrist with the handkerchief held in his teeth.

One by one, the four piles of tinder were fed into the little fire. Within two minutes, sticks as large as his finger were burning.

The body, following some foolish program of its own making, had now ceased to shake and Stettler, whose mind had never quivered, felt better matched to it. He felt, in fact, much better about everything. His chances of getting out of this, he calculated, were a hundred to one. What the hell, in a country like this, a man faced chances like that every day that he decided to get out of bed.

He dragged a few larger branches from nearby deadfalls and added these to the fire. The heat from it was now appreciable. It beat into him. He sat for a considerable time and thought about nothing whatsoever.

In half an hour, he was warm again.

With a good deal of pain, he removed his mackinaw and then his shirt. He tore the shirt up the back, tail to collar, pulling out a strip about six inches in width. With the strip he made a sling for his left arm. He then pulled on the torn shirt again and buttoned all its front. Finally he got into the heavy jacket, the right arm sleeved, the left, with its sling, inside the coat.

Stettler next spent an extra hour in gathering firewood. The moon was setting and darkness gathering thickly just beyond the fire's glow so his woodpile grew slowly. He did not cease gathering wood until he had enough for four, perhaps five hours of burning. That done, he lay on the ground, facing the flame and quickly went to sleep reflecting that, so far, he had not thrown away any good cards.

Pain or cold awakened him every hour through the rest of the night, but when the slow, reluctant northern dawn came he was a little rested, a little stronger. He blew the fire into a brief life, warmed himself again, and then reconnoitered his position.

The timber crowded Stettler's nest at the meadow's edge and he could see no ridges of the hills from this point. He considered walking to open ground where he could take a bearing on the hills but chose instead to retrieve his boot from beneath the horse.

He spent almost an hour in finding a fallen pine firm enough to use as a pry, dragging it to the horse and limbing it with his knife. Using another piece of log for a fulcrum and several chunks for blocks, he lifted the carcass from the ground, an inch at a time, readjusting fulcrum and pry each time. It was almost noon before he got the boot out.

Stettler built another big fire, stripped himself naked, dried every piece of clothing, then carefully and slowly dressed himself again.

He further prepared himself for the walk.

He had dried all the remaining matches thoroughly beside the fire. Using the foil of the cigarette package he rolled each match individually in the paper's folds, making one roll of six matches and another small roll of four. These he placed in separate pockets. He would spare no matches to light his remaining half dozen cigarettes but would use them only for fires at his rest stops.

He would, he knew, walk slowly in riding boots. The cowboy boot with the high heel and pointed toe was designed to be slotted into stirrups. For walking, they were comfortable enough for short distances but in any protracted hike they pinched. Since he would be walking fifteen miles or more he could expect his feet to swell. By nightfall, he would have to fashion some type of boot jack to get them off and, once removed, he might be unable to get into them the next morning. Leaving his feet in them the blood flow would be constricted and, except when warmed by fire, his feet would be painfully cold. If it dropped far below zero, they would probably freeze.

Reflecting on these matters, he decided to remove the boots once again. Once more he dried the socks. He examined his delicate little blue-veined feet with care. He pared the toenails shorter, then carefully slotted the feet back into the boots.

It had been an admirable program of preparation and, like many such programs, far too good. He had not been watching the cloud which had thickened, darkened and dropped. By the time he was ready to walk at almost noon, the first snow of the new winter was falling, flakes big as the breast feathers of a goose. There would be no landmarks. The man would move through endless curtains of silent white snow which would hide everything beyond a distance of twenty feet.

He recalculated the one hundred to one odds he had given himself earlier. Forty-nine out of fifty seemed a more reasonable figure, now.

He lit one cigarette from the embers of his first fire and began to walk.

A great deal of nonsense, Stettler knew, was talked about the instinct of some men to find their way home. Morton Dilloughboy had such a reputation in the Namko Country. Even in strange country, Morton invariably abandoned the horse trails when traveling and would almost always disdain to follow his own tracks in returning, choosing instead to break new trail. Stettler himself had observed the phenomenon but by observation and, later, by some skillful questioning of Morton, had discovered the method. Morton, casual and unheeding though he seemed, always counted the creeks he crossed on the way out and recounted in returning. This reduced his margin for error to the comparatively minor one of determining whether he was upstream or downstream of his destination and there was usually a recognizable landmark at the last creek to provide him the clue.

This practice was not available to Stettler. He was somewhere on the high ground, the source of most of the slow creeks that trickled down the Namko plains. He could not have counted any that he had crossed during the ride nor known which way they flowed.

He could have backtracked to his ranch, hoping to follow the thoroughbred's prints before the falling snow obliterated them but, if only for the reason that he was Stettler, he did not do that. He set out to walk to Frenchie's place. That had, after all, been his objective.

Calmly, he began to walk, trusting to whatever instinct the human animal retains for direction. He walked slowly, that he might not sweat, that his clothing would be dry, but the falling

snow melted on his shoulders and his back and slowly soaked the
jacket and shirt. Once every second hour, as he could best calculate
the time, he stopped and, with painful care, used one more match to
light a fire and dry himself.

When the snow grew lighter in late afternoon he was in meager
black spruce trees at the edge of a muskeg of indeterminate size.

This, he calculated, would be the one lying at the northern edge
of Frenchie's cattle range. It was a dismal region, black trees,
black water and usually mournfully silent, the land being fit to
nourish nothing more than three or four ravens. Morton Dilloughboy, who found a challenge in such scenery, had named it the Blue
Danube Swamp.

Stettler avoided the flat ground, which quivered when stepped
upon. He wanted to keep his boots dry. The boots had been dried at
each fire, but his feet had now swollen within them and he knew he
must wear them until he got out and could slice the side stitches and
peel them away. Neither were they completely dry when he hit the
Blue Danube. A blister had formed near the heel of each foot,
broken and then bled. He had felt the blood creep down the soles of
his feet and pump up and down between his toes. But they were
boots that were almost dry — in this game, a good card he could not
afford to throw away.

So he crossed none of the many deep bays of swamp grass which
were indented on the sides of the swamp but moved, carefully,
among the black spruce at the swamp's shoreline. He stepped
carefully over the exposed roots which frequently were of a pattern
to snatch a careless foot and leave a man with a torn ankle ligament.

Through the forest his progress had been a notch above a slow
walk. Now his pace had dropped to a crawl.

The muskeg, like all of its kind, had been a lake a few thousand
years ago. Being stagnant, it had produced mosses and other
growths faster than they could decay and by a slow process the lake
was thereby transforming itself into soil. Given another few
thousand years of natural process, or ten years and a half million
dollars' worth of draining and ditching, it would be a meadow to
delight cows, horses and prairie chicken. Stettler was just another
man whose time was not right.

He knew that a draw ran off the southern side of the Blue
Danube. Once he hit that depression, it would point him toward

Frenchie's. As he rounded each peninsula he expected to find it. He did not, for the good reason that this was the wrong swamp. He circled it all and came, at last, to the point at which he had begun. What swamp it was he knew not. Maybe nobody knew. There were many that remained nameless.

The snow fell heavily as he prepared again for nightfall. In fast fading light he collected wood and then, hunkered beneath a tall spruce, lit his fire and sat there with his hunger and his pain. When the fire was firmly set he made one more trip to the swamp's edge, drove the heel of his boot into the wet ground and, kneeling, drank the black water that filled the boothole. Lifting himself, he saw the black mud caked on the shirt and the hand of his good arm, which he had used to support himself. His face, he thought, must be as filthy. He tried, clumsily to wash himself with snow but the mud could only smear and streak.

Dirt and the smell of his own sour sweat made Stettler remember things he preferred to forget. During the war he had found himself attached to an American outfit which liberated the concentration camps at Dachau, and for two days he was among those set to guard the living and the dead, they being scarcely distinguishable except that the living made mewing sounds. Stettler had agreed with the American sergeant who said, "We should pack them all in a hole and run a bulldozer over them."

"You couldn't be more right," said Stettler. He had been astounded when he came to realize that the American was talking about the SS camp guards, who were being held prisoner in a corner of the camp. Stettler did not find the SS lovable, but then, few people were. He had no desire to bulldoze them underground. They were, after all, recognizably human and, he considered, probably like himself; they weren't in that war because they had chosen to be. It was the concentration camp inmates whom he found so revolting that they frightened him.

On the second day at Dachau, he recalled, a dry storm was blowing, a warm eye-stinging blast of air over the Alps from Italy. Munich people called it the *Foehn* and said it made men mad.

Stettler had been about to address himself to some K-rations when he found himself surrounded by the camp's animal life, scarecrow men, loathsome caricatures, slack-jawed, whining. He shouted at them to get back and waved his rifle at them, but they moaned and looked at the K-ration cans. He flung the cans at them, trying to break the stick bones of these monstrous creatures, and then he fled, went AWOL for two days and was transferred back to the Canadians who were killing normal-looking men in normal ways.

Through the night the concentration camp's prisoners visited him again in the mountain swamps behind Frenchie's place, and he wished, once again, that he could kill them all.

The stars came out during the night and it froze.

At dawn, he broke ice in his boothole to drink again.

Since there was a dawn in the clear air he could take direction. To the south, he knew, he must cut creeks, trails or tracks. He walked due west for half a mile to place himself beyond the edge of the nameless muskeg and then, carefully placing one foot in front of the other, began to walk south. His stomach ached from hunger and he was now very tired. His odds, he felt, had dropped again. They were now no better than even money.

He counted as he walked. Five hundred paces slow walk. Five hundred paces fast. Two hundred paces at a trot. At the end of each sequence he leaned against a tree, breathing deeply and did not move again until the freezing air penetrated and he was near to shivering.

Moving slowly, he detoured from time to time around small swamps and deadfall or thick, second-growth pines. He made for the south.

The sky clouded again and light, fine snow began falling, but before this took away his sun, he had hit the edge of a large opening, rimmed with the sharp spires of a thousand spruces and recognized that he had hit the Ildash.

The Ildash he knew. It was a region of swamp, meadow and forest which made a patchwork triangle north of the ranches of Frenchie and Smith. By bearing right, he should find Frenchie's creek.

What he could not estimate was the energy that remained in his body to walk those miles.

Without a broken shoulder, or in milder airs or with better boots, he might have been able to travel for days. But his was a small body. The energy reserves were scant. He had, he knew, used a lot of that treasure and he did not know how much remained. There was no longer any pain. The brain had long since manufactured enough endorphins to cancel out all the agony of the broken shoulder and, with it, all the bobwire cramps that go with prolonged hunger.

But the lack of food had cost him heavily. He knew that. His body's meager supply of fat had quickly been burned away and he was burning calories from muscle tissue.

He now calculated his chances as being no better than one in four.

Stettler trotted, he walked, he stood, he walked, he trotted and he stood again, and the easy snow came down upon him. He did not let himself sweat, and his thoughts, encased as he was within a soft white world of a few hundred feet visibility, remained essentially tranquil. He knew only that one more walk, one more trot, would bring him to a trail, a fence, a wagon road, which would border on Frenchie's place.

At the end of more than four hours he finally found something familiar, although it took a minute or more for him to adjust his mind to what he saw. It was the embers of his own campfire. ''I'll be damned,'' he said. It was his only comment. Stettler was not a complaining man.

He again started walking, again making south as he could best perceive it to be. He shambled, lurched and sometimes fell but never wavered in his purpose nor, as he imagined it, lost his capacity for calm, rational and logical thought.

This comfortable illusion did not leave him even on the occasion when Smith rode up to him. Stettler had leaned against a tree to rest. He no longer trusted himself to light a fire. The warmth of it might seduce him to rest beside it forever. Instead, he would pause and hug a tree for a time.

He saw Smith riding up on a black horse which had two white stockings on the front legs. Smith was wearing a new, large hat of lemon yellow. He was spurred, and the spurs rang like little bells.

Stettler wiped his dirty face and waited, wondering why Smith came on without seeing him. When Smith was a hundred feet distant the horse blurred, shifted and changed into a hunchbacked moose. The pale antlers were where Smith's yellow hat had been. The spurs jingled no more, for there were no spurs, no bells to ring.

The bull was more startled than Stettler. It stopped, snorted, turned and galloped away. A moose cannot gallop as fast as it can trot, but when badly frightened, it tries to gallop.

The panic remained with the animal. Stettler remained a rational man. The matter should not, after all, have surprised him. The energy was running out, and the mind now couldn't cope with much more than the rise and fall of his boots. Faced with an unusual object, in this case the bull moose, the tired mind offered up a dream, dreaming being less taxing than the recognition of reality. A silly damn thing, a man's mind, he told himself and reached for his last cigarette.

The cigarette he found but the last match was gone. This puzzled him. He had used but one match for each fire and never sacrificed one for the lighting of a cigarette. Somehow, he had used them all, but when? He tried counting his fires, stop by stop. No matter how many times he counted, the number came to eight. There should be two matches left and there were not. After a time he left the riddle unsolved, pushed himself away from the tree and again, as always, he walked, his head down, watching the toes of his boots slide in and out beneath him on the ground.

For two nights and two days, it had been an immaculate performance by this man. He had not been guilty of a single avoidable error. Except for the chance of the choking snowflurries, he would long since have arrived at Frenchie's or at some other ranch. In his own area, where the meadows, the swales and the islands of trees were as familiar as furniture in a living room, he would have found his way even in snow. Riding the horse to death had been, of course, a foolishness but, being a private foolishness, beyond the knowledge or the guess of any other man on earth, it did not matter.

He considered all this without rancor, bitterness or anger.

Some men could rail against bad luck. The more foolish among them, he had observed, could be roused to anger by being dealt a poor hand at a card game, a trait of his fellow man that never ceased to secretly astonish him. As the cards were dealt, you played them and eventually you ran them out. He had been dealt poor cards, but he had played every hand superbly in a game in which the bluff does not win a single trick.

He was, he realized, running out of chips and couldn't stay much longer in this game. There were no more fires to dry his clothing and the falling snow had melted into them. The heat of his slender body leaked rapidly away.

He indulged in one brief sleep on dry ground beneath the shelter of a large pine. A few minutes nap should be his due, he felt. When he awoke it was dark. There was cloud cover. No moon or stars showed. He could go nowhere. Nevertheless, Stettler declined to die, for the moment at least. He shuffled in circles around the tree's trunk for a time, dropped and slept and then repeated the process. He saw another grey dawn arrive in that vacant land and, being able to perceive some difference of light between the east and the west, he set his course. Again he began to walk to Frenchie's through the Ildash.

Stettler set his mind on hold. Even counting the steps had become tiresome. The man simply moved, holding to nothing more than the placing of one foot before another.

Once he found himself staring at an open, brown plain, marked by strange conical shapes. It was an extraordinary sight, unlike anything he could remember in the Ildash. He watched it for a considerable time. After many long and deep breaths the brown plain resolved itself into the pine needles of the forest floor. The strange hummocks were pine cones. He had, he realized, fainted and fallen beneath a tree.

Poking his hands on the ground, he pushed himself upright, stood, wavering, and then began walking again. It was not much of a walk, but by this time he was no longer much of a man. Could he have seen himself, he would have been reminded of the half-men in Dachau. His eyes were lusterless, his body sloped forward as if moving against a fitful wind, his mouth was slack. From time to time, he gave off hard grunts and thin whining sounds.

It was in that condition, late in the morning of the fourth day, three and a half days after leaving home, that Stettler found a wide, well-marked wagon road. He trod in one or the other of the two deep ruts for almost a quarter of a mile. He then staggered back into heavy second growth timber, his mind shorn of any recollection that his feet had ever touched that road.

Dark curtains were flapping left and right of his eyes when he stepped into a pile of logs which flung him on the ground. He lay there for a time unconscious and came back into the world unwillingly. He recognized the return of the world and what was real, but he recognized it with regret for there remained the whisper of a memory of the place he had left, which was peaceful and where the soul had rest. Well, it was the world again, and he was in it.

Stettler reached for a log to draw himself to his feet. It felt strange to the hand. When he was standing weaving on his feet, he found that he had fallen beside a split rail fence. He touched it, rail by rail, and looked along its zigzag to where the panels leaped a small creek and jogged into a patch of trees.

He knew this fence. He had helped to build it. It was the fence around Smith's home place. He could recognize his axe work where the logs were notched.

Remembering his moose, Stettler kneeled and examined one of the notches with slow care, running his hand on the cut wood. It was real. It was also real that in some way he could not remember, would never be able to remember, he had walked to within a few hundred yards of Smith's house.

He sensed blood running down his face. In falling, a fence rail must have put a crease in his scalp. Stettler lifted his one good hand to wipe away the blood from his eyes. No blood came away and he wiped again. The hand was wet, but it was wet with tears. He could not have been more surprised if they had been pearls. Tears were things he had not known since he was a very small boy.

The slim, ragged hank of man leaned against the fence and wept for many minutes. When the tears ended, he began a series of very deliberate preparations. First he washed his face and both the good and bad hand with snow.

He peeled off the mackinaw, undid the sling in which the useless arm rested and ran it through the sleeve of the coat. Getting the coat in place again was a process that took almost ten minutes. He put the left hand in the pocket of the coat. Stettler buttoned all the buttons. He wet his hair with snow, and combed it with his fingers. For half an hour the strange, wasted little figure preened itself in the snow. Then he walked the quarter mile to Smith's place and, leaning against the door post for extra support, knocked loudly on the door.

When Norah opened it, a blast of warm air, rich with the smell of baking bread, swept over the man. He felt his knees folding. He grabbed the side of the door and looked at her. He saw, first, twin images of her flushed face. Then they merged into one.

"Stettler," she said. "Jack. For God's *sake* man."

Norah's face was an open door into her heart. Every mood revealed itself. As a child she had been teased about it, as an adolescent she had tried, with quiet desperation, to become remote and inscrutable. When it didn't work, she abandoned the effort as hopeless and let the light of her nature shine through. Smith said it didn't matter anyway, since she never played poker.

Standing at the door that soft, round and plastic little face betrayed on the instant everything that she felt, and these were dismay, pity and horror. The man read every one of those messages and could have struck the face with his fist to wipe them away.

He felt the sap run in him again. The knees were straight. His voice, although it had a rattle like a raven's, came out loudly.

"My horse left me. I was on the way to Frenchie's. Could I borrow a horse from you."

"Come in man. What's happened to you, Jack?"

He had rehearsed his lines and he repeated them. "My horse left me. Have you got one I can borrow."

"Come in, for God's sake," she said. She reached out and touched his arm. "Come in."

The black curtains moved away. He could see her clearly now, a flustered woman, her soft, foolish face full of worry and question. For just a moment, all his strength returned and when he spoke again he spoke not in the bubbling rattle but with the harsh, brazen voice that people knew to be Jack Stettler's.

"If you're going to lend me a horse, I'd appreciate taking the goddamed thing and going," he said.

Her eyes never left his but with her left arm, wordless, she gestured toward the corral.

He pushed up one stiff forefinger to tilt the brim of the hat he no longer had and ground out one grudging word. "Obliged."

He turned on his heel, but turned too fast. He took just three steps on the snow-covered path of the yard and the blackness swept in from all sides. The ground tilted beneath his feet, and the last thing he saw was the packed snow of the path flinging itself against his face.

When he came to she had dragged him into the living room, cut his boots off, undressed him, covered him with blankets and was packing hot water bottles beside him.

"You're gonna be alright, Jack," she said. "When Smith comes we'll get you to a doctor. You'll be alright."

"Can you hear me, Jack?" she said, when his eyes opened.

He could hear, but he pretended not. He could not trust himself to speak. He lay unmoving, unspeaking, granite eyes turned to the pitch-pine ceiling while within a hurricane raised dust in that acrid soul, the wild winds of rage, of humiliation, of defeat. He was, in the end, no better than all the rest of them. He was, like them, damned by the eternal human curse of frailty.

# A Day With
# a Deer, a Bear
# and Norah Smith

ON A JUNE morning which sang of summer with golden throat, Norah Smith and a roan gelding named Tackatoolie were churning up dust and turds in the horse corral. It was a half stampede. Tackatoolie was a tall horse. Norah was short and two months pregnant besides. Each time she tried to slip on the hackamore he tossed his big head, which was shaped exactly like a claw hammer and contained about the same amount of brains. This would bunt Norah a couple of feet and permit him to run to another corner of the corral. She would follow, saying sweet things and sometimes swear words through her white, even teeth.

She was making her fifth or sixth try when she saw that her husband had been watching the performance through the bars of the corral gate.

"Damit," shouted Smith, "stop lettin' him push you around. You're spoilin' that horse."

While her attention was thus distracted, Tackatoolie butted her with his head and she fell into a pile of fresh horse turds and dirtied her one good pair of slacks. She threw the hackamore on the ground and walked out past Smith with tears in her eyes. He noticed that. He followed her back to the house and upstairs, where she was taking her old, faded blue jeans off a peg and snuffing back tears. Smith never claimed to be a man who understood women well. He knew that under usual circumstances they were unpredictable, and when pregnant, damn near impossible. Nevertheless, he tried to cheer her up as best he could. He spoke to her in the friendliest way imaginable, pointing out that all her troubles were in her head, but that did no good. She started to bawl and after a while he left her to get over whatever it was.

It was a day that had begun badly for Norah hours before her encounter with Tackatoolie. Bearing the third Smith, she was still subject to morning sickness and had puked in the yard before setting about shaving feathersticks from jack-pine kindling to start the morning fire in the kitchen stove. As was expected in the Smith house, she was first up. When she brought out the castiron skillet for hot cakes and saw the dawn reflected in its greasy face, she was sick a second time. When she came back, Smith had arisen. There was an absence of comfort in the sight of him. He had not shaved for two days. He wore Stanfield's button-ups and jeans with a boot on one foot and a sock on the other. Smith was never bothered that he could not find both boots when he woke of a morning. He would pull on whichever he found and then make his morning perambulations around the downstairs floors drinking coffee and talking, from time to time, about some obscure subject which had seized his attention upon waking.

Even in winter his bootless foot never seemed to chill although the temperature at floor level might be an even thirty two degrees Fahrenheit. From time to time, he would observe that, by God, one of his boots seemed to have gone missing. She would answer that it was under the bed, upstairs, as always. That he would accept as being just another contribution to the great national debate about the twentieth century belonging to Canada, giving her no more serious attention than reasonable men give to high-priced teams of economists. Often as not, should he choose to go outdoors, he would pull an overshoe or some other mismatched boot over the other foot and walk gimpy for half a day.

He was leaning on the counter by the sink, sipping his second cup of coffee and looking at his favorite mountain, when she first spoke to him.

"Do you know what day it is today, Smith?" she asked.

He thought for a moment. "Monday?" he said. He was not sure. Mondays on a ranch are pretty much like Tuesdays.

"No, I mean another kind of day."

A ripple of uneasiness spread on the calm surface of his mind. He thought quite a long time. "Mother's Day?" he said.

"That was a month ago."

"Oh."

"It's our wedding anniversary," she said.

"Oh. So it is. I'd forgot."

"You also forgot to bring Roosevelt home from the Larsens' yesterday."

"Well," he said, "I didn't exactly forget. I remembered when I got there but when it was time to leave I had sort of lost track of him.'' He sucked up some more coffee. ''It is alright anyhow Norah,'' he said. ''I figure Roosevelt wanted to stay over with them for another day or two anyhow. Otherwise he would have been at the truck when I pulled out.''

''That's not for him to decide, he's only a kid. He should be here for his school lessons this morning.''

''Margaret Larsen will probably give him some lessons. You can have a sort of holiday. You will only have Sherwood to teach today.''

''I will not, because we are all going out to the McQuarries' today.''

''Oh.''

''Will you stop saying 'oh.' You have known for two weeks that we were goin' to the McQuarries' today.''

''I might have known it but my mind never got really roped into it. It sort of caught me by one hind leg and I shook off the lassrope. I have been spending my mind more on the national debt and things like that. I have gone on to bigger things.''

''You bloody well do remember. You promised to show him the old survey stake. The one he can't find.''

''McQuarrie couldn't find his own bellybutton using both hands and holding a flashlight in his teeth.''

''Why do you dislike the McQuarries?''

''I don't dislike them. Damit, why can't you get that in your headbone. I do not dislike the McQuarries.''

In honesty, of which she carried the share of ten ordinary Canadians, Norah had to admit, however privately, the truth of that statement. Nobody disliked the McQuarries, who were honest, charming, gentle, mild, well-bred, well-educated and naturally intelligent. It was just that people would not take them seriously.

The Smiths had been the first to meet Colin McQuarrie who came into the country having read many books including *Swiss Family Robinson* and the *RCAF Survival Manual*. Norah, who liked him, quickly perceived that his failing was that he could not help believing what people told him. Smith, if he perceived that fault, was less forgiving.

On his first morning at the Smith ranch, McQuarrie had politely requested a horse with Arab blood, but not too hot-blooded. They ran in a wise, patient and notoriously lazy gelding named Stanley Steamer, from the dude string. That was only polite. Then McQuarrie insisted on saddling his own horse.

Smith came out to inspect the job, closely followed by Norah, whose instincts urged her to do that.

Stanley Steamer was all right in the saddle, as Smith tested by shoving four fingers under the cinch to check the tightness. His bridle, however, had been, with much lacing and unlacing and turning of buckles, installed upside down. Stanley Steamer was restive, but he accepted it as one of those things. He had known many dudes.

"Yep," said Smith. "Just right." He checked the cinch again. "You had to let some air out of him before cinching up, I guess.'

McQuarrie, who had read about that too, admitted modestly that he had performed the knee trick.

"There is just one small thing," said Smith.

"Oh?"

"Yeah. That is, if you don't mind my mentioning it."

"What's that?"

"Well, just a small thing. That there bridle."

"Something wrong about the bridle?" said McQuarrie.

"No. Nothing wrong. Nothing wrong at all. A perfect job. On the right horse. On a stud horse that would be exactly right. However, this here horse is a gelding. With a gelding or a mare, you put the bridle exactly the opposite."

"Sorry," said McQuarrie. "My mistake."

"An easy mistake to make," said Smith. "Made it many times myself. The simple rule is, don't never bridle a horse without you look under the tail first."

"Let me get that bridle, Colin," said Norah. "They're tricky." She rejigged the buckles and the lines, hearing over the shoulder McQuarrie trying to make conversation.

"Would there be some Percheron in that horse?" asked McQuarrie.

"Exactly right. We breed into the Percheron for big bone, so they can pack. Then we cross with shithouse rat, for the smarts. In Stanley Steamer the rat strain seems to be plumb wore out."

Norah led Steamer over. "He's ready to travel, Colin," she said.

Colin thanked her. He was a man who said thank you most of the day. A bread-and-butter man, Smith called him.

Despite such puzzling introductions to the ways of the Namko Country, McQuarrie and his wife had moved there and bought the old Soap Lake Place. It had been abandoned by the first settler whose bowels were unequal to dissolved sodas. Almost all the Soap Lake range rights had been acquired by neighboring ranches and little remained of the ranch but a grey, two-storied square log cabin, a log barn which was sounder, a mile of fence, a horse corral and a piece of bottom land beside Soap Lake Creek, which was big enough to nourish a Nubian goat and a Newfoundland dog but not much more. It suited them perfectly because of the view of Kappan Mountain, an asset most settlers thought came for free. McQuarrie graveled the road to the old house. He had a bridge built across the creek, restored the house and installed running water, a septic tank and twin kitchen sinks. He got a tractor, a diesel electric light plant, a matched pair of Bouvier Flanders dogs, twelve Mongolian pheasants that died, one goat which didn't and a sincere, enduring relationship with his banker.

For horses, he bought two golden-coin palominos. Namko never had parades, only stampedes. He bought palominos anyway.

His wife was a woman with a voice like silver bells and her thoughts were gold, twenty-four carat. She hired Indian girls, from the Reserve, to serve as housemaids. Three left, without notice, so she hired a fourth. How else, she said, could the McQuarries learn to speak Chilcotin, the original language of the land and a bounden duty upon the whites that they should speak it? None of the local Indians had ever had that idea. She brought it into the country fresh and they were, a year later, still examining the idea thoughtfully. Chilcotin is one of the dialects of the Athapaskan language and foreigners who understand it, and they number below six, say it is more impressive, more precise and far less bastardized than English. However, verb tenses alter in every context and there is also a requirement for inflection, as in Cantonese, to provide full meaning to what is being said. At the end of ten months the McQuarries had a grasp of about seventeen words and didn't know how to say any of them.

Their favorite was the Chilcotin world for 'hello' but they pronounced it like the word for 'drunk' and quite misunderstood the response it brought.

"It would be awful if we didn't show up today," Norah said to Smith that morning. "She's getting up dinner for us at twelve o'clock."

"Don't she normally cook dinner? What do the McQuarries do about eating if there is no visitors? Don't they eat when they're by themselves?

"That's what I mean. You don't like the McQuarries."

He sighed. "I have never known anybody with logic like yours," he said. "All I said was that I figured she would cook dinner at her house whether there was any Smiths in it or not. Somehow that turned into me not liking the McQuarries. How do you arrive at conclusions like that? There should be some sort of a prize for thinking of that kind."

"Well anyway, we have got to go."

"As for my logic," he said, "it works in an entirely different track. Now, in my logic, if you and me and Sherwood are goin' to the McQuarries' today, then Sherwood ain't goin' to get any school anyhow. And neither would Roosevelt, if he was here. So Roosevelt stayin' over a day or two at the Larsens' don't make the slightest difference to him or you or me or anybody in the world."

"You can always twist things somehow."

"You didn't see my other boot any place, did you?" he said.

"It's under the bed."

"Are you sure?"

"Yes. I saw it there when I got up."

"I looked, but I never saw it there."

"It's there."

"Well, I will look again then. Maybe it was lyin' underneath something else."

He went upstairs. Sherwood, their oldest boy, came down.

"We're going over to the McQuarries' today, Sherwood."

"Ugh," he said.

"Why are you making that face?"

"She always talks to me so much."

"Sherwood. Mrs. McQuarrie is a very nice lady."

He answered in calm, conversational tones much like Smith's.
"Oh, yes," he said, "she's nice. But she's an awful talker. Is
breakfast ready?"

She cooked Sherwood's hot cakes soggy, the way he liked them,
and had Smith's turning from brown to black, the way he liked his,
and then she noticed they were both missing. She found them
monkey wrenching some equipment in the toolshed. She noticed
the truck was missing.

"Where's the truck?"

"I loaned it to Frenchie for a couple of days."

"What'd you do that for?"

"I didn't figure we had any use for it and he needed it."

"How do we get to the McQuarries'?"

"Well, we will just saddle horses. It is almost as quick, going
over the jack-pine ridge."

"Oh, hell."

"And a nice morning to travel saddle horse, too," he said,
casting his eyes over the June morning which was, in fact, one of
the better mornings of that year.

When it was time to go to the McQuarries', Smith had gone
missing.

"We gonna go without Smith?" said Sherwood.

"Too bloody true. He can find his own way over."

"Smith can find his way anyplace," said Sherwood.

"When he chooses. Come on, Sherwood, we'll trot."

Knowing as he did that there was far more time in this world than
was known to wives, Smith had saddled up and ridden to the draw
on Oregon Jim Creek. He had cut deer sign there a few days before.
An hour's hunt, he thought, would soothe his mind, which was
getting heavy with domestic disputes.

Deer on Smith's range had faded away after the huge influx of
moose during the thirties and sometimes a year or more would pass
without them shooting one on the Home Place. He missed them,
both because they were not ugly and stupid as were the moose and
because in the hot weather the family could eat almost a whole deer
before it spoiled. Much moose meat spoiled in summer unless
made into jerky. Of late it had been difficult to coax Norah into
making jerky.

The deer in the draw were probably a bunch moving late toward the beautiful meadows above timberline and by today might be gone, but it was a worth a ride to see if perhaps they had hung up there. Anyway, the air was good this morning, the ground was dry, the meadows were green and the snows on the mountain reminded him of newly starched white sheets. He loved to get between white sheets occasionally, sheets starched so hard that they almost crackled. Particularly when dirty, and before bothering to take a bath. When a man came home dog-tired and smelling like a bush-tail rat and dove straight into starched white sheets for sleep it made him appreciate the joys of married life.

He tied the horses in a poplar grove at the edge of the meadow and walked the side of the draw on a dusty path made by the feet of his horses and cattle. There, among the prints of the domestic stock, were the neater prints of deer.

Canada geese in a nearby pond began to raise a kalakalowa. They were talking to a pair which was circling to his right. He squatted in the track and watched the two flying birds swing in a broad turn. They came past him up the draw, not a hundred feet from him. Because he was still, they had not noticed him but in passing one turned his head and looked him straight in the eye.

A quarter of a mile further, he spotted the ears of a deer which had bedded down beside a deadfall on the creekside. He stopped, but the deer had seen him first. When the doe stood, he saw that her coat was dull, her flanks thin, and he guessed that she had a fawn hidden in the grass near her feet. She was not worth shooting but she was company of sorts. Smith stood, unmoving, watching her calmly and she, as calmly, watched him. In an instant there passed between those two living creatures the agreement to truce, that no man has ever explained, the silent compact that there was, at this particular time, at this particular place, no hunter and no hunted. She paced, a few steps right, a few steps left, of the hidden fawn.

"Now mama," he said. "Why don't you pick up that little guy and move along?" She stood, fanned her ears toward the easy sound of his voice, but did not go. "It's a dry doe I'm looking for," he explained.

Then the buck stood. He had been sleeping at the creek's bank. His antlers did not yet have their full season's growth but in their heavy velvet, which was lustrous in the new sun of the day, they were a glowing crown.

The buck had not been startled into wakefulness. He seemed to have risen, fresh, clean and brisk, for no purpose except to enjoy the new breeze which had begun to walk down the draw. He was a perfect animal enjoying a perfect morning.

Slowly, so slowly that the doe did not spook, Smith drew down the rifle on the buck. He brought the bead of the front sight flush to top of the notch in the backsight and centered it just back of the shoulder. This was where he almost always took his shots. It spoiled some meat, but the country had much free meat in it. When he was younger he used to take head shots and being a good shot, usually connected and spoke of it later in a modest way. However, he had once taken a shot at a perfect four point which ran. He thought he had missed it until, weeks later, he found the carcass of the starved animal with the lower jaw all shot away. He had never spoken of this to anybody and he had never taken a head shot again.

This time, however, he didn't want to shoot into the chest cavity so he shifted the sight to the neck. If a bullet didn't snap the neck or cut the main artery, the deer could keep going and good luck to him. He held his breath to squeeze off and the world stopped turning for him. When a shot is good, a man knows it before the last of the pressure is off the trigger. This was that kind of shot.

When the buck went down Smith didn't bother to jack a second shell into the chamber. He walked forward slowly and waved again at the racing doe and her fawn, who did not look back at him. He stepped across the creek, moving deftly from one boulder to the next, scarcely wetting his boots.

He found the buck as he knew he would find him, stone dead. The deer had dropped in a little heap, his proud head falling back over his body.

Smith knew that the buck had died full of the joy of life and believing the terrible lie that he would live forever. It had been quick. The deer had known no pain, no fear, had not had even one instant for the immense regret of things in this life which he might have done and hadn't.

From full life into eternal death the translation had been instantaneous, like somebody switching off an electric light. It was a wonderful way to go and Smith hoped to God that somebody would do as much for him when the time came, although he surer than hell wasn't ready to go yet.

Smith took great care in gutting out the animal. He rolled his sleeves to his elbow. He worked slowly, pausing once to put a new edge on his knife. He hung the four clean quarters from poplar branches. He would bring a pack horse over tomorrow for them. He washed his hands and arms in the sands of the cold creek. There was scarcely a drop of blood on his shirt.

In a small pouch made from a piece of the hide he carried away the fresh liver and presented it to Mrs. McQuarrie when he rode into the Soap Lake Place an hour later to join Norah and Sherwood. Mrs. McQuarrie remarked on the lovely brown eyes of a deer she had never met, but she accepted the liver.

Smith and Colin McQuarrie rode for an hour to look for survey stakes. Smith could not find one. The trees, he said, were creeping down on the grass and had been doing so for ten years or more. Unless they had a damn good twenty-mile forest fire pretty soon, and threw the Crown's minister for grazing permits into the middle of it, the whole country was damn near ruined.

"I guess I'll have to bring in a surveyor from Williams Lake," said McQuarrie as they sat at the dinner table, eating roast beef proudly flavored with wild garlic which Mrs. McQuarrie had plucked in their horse pasture.

"Expense for nothing," said Smith. "You can see your meadow. If you want to throw up a fence, just build her wide."

"Everybody's fences get wide in this country," said Norah. "Just build along the nearest jack-pine ridge at the edge of your meadow."

"That might make for trouble in later years, mightn't it?" said McQuarrie to Smith. "I would feel uneasy about doing that."

"Hire a surveyor then," said Smith. "At least he'll feel easier about his business."

McQuarrie talked about his breeding stock which, along with grass, is the second of two essential items for ranching. He had none yet but had been reading much literature about the Hereford, the Charolais, the Sementhal and the other strains of beef cattle. What did Smith think of them?

"Did you ever think of keeping sheep?" asked Smith, mildly.

Norah was reminded that at times she hated this man she married and never more so than when he said such things in sweet deception. McQuarrie didn't know and couldn't see where sheep men ranked in Smith's estimation. She knew well Smith's sure order of priorities. The only truly good men were those who kept horses, although it was understood that they also had to keep some beef cattle because you couldn't make any money with horses and you could, some of the time, with beef.

Men of the next rank admitted dairy cows to their herd and the class below that raised pigs as well and had a lettuce garden. Sheep men were far down the list, being little better than farmers who wore overalls and had shoes with laces. Smith recognized that below the farmer class there were other trades in the world, carpentering and logging and school teaching and politics, but these were so far beneath his field of vision as to be not worth dividing into classes.

"Do you think sheep would do well here?" said McQuarrie.

"Who can say," said Smith. "It suits for some people."

Norah left and began rattling dishes in Mrs. McQuarrie's sinks.

The McQuarrie kitchen was a magnificent place and Norah was soothed by standing in the midst of it.

Norah had her share of the moral flaws common to the human character, but of one particularly corrosive sin she was free. On that imperfect and imperfectible little soul there was not a single strain of covetousness. She could enjoy other people's good fortune almost as much as her own.

In the McQuarrie kitchen there was running water, both hot and cold, cupboards with birch paneling, an Osterizer, and a pop-up toaster, which operated from a gasoline-fired, 110-volt system. There was a propane stove, which had all the knobs and a pilot light that worked.

Her hostess joined her and they began to clatter dishes together.

Mrs. McQuarrie, for all the china hands and voice of violets, had depths of thought too.

"I don't think Smith likes sheep," she said.

"Why do you say that?"

"I just got that impression."

Norah washed and Mrs. McQuarrie dried.

"Norah, will you tell me something?"

"Sure, if I can."

"Tell me what a rancher is."

Norah laughed. "Anybody who will catch a horse to ride rather than walk to his front gate."

Mrs. McQuarrie's voice was fainter, tighter.

"But we're not ranchers, are we?"

"Why sure. Everybody here is a rancher."

"We are strangers."

"You are not. Everybody likes you. You're some of the most popular people in the whole country."

"Popular strangers," said Mrs. McQuarrie.

They changed the subject.

From the living room came Smith's voice.

"My old dad had sheep once."

"Did he have trouble with foot rot?"

"Not a bit. They all died first winter before the foot rot could start."

"Too bad. Did he run out of feed?"

"No. There was lots of feed. What happened is he went to Oregon to buy a stud horse and got on a real bat. By the time he got home the sheep was all gone to the wolves and the weather. I always remember after he come home somebody asked him how his sheep were doing. He said, 'I never had fewer and I never felt better about it.' "

"I suppose when a man has nothing he must gain a certain sense of freedom," said McQuarrie.

"If we didn't have to keep horses and cows on these ranches we would all be free and happy men," said Smith.

Norah came into the living room. "It's time we started home," she said, shortly.

Sherwood, who had been studying the ads in a *Western Horseman* magazine, stood up and shook his pantlegs over the tops of his tiny riding boots. He was quiet like Smith, but neater. "I guess it's about time I pulled out," he said.

"Pull out where?" said Norah.

"He is taking a message to Frenchie for me," said Smith. "I'm going to meet Frenchie to pick up the truck at the store tomorrow. There's some stuff I got to cart back home from there.''

''Why can't you go over to Frenchie's?''

''Because I am expecting Narcisse Peter to buy a horse from me today at our place.''

She said no more. They went out to their horses. McQuarrie's wife, who felt the loneliness of the range pressing in on her again, was offering up little trills and cheeps of polite dismay that they were going so soon.

Sherwood was riding a big bay. It was tall. So tall, Smith sometimes said, that the connection between its brain and feet was too distant. Sherwood had to lead it to the side of the corral and climb up one log in order to get his foot into the stirrup. ''See you later,'' he said, and trotted off.

Norah called after him.

''Sherwood. You come home right after supper at Frenchie's. You hear me?''

''Sure,'' said the boy, tossing the word over his shoulder.

''I bet he don't get home till pretty near dark,'' she said to Smith.

''Probly.''

She watched the big horse and the tiny boy, going into the wide and empty that would soon swallow them silently.

''Gee. He seems so young, to be off all by himself on a ten-mile ride.''

''He's small for his age,'' said Smith. He got into his own saddle. ''How old is he now anyhow?'' he asked.

''Ten.''

''Oh, ten is he? I had forgot.'' Smith waved a hand casually at the McQuarries, and went away at a fast trot. He was almost into the timber on the edge of the Davie Allen Meadow before Norah caught up to him.

When they were walking their horses, side by side, she said, ''Why did you say that about sheep to McQuarrie?''

''I was just keeping conversation going.''

''But you despise sheep and you know it.''

''What difference does that make? If he likes them why should I try to make him sensible?''

''You were making fun of him.''

"I was only keeping conversation goin'. I was participating."

She grunted. Ten minutes later she said, "What's a rancher, Smith?"

"Now what kind of question is that?"

"Well, Mrs. McQuarrie asked me and I couldn't tell her. So you tell me. What is a rancher?"

"Mort Dilloughboy's got it best, I guess. He says ranch country is where the places are far enough apart that every man has got to keep his own tomcat."

"So Morton is a rancher, then."

"Oh, sure he is."

"Morton has never raised anything on his place except mortgages. Every year he loses more cows than he gets calves."

"I never said he was successful. I said he was a rancher. Morton is a failed rancher but he is a rancher anyhow. Anybody in the country will tell you that."

"But they won't tell me why," she said.

"Because if you have to ask why about a man, then he is not a rancher," said Smith. "It is a question that just answers itself without being asked. The very best kind of question there is."

"And Colin McQuarrie is not a rancher."

"Well, what do you think?" said Smith. "As I say, it answers itself."

Yes, she thought, Morton, who did everything wrong, was a rancher, because he was a good old boy, a delightful drinker, a teller of fine stories and a horseman. He was one of the brotherhood. So was Stettler, sour, dour, Stettler, a mean, cold man whose smile was like a ripple on a slop pail. Stettler, too, was one of them. And Colin McQuarrie, successful or unsuccessful, drunk or sober, helpful or helpless, was not. Like Arch McGregor at the store, like almost everybody on the face of this great earth, he was not and, almost certainly, he would never be.

Two miles from their home place they came upon the bear.

"Look at that dirty scut," shouted Smith. He jumped off his horse and threw its reins to Norah. "I am goin' to civilize that bastard," he said. "Right here and now." He reached out a hand for the gun, forgetting that he'd dropped it off at the house after shooting the deer.

"Give me a gun," he said.

"There's no gun on this saddle."

"Well why not, damit, why not?"

"Don't blame me. Why did you leave it home."

"Damn. Damn, damn, damn. Look at that black bastard eating my cow."

"That's the carcass of that old cow that aborted. That bear didn't kill her. Leave him alone, Smith."

"Eatin' one of my cows. Son of a bitch."

"Leave him alone."

Smith took a few steps away from the horse and toward the bear. The black bear looked up at him from the ripe carcass of the cow and then returned to his feeding.

"Look at him," said Smith, "won't even stop eatin' when we're here. Dirty, greedy bastard."

"What are you so mad about? It's only an old rotten carcass. He never killed that cow."

Smith looked around for a rock. There were none handy so he tore up a clod of earth and, running a few steps toward the bear, threw the clod at it. The bear had not had clods of earth thrown at it before. It was a simple, unsophisticated bear from the mountains who had never made the acquaintance of any ranchers. It looked at the flying clod of earth and batted at it with its paw.

"Stop it, Smith," she said. "These horses are getting excited."

"Ride back to the house and get my gun," he said.

"I will not."

"Hurry. Go back and get the gun. It's only a couple of miles. I'll keep teasing him here until you get back." He threw another clod of dirt at the bear.

The bear stood up and took its first good look at a rancher.

The horses, now with a good sniff of the bear's scent, snorted and danced.

"Get on your horse, you damn fool," she said.

Smith threw another clod at the bear. "You miserable, dirty black bastard," he said, "if I had an axe I'd go after you right here and now. Go on back to the house, Norah. Get my gun." The bear pushed its head forward and moved it, snakelike, from one side to the other.

Norah brought her own horse and Smith's under control to ride toward her husband. The lines of her bridle were long. She used the free end to lash Smith across the shoulders.

"Ouch," he said.

"Get on that horse," she said.

"Oh alright," he said, "alright. I s'pose he wouldn't stay until you got a gun anyhow."

He mounted and they rode off, leaving the most puzzled bear in Namko Country still standing. When some distance from it they saw it drop back to its front legs and waddle off into the jack pines. Smith shook his fist at it. "Next time," he shouted, "I will have a gun and you will become a Christian in one hell of a hurry."

There still being daylight, he considered taking a pack horse over to the draw to pick up the deer quarters but instead he took the gun and went back to look for the bear.

"What if Narcisse comes?" said Norah.

"I have waited for him three days, he can wait for me three hours."

"I thought that was the reason we had to send Sherwood down to Frenchie's, because you had to meet Narcisse."

"Talk about twisting words. Jesus. You should be in Parliament. Just make sure if Narcisse comes, don't let him go. I want to sell him a horse. We can use the money."

The bear scooted for the timber as soon as Smith appeared the second time. Smith tried to track him, but the ground was dry and he had no dog so he rode over to one meadow to look for horses and to another to look for cows. He found none. It didn't matter. It was a good day for riding.

Spring was Smith's favorite season. In spring a man looked forward to two summers and only one winter. People said the fall was cleaner and prettier, but in fall you faced two winters and only one summer. The range was preparing for sleep in russet twilight when he got back and Norah, whose clothesline had broken again, had not started supper because she had been obliged to do the wash a second time.

Narcisse was there however. Narcisse had spoken little to Norah. He liked Smith but could barely tolerate his woman whom he found a noisy, clattering creature. It was a pity, Narcisse thought, that Smith couldn't have found himself an Indian woman or, failing that, have taken a stick to the white woman whom he'd picked. However, being Indian, Narcisse was polite and he forebore from ever indicating his feelings about Norah. "I figured Sherwood might get home before dark," she said to Smith.

"Oh, he would hardly have made it by now," he said. "You better throw something on for Narcisse and me. I guess the last of the meat is gone, en't it."

"I thought you were gonna bring that deer in."

"Oh, it would be too fresh anyhow. Throw on a lot of macaroni and cheese. If there is enough of it, maybe Narcisse and me will not notice that there is no meat in it. You'll eat, Narcisse?"

"I got to go real quick," said Narcisse.

"Nobody has got to go real quick until they're killed," said Smith.

"I'm s'posed to be in that place Pella Coola."

"Bella Colla. What are you doin' there?"

"I'm lokkin'."

"Ah. So you're a logger now, Narcisse. Well, that is probably smarter than bein' a cowboy. But I tell you Narcisse, you will not like it for long."

"How much money do you make, Narcisse?" asked Norah.

Narcisse, who knew exactly, said he guessed it was about twenty dollars a day.

"Twenty dollars a day," she said. "Imagine. What would it be like to have twenty dollars cash money comin' into the house every working day?"

She was talking to herself. They realized this, so paid no attention.

"I tried logging for a few months after the war," said Smith. "It is a poor kind of life. Whistles blowin'. Everybody hollering. And nothing but goddamed trees around you. How do you like the Bella Coola yourself?"

"It's OK, I guess."

"A dark, wet stinkin' place," said Smith. "It is no place for people like you and me, Narcisse."

"Sure lots money," said Narcisse.

"You will get over that feeling," said Smith.

"Just like Smith, you'll get over being interested in money," said Norah.

"Surely there is some coffee," said Smith to her.

She brought them coffee.

"You didn't happen to spot Sherwood when you came across, did you?" she said. Narcisse agreed. He had not spotted Sherwood.

"Narcisse," said Smith. "How'd you like to buy that little buckskin mare, the one I call Dancer."

"I don't think I know that horse."

"Great horse for kids," said Smith. "Put one of your kids aboard Dancer and he will really get smartened up in a hurry."

Narcisse sipped his coffee with pleasure and lit a tailor-made cigarette. He enjoyed conversation with a smart man.

"Maybe I come back for her in ten years," he said.

"She might be past her peak then," said Smith.

"Maybe I do like Ken Larsen says about his wife. He keeps her until she's forty and trades her in on two twenties."

"Ken will find out he ain't wired for two-twenty," said Smith, but that went past Narcisse; there was no electricity on the Namko Reserve.

"Then there is that young stud I got," said Smith. "He is just like his father. I don't want two studs, I might as well sell one of them."

"S'pose I had two studs like that," said Narcisse, "I would sell two of them."

Nicely done, Narcisse, said Smith to himself.

They amiably exchanged stories and insults about their horses and other people's horses for twenty minutes, sometimes becoming grave while they spoke respectfully about Namko horses long dead. It was the accepted wisdom that all the best horses were the horses of memory, not those now living.

They both smoked and sucked up coffee.

"Well," said Smith. "Have you found a horse you do want?"

"Yeah. I find him."

"What one?"

"It's that horse got that funny brand."

"You mean he ain't got my brand."

"No, that funny brand."

"You don't mean that old Lazy Z Bar horse I got years ago? Two white stockings, bay? White star on his face?"

There was no answer.

"That is the only horse I remember that I never got around to branding. Except young stuff, of course. A brand like this?" Smith went to the counter and found a pencil and discarded cigarette paper package. On it he drew the brand.

"I guess," said Narcisse.

"Well," said Smith. "Who would have believed it? I thought old Lightning Rod was dead three years ago. Wherever did you find him?"

"He hangs around that Happy Ann Meadow," said Narcisse.

"Still alive!" said Smith. "Imagine. Twenty or twenty-two years old at the least, and he toughed out three winters alone. By jing, I think we could all learn something from that old horse. In fact, I plan to think about him when I am ninety-three years old myself.

"Think of that, Norah. Old Lightning Rod is still around."

"I am thinking of it," she said.

"I guess he ain't worth much that horse," said Narcisse.

"Worth much! Worth much? Why, he ain't worth nothin'. Nothin'."

"He's good enough, I guess."

"He is not good enough." Smith leaned forward in his chair toward Narcisse. "Let me tell you about that horse. For one thing, he is so old that you will not get any use out of him."

"That's OK. I go to Bella Coola anyhow. I don't use him much."

"Then why do you want to buy the horse?" asked Norah.

"I ain't got no horse now," said Narcisse.

"That's a good answer," said Smith. "But you interrupted me. I want to tell you some of the things that are wrong with Old Lightning Rod. I won't be able to tell them all, because I can't remember them all, but I will scrape together as many as I can in the next half hour . . ."

"I am going to ride out and meet Sherwood," said Norah.

"When it's near dark? Why?"

"He'll be on the trail, won't he?"

"Anyway, your horse isn't in the corral."

"Did you turn him out?"

"Yes I did."

"Why'd you do that?"

"I didn't expect you would take a notion to go riding saddle horse tonight. All is well, Norah. He will be home as soon as he gets here. Have you got enough supper on for him too?"

"I opened three big tins of beans and there is bannock from this morning."

"Good. Then all is well. Now, Narcisse, one thing above all else about that horse. He is lazy. Rustling his own grass for three winters is the most ambitious thing that horse ever did in his lifetime. Also, in case you didn't notice, he has a bog spavin."

"I don't want to pay much money for a horse," said Narcisse.

"Did I say one bog spavin? I meant to say two. Two bog spavins. And as I remember it, a split hoof."

Norah went out. The evening star glowed. She made her way to the horse pasture, stumbling in the hummocks made at the creekside by the animals' hooves. She thrust through the heavy willows that tried to switch her face and claw her. Neither seeing nor hearing any horses, she came back across the creek, losing one boot in the mud and fishing it out only by feeling around in the slop. She walked to the gate and peered into the dark trees out of which Sherwood should come. Only the darkness of the night rode silently in from the eastern horizon.

When she came back to the house the kitchen was empty, the pot of beans boiling over. She set the beans at the back of the stove and covered them with a plate. She wasn't hungry. She made a cup of tea, turned on the radio and tuned in a children's choir on one of the evangelical radio stations broadcasting from the United States.

At eleven o'clock she thought she heard a halloo and went to the door, but it was a coyote yelling up by the draw. At eleven-thirty she heard another. This time it was Smith and Narcisse, driving a dozen horses to the corral, a plunging dark mass tearing the creek waters apart and cracking the rocks with their sparking hoofs at the shoreline. Smith was hazing them with his high, artificial yell. Half an hour later there was more racket when they turned them out again to the horse pasture. She ran to the door as the horses went past.

"Did you keep my horse in the corral?" she said.

Smith trotted his horse over to her. "Yeah, he is there. Not that there is any point riding him, but he is there."

"Sherwood isn't home yet."

"Well, maybe he is staying over at Frenchie's for the night."

"He should be home long ago."

"Not if he is stayin' at Frenchie's, he shouldn't. He can't sleep at Frenchie's and be at home here at the same time."

"I'm worried, Smith."

"All is well, Norah," he said.

"You always say all is well."

"And you always say all is not well. It is just the difference of our temperaments."

"Well, I am going to ride to Frenchie's right now."

"Leave it, leave it be, will you. I will ride over, since you insist."

He started for the door.

"Are you going now?"

"In a minute or two. Give him twenty minutes more. If he ain't here, I will ride over. Both Sherwood and me can spend the night at Frenchie's, if that's the way it's got to be."

Half an hour later he came back to report that Narcisse had gone with a horse. Narcisse had taken old Lightning Rod after all. Smith would have felt badly had the rest of the country learned of him selling such crowbait but he had resolved the problem by making a gift of the horse. This preserved his reputation. People said that there were times that Smith would not sell you a horse, but he might give you one.

"You are no businessman," Norah said.

"I never claimed I was. I am a rancher, not a businessman. Sherwood is back?"

"No."

"Alright then, I'll go."

"I am going to ride with you."

"Go to bed and stop worrying."

She looked at him, silent. He fidgeted. "Oh alright. We will both go. There is no need for it, but we will both go.''

"You got your horse in the corral too?''

"Yeah.''

"Why'd you keep him in, if you wasn't worrying yourself?''

"I am not worried. I do not worry. You can do enough worrying for any two normal people. There is no worrying left for me to do around this place. Now, just so I don't fall in a fainting fit, I am gonna eat one plate of beans and then we will go, OK?''

She went out, and was back in the kitchen before he'd taken a bite. "You better come out, Smith,'' she said.

Sherwood's horse was in the yard, the saddle empty. It had stepped on one line and broken it off; the other was trailing. "Oho,'' said Smith. He spoke gently to the horse. "Now boy, now boy, now boy.'' He walked slowly toward it.

It backed away, trod on the remaining rein and he grasped the bridle. "Now boy,'' he said. "Now boy.'' He looked at the shoulders. The horse had been lathered up; the hair was stiff with dried sweat. He examined the saddle and walked around the horse while Norah held its head.

"He ain't scarred up and there is no mud on the saddle,'' he said. "No doubt all that has happened is that Sherwood got off him for a minute and then couldn't get back on again. He's a tall horse. Sherwood has to make quite a jump to get into that first stirrup.''

Norah made no answer.

"Put a new bridle on him,'' said Smith. "We will lead him back over the trail. Sherwood will be a little tired of walking when we get to him. I think he will be pleased to have a horse to come back on.''

Before she found the other bridle, however, Sherwood walked into the yard with his chaps slung over his thin shoulders. He was whistling. She reached the kitchen door almost as quickly as he did. Smith was inside.

"Well, Sherwood,'' Smith said. "You are late for supper.''

"I'm sure hungry,'' said Sherwood, and slung his chaps on the peg. Norah followed, a step or two behind the boy, as he walked to the stove and slid the plate aside on the bean pot.

"Only beans?'' he said.

"There will be meat tomorrow,'' said Smith. "Let us eat. You had better have something too, Norah.'' He sat in the chair at the head of the kitchen counter and Sherwood sat on the bench at one side.

''We've been worried, Sherwood,'' she said.

''What about?''

''Yes,'' said Smith. ''That is what I have been saying. What about? Let us have the beans, Norah. They are not the finest food on earth, but we can think about oatmeal mush while we are eating them and feel lucky.

''Mind you, Sherwood,'' he continued, ''I was surprised when your saddle horse came home before you did.''

''Oh, that was just a couple of miles up the road,'' said Sherwood. ''He startled and I went over his head.''

''Oh yes ...?''

Smith wanted to hear more. Sherwood, sensing this, took his time in answering.

Norah brought the bean pot over and filled their plates and stood waiting, as Smith was waiting, for the answer. Smith pretended not to be waiting, but he was, she knew.

''There was a bear come right up the path toward us.''

''Ah. That bear. I imagine that would be the bear that I was educating this afternoon.''

''I was trottin' old Bud and he never saw the bear until we was almost on top of him. So when he stopped, I kept goin', right over his head.''

''... Yeah ...''

''Old Bud, he went one way. The bear went 'woof' and he went the other way.''

''What did you do, Sherwood?'' said Norah.

Sherwood considered his answer before delivering it. ''I just sat there in the trail feelin' lonely,'' he said.

When she looked at Smith, he was laughing, silently, bubbles of amusement rising from his thin gut but making no pop when they came out his mouth. He spoke to her. ''I like that,'' he said. ''Feelin' awful lonely. I like that.''

These words he spoke to Norah, but he went further. He turned to the boy and paid him the highest compliment it was within his power to utter. ''I admire your style, Sherwood,'' he said.

"We are lucky Sherwood is alive," said Norah, but Smith paid her no heed and continued an amiable conversation with Sherwood.

"Sherwood," he said. "You know, it wouldn't surprise me if you was to make a rancher some day."

Norah, who was still holding the pot, said, "Yes, Sherwood, you will be a rancher some day."

They both looked up at her. Up to this point, they had been paying her little attention.

"You will be poor and you won't know the difference," she said. "Your house won't ever have a flush toilet and you will dress like a bum."

"But, then," she continued, dropping her voice, "that won't matter, will it? Because you will be a rancher, like your father. And no matter how tough things are, you will always have the satisfaction of knowing that you are superior to all the poor, non-ranchers who infest the rest of this world. You will be like Smith. Smug." She repeated, in even softer tones, "Smug." She said it a third time. "Smug."

She carried the bean pot toward Smith but instead of pouring it on his plate she poured the whole steaming mess into his lap, and once more, sweetly, she said, "Smug."

Smith tore open his belt and slapped the pants to his knees to avoid scorching the family jewels. Sherwood, too, was on his feet.

"Holy God Smith!" said Sherwood.

Norah smiled again. "Good night, gentlemen," she said, and went upstairs to the bedroom.

"Smith," said Sherwood. "Smith. What did she do that to you for?"

Smith looked at the hole in the air left by his wife. "She must be mad about something," he said.

Taking a table knife, he began to scrape the beans from his pants to the floor. "Your mother should have been a gunfighter. She has the fastest draw in the west. You better hunt another can of beans from the cupboard."

Thus the day ended, shortly after midnight.

It had been a good day for the deer, although short, and a confusing one for the bear. Norah's day had been poor. Smith's day had been, as usual, not bad.

But for Sherwood the day had been immense, grand, huge beyond his imagination. He knew that even when he was an old, old man, he would still remember this day, the day his mother dumped the plateful of beans into Smith's lap, on purpose.

# SARAH'S COPPER

WHEN JOHNNY QUA knocked the tail lights off the traveling salesman's Buick, the first thing anybody said was that he was an Indian.

"The Indian went right through the red light," said somebody on the sidewalk.

"He probably thought it was a sunrise," said somebody else.

Johnny pried open the door of his old International half ton and walked to the point of impact, the red rubies of tail light glass crackling under his boots. Sarah, his wife, got out of the passenger side just as another comment floated off the sidewalk. "Probably been all day in the beer parlor," said the spectator.

"He ain't had nothin' to drink," said Sarah.

The man shrugged and walked away. It was not a conversation worth continuing or an accident worth any more watching, not even on a quiet weekday on Oliver Street.

The salesman flung his door open and got out, leaving the big motor mumbling and the music playing out the twin speakers of the car radio. He looked at the shattered lights, the twisted chrome, the torn fender and swore.

"I'm sorry I hit you," said Johnny. "It's my fault, I guess."

"You are goddamed right it is your fault."

"Funny thing, I never see that light. I guess it's new light they got here."

"You got eyes, haven't you? I thought you people were supposed to have great eyesight. Can't you see a bloody street light?"

"He said he was sorry," said Sarah.

The salesman did not welcome the contribution. "Listen," he said, "I earn my living driving this car." He stressed the word 'living.'

"We use our car to make a living too," she said.

The salesman looked at the shabby old International—a cracked windshield, rotting fenders and loose doors—all stuck together with dried mud. His silence was eloquent. When Johnny couldn't produce proof of insurance, the salesman called for the police and they were, in a short time, attended by a constable recently graduated from the Regina school who clearly had expected there to be more to police work than broken tail lights on Oliver Street.

The policeman quickly established that the salesman carried half a million dollars worth of public liability and that Johnny had none. Having stood downwind of the Indian long enough to sniff for alcohol, he informed Johnny, briefly and unemotionally, that the truck was impounded and would remain so until he bought insurance and brought his pink slip to the station.

"That ain't paying for my damage," said the salesman.

"Maybe we pay you now," said Johnny. "I got twenty-five dollars."

"Twenty-five dollars!" said the salesman.

"Ain't much damage I don't think."

"On a Buick?"

Sarah said, "It's an expensive car, Johnny."

The policeman drew the salesman a few paces away. It was not far enough that the Indians would not be able to overhear, but it was a gesture. If they chose to listen, it was their business. They had, in any case, been implicitly removed from all dialogue since the policeman first arrived on the scene, the two white men having conversed with one another past the faces of the Indians.

"You could be a long time collecting," the policeman told the salesman.

"I could collect from a white man fast enough."

"If he wants to go back and sit on his reserve there is nothing in the law that can touch him," said the constable. "You can't sue, you know."

"And probably hasn't got a pot to piss in or a window to throw it out of," said the salesman.

He took Johnny's twenty-five dollars and they all went to the station to make out accident reports.

"You want any help on that, Johnny?" said the policeman.

"We can read and write, you know," said Sarah.

The salesman looked at the policeman, just long enough to tell him that he was sorry to see a man taking lip from such a sulky little bitch. Then they began to discuss road conditions to Prince George, the Prince George hockey team's achievements and the latest series game in Quesnel. They were still engaged in amiable conversation when Johnny and Sarah handed over the forms, which were wordlessly accepted.

For the rest of that afternoon Johnnie and Sarah had the opportunity to re-examine the Indian's place in the modern industrial state. They did not, of course, have one. Johnny had bought the truck with money he had made from a hay contract. Being a reserve Indian and capable of eluding bailiffs should he choose or forget to make time payments, he had been obliged to pay all cash for it.

Even this had not been without difficulty. At the first used car lot to which he had gone, the salesman had demanded to see the cash before he would talk with him. Johnny had turned on his heel and walked to the next lot where he bought the first clunker they showed him. He had gained some satisfaction by driving it back to the first lot, parking beside the gas pumps and jerking a thumb to tell the salesman he wanted his tank filled. But it had been a second-rate victory; it was, after all, a third-rate truck.

Having spent all his money for the truck, some gas, some groceries and two new tires, he had left the matter of buying insurance to tomorrow, a portion of time not made inconvenient by immediacy.

Now, however, when the law required the proof of insurance in the hard here and now, he had no money to buy it. He could not buy the insurance on time, for the same reason that he could not buy the truck that way.

He had a contract to haul poles for a rancher near One Eye Lake, but the rancher was uncomfortably habituated to the old Indian custom of drawing money ahead on contract work and he now never advanced more than enough for a week's groceries. The Indian Department, whose children they were, might have advanced the money for insurance. But Johnny was not destitute. He was the owner of a truck, one of the few Indians on Namko Reserve who had such evident affluence. Therefore, he was not eligible.

All with whom they dealt were hard put not to be brusque in their replies. A century had gone by since the whites had herded these people onto the reserves, put their hands on nice, new ploughs and told them to go ahead and push and everything would work out. The buggers still wouldn't push them.

"You remember that big meeting the college bunch had up

here?'' said Johnny to Sarah. ''All the time they keep saying, 'The Indian people have got to tell us what they want.' Here's me. I know what I want. I want insurance on my truck.

''It's always the same. S'pose you tell them something you want, it don't never work. You tell them some one thing, they never like it.''

''Lay off that Uncle Tom talk,'' said Sarah.

He proceeded to irritate her further. ''Lo, that's my name. Lo the Poor Indian. Most famous Indian ever was, ain't it?'' He crooned a little lament in Chinook, ''Halo muckamuck, halo chickamin, nika sick tumtum.''

She grew dark and broody, so he stopped it. She was, Johnny calculated, probably smarter than he was and certainly she was better educated, having passed Grade Ten. Also, she maybe had more push than he did. But as a wife, she was not amiable. They had been married less than a year and already he knew that. She was also strange, even for a Kwaguleth.

The Kwaguleth were a coastal nation who knew everything about the sea and cared little about the land. It was said that they thought themselves better than other Indians. The Kwaguleth themselves always denied that they held any feeling of superiority, but they were all sensibly aware that there was a great deal of evidence to that effect.

That Sarah and Johnny had met was a mere accident, created by an all-Indian baseball league playoff at Mission in the Fraser Valley. That they had married was a surprise to all, and in the case of all close relatives, a considerable disappointment.

They did not look alike. She was small, round, and, in her early twenties, running rapidly to fat. She wore large eyeglasses of grey metal frames and there was much grey metal in her teeth. He was long and straight as tap water, his skin was dark and, as was common to some of his people, would be almost black in his old age. For teeth, he had a mouthful of pearls. Every young girl and several women on Namko Reserve had watched him and waited for him while he matured in heedless good health and cheerful spirit. What, they asked, did he see in Sarah?

They could not speak to one another in their own languages, so they conversed only in English. For the kids who had gone to school, this mattered little; English was, in any case, the first and almost the only language. But in the fifties, many of the older Chilcotins on the Namko Reserve knew only a few dozen English words. They spoke to Sarah not at all. They might not have spoken with her much even if she had mastered that wildly intricate language in which no verb was consistent from one sentence to the next.

The pan-Indian movement of the sixties was scarcely to be glimpsed at this time and the Chilcotins were in no hurry to adjust themselves to any such thoughts. To them all other Indians and, occasionally, whites as well, were known by the single name of Shuswap. The Shuswap were people of yet another language group who lived to the east of the Fraser River, but Chilcotins had fallen into the custom of using the word to describe anybody who was not one of their own. Johnny's wife was called, sometimes within her hearing, the Shuswap woman Johnny Qua's got. They lived lonely in a two-room place on the edge of the Reserve. It was unusually ugly: two-by-three studs—unseasoned timber which had split and warped—for the walls, imitation brick siding on the outside, cardboard substituting for glass in some of the window panes, which was accentuated by the gingham curtains that Sarah starched and ironed. There were no fences in the Reserve, horse corrals excepted, so the boundary of their yard was unclearly defined; neighboring dogs used it for both copulating and fighting.

When they got home the day after the accident, having hitched a free ride on the Stage, she fried meat and potatoes for him and went to the bedroom, closing the door behind her. Half an hour later, while he was drinking coffee beside the stove, she opened the door and called him.

"Maybe I got something for you, Johnny."

When he came in she was sitting on the bed, her feet in the shallow tin trunk she had brought with her from the coast. In her hands was a copper, a shield-shaped piece of metal black as charcoal and scrawled on the face with crude designs.

"What you think of this," she asked.

"Not much," said Johnny.

"You mean it don't look like a truck?"

"Don't look like anything," he said, "just an old piece of black metal. What's that on it, somebody's face?"

"It's Nungamela, that's his name. It's my copper. Comes to me from my mother's brother, old-time way."

"Now look, us two are just two Indians, talking together and Custer can't hear us. Tell me what it really is."

"It's a truck, that's what it is. We can sell this for enough to get the truck back from the cops. Enough easy. Maybe it's worth thousands."

"There is nobody in this country goin' to pay thousands for that thing. I can tell you that. I ain't no businessman, but that I can tell you."

"You ain't no rich white man either, Johnny. The antique shops in Vancouver will buy it."

"Totem poles I can see, maybe," he said, "but not that."

She reached into the blue tin trunk, poking beneath the white confirmation dress that would never fit her again, the Bible she won in Grade Five at Mission School, the few dresses and her one pair of high heeled shoes. She brought up a photograph, cracked, faded, lumpy with the gobs of glue which held it to a cardboard backing. The photograph was apparently not an original but a photo of a photo taken at about the turn of the century. It showed half a dozen Kwaguleth in full regalia, standing sober, shoulder to shoulder, like children posed for a class photo. Behind them was an old Indian long house.

"You see there's writing on the pole at the corner of the big house?"

"Yeah, sort of. I can't read it."

"I'll tell you what that says. It says, 'Chief Klackawa broke a copper worth eleven thousand blankets.' He broke it and it was worth eleven thousand blankets. That's maybe like eleven thousand dollars in money today."

"What for did he break it?"

"He broke it because it was worth eleven thousand blankets and he was a high chief, that's why he broke it."

"I don't understand," he said.

"You aren't s'posed to."

He sat on his heels and looked long at the picture.

"I don't s'pose," he said, pointing to the other side of the house, "that there is another sign over there about Chief Klackawa goin' through any red lights, is there?"

She laughed, pushed him over backward with her foot. "Nothin' but a Chilcotin savage," she said.

He sat on the floor, his hands braced behind him, palm down on the lino. "Your ancestors broke coppers, I break GM trucks, that's all I said."

"We'll hitch into the Lake, take a bus to Vancouver and sell it," she said.

"No, we won't."

"We can, I tell you. It don't matter how crazy my ancestors were, there is white men around today just as crazy."

"I didn't say whether we can or not. I said we won't. That's yours."

"Johnny, it don't mean anything to me."

"It's your family's. It's part of them. It ain't for me or for fixing up trucks."

"It don't mean anything to me, Johnny. It's just a piece of stuff from the old, crazy days. If it was important to me, I'd tell you it was."

"You would tell me, would you?"

"Sure I would tell you. The copper don't mean anything to me. The picture is different. It means something." She held out the picture and pointed to one of the dim figures who stared bleakly out of the last century. "That man was one of my ancestors."

"What's your mum and dad gonna say if they hear we sold this thing?"

She answered that they couldn't think much worse of him than they did already and because of the way she said it, with that warmth, that understanding, that stuff called love, the voice that the other people never heard her use, he accepted that explanation with a laugh. Two days later they got off the bus in Vancouver, the driver recommending to them the North Coast Hotel near Skid Road.

"You mean they got reservations for us here too," said Sarah.

"All I mean is, the Indian people often stay there," said the driver.

"If it's cheap, it's good," said Johnny, and led her away. They were almost an hour finding the place, although it stood but twelve blocks from the bus station.

"Cash in advance," said the clerk. "No booze and check out by five o'clock or you pay for an extra day."

Sarah signed the register "Chief Klackawa and One Klootch," but the clerk, having counted the money, did not retain enough interest to read what she had written. They slept badly with a broken neon light hissing by the window.

The day was worse than the night, for they made the familiar discovery of travelers from the lonely places of the province. In the city, where everything is, everything is hidden by the force of numbers. A skilled man may track and find a single deer in a thousand acres but he is helpless to find one particular salmon among the thousand on an acre of spawning beds. Ranchers, cowboys, trappers, prospectors and other such people from the back of beyond had devised a system for coping with Vancouver, one which had nothing to do with telephone books or street maps. They obtained guides. Usually they carried the street address of one friend or acquaintance and they caused themselves to be delivered, unannounced, to that doorstep. Thereafter, the friend arranged all their business and social affairs and those which he could not arrange were simply left unconsummated for another year. Neither Sarah nor Johnny had a friend in the city, so they walked the streets, Johnny carrying the copper in its wrapping of brown paper. There must be ten, perhaps twenty antique shops in so large a town; chance could not help but deliver them to one.

Chance first delivered them to three pawnbrokers for conversations of mutual and total incomprehension. By noon, they had strayed to a section near the financial district and found four shops called "Antique." Two dealt in period furniture, one in turquoise and the fourth was a coin dealer. The coin dealer directed them to the city museum and drew a map on the brown paper wrapping of the copper but they became lost so long, so far, that Sarah agreed promptly when Johnny announced that it wasn't worthwhile anyway, museums didn't buy things, they were government places. Governments only took things. She had worn her high heels to Vancouver, a bad decision, her foot had blistered and she had begun limping. Her dress, which was of synthetic cloth, was wet beneath the arms and down the back; they had chanced upon one of Vancouver's occasional hot days when the humid air was steaming in the sun. The people who could had fled the downtown for the beaches or their gardens in the suburbs. Those who remained downtown were irritable because they had to be there.

By midafternoon, they had found only one Indian specialty shop, operated by a Mr. Balkarian. It was his custom to cast himself at the feet of any customer and to drive for the throat of any who wanted to sell to him. His supplies were, in any case, ample. He kept several carvers of indifferent talents in his debt and had learned to enhance the antiquity of what they created by aging their products for several days in a smokehouse. Balkarian had heard of coppers but, being a student of the dollar rather than of the culture, he cared little about them. He offered twenty dollars, permitted himself to be bid up to a hundred and then let it be known that there were limits to his philanthropy and that he was already serving as the sole financial support of a dozen hapless Indian families. The hundred dollars was about twice what Johnny thought the thing worth, but before he could accept, Sarah snatched it from the counter and walked out the door, leaving him with no choice but to follow. Balkarian did not pursue.

Only a few doors distant, opportunity plucked at their sleeves once more. A and B Traders had only one basement window showing to the street, but this was set with a handsome Tson'qua speaker's mask. Within, the place was dusky and, being below ground level, almost cool.

A.B. Puddicombe, owner, manager and sole employee of A and B Traders, held the copper at arm's length. "A beauty," he said, "and a heavy one, too." Because he was old and his arms tired quickly, he stood the copper on a table, held the top with one hand and continued to look at it. "Does it have a name?" he asked.

Johnny, who could not remember, turned to Sarah. Her face glistened with sweat and her glasses had fallen down on her short nose; she was pushing them back with her thumb.

"Ain't no name," she said, " 'sa copper, that's all."

Johnny felt both apprehension and exasperation. She could speak perfect and unaccented English. When she dropped the grammar and picked up the Indian dialect tone there was usually unpleasantness in store for someone.

"Some of them had," said Puddicombe, "some of them had."

"Might be you want to buy it from us," said Johnny. Now, as throughout the long day, he played the role of owner and seller. That was, Sarah said, a man's work.

"I'm not a store," said Puddicombe, "I buy on consignment."

"What's that?"

"Somebody orders something, I find it for them. For a commission. I'm a commission buyer."

"Ain't nobody wants to buy one of these here coppers?"

"I'm sure there are. But you'd have to give me time to find a buyer."

"Don't got time. We need money right now."

"Anyway, I wouldn't sell it for you right now."

"Why not?"

"Because I would be cheating you, that's why."

"Never stops nobody else," observed Johnny.

"No, I mean that. Have you any idea how bad the fishing's been this season for the coast people? They're selling off these things for next to nothing. Believe me, it's not the time to sell."

"But we got to sell, now."

"That's what everybody says. That's the trouble, don't you see? Keep it for a year. A year from now, I can get you a good price for that. A good price."

"I can't eat food somebody's goin' to give me next year," said Johnny.

"You give us somethin', we'll take it," said Sarah.

"It's yours then," said Puddicombe, who had suspected so from the start.

"Yes," said Johnny.

"You buy from us cheap, you make lots of money when you sell it yourself," said Sarah.

"When you sell it next year," said Johnny.

"I do business only one way," said Puddicombe.

"It's only old thing kickin' around," said Sarah. "We know it ain't worth much money."

Puddicombe, before he diverted his retirement years into consignment buying, had been twenty-five years a schoolteacher and he kept the distressing habits of the profession. Given an opportunity, he could no more resist the temptation to lecture than a longhaired dog can abstain from rolling in rotten fish.

"You shouldn't say that," he said. "These were articles of great prestige."

"It's all old stuff for me," she said.

"You have no idea," said Puddicombe, "these traded for fortunes. Reputations were made and lost in coppers. At a big potlatch, a chief might throw his copper into the fire or into the sea; he might break it. When he did he was greater than all the other chiefs that he had shamed. There was something (he held up his thin, blue-veined arms), something magnificent about it all."

She pouted and her face grew dark and muddy. "I don't know nothin' about that old stuff," she said. She limped to a chair, sat down, pulled off one shoe and felt a blister with her fingertips.

"What would you do s'pose you was me, and needed money?" said Johnny.

"There is one thing you might try," said Puddicombe. "It's only a chance, but what have you got to lose by trying?" He pulled open the door of a shabby desk, rooted about with his slender fingers, and brought forth a business card.

"This man," he tapped the card with one long finger, "has a lot of money. A great deal of money. And he's an impulse buyer. If you happen on him just at the right time, he might buy it on the spot. Take a taxi to this address. I'll phone and tell him you're coming."

"How much you s'pose I ask?"

"How can you put a value on a copper? There's a dollar's worth of metal in it. Most of them were hammered out of copper sheathing on old ships' bottoms. In the old days, the famous ones traded for the ransom of kings."

"It ain't the old days," said Johnny.

"It's awfully hard to suggest anything to you. Why don't you start at two thousand dollars."

"Two thousand!"

"A man with a lot of money will sometimes buy for two thousand when he won't for two hundred. There's prestige involved. It's all really part of the same picture."

"Two thousand dollars," said Johnny.

Sarah took the copper from the table and limped toward the door.

"We'll get a taxi," she said. Johnny walked after her, rattling the change in one pocket with his hand.

"Good luck," said A.B. Puddicombe.

"Thank you," said Johnny.

Sarah was already out the door.

At Arnie Weller's apartment it was the cocktail hour. He, his wife and two other couples were about to leave for the football game. The Lions Football Club had but recently been established in Vancouver and the populace treated it with a respect that ancient Sparta had reserved only for warriors who fought at Thermopylae. The living-room radio was already devoted to arcane discussions about strategy and tactics for this night's game and the couples divided their comments between discussing the qualities of the teams and the qualities of the radio commentators. Football being central to the scheme of human affairs at the moment, people who were close enough to utter public comments upon the performance shared in the team's general public acclaim, and even those so far removed that they could do no more than comment upon the commentators enjoyed some elevation of status.

Status had been a lifetime pursuit for Arnie Weller, there being not much else to chase when you have inherited a fortune. His clothes had status and so had his manners, both being almost flawless. He had attended many universities, but he had never had to meet a payroll or be on one, so his lack of ability to ever do any single thing well went unnoticed for forty years. He had married the prettiest and silliest girl in town and she found in him nothing wanting. They were the pleasant and inoffensive rich. If they had done the world no good it could be said with equal truth that they had done it no harm and for this they were envied by both the successful and the unsuccessful in their circle of acquaintance.

Candice Weller was startled when the two Indians' arrival took the form of a hesitant tap on the apartment door. The high-rise was among the first of the city to be supplied with an intercommunication system and a buzzer system to the locked lobby door.

Johnny and Sarah had pondered long before the arrays of buttons and speakers. They had found a solution in following another couple for whom the buzzing door had swung open. The four people rode up the elevator in an atmosphere of clammy suspicion, all with eyes fixed upon the numbered lights at the front as if expecting a message from God to be written there.

"Oh, you're here to see Arnie," said Mrs. Weller. "Do come in." She called Arnie twice. He was in heated argument with one of his guests, insisting that the Lions must take to the air.

Mrs. Weller would have offered the couple a drink, but she had heard somewhere that Indians could not or should not have it. Arnie resolved the matter by taking them away to a corner of the living room. "Mr. Puddicombe tells me you have a copper."

Johnny unwrapped the parcel and handed it to him.

"My dear, your foot is hurt," said Mrs. Weller with a squeak in her voice.

Sarah looked down. The blister had broken and a drop of blood had eased out through the shoe onto the broadloom.

"It ain't nothin'," said Sarah.

"Do sit down. Let me get you something for it."

"Ain't nothin'," said Sarah.

Sarah took the evening paper from the nearby coffee table, laid it on the floor and placed her small foot upon it.

"Isn't it hurting awfully?" Mrs. Weller asked, but Sarah did not answer. She watched Johnny, Arnie and the copper.

"Is it a name copper?" asked Arnie.

Johnny was trying to remember the name Nungamela, but it then occurred to him that perhaps he was confused and Nungamela had been the name of the famous copper that was worth eleven thousand blankets. He looked enquiringly at Sarah.

"It's just a copper," she grunted.

"Well, of course, who could know now," said Arnie. He held the piece at arm's length and squinted at it.

"I hope you're not thinking of hanging that in the living room," said Mrs. Weller.

"How about the summer place?" he asked.

"If it's in the TV room," she said.

Arnie held it aloft to his guests. "What do you think of this?" he asked.

They showed little interest. "If that's where you get your kicks, Arnie . . ." said one.

"Well, I like it," he said.

"We've hardly got time to get to the game," said Mrs. Weller.

"This won't take long." He looked at it again. "Yes," he said, "I like."

"How much Mr. Squaw?" he said.

Johnny looked at Sarah, but her eyes remained fixed on the carpet. He shuffled his feet.

"Name a price," said Arnie, "I can only say yes or no."

Johnny spoke without conviction.

"One thousand dollars?" he said.

"Done," said Arnie.

"Oh, Arnie," said Mrs. Weller.

"It's for my room, not yours," he said. He seated himself at a nearby table, pulled out a checkbook and a pen.

"The name's Qua," said Johnny. "Q-U-A."

Arnie wrote and stood with the check in his hand.

"There is one thing more I'd like, if you don't mind."

"What's that."

"Well, it's just a little thing. When you make out the receipt, would you be good enough to write a little statement on it that you're Indians."

"You don't know we're Indians!" said Johnny.

"Well, there's on-reserve, there's off-reserve. I just like it on my record, that I bought from genuine Indians, registered under the Indian Act."

"You want I should write that down?"

Sarah stepped off the newspaper, reached for the copper on the table and held it in her two hands.

"Yes," said Arnie. "If you don't mind, I'd appreciate it."

He turned when his wife uttered a small shriek. "What are you doing?" she cried.

All of them, even the guests beside the liquor cabinet, turned to Sarah. Bracing it across her knee, she was bending the heavy copper back and forth.

"What are you doing?" shouted Arnie, as the torn metal finally parted.

She stood before him, her glasses fallen half-way down her nose and looked up at him. She threw the two pieces clattering at his feet and loudly, clearly, spoke a few throaty words of Kwaguleth.

"What did she say?" said Arnie to Johnny.

"I don't know. Her language, it's different from what I talk."

Sarah spoke, again clearly. "What I said was, 'I break my copper in front of you.' "

"What do you mean?" said Arnie.

"This is madness," said his wife.

"You don't expect me to buy this when it's broken," said Arnie.

"Ain't no reason for you to pay anything," said Sarah. "Ain't nothin' but an old piece of metal."

She turned and walked to the door and Johnny followed.

"What do we do now?" he said.

"We go," she said.

"Have we offended you in some way?" said Mrs. Weller. They did not answer her, but opened the door and walked out.

"Wait a minute," shouted Arnie, "wait a minute." He walked toward the door, but it closed in his face.

"This is madness," said Mrs. Weller. "It's madness."

"You made quite a deal, Arnie," said one of the guests.

"I paid their price without a question," said Arnie.

"You mean, that's why she broke it and threw the pieces at you."

"You're unfair," shouted Mrs. Weller, "terribly unfair. Arnie paid their price and never haggled. He was handing them the check."

"Yeah, sure," said the guest.

Mrs. Weller looked at the four guests standing beside the liquor cabinet, and saw the light of pure malice shining in every eye. More quickly than Arnie, who was sometimes less than swift in new social situations, she saw that a story had been born and that nothing would ever kill it. Weeks, months, years from today, their friends would snicker about how Arnie dealt with Indians. It would be told openly and conveyed in silences; it would grow beyond all imagining in shape and form. In the fine raiment of her husband's reputation there was a rent that would never be mended. She almost wept.

"You're being unfair," she said, "unfair," and the four guests all smiled their fearsome smiles.

Down on the marble steps of the lobby, Sarah had a catch in her voice when she spoke.

"Oh, Johnny," she said, "I threw away your truck."

He looked at her, sad and small, shabby, near tears, standing by the shining brass door. When he spoke, his voice was gentle.

"I don't know what you done up there, Sarah. I don't know. But I figure you done it real fine, in the old-time way."

She was so overcome that she reached out and touched him, even though this was a public place. She laid her hand, palm forward, on his chest. "You're a good man, Johnny Qua," she said, and because she had touched him, he now touched her, laying his fingertips on that hand. He said nothing, but he smiled at her.

Then he jingled some change in his pocket with the other hand.

"Besides bus fare," he said, "I figure I got enough to buy you dinner at a Chinese restaurant. Let's go."

He took a step or two, turned and saw her still standing there with wet eyes.

"Come on, High Chief," he said.

She walked with him down the busy street and after a while, remembering another old-time way, she dropped back and followed him at a distance of three paces.

None of the people on the street paid them the slightest attention. There were always one or two Indians on the streets.

# THE OWNER
## OF THE GANG

IN A COUNTRY where many men had only one nickname and some
had to get along with none, Frenchie carried two nicknames. The
usual one was Frenchie, but he was also called, behind his back,
The Owner of The Gang. He was called The Owner of The Gang for
the same reason that an old Indian woman whose total worldly
possessions were one old, dry cow was known as The Cattle
Queen. The humor of the Chilcotin is not always kind.

The Gang Ranch everybody knew, and more than one man
dreamed, in still and private moments, of owning it. It had been
founded during the original Cariboo Gold Rush by two American
southerners, Jerome and Thaddeus Harper. That more than a
century and a quarter later the Gang's cows still bore their brand —
the JH-joined figure — was in itself a monumental tribute. The
Gang was a symbol of everything that was old and good and big
about ranching. But above all, it was the Gang's size which was
awesome. The Home Ranch, built where Gaspard Creek meets the
Fraser River near the junction of the Chilcotin River, amounted to a
village in itself, complete with school and post office. There were,
in the Gang, 38,000 deeded acres and hundreds of thousands of
other acres held by various forms of lease, grazing permit and
strong moral right. The ranch extended over grasslands, forests
and mountains. Taken all together, they made the Gang about a
tenth the size of Belgium.

Frenchie, on the other hand, held full and indisputable title to
just one hundred and eighty acres. He had a few hay leases on
scattered swamp meadows. Besides these he held what could be
best called a strong moral authority to share open range with the
other cattlemen of Namko. He could have owned more but he had,
as his wife said, the instincts of a true peasant. He could never
permit himself a debt. The few morsels of land he owned had been
paid for in cash; so also did he pay cash for his secondhand hay
machinery, his secondhand saddles, his secondhand truck and,
from time to time, his secondhand clothes. Since all the money he

ever had he had made one dollar at a time, nothing came quickly.

Made bold by whisky, Morton Dilloughboy once commented on this highly personal matter while waltzing with Frenchie's Wife at a Stampede Ball. "He thinks if he works hard enough he can be the richest rancher in our graveyard. But there ain't that much work to be taken out of the lifetime of a single man." She might have shrugged. That would have been a usual response. She chose to answer. "Neither death nor even God Almighty would be so presumptuous as to try to keep Frenchie off his own property," she said. "He'll stay and haunt. If only for the reason that he wants to be sure that two hundred years from today there is somebody of the Bernard name riding the Bernard range."

The Bernards had four children who had survived on a diet of moosemeat and beans, children who were, like the old machinery, repaired at home when ailing. When The Owner of The Gang became what he was never cut out to be—rich—there were three boys at home—Adelard (usually called Delore), sixteen, Hector, fourteen and Robert, nine. The daughter, Marilyn, had escaped by marrying a wealthy American hunter and going to live in luxurious debt in Cleveland, Ohio.

Since she would, by the nature of things, marry and produce children of another name and another family, Frenchie was able to bear the loss of her with some fortitude, strong family man though he was. Marilyn came home from time to time for visits, self-assured and well-dressed. Men in Namko wondered why they had never noticed that the Bernard girl was both pretty and clever. Even Frenchie was moved to philosophize to his wife. "Marilyn has learned to be intelligent," he said. Then, naming the other two boys old enough to be identifiable in character, he added, "Hector, on the other hand, is naturally smart. As for Adelard, Adelard has the fire." His wife said nothing.

As it happened, Marilyn made a parallel set of judgments to her mother, also privately, also in the same week. "Dad admires Hector. He loves Delore. And he tolerates me." Her mother offered no comment. To her, talk was silver and silence was gold.

Only at night did Frenchie's Wife speak and then it was to read to the children, a custom as unalterable as it was, at times, puzzling, for she read, it seemed, as much for her own hearing as for theirs.

Simple stories written for the young alternated with some of the more intricate works of classic literature. In the great killing winter of 'forty-nine when half the cattle starved to death, the family heard *Anna Karenina*, a chapter at a time. For the youngest of the brood in that year, it could have done little unless to plant in his mind the thought that Russians were associated with winter die-offs.

Frenchie traditionally paid scant attention to evening readings, particularly when he realized, shortly after she began, that she was reading fiction, which was all lies from start to finish. He himself could scarcely summon up much belief in printed material which claimed to be true and, in the ultimate, could never fully believe anything printed until and unless it appeared in the *Free Press Prairie Farmer* or *Western Horseman*.

His change of fortune began when Frenchie and Smith were taking the beef drive to Williams Lake one fall. On the saddle, near the headwaters of the Tstulantanko and the Beaver, Frenchie picked up some colored rock near their camp.

"If this was molybdenite that hill would be worth a fortune," he said.

"If we had some ham, we could have some ham and eggs, if we had some eggs," said Smith.

"I mean it. I was reading about that stuff in *Prairie Farmer*."

"Did they mention this hill in *Prairie Farmer*? Because that rock has been seen by every beef-drive crew that went over this saddle and it never excited them none. Except Morton once packed a hundred pounds of it back to build a fancy fireplace and then got too tired to mix the cement."

"Molybdenite is something new. It wasn't worth much until a year or two ago."

"What the hell," said Smith. "Let's pick up a piece and take it into the Lake and ask somebody."

In the Lakeview beer parlor two weeks later they sought professional help from Eddy Grainger, who went prospecting now and then to get away from his wife. "Just pretty rock," said Eddy.

There the matter might have ended except that, after they left the beer parlor, Eddy, who had become very drunk, prowled the tables demanding people tell him what route the Namko beef drive came over. When this word reached Smith and Frenchie, it was enough for them to spend five dollars apiece for a Free Miner's License, and instead of trucking their horses and themselves back to Namko they rode out under cover of night, skirted the highway most of the way home and pounded their stakes into the colored rock of the hill. At home, they invited their fellow ranchers to also stake. An expedition was formed, everybody glad of an opportunity to forget cows and fences for a few days. They staked all the outcrop and camped there three nights, admiring the sun by day and the moon by night and telling lies about their horses. They had a wonderful time.

Larsen was then delegated to go again to the Lake and check the rock against somebody not as drunk as Eddy Grainger. He did this and the episode seemed to have run its normal course when he returned and reported that it was molybdenite all right but low grade and not much better than could be found in highway cuts a few miles from Oliver Street.

"If the claims are no good, it's not right that everybody should lose," said Smith. "Let's toss coins until one man has it all. Then he'll be the only loser and the rest of us will have nothing to lie about when our wives ask."

Frenchie ended up with all the shares. He took them home and put them in a bureau drawer, saying nothing about them to his wife.

Such are the cycles of economics, whether for a nation or a bunch of colored rocks. The first men who noticed the rocks took a mild interest then forgot them. Smith and Frenchie first took a stronger interest, lost it in the beer parlor, retrieved and expanded it later to include their neighbors and then again allowed it to subside to zero. There were more cycles to come.

The next cycle commenced in the fertile mind of one Willi Taube, prospector, child of a miner's home at Timmins, Ontario. Willi was prospecting when he arrived one day in Namko, although he did not so inform the inhabitants. He was, he told them, hunting moose.

His prospecting equipment consisted of one case of Queen Anne Scotch, several dozen beer, a couple of cases of clay pigeons, a thrower and a shotgun. This is what he usually carried for prospecting. He hated climbing around on rocks. He was easily lost if more than one hundred yards from the sound of highway traffic. He was afraid of wolves, bears, cougars and even coyotes and the thought of spending a night anywhere except in his own or somebody else's bed drove him to distraction. There were plenty of people who enjoyed that sort of thing, he felt, so let them go right ahead and do it. When they dug something out of the ground he and his partner, a good, solid, bucket-shop operator of the old school, were willing to find people who would throw money into the hole. This, he considered, took a great deal more skill than whacking away at the stony face of British Columbia with a hammer and a drill.

Harry Smith, as his bunco-artist partner was currently calling himself, was at this time waiting in Vancouver with several thousand dollars they had pried out of an unusually foolish doctor in Moose Jaw. It was Harry's job to arrive, waving money, whenever Willi found another mine.

"There is a place called Namko," Willi had said. "I like the sound of it. There must be some ore in a place with a name like that." Harry did not say nay. It was his view that Willi's IQ was only high enough for him to remember what an IQ was if he was told twice, but he also knew that Willi had peculiar skills not common to most mortals, and that these were the stuff that manured the great money tree.

Willi arrived at the Namko store on mail day and enquired diffidently and not too earnestly about hiring a guide for hunting moose. It was a discomfort he wanted to avoid, but one had to start somewhere. Next he brought out his equipment, the clay pigeons, the thrower and the shotgun. These he generously shared with all comers and, since all the men of the country liked guns and practically none had encountered the sport of clay pigeon shooting, he soon collected a large number of devoted admirers. He next brought out the Queen Anne Scotch and by nightfall he knew there was molybdenite ore at the headwaters of Tstulantanko Creek and that Frenchie Bernard held all the claims that had been staked there. The rest of them thought he had been asking about moose all that afternoon and evening and were surprised when, instead of hiring a guide, Willi drove off to Williams Lake. He said he needed more supplies but the supplies he needed were a compliant geologist, Harry and a helicopter.

Within three days they had examined the claim, where the geologist admitted that there was here possibly, not probably but possibly, an anomaly and that he was prepared to testify to that. Anomaly is a word commonly used to describe an abnormality in a geologic formation which may contain mineral enough to make a mine. It is like turpentine under the tail for some who bet on penny mining stocks although professional promoters such as Willi Tabue agreed privately among themselves that an anomaly was really like a bellybutton, everybody had one.

One week later Willi and Harry arrived unannounced at Frenchie's ranch with bundles of currency discreetly distributed through Harry's socks and shirts in the suitcase. They came unannounced, but not unexpected. They had failed to reckon with the Moccasin Telegraph. A party of moose hunters had seen the helicopter land on the saddle of the far hills and had talked about it in Arch MacGregor's store. Larsen, in Williams Lake for tractor parts, had spotted Willi driving past on Oliver Street. Driving across the Chilcotin plains Willi and Harry had stopped and asked the driver of the stage for advice, namely, ''How much more of this shitty road we gotta take?'' He had preceded them into Namko and dropped the word together with the week's mail. None of these reports came in with precise accuracy. The Moccasin Telegraph might, as some have claimed, tell of the death of kings within minutes, but when and if it did, one could be sure it would report the death of the wrong king in the wrong country. Usually, it was not so much a transmitter of information as a bearer of portents and omens. Like clouds in the sky, it could foretell coming events, but without precision.

Also, Moccasin Telegraph was often interesting at the expense of being factual. Men used it as a framework for telling larger and better stories.

This chanced to happen in the Namko beer parlor, a collection center of the many reports that were to make their way to Frenchie. Arch MacGregor had been moved to reminisce about another mining promotion, in another part of the country, in another era, when a promoter had boasted about how he manipulated a goddamed stupid, pea-souper Frenchman. Henry James, at a nearby table, overhead only part of Arch's story and shaped his own understanding of it. When next day he drifted in to Frenchie's for coffee, he drew Frenchie's Wife aside and murmured to her about what those mining bastards were saying about Frenchie.

When Willi and Henry entered the kitchen, Frenchie was jovial. "Ai, you remember me eh, dat damn pea-souper," he said. It was a heavier accent than anybody in the Namko Country had heard from him for years. It was heavier than Willi had heard from him ten days before, but Willi was not all-the-way smart.

Frenchie's Wife murmured politely as introductions were made and offered coffee. The visitors sat on the shabby sofa. Frenchie urged them to hunt moose, spoke eloquently about 'dat fancy big car dey got dose guys' and told a long and not very funny joke about French Canadians. Willi told a joke. Frenchie told another. Harry cleared his throat.

"Do you think it might be an idea to tell Mr. Bernard why we're here?" he said.

"I was coming to that. You see, Frenchie, we're both in the mining business."

"De mining business, well by damn." Frenchie turned to his wife. "You 'ear dat, dese gentlemen are miners."

Before Willi could continue, Frenchie revealed that he, too, was a miner of sorts, having staked claims at the head of a nearby creek. Did they know where he might get an opinion on that ore?

"We examined it, and we think it has some possibilities."

"You see it?"

"We flew in there," said Harry, shortly.

"Flew in."

"Well, not exactly, we didn't fly, we used an airplane," said Willi.

Frenchie laughed and shook his head. "You guys, you are too fast in the head for me."

Harry drew a paper from his pocket. "We like a fast, clean business deal," he said.

"You and me bot', dat's de way for me too."

Harry spread out the paper. "We want to buy out all your claims." Frenchie looked at the paper and shook his head, up and down.

"Name us a fair price and we'll pay it," said Harry.

"And no bargaining?" said Frenchie.

"No bargaining. If it's fair, we'll pay it."

"If it's fair, you pay, hokay. But dere is no bargaining, eh. None. Me, I ham no good for bargaining."

Frenchie's Wife walked out to the kitchen and stood by the window. Her hands were trembling. She put them on the counter.

"Two thousand dollars," said Frenchie.

His wife lifted a hand to her mouth and bit it. There were tears in her eyes. They were for her, for her husband, for the whole damned ignorant and backward land of the Namko.

Less than half price, thought Willi. Aloud he said, "Now that's an interesting figure."

"Just a minute," said Harry, who had his professional pride at stake. He had never yet let a mark name his own penalty.

"Wait a minute for what?" said Frenchie. "You done all your investigation, ain't it?"

"Well, there are things to be considered."

"OK, I withdraw that price."

"Withdraw?"

"Yes. Withdraw. There is a new price. Four thousand."

"Mr. Bernard, you must be joking."

Frenchie, who was rolling a cigarette, paused to light it and blow smoke in their faces.

"OK, withdraw again. Eight thousand."

"We're not here to play games, Mr. Bernard."

"Sixteen," said Frenchie.

Before Harry could open his mouth again Willi struck him on the arm. "Shut up you goddam fool," he said. "Sixteen thousand we accept, Mr. Bernard. We pay it. OK? We pay it."

"OK," said Frenchie. "Sixteen." He took the five thousand in cash they carried and a check for eleven thousand more and gave them a paper promising delivery of the claims the day he cashed it at Williams Lake. They left, declining the offer of a second cup of coffee.

"You were brilliant!" his wife said, as the big car bumped out of the dirty yard. She had never paid him such a compliment before.

"I didn't do so bad, I guess."

"You were brilliant. But watch out. Did you see the look that man called Smith gave you?"

"He wasn't happy."

"My father had a way of describing that look. He said it was the look of a man who is measuring you for a coffin." But he did not hear her. He stood with fifty one-hundred-dollar bills in his hand

and eleven thousand in his head, looking out at the grass, the jack pines and the far hills, feeling the Bernard ranch growing under his feet.

He took Delore to the Lake with him two days later for closing the deal, speaking expansively of land, of new breeding stock and of a two-thousand-dollar bull. The boy's answers were monosyllabic. Kids had no sense of the proportion of anything. Still the kid was sixteen; Frenchie had been earning his own living for a couple of years by the time he was sixteen. It did not occur to Frenchie that Delore had also.

Frenchie talked about tractors. It was perhaps time to get the first. There'd be work enough for one.

"What is Mother getting out of this?" said Delore.

"She gets everything I get. She's my wife."

"What half? The bull? The tractor? Or the High Meadow?" Frenchie grunted.

"She could use a gas-powered washing machine."

Frenchie stirred uneasily. "That fan belt's squealing," he said. They pulled off to the side of the road and experienced the usual joys of bloody knuckles, turning the adjustment on the generator with the aid of a rusty, rattling Great American Fitzall wrench.

The rest of the trip was made in silence and Delore remained silent while Frenchie, Willi and Harry did what was supposed to be the last of their business in a room at the Lakeview hotel.

"Here's a bonus," said Harry, who was smiling, although only in the mouth. He tossed Frenchie a packet of shares. "Two thousand shares," said Harry.

"I don't want to buy shares in anything," said Frenchie.

"It's a bonus," said Harry.

Frenchie examined the papers. "These are a dollar a share. That's two thousand more dollars."

"It's a superstition," added Willi. "We have always had the discoverer holding shares. Take them, it's for our luck."

"Two thousand dollars for luck?"

"It's nothing but twenty pieces of paper right now," said Harry. "We won't get listed on the market until we've done some drilling. When we're through drilling, you might still have only twenty pieces of paper."

"On the other hand," said Willi, "you might have twenty or

thirty grand. Pyramid went on the market at seventy-five cents and sold above fifteen dollars a few weeks later.''

Frenchie tucked the papers inside his denim vest. There was no pocket to take them. They poked out from his open shirt collar. ''Two thousand,'' he said, ''is what I bought my place for in 1941.''

After he and Delore went out Harry said, ''That son of a bitch.''

''You got a small mind, Harry. You're so sore about sixteen thousand that you forget we're working for fifty or seventy-five.''

''No goddam mark is gonna go away laughing at me.''

''He's doing a sixteen-thousand-dollar laugh up at the bank right now.''

''He took the stock,'' said Harry. ''He didn't spit out the hook.''

Willi and Harry went promptly to work the day after the Williams Lake deal, with well-directed energy and calm deliberation as befitted their professional status. They were as confident as a Christian holding four aces, as indeed they did, two of them being up the sleeve. A diamond drill was lifted into the claim, and by separate flight, drill cores from another location.

This is not easily done by most people, but Harry, after all, was a man who had sold leaden gold bricks to a retired prairie farmer not once but twice, on occasions separated by three months, and had the old fellow come back a third time and plead for another chance to get a good one.

Rumors were judiciously circulated while both partners remained vigorous in their denial that there was anything special about Saddle Rock Resources. The stock was floated gently on the market. Being fearful of the warehousing routine, which required heavy bribery of a stock salesman, they chose instead the device of high closing.

Using venture capital supplied by an unusually credulous dentist in Toronto and the cooperation of a floor trader, they ensured that the sale at the end of each day was a cent or two higher than the day before. In the shorthand of newspaper stock pages, this reflected a steady demand for Saddle Rock Resources. People notice these things. There are, indeed, people who notice little else in this world. Within a month, the high closing phase was ended, and the reports of the drill core having been released, the stock moved without need for manipulation. On a stock market, all the many and complex emotions of man have been reduced to two — fear and greed. Harry and Willi referred to these in terms of the little figures in a Swiss weather clock.

At the third week, Willi, who had a sense for emotional states of the investment community, announced, ''Hansel and Gretel have come out their door and the wicked witch is inside.'' The partners promptly began to unload their own shares.

''I only hope to God that damn rancher is buying what we are selling,'' said Harry.

''Don't let personalities interfere with your business judgment,'' said Willi.

''It's a matter of professional pride,'' said Harry.

''Well, don't brood about it then, do something.''

''I did,'' said Harry, ''but is it gonna work? ''

Harry was gifted with the eye of a good detective and, brief and unhappy as his time in Frenchie's home had been, he had determined that *Prairie Farmer* was the only newspaper there. With the aid of a friend who had a print shop, he produced a tear sheet purporting to be the front page of *Prairie Farmer*, and by judicious study of the mail times, got it delivered to Frenchie's mail box in Namko.

Well for Harry that he did. Frenchie had occupied himself with many things these weeks, but none had had any connection with stock markets.

He had paid one-thousand-dollar options on a half-dozen patches of grass and bought a shiny, new tractor. He had even bought a gasoline washing machine for his wife, but being from a secondhand store, it broke the third time she used it. Frenchie ordered Delore to fix it, and when the lad could not, said he would get around to doing it himself some time soon. The machine stood large on the ranch house porch where Frenchie frequently bumped into it and cursed it.

As for his two thousand shares, he had thought little about them. A week or two after they were listed, an edition of a Vancouver newspaper had wended its way into Namko and he read there that they were selling for seven cents. This indicated nothing to Frenchie except that the mining men were losing at a rate of nineteen to one. He considered himself the only man who had made money from Saddle Rock Resources.

He was, therefore, thunderstruck when Harry's ersatz clipsheet came, showing the stock to have climbed to one dollar and ten cents (which was true) and quoting experts to the effect that the Saddle Rock properties gave promise of becoming another Sullivan Mine.

"I'm going to Kamloops," he told his wife.

"To buy that bull?"

"To do business," said Frenchie, who was already pulling on his boots.

"Don't forget to get rings for the washing machine motor," said Delore.

"This is not the time to think of goddam washing machines," said Frenchie. He was gone within the hour.

He never did become a millionaire, but he touched the wand of gold in those next few days.

The stock had a glorious run and could be seen, marching across a screen, in the Kamloops brokerage offices. Until the distant and unseen Willi and Harry had disposed of their all, leaving Saddle Rock Resources to dip, flutter and then go off the board in a screaming dive, Frenchie was drunk as he had never been drunk before, on money.

Ken Larsen, who chanced to be in Kamloops that week, picked him up from the police. They had found him down by the tracks and given him shelter in the cells for a night.

When Ken delivered him to the ranch house he was drunk again, this time on whisky, and he would not leave the truck until Ken gave him two more bottles, one for each hand.

He staggered into the house, speaking to no one, and dropped in the overstuffed chair with the broken springs. His wife silently brought him a pitcher of water and a glass and left him there while she cooked a meal for the boys. They ate in the kitchen, leaving Frenchie to the darkening living-room in the fading light of the day.

"Nothing goes well forever in this world, boys," she said.

"Goes well?" said Delore. "How bad has it gone?"

She knew, he realized, because there had been a brief tumble of blurred confessions from Frenchie while the husband and wife were alone in the living room.

"Your father fell off a rainbow," she said.

"Did he blow all that money on the mining stock?"

"He did more than that. Your father is in debt to the bank, for the first time in his life."

"How could he be so stupid?"

"It's his nature," she said. "Your father only knows how to buy. He cannot sell. He was still buying after it fell back to two cents. It's not his fault. It's the way he was made."

Wordless, the boy turned and went to the upstairs loft where he made his bed with the two younger boys. She heard drawers slam. She wondered at the sounds, but it was not until he came back downstairs, the cheap tin suitcase in one hand, that she knew that their family was forever changed. He was, after all, the father's son with the father's head. She pressed two hands together, palm to palm, fingers toward the floor, but that and that alone was her only wail of anguish.

"I'm pulling the pin, Mother."

Frenchie, sprawled in the chair, lifted his head and focused his small red eyes on his son and heir. For a moment, no more, he hesitated while pride, compassion and shame battled within him. Pride won, and he chose to walk upon his heart.

"To go to the rodeo circuit, I s'pose."

"To go, and not to come back," said Delore.

"This is not a time for talking," said Frenchie's Wife.

Frenchie waved her down. "Go," he said to his son, "go and be a goddamed rodeo bum. Go."

She drew the boy to the kitchen.

"Don't say things to your father that you'll regret," she said. "He's drunk. He's very, very drunk."

"Yes, he's drunk. And when he's sober, he will still be exactly the same man, the most selfish son of a bitch the country ever knew."

"Do not say things you will regret."

"Regret, hell. You can have him." He cast a hand toward the rumpled heap of man in the chair. "There he is. The Owner of The Gang. Welcome to him."

Frenchie started out of the chair, fell back, dropped his head and closed his eyes.

Adelard walked to the door and his mother followed him. When he opened it she rose on her toes and kissed the side of his cheek. Her voice was, as usual, calm, composed.

"Write to us sometime, Delore," she said.

The boy for the first time seemed awkward and unsure.

"Yeah," he said. "Yeah, sure." He kissed his mother's cheek and walked out, closing the door quietly behind him.

She turned to the other two boys. "It's early to bed tonight, boys," she said.

"You gonna read to us?" said Robert.

She focused on his words slowly, as one awakening from sleep.

"Oh, yes," she said, "of course. It is time, isn't it?"

She moved the hissing gas lantern to the small and bare round table at the corner of the living-room, lifted a book from the wooden shelf on the wall, and finding her page from the previous evening's reading while they drew up chairs to each side of hers, she began to read from *Robinson Crusoe*.

> Our ship making her course towards the Canary Islands, or rather between those islands and the African shore, was surprised in the grey of the morning by a Turkish rover of Sallee.

She spoke calmly, evenly, without emotion, letting the clear English words tell the story by their own force.

> We plyed them with small shot, half-pikes, powder chests and such like and cleared our decks of them twice. However, to cut short this melancholy part of our story, our ship being disabled and three of our men killed and eight wounded, we were obliged to yield and were carried off all prisoners into Sallee.

Unwavering, that warm and lovely voice filled the dark and cold little room, and as she continued, even The Owner of The Gang lifted his head and seemed to listen.

# THE LAST
# DAY OF VIOLENCE

NO MAN IN the Namko Country was noisier than Morton Dilloughboy and none quieter than his son Abel. It was when the hour of the
day matched Abel's temperament that Smith and Norah came upon
him, in the languorous peace of the long northern twilight. This
was the time when the creatures of day fell silent but those of the
darkness were not yet roused, when the punishing heat of a July day
faded but the chill of the night had not yet descended. The
gloaming — nature's hour of truce.

The Smiths were riding to the annual three-day Stampede in their
rubber-tired wagon, with grub, kids, tents, bedrolls and hay piled
in the back. The great Stampede itself was a sort of truce in that
land, a time when business matters were discussed lightly or not at
all, when fistfights were rare and when all territorial boundaries
were let down, even as to separating one rancher's camp from
another on the jack-pine hill above Stampede Ground where they
congregated. No social event of the Namko calendar equaled
Stampede, not even Christmas. Men and women came to it gladly,
forgetting for those few days the latest atrocities committed upon
them by banks, by bureaucrats and by the democratically elected
governments whom they had chosen to set in authority over
themselves. So the old wagon was freighted with contentment
when it rolled out into the Beyond Meadow where, in the fading
light, they could see Abel Dilloughboy, saddled up on a grey mare.
Smith stopped the wagon.

"Shall I come over with you?" said Norah.

"No, maybe better I walk over myself."

Smith walked across the grass to where man and horse stood,
waiting.

A rope stretched from the horn of the grey's saddle to a whitened
deadfall log which Abel had been dragging. Beyond, Smith could
see a pile of such sticks. Further, dimly visible in the fading light,

was yet another pile. Man and horse had been at work for a full day, perhaps more.

Smith stopped before he reached Abel.

"Hello Abel."

The man on the horse bobbed his head, but did not answer.

"It's good to see you Abel."

"Nice to see you, Smith."

Smith looked at the cold decks of deadfall.

"You been pretty busy."

"Just tidying the place up some."

"Sure looks good," said Smith. He tried to make it sound sincere. "Very nice, Abel. You are making this meadow a real nice place."

The Beyond was like a hundred, a thousand other natural meadows. Coarse grass, patched with Red Osier brush, islanded with poplar groves and, at the edge where the jack-pine forest stood, stippled with dead pines. It needed the deadfalls cleared about as much as it needed its grass combed, but how could a man say that to Abel?

"You're coming to Stampede of course," said Smith.

The man on the horse shifted in the saddle, uneasy, and screwed his face in a knot.

With a forefinger he pushed his steel-rimmed glasses back to the ridge of his nose. The glasses, broken twice and mended loosely with tape, were set on a pudgy, almost childlike face, a soft face, vaguely formed, it seemed, except for a white scar that made a half-moon mark on one cheek. Abel was a pudgy man and, although he spent many hours in the saddle, his ass was fat. His voice, when he let it out, often wavered and sometimes the words were slurred.

He answered Smith in his usual way, which was to agree. Abel was not known to use the word no.

Smith had now approached more nearly and stood with his hand on the withers of the grey.

"That would be nice, to come to Stampede," said Abel.

"So you're coming?"

"I got to get through this job first."

Smith scratched the ground with his boot and spoke at the crease he had made. "A lot of your friends will be there. They'll be expecting you, Abel.'' When Abel did not answer he continued. ''You have a lot of friends in this country, you know. I guess you know that, don't you, Abel.''

''People are nice to me,'' said the man on the horse.

''Norah and me, we'd be real pleased if you could bunk down in our camp. You could just turn that horse loose and let her go home on her own and come down with us on the wagon.''

''Sure,'' said Abel. ''Sure, I'd like to do that. But I got to get this job done first.''

''We could wait for you, while you finish up that load.''

''No. You go on, Smith. Maybe I could get down tomorrow. Or the next day.''

''A lot of people would like to see you, Abel,'' said Smith. ''We'll be expecting you.''

Abel did not answer. Smith slapped the horse on the withers, a gesture of goodbye, and went back to the wagon.

''Is he coming?'' asked Norah.

''He said no bloody way was he coming.''

''No he didn't. Abel doesn't talk that way.''

''He said it, in his own way.''

''He won't come because he can't take violence.''

''Violence?'' said Smith. ''What is violent about Stampede? That is, if you don't happen to have been born a horse.''

''You know what I mean. Anything that's rough bothers him. He won't even help when there's branding and castrating to be done.''

''Now that you mention it, that's true.''

''Oh, don't act so damn stupid. You know that as well as I do.''

''Leave it, Norah, leave it lay. Look at that sky. Did you know I arranged it personally for you?''

But the subject of Abel Dilloughboy could not so easily be set aside. That night, as a half a dozen men and women gathered by Ken Larsen's bonfire, the pale specter of that middle-aged, empty-eyed boy was among them again, as he so long had been.

His mother, Morton's first wife, had taken him when she took leave of Morton. Mother and child had lived in Calgary while in Namko the memory of them faded.

Morton revived memories of the boy during the war years when it was learned young Abel had joined the army, had risen to the rank of officer and gone overseas. Morton himself had served in the cavalry during the First World War, happily if he were to be believed, and he never tired of repeating that it was only the cavalry that had lent some class to what might otherwise have been a vulgar brawl. Thus, through Morton, people had become caught up in the military career of a boy some had forgotten and most had never known. They were saddened when he was listed missing in action, relieved when he was later reported prisoner of war and slightly elated when, after the peace, it was learned that Abel was coming to Namko to run Morton's ranch for him. It was no hero but a large and awkward child who came back to Namko. "I guess Abel had a bad time of it during the war, but he's coming out of it now," Morton would say. It was two or three years before Morton ceased saying that and tacitly agreed with what the rest said, that Abel had a right to his own place in the world, meager as he chose that place to be. He was amiable, inoffensive and, from time to time, when he didn't forget or simply drift off the job, helpful in chore-boy work at whichever ranch he chanced to come to rest for a time. He built his own cabin on a corner of Morton's land, where he came and went as he pleased.

At the fireside on the eve of Stampede, they speculated again as to the mystery of which he never spoke, and, indeed, of the greater mystery of what kind of man he really was.

"He would never talk to Morton about the war but he did, once, just come a little close with me," said Larsen. The group around the fire was small. Morton was absent. They were warmed by whisky. It was a time of confidences.

"It came up when I got just slightly sore at him one day. He had promised to help me brand and then wouldn't do it. 'Ken,' he says, 'I have had my last day of violence.' I told him I was sorry, I could understand that. He went on, like I had never spoken. 'People can insult me. I will just take it. People can knock me down. I will just lay there. I can't ever be violent again.' So I put him to mending fence that day but he forgot what he was doing and wandered away and when I went to pay him a month later he couldn't remember anything about doing any work for me."

"They had no business putting a boy like that in the army," said Margaret Larsen. "They could see he could never make a soldier."

"Funny thing is," said Smith. "He was a good soldier."

"You said you never knew him overseas," said Norah.

"Never did. But the name Dilloughboy is easy to remember and I heard about him, more than once, by the army grapevine."

"What did you hear, Smith?" said Larsen.

"That he was the best field officer in the whole damn Canadian army. That's what I heard."

"Be damned," said Larsen.

"In case you don't know it, Ken, field officers are the ones who win the wars that the staff officers are trying to lose."

"Let's not talk about him anymore," said Norah. "Abel wants his privacy and he ought to have it."

Ken kicked the firelogs and they watched the sparks fly upward to be pinched out, one by one, by the darkness, the black, uncaring emptiness that eventually claims everything upon the earth that moves.

The faint spark in their world which was Abel still burned dimly in the little world of Namko but they could not trace it to its source, nor make any calculation of its gyrations. Had they been so gifted they would have known that he had been a participant in both the starting and the stopping of that titanic conflict of armies.

Abel blamed a friend, Desperate Desmond McCue, for starting it. He and Desmond were stacking tins of Libby's Pork and Beans on the shelves of a Calgary supermarket on an August day, when Desmond, a freckled jug-eared kid who had been recruited to the job by Abel, gave way to one of his occasional fits of despair. In Desmond, despair alternated with vast and often illusory enthusiasm.

"There has got to be something better than this to do in the world," said Desmond.

"It's steady work," said Abel. In Depression days, that logic was unanswerable.

Desmond began juggling two and then three cans of beans, a grave offense had it been noted by the supermarket's manager.

"Don't you feel that flatness about everything?"

"Flatness? I suppose . . ."

"Yes. Flat. Nothing moves. Nothing changes. Ten dollars a week now. Next year, ten-fifty maybe. And in a hundred years, maybe a gold watch."

"I think maybe that sort of thing suits me," said Abel.

"I tell you what's needed," said Desmond. "What this country needs is a damn good war."

Within hours the German armies invaded Poland and, throughout the long war that followed, it was Abel's morbid joke to blame his friend for everything that happened in those long years.

What Abel was doing was, like everything else done in the supermarket, neither dangerous, exciting or even mildly interesting. He was stacking cans of beans into the tallest display terminal yet attempted in that establishment. The pyramid collapsed and one tin cut half a biscuit out of his face.

This was a far more serious matter than might be instantly appreciated. It was a condition of Abel's employment that he equip himself with a dark suit, a necktie and enough white shirts to be cleanly clad in one each of six mornings of every week. Abel had bought two white shirts when he launched himself in the business world, and his mother, who worked at the Five and Ten, washed one each night, always leaving one in reserve. She could not get the blood from one shirt on the night of the Libby's beans episode and had burned the other with the iron. There had been a tense few hours that night, ending only when Abel bicycled across half of Calgary and borrowed a shirt from an old schoolfriend. It all took so many hours, and several dollars too, so he had forgone the attention of a doctor. The cheek cut, left unstitched, never closed and he was left with the scar.

In the first week of the war, Desmond enlisted. "You know what?" he told Abel. "I have an ambition. Some day, I am going to march down the Wilhelmstrasse playing my old man's bagpipes."

"I don't think I would fit into the army," said Abel. He was a pudgy kid, unathletic and uninspired to such contests, and most would have agreed with him. But he was saddened when Desmond left on his long march to the Wilhelmstrasse. Perhaps for that reason, perhaps for the reason that he customarily did as other people told him he should do, a week later he, too, took the King's shilling.

It is not a matter of surprise that Desmond did not play his father's bagpipes in a victory march though Berlin. Nobody did. When it ended, neither victors nor losers gave a damn about band music and parades. What is beyond surprising is that the army made use of Abel Dilloughboy and Abel made use of the army. If there be any explanation for such incongruity it may lie in the old saying that war makes a good man better and a bad man worse.

In the beginning, it was chance playing its familiar vital role in the conduct of war. Three weeks after enlistment, Abel was plucked from the ranks of the recruits and sent to an officer's training school. What lay behind this extraordinary decision by the Canadian army was a confused situation at the war's beginning which saw a number of young men fling themselves into the arms of recruiting officers without first informing their parents. Some of these enthusiasts were sons and nephews of the country's upper class who should, in the normal course of affairs, have begun army careers as they began other careers — with the clear understanding that their future was in the executive ranks.

One lad who had cast himself into the ranks instead of seeking a fitting position in the officer corps was a Dilloughboy whose father that been a colonel in the First World War. Inquiries were made, things were said quietly in the right places, matters were set in train with the result that the army decided that the colonel's son had talents beyond those required of a private. Naturally, when it came to plucking him from the ranks, they picked the wrong Dilloughboy. It was an uncommon name and the army was still small; as military errors go it was one of the more forgivable.

The error was discovered too late to turn Abel back from the Officers' Training School. Those who had been in charge of the screw-up promised to rescue the other Dilloughboy some time later. Privately, one of them remarked that one Dilloughboy would probably serve the army as well as any other.

Nothing in this was of itself calculated to make a soldier out of Abel. Like multitudes of others who found themselves in uniform in September 1939, he had some idea where of he was, but very little idea of how he had got there. He nourished no ambition for parades or medals and he held no particular animosity toward the German nation whose environment he was being sent to spoil. Luck dealt him a second ace in the regimental sergeant major who ran the Officers' Training School.

The RSM had fought for the Americans in Vladivostok and for the British in Mesopotamia. The rest of the dull period between the first and second big wars he spent in the Canadian regular army, which was then one of the smallest in the world. This had earned him the rank of RSM, generally considered the most enviable position to hold in any regiment of any army of the world, combining the enjoyment of noncommissioned status with all the privileges of commissioned rank.

At the training school, the RSM had already bullied several sets of officer cadets through their training and he found himself vaguely dissatisfied with the stuff the army sent him. They were all young men from stable homes of the upper-middle class. They were polite, energetic and had nice even teeth. They did well properly. It was his suspicion that not one of them could tell shit from shinola because in his experience wars had very little about them that could be satisfied by good breeding and orderly team sports.

On the eve of the first class to include Abel, he noted the Dillougboy dossier, the briefest on the pile. All it said was "Grade 11, Mother divorced. Safeway store clerk."

"By God," said the RSM, "I've got one that isn't kennel-bred."

He introduced himself to the cadets in the usual manner, appearing at their dormitory fully dressed at the first notes of the morning bugle. He chanted, "*I'm* up, *I'm* up, *why* aren't *you* up," and vaulted down the room from bed to bed, treading on the sweetbreads of anybody that still lay there.

Later that day, when he located Abel among the many, he found him wanting and weedy. All that had titillated his interest the previous night was lost. Damnation. Somehow, he had wanted this one to be better. However, the RSM was a man of many talents and one of these was the training of retrievers for field trials. He had, at one time, as a result of an ill-considered promise, found himself burdened with the task of training a friend's dog which was not a Labrador, a Chesapeake, or any other type of retriever whatever. It was a mongrel, predominantly Border Collie. It is a testimonial to the RSM's patience, perseverance and guile that he not only trained that dog but one glorious day entered him in a picnic trial as a New South Wales Retriever and won top place.

Using such extraordinary skills, he set out to make Abel an officer. He did so by treating him with an intolerance that required the most imaginative degree of delicate balance, day by day. He never presented the cadet with an insuperable task, but they were all almost so.

The night before the commission lists were to be posted he took Abel aside and spoke to him, for the first time, as a human being.

"You know I've put your name in for commission," he said.

"Yes," said Abel. He had gained confidence in those few weeks. He was not surprised to be among the two-thirds of the class who graduated.

"I gave you a bad time, but that was to see if you had the makings," said the RSM.

"That's OK."

"Anyway, I wanted you to know what it was all about."

"If you're that interested, why don't you give me some advice before I go out of here?"

The RSM was startled. It had never occurred to him that more could be expected of him than offering the gratuitous and even fulsome compliment that he had.

"I gave you advice the whole course."

"But never as one man to another."

"By damn," said the RSM, "you are a one." He thought a while. "Alright, I will," he said. Then, because he did not yet know what to tell Abel, he thought some more.

"A slow decision is no decision," quoted Abel from the lectures.

"All right then, the first thing that comes to my mind. Remember this. Every son of a bitch in this war is your enemy except the men right around you."

"I don't remember you saying that during lectures," said Abel.

"Never said it then, never said it now, sir," said the RSM.

Abel applied his thought processes, which had remained simple, to the RSM's advice. Clearly he had to obtain the loyalty, even the affection, of the platoon which was placed in his command. He sensed that an officer did not obtain it by drinking in the Sergeants' Mess, although it was a privilege to be invited there, since a non com's mess was invariably superior to an officer's mess. Very few men, he thought, were like Desperate Desmond who found some glamor in uniforms, bagpipes and guns that made loud noises. There had to be something that encouraged a soldier to accept your orders to stand out and be shot at by somebody else, but there seemed precious little with which to buy him. The promise of promotions might affect a few, but for every man promoted to corporal or sergeant, there would remain at least six others who thought themselves more deserving. All ranks received the same pay and money could never be an inducement.

Out of it all, he concluded that what soldiers despised most was haywire equipment, unplanned idleness and unnecessarily bad food and shelter. While some of his fellow junior officers sought to let their light shine before majors and colonels, Abel cultivated the good will of quartermasters and billeting officers. When supplication failed, he stormed and shouted. When necessary, he borrowed without intention of returning. It was a ceaseless and tiresome effort. The results were small, but they were noticeable to the important people, the men of his own platoon. B Platoon was invariably a trifle better off than all the others. Under canvas in rainy weather, B Platoon was found to have occupied the high ground where a man could be damp instead of sodden. Men got boots that fitted and rifles to which the ardent patriots of the munitions plants had remembered to attach all the working parts. When they shifted to barracks in England and first learned about cold, Lieutenant Dilloughboy arranged the displacement of an entire carload of Welsh anthracite.

The coal seizure proved that Abel had learned not only some elements of that quality which is called leadership, but had also come to understand bureaucratic process. The carload of coal, which was being winnowed away exclusively by B Platoon for warmth and for trading with neighboring farmers, could not easily be hidden. Abel achieved concealment by attaching himself, part-time and voluntarily, to quartermaster stores, where he arranged documents to prove that the coal did not exist. By some leap of the intellect he had perceived the single important rule of bureaucracy — given a choice between the evidence of his senses and the evidence of paper, the bureaucrat will choose the paper every time. So his men wintered well.

He worked them harder than did most officers but found more time to give them, officially or else illegally, for leisure. The standing rule was that a man who was idle should be given a pass, but that a man should never appear to be idle while on duty. Sergeants and corporals adapted well to the system. Whenever observed, B Platoon was busy. The impression was conveyed that if B Platoon were not seen, then it must be just as active in some other place.

They were outstanding in some small exercises carried out under the eye of an English brigadier who called them colonials. While the brigadier was observing him, Abel ordered a detachment to move slowly south along an embankment, cross it casually, double back at full speed through a swampy ditch while hidden from view and emerge unexpectedly on another portion of the mock battlefield.

"Jolly fast going," said the Brigadier when the detachment, dripping mud and weed, flung itself back over the embankment. "Take a note of that," he said, speaking to one of the staff officers who accompanied him.

Three junior officers had also watched the maneuver and all were convinced of the truth—that Abel had hidden a second detachment of men a quarter of a mile down the embankment and that the men who emerged at one end were not those who had disappeared at the other. The brigadier, however, a man of senior rank, had expressed approval and none of the junior staff officers cared to dispute him.

What they did not know was that the English brigadier was a downy old bird who had seen the trick played half a dozen times before and admired it every time.

On the next day's maneuvers, Abel did a more grievous thing. His platoon anticipated an attack by the opposing team with such prescience that somebody took the trouble to find out how and discovered that Abel had simply donned a staff captain's uniform, walked into the opposing team's headquarters and examined their plans, some two hours before the event.

A group of Canadian officers protested this action to the English brigadier, appealing to his sense of fair play as a referee. "I quite understand your position, quite," he told them. He added, "When you chaps come into action with us, we shall do our best to find you some sector of the front where the Germans have promised not to play any tricks on us." He wrote Abel's name into his report and Abel was promoted to captain.

In Italy, Abel was reunited with Desperate Desmond, who had lost neither his flaming spirit nor the bagpipes. He was a private still, or, more accurately, again. From time to time the army had elevated him to corporal but he invariably lost his stripes in cheerful drunkenness.

"How do I get used to calling you 'sir?'" asked Des.

"Half the men call me by my first name when we're alone," said Abel. "If you do it when a senior officer is looking, I'll put you on charge."

"You look different," said Des.

"Who wouldn't be in this place." said Abel.

The command post was at the bottom of a slope of the Apennines on the Adriatic Coast, in an Italian hamlet of a justifiably obscure name. There were only half a dozen houses. They occupied five of them. The sixth, a couple of hundred yards away across a rolling field and a hundred feet higher, was held by Germans, who had many guns.

"We've been sitting here two months," said Abel.

"I'll play them the pipes," said Des.

"That will be just enough to start them shooting. Leave those damn pipes alone. We have a sort of an agreement across here. Everybody shoots a few rounds across morning and evening so we have something to report and for the rest we keep it quiet."

They exchanged experiences, which were chiefly those with women, creatures with whom they had never aspired to intimacy while they were still kids in Calgary. Desperate Desmond had frolicked joyously and without discrimination and had been educated in the care and treatment of the clap. Abel's experiences had been few, but of much warmth.

"You're a handsome bugger, you know," said Des.

"Not me."

"Yes. You. You're different now. It's your face. There's something strong and peaceful in it, if you know what I mean. And that scar on your cheek, it's distinguished. Do they ask you about it?"

"Yes, they do. I tell them I got it stacking cans of beans in a grocery."

"Which of course they won't believe."

"No, they don't." More than one Englishwoman had taken Abel warmly to bed because she didn't believe the bean story but could not resist a strong man who didn't talk about war and shooting.

''Keep your head down in daylight and I'll get us out of here some day soon,'' said Abel as Des was leaving.

''Out which way?''

''Out back that way. There is no way we are going to go up that hill.''

''When do I get to march down the Wilhelmstrasse?'

''Bugger off,'' said Captain Dilloughboy.

Two weeks later, they were ordered up the hill, a performance which somebody had decided would break the Gustav Line and end the war. Abel called in the lieutenants of his three platoons and talked at them gauntly.

''Just so everybody knows what's what, there is a general attack the morning after tomorrow and this company is not going to move,'' he said.

He had come up from Command Headquarters, a mile to the rear, just half an hour before, his face unnaturally pale.

''We are supposed to go up that hill, but we are not going,'' he said.

''Are you talking of a mutiny, sir?'' asked a lieutenant.

''You can call it that if you want to. I couldn't care less.''

He pulled out his map and showed them, as he was supposed to do, the form of the general attack on the Gustav Line. He then told them, as he was sworn on oath never to do, how they should disobey the orders.

''There are no planes coming and there is practically no artillery support, and I wouldn't object even to that if there was a hope of us getting to that German command post. There isn't. We have lived with this piece of Italy here and all of us know that.''

They all did, and they all listened silently to the man who proposed to save their lives and destroy their reputations. Not one of them wanted to walk up that hill, and not one could tolerate the thought of what would happen when they didn't.

''The classic case of no way out.'' said one.

''That's probably just about it,'' said Abel.

He poured them coffee and they sat, lonely, frightened, looking into the dark liquid.

''We are going to fake the attack,'' said Abel. ''We will throw a lot of fire into the air, the men will go out a few yards and then come back. I report we're pinned down and can't move.''

"What about other sections of the line we're supposed to be taking pressure off?"

"Screw the other sections of the line. In this war, as far as I'm concerned, every son of a bitch is my enemy except my own men."

Jesus, they said. Oh God, Abel. Appeal up the line over the colonel's head, Abel, they said. He blew air from pursed lips and shook his head.

He went on, quiet, businesslike. "The next thing you need to know is that it won't be long before they know we're faking the attack. When that happens, somebody will come up and take me away and shoot me or promote me or whatever the silly bastards do. Then you're going to have another officer who will order you and the men in. That's what you'll have to decide for yourselves." He spread his hands. "That's why I'm telling you all this tonight."

Jesus Abel, God Abel, there must be another way Abel, they said. He dismissed them and one by one, they shook his hand, because he had given them a couple of extra hours without death and pain, because he was doing what a man had to do in an impossible situation or, perhaps, just because he was Abel Dilloughboy. They did not speak but they shook the hand hard.

Abel tried to sleep but could not. He prowled around in the ruins of whatever damn village this was, talked inconsequentials to one or two of the men on guard and finally relieved a guard at the corner of the old barn who was engaged in a bout with dysentery.

While in the cow barn he saw a figure coming down from the German positions. He was about to fire when he first saw the man, but then a rise of the ground hid him. On the near side of the rise the figure appeared again. This time he did not shoot because he recognized a Canadian uniform. The man paused, sniffed the air like a setter casting for bird scent, came on again and entered the cow barn.

It was Desperate Desmond McCue and he was drunker than fourteen hundred dollars.

"Don't tell the captain," he said.

"I am the captain."

"Then don't tell yourself," said Desmond. He giggled. "I have been drinking with the enemy," he said. "Now that all those good times are over, I think I will have me a small sleep."

He circled, uncertainly, like a dog making a bed in leaves and was about to lie down.

"On your feet," said Abel.

"Jeez. Abel. It is you."

"When you speak to me, say 'sir'."

"Sir. Yes, sir." Des stood teetering. On his face was contrition and in his heart, the pure joy of fun, fun which could not now be taken from him.

What he wanted to do, Abel thought, was to break that silly childish face with fists. As a drunk, Des was coy; when sober, he was yet but a boy. He had all the awkward charm of a boy and, selfish, unheeding, took the benefit of years and of experience not to advance from the role but to play it more strongly. The impulse passed, he told Des to sit, and sat beside him and listened to the juvenile story Des had to tell him.

Some sort of communication had been established across the lines sufficient for Des to learn that the Germans had schnapps and Italian brandy and were doing the right thing by those commodities. Trusting to luck, which had guided his life to that day, he had calmly walked across to the German command posts and found therein a merry band of Saxons whose lieutenant—luck again— was none other than Willy Schumaker, with whom he had played peewee hockey in Calgary during the early thirties.

The Depression had carried the Canadian Schumakers back to the Germany they had left a decade before. Hitler had arranged that Willy, like Des and Abel, should find joy through strength in armies. Here, as Des said, they all were.

"He 'members you. Got a message for you from Willy." Des dropped his head, trying to remember the message, and was almost carried away into sleep. Abel had to shake him awake and ask for the message. "Willy says we're showing ourselves too much in daytime, says we gotta keep down or he's gotta start shooting during daylight."

By this time the soldier relieved by Abel had returned to his post, lighter if not stronger. He looked at Des in puzzlement.

"Let him sleep here," said Abel. "I'll be back to collect him in a while."

Abel shook all his platoon commanders awake, one by one,

explaining to them that in war there are no impossible situations. He took one lieutenant with him and a dozen volunteers, carefully selected, from the ranks. One man was detailed to pour coffee into Des and, if necessary, work him over with wet towels.

Within an hour they were ready, boots and brass shining. Abel, in his dark-blue mess uniform, carried a swagger stick. He thrust the pipes into Desmond's hands.

"If you can't play us up the Wilhelmstrasse, you can play us for a party," he said.

"What?" said Des. "What, what?" A suspicion lay within him that he had missed something important, but he was too fuddled to think long upon that or upon anything else.

"We're going up to have a drink with Willy," said Abel.

"Play us 'A Hundred Pipers and All and All,' " said the sergeant.

Thus, one day to the hour before the scheduled attack on the Gustav Line, this gaggle of officers, NCOs and men walked up the hill to the sound of the pipes. They were halfway to the German post when a machine gun fired over their heads. A sharp voice was heard and the machine gun stopped. Des faltered when the gun fired. "Keep playing, damn you," said Abel, and the wail of the hundred pipers resumed.

"That you, Willy?" said Abel. He walked into the glare of a bright light from the German position, clad in his blues, swinging his swagger stick, the others, all unarmed, straggling along behind him.

"Abel, for Christ's sake, are you out of your mind," said Willy.

"We're just gonna have one quick drink and go. It's my birthday."

"Go back," shouted Willy. "Go back. Don't you think there is anybody else on this front watching us?"

"One fast drink," shouted Abel.

The dip of the ground then hid him and his men from Willy's. The fourteen ran through the dip and up the opposite slope, pulling grenades from their blouses as they moved. Two grenades, rolling on the floor at his feet were the last things that Willy Schumaker, star of the Calgary Peewee Hockey League, was ever to know on this earth.

By the time Des stumbled up, dragging his sighing pipes and crying, the action was ended, the Gustav Line turned and, presumably, the Second World War won.

"What have you done?" cried Des. "What have you done to Willy?"

"What have you done 'sir,' " said Abel.

"Sir," said Des.

"Get up there and get behind that German machine gun," said Abel. "We'll be counterattacked within half an hour."

The news that all three platoons of B Company had occupied their objective twenty-four hours ahead of time caused a vast peeing of pants in the regimental and in the divisional headquarters. An army is nothing if not bureaucratic and like all bureaucracies, holds the view that it is better that a thing not be done than that it should be done in other than the form made and provided for. Abel demanded, pleaded, wept and raged, trying to win air or ground support for a further attack on the flank he had exposed, but little was done to aid him and the company resigned itself to defending what it had won.

The general attack next day was an unmitigated disaster from one end of the Gustav Line to the other. When the last spasms of the aborted offensive ended a few days later, the army was hard put to decide whether Abel should be given a field promotion to major or court-martialed for disobeying orders.

But they could not punish him. He was the only commander on the front who had attained his objective and he had done it with almost no casualties — two dead and four wounded. They gave him the Military Cross and told him not to do it again.

He had not stopped the war, after all, but then, neither had the war stopped him. The little battle on the tag end of the Gustav Line, his own private campaign, had been a gut-wrenching business for them all, having as it did, elements of heroism, cowardice, duty, mutiny, loyalties, betrayals and plain damn foolishness, all of the stuff the fighting men knew before the walls of Troy. It ruined Desperate Desmond. He spoke to nobody for days afterward and even refused strong drink. Within a month, he was invalided home with a bleeding ulcer. He and Abel promised to write at their brief, unemotional parting. They never did.

Captain Dilloughboy continued strangely at peace with himself in the world composed almost entirely of enemies. He became leaner yet, almost thin, but his shoulders didn't fall forward. He was quiet, but vigorous.

As the regiment shifted back and forth along the line and, in time, back with the Division to western Europe after the Normandy landings, the old guard of Company B were drained away in slow but persistent leakage—sickness, transfer and casualties. Soon there was scarcely anyone left who called him by his first name except his favorite sergeant, a short, squat, little fellow once attached to an armored regiment where he had acquired the name Short Wheelbase. He was now called Wheelbase.

The replacements who came to the platoon were in awe of Abel, for his reputation had spread. They could not conceive of calling him by his first name. They called him 'the Old Man' and discussed him earnestly. He grieved for them for, as they came in, the casualty list went higher. He had gone through much of that war by this time with unusually low casualties and now, when the end of the war could be seen, he began losing men. He tried to teach them in days what other men such as Wheelbase had learned in years. "Remember," he would say to each recruit, "over here, there are a lot of people who want you killed. And they aren't all on the Canadian general staff." But there wasn't time for the new men to learn. They died before he could get to know them.

In time, he too became careless, and one morning in Normandy, amid more than usual confusion of battle, he and five others became separated from the rest of B Company. Walking a footpath behind a hedge, defying his own rule to never use paths, one man trod on a mine. The mine killed everybody except Abel, who was nicked by a few fragments of metal, and Wheelbase, whose left hand was carried away. Abel worked over Wheelbase for a time, applying a tourniquet and then bandages from the kit he always carried while in action. After a time the sergeant came out of shock and the two of them resumed the search for their own positions. He was almost carrying Wheelbase when a German patrol picked them up and they were both delivered to a nearby field-dressing station by stretcher.

The triad system operated at the dressing station and the orderlies separated all brought there into the dead, the ones sure to die and those who might be saved. Abel had used the last of his energy in dragging Wheelbase along with him and had been bled upon copiously. They judged him a goner and left him lying on a hillside, promising to find him a padre. Wheelbase was taken down to the tent for attention by a doctor.

A captive now, the last of his men taken from him, a peace passing all understanding covered Abel Dilloughboy like a warm dry blanket. For the first time in four years he was no longer responsible for anybody, not even himself. When the orderlies should come back for him in an hour or more and find him fixable, the doctors would wash and close his cuts. His feeding, his shelter and his transport had become the responsibility of Adolf Hitler and his servants. There were no decisions left for him to make.

The past few days had been the worst of the war for Abel, for the regiment had been vigorously bombed by friendly aircraft. The second time the Allied planes had plastered his position, he had been almost hysterical with rage and had ordered the men to shoot at them. They had no weapons that could hit Typhoons, but it made them all feel better to try knocking one out. In the third attack, Abel and his men just lay in the dirt and moaned.

The agony and the terror now seemed far from him and strangely unimportant. He observed the bombing, at a distance of space and time, with idle detachment. He was doing so when a flight of Typhoons swept in firing rockets at the German field-dressing station.

Again, all around Abel was war and the confusion of war. He might have taken shelter nearby and waited out the brief attack. He must have considered doing so. That he did not reflects the fact that whatever Abel may have done independently of the army or in opposition to the army, the army had also done things to him. It had introduced in him habits of action that could not easily be dropped. He did not take shelter but ran. If any of the Germans noticed him going, they were too busy with the war to chase him. In a few minutes he was free of the Germans and again a prisoner of the habits, rules, customs, traditions and loyalties of His Majesty's Canadian Army. He went looking for his company.

A mile or two distant, he went to ground in a small French farmhouse, where an old, old, Norman-French lady in a poke bonnet bathed him, bound him up, prayed for him and hid him in the hayloft while her old husband bleated in terror and dismay.

Abel was tired enough to have slept well, but he had been tired for three weeks. Sleep, it seemed, had deserted him when he most yearned for her. He had left her somewhere, in Italy, in England, in Calgary. She sulked and would not be reconciled.

About midnight he crawled out of the hay and found the Pole Star in the sky so that he could, once more, strike for the West. There was a lamp burning in the farmhouse kitchen. He had intended to slip away unnoticed, but since the old people were awake, it seemed but decent to thank them.

The old man spoke a little English. "You will take the German?" he said.

"No. I go back to Canada line, back to Canada army."

"But you take the German."

They pleaded with him, she in French and he in inscrutable English, for what he could not know until, from the cellar, they brought up the young German deserter whom they had hidden there.

"Germans come, bang, bang," said the old man. He shot at his old wife with one pistol finger and then at himself. "Bang, bang," he repeated.

"I am not in a position to say no," said Abel.

"*Encore, s'il vous plait?*"

"I said yes. *Oui.*"

He and the German walked west together toward the light of artillery fire in the western sky. The German, he noticed, still had his bayonet on his hip. He pointed to it and held out his hand to take it. It was an error; it gave the young German ideas which he had abandoned a few days before. He displayed the bayonet point first and indicated that it was Abel, not he, who was the prisoner. There was a short and violent scuffle. When it ended, Abel had the bayonet and the young man was, again, a prisoner, and, again, apparently happy to be so.

They kept off the roads, where transport could be heard rumbling. When they heard German being spoken nearby, they lay down together in the mud. Abel held a finger to his lips and for emphasis, pointed to the bayonet he carried. The other nodded agreeably.

Sometime in that long night, perhaps at one A.M., perhaps two, they crawled into a haystack. The deserter promptly slept, curled up with his knees near his chest, leaving Abel with another impossible situation. He wanted to sleep and sleep was ready to take him; indeed, it would soon take him whether he chose it or not. He would not or could not trust the German and was too befuddled to walk away from him. Dreams began to form before his open eyes and when he snatched himself back from the precipice of deep sleep his heart pounded and he was wet in cold sweat. In the end he sought to solve it all by stabbing the other with the bayonet and, perhaps because he was too long gone in exhaustion, made a poor job of it. The German took all the rest of that night to die.

It was the longest night Abel would ever know.

The boy brought out papers. A boy he was. Only seventeen. There were pictures of the parents, farm people, and a little brown-haired girl who must have been a sister.

They had no more than half a dozen words in common and conversed mostly by signs. Abel would tell the parents? Yes, he would. He would tell them that he had been a good boy, a good soldier? Oh God, yes, anything, anything.

In the first light of dawn Abel was sobbing and shouting. ''I forbid you to die. You understand? You are under my command and I am your officer. An officer. Forbidden to die. *Verboten.*''

The boy gave a thin smile and said, ''*Jawohl, Herr Ober,*'' but soon after that he was dead.

Abel walked to the edge of the nearest road where the transport vehicles were still moving. He flagged down the first he saw, which was a 1500 WT loaded with a few men from a Panzer group.

A young lieutenant, unshaven, red of eye and hoarse of voice, was riding in the back of the truck with his men. He addressed Abel in perfect English.

''What are you doing here?''

''I'm surrendering.''

''You have no business surrendering,'' said the lieutenant. ''The Canadians are moving up here in an hour or so. Sit there and you'll be picked up by your own people.''

''I'm surrendering,'' said Abel.

The lieutenant was exasperated. ''We are very tired and we have no time for prisoners,'' he said. ''There is no room for you in the truck.''

''Shoot the bastard and let's get moving before the planes start,'' said a German sergeant. Abel heard the word 'shoot' in German.

"You can shoot me if you want to. I don't care. Or you can take me prisoner."

"Get in," said the lieutenant.

Abel tried three times to get over the high tailgate of the truck. Finally two men got out, took his elbows and lifted him in.

"Thank you," he said. "Thanks very much. *Danke schön.*"

Thus Abel was carried away a second time into captivity and this time he looked as he had once looked, a small man, a frail man, a weak and nothing man.

The lieutenant saw that there were the stains of tears on Abel's cheeks and was reminded of reports that the Canadians had run short of reserves. They must be sending over the weekend soldiers now, he thought. This one looked like a store clerk. Aloud, he spoke with kindness in his voice.

"Had enough, eh Canada?"

"I wasn't cut out for this sort of business," said Abel Dilloughboy.

# HOW TO
# RUN THE COUNTRY

KEN LARSEN LEARNED that he was expected to run the country
while he was on his back under the old Dodge truck, calling
loudly upon his Maker to destroy Detroit utterly. Since he had
crumpled the oil pan by his own stubborn insistence that the
truck would not high center on a stump in a cow trail, his
blaming of Detroit was quite unfair. But, then, so many things
in this life are.

He had brought the truck into the old log barn next the
Namko Store with the crankshaft making whinnying sounds
against the folded metal and for two hours he had been
monkey wrenching it. His wife, Margaret, stood beside the
oil-drum heater, which was at last throwing off a good
chinook. Smith was also there, lending counsel and, occasionally, actual help. Smith had no reason to be there. That
was one of the reasons he was there.

Arch MacGregor so found them. The light of two hissing
gas lanterns cast vagrant shadows on faces, logs and the
great bulk of the big truck—a coven of twentieth century
witches celebrating the coming of the industrial age to
Namko. Arch could not see Larsen at first, because nothing of
Larsen showed but two shadowed legs and feet protruding
from the truck's front.

"Is Ken here?" he said.

Smith pointed at Larsen's boots. "He is dreaming, tonight,
of his dear one," he said.

Arch spoke to the legs and feet.

"Ken."

"Yeah."

"I have been looking for you for two days."

"And I have been here for two hours, right beside you. You
should pay more attention to your customers. Where is that
mechanical genius of yours, Herb? Why ain't he doing this?"

"He ain't here."

"I don't need somebody to tell me that Herb ain't here. I can figure that out for myself. Where is he? Is he drunk again?"

"No. He went moose hunting."

"Well, that is nice. He has taken up a second hobby."

"I gotta talk to you, Ken."

"Goddamed gasket's gonna leak. All I can do is gum it up some and keep adding oil."

"I said I gotta talk to you."

The faceless voice floated out from the mud that clogged the fenders. "One thing I gotta agree with Herb. He says there are only two kinds of people in this world who make their living lying on their backs, and I don't get any kisses."

"Ken. Will you get the hell out from under there? I have got to talk to you."

"Talk, then. I would be happy to listen to anybody. Unless he was one of them rotten bastards that hung this pan so low. Go ahead. Talk."

Arch squatted and spoke down the wheel well.

"What I wanted to tell you is that you are now the Liberal candidate for Chilcotin riding in the election."

"What election?"

"The provincial election, for God's sake."

"Oh, yes. That's right. I forgot about it. Say, pass me that box end, will you? Reach over with your hand, there's a bunch of them there. Not that one, the young one. Thanks."

"I am not fooling, Ken. The provincial headquarters called me and asked if I was president of the Chilcotin Liberal Association. Naturally, I said yes."

"Naturally. If they had asked you if you was president of the United States, you would have said yes to that too."

"That's right. Somebody has to carry the load. So, in my capacity as chief Liberal of Chilcotin, I have held a nominating meeting and nominated you."

There being no answer, Arch repeated. "So I have nominated you as the Liberal candidate."

"By damn, I've cross threaded it."

"Did you hear me?"

"Yes. I hear you. Lovely conversation. No. I didn't cross thread. She's just burred. I will persuade it some. Hand me the hammer."

Arch found the hammer and passed it under the front bumper. Larsen snorted and blew and made ringing sounds with the hammer. ''Engineers who build trucks are like the nose and heel fly. They are put on earth to make our character stronger.'' After a minute, he rested and asked for a cigarette, which Smith rolled for him, and then, still prostrate beneath the Dodge, sucked on it and blew sky-blue smoke which crept among the grease and steel and sifted out into the room.

''Did you really tell them that Arch?''

''Yes. I did. Why not? You're a good Liberal aren't you? You told me so.''

''Yep. Always have been.''

''OK then. You are the candidate for Chilcotin this time around.''

''Like hell I am.''

''You are, I tell you.''

''By damn. You know, the only thing for this is a weld.''

''A what?''

''I am going to have to weld, sooner or later.''

''Will you keep your mind on what I'm talking about? I have got to phone them back and confirm this and it's gotta be tonight.''

''OK, phone.''

''And tell them what?''

''Tell them to go pee up a rope, of course. What the hell. She'll hold well enough to get us home. Margaret? You ready to go?''

There was no answer. Larsen dragged himself out, rolled up and off the cold earthen floor of the shed and stood. Margaret had remained unmoving, her hands over the stove. He slapped the old truck on the fender, which quivered at the touch.

''Now will you take us home, you cantankerous old beast?''

''Ain't you even flattered that the party wants you to run?'' asked MacGregor.

''Yeah, I s'pose I'm flattered. Some. But I have noticed that flattery butters no parsnips. Anyhow I have now enjoyed all the flattery I am gonna get and it is time to go back and look after my cows. They don't flatter me, but they keep groceries on the table.''

"Now," said Smith. "If that ain't a strange thing. Here is Ken Larsen, who knows all about running the country. I know he knows. He has told me how to run it. A hundred times he has told me. They ask him to do it personally and he passes it up.''

"I am a rancher. I am not a politician.''

"But I have seen you clear up the whole Russian situation in a single evening,'' said Smith.

"Come on Margaret," said Larsen. "Let's get on our horse.'' To Arch he said, "Why in the name of God would they ask me anyhow?''

"Well, I used your name and they liked the sound of it, that's all, I guess.''

"If they like the sound of Larsen, why don't they get that old Larsen that used to log in the Bluff Lake Country?''

"He's a thousand years old now and he lives down in the Okanagan now.''

"That don't matter. He's honest. He's respected.''

"Ken," said MacGregor. "The truth is, I have already told them that you accepted.''

"What the hell did you tell them that for?''

"I couldn't find you and the nomination time was running out.''

"I was right here. Right beside the store. All you had to do was come down and I would have told you. And you knew the answer anyhow.''

"Well the fact is I told them you had accepted.''

"Oh well. That is no real problem. Just phone them back and untell them.''

"Amazing," said Smith. "It is like Moses telling the Jews he don't know where the Promised Land is and, if he did, he wouldn't lead them anyhow.''

"I ain't never found no Promised Land. All I found was Namko in the Chilcotin. A different sort of place.''

Margaret spoke for the first time. "Aren't you honest? Aren't you respected?''

"I am also smart in the head and that means I am not gonna get mixed up in no politics. Anyhow, the government is gonna win this seat."

Margaret spoke with her words spaced. "You have got a chance to be one of fifty-two men who govern this province, and you won't even try it."

"That is just about the size of it. Now come on, Mother, let's get home."

"You won't even try."

"What has got into you? What is politics to you?"

"If my father had your situation . . . and your friends . . . and your opportunity . . . "

"How did your father get in here? Your father didn't have anything to do with politics. Didn't you say he was a tailor?"

"Yes, he was a tailor. But he was a politician too, even if he was just a tailor."

"You took the wrong meaning, Margaret. I have got nothing against tailors. I prefer them, in fact, to politicians."

"That is the kind of remark my father would never understand."

"I don't know what you are driving at," he said. He often did not and held firmly to the belief that much of what women said and did was too obscure for any man to bother to seek understanding. But Margaret spoke on, and this time he listened while the oil-drum stove thrummed and glowed and the bitter wind howled in the eaves of the shed.

"He was a humble tailor, that's the word, a humble one, in Moncton, New Brunswick. And that is a humble town to be humble in. He was Polish . . . "

"Yeah. I remember you saying he was a Pole."

"And his English used to embarrass my mother. Of course, she was English and they embarrass easily about grammar. But it used to embarrass us children too. He was just a funny looking little man from Gdansk. He didn't have any proper education and he never understood what politics was all about."

"Well, first generation off the boat. He couldn't have much chance to get involved," said Larsen.

''He did get involved. He joined a party and he worked for it. He worked for it. Do you know what that means, Ken Larsen?''

''No. No more than I know what put the burr under your saddle.''

''A worker was all he was. Never in the inner circle of the party. Just a faithful worker. But when he got to be very old, the party rewarded him. They rewarded him for long and faithful service. They nominated him as a candidate.''

''I never knew that.''

''That was when he learned about politics. There was an independent running in that election and the independent was the real party candidate. He got all the party funds and all the secret support. But the party had to have an official candidate and they needed somebody absolutely hopeless. To carry the flag. And that was my father. The goat. The most hopeless candidate they could find. He was given the opportunity to run all on his own. With no funds and no support, and all the knowing men of the party snickering at him behind their hands.''

''Would you like me to get mixed up in that kind of a trade?'' he said. She ignored him.

''He didn't get enough votes to put into one of his thimbles. I don't know who voted for him. The family, I guess, and a few dozen old friends. Lots of men get defeated in politics but my father didn't get defeated. He got a public humiliation. He was a great big public joke.''

Smith, who had been looking at her intently, asked, ''Did he know what was being done to him?''

''Yes. I think he did. Not at first, of course. But before the campaign was over, yes, he knew. But the thing is, that didn't matter to my father. He just fought the good fight anyway. And after he was beaten, he smiled. By God, he smiled. And he walked around to the other headquarters and he congratulated all the other candidates. Because he was proud. By God, Ken Larsen, he was proud, even to be a sham candidate. And what's more, he kept on smiling, and he kept on working for his party, right up to the day he died.''

She went on with the threat of rain in her voice and the three men, still, intent, watched her. ''My father was a great Canadian, damit. It didn't matter so much that the country never noticed him.

Lots of great Canadians are never noticed. But we could have noticed him. We could have been proud of him instead of being embarrassed by him. We could have told him how great he was, even if we didn't know it at the time. But we never did and now he's dead and I can't tell him that. I can't ever tell him now.''

"You amaze me Margaret," said Larsen.

She turned to him. "And you, you big fat turd, you won't even try." She walked to the truck, dragged the sticky door open and said, "It's cold. Let's go home." With two tries, she got the door closed and latched and sat on the cold plastic seat, her face seen dimly through the dirty windshield in the light of the gas lanterns.

"I have never seen her act this way in my life before," said Larsen to the two men. He dropped his voice. "She must be coming to the change of life."

The others looked at him but did not smile or answer. He shifted his feet uneasily, walked to the driver's side of the truck and spoke through the open window.

"You want to see me get into that kind of business?"

Her voice came out of the darkened cab. "I'm cold and I want to go home."

"You can decide it. You can decide it right now. You say the word, tell me to forget all about the ranch and go politicking, and I will go."

There was no reply.

"You know how much work is ahead of us this winter. You want me to drop it all for politics, just say so."

Again there was no reply.

"Say the word," he said.

"I would never tell you to run. Never in ten thousand years," she said.

"Well, damit, I will run. Whether you say so or not. I will run anyhow."

"That's the spirit," said Arch.

Larsen pulled at his lip, looked at Arch and at Smith. "I don't know exactly why I am doing it. But I am gonna do it."

"See you tomorrow," said Arch. "There's campaigning to do."

"Yeah. Yeah. OK. First thing tomorrow."

Larsen looked at the truck, the silent wife and back to Arch. He whispered. "I will do it. But I tell you straight. I won't ever be able to take it as seriously as her old man did."

"Well, that's done," said Arch. He passed a paper to Smith. "Here, Smith, you sign as seconding the nomination. I'll get the other names we need tomorrow."

"I'm not a member of the Liberal party," said Smith.

"Who is, in this country? Just sign it will you? I've done my part, now do yours."

Smith signed.

In such a straightforward manner did the Liberal candidate for Chilcotin appear to be chosen, involving no more than three reasonable men, an interfering woman and a dinged oil pan—a simple process.

The nomination in the Namko Garage was no more than one small white-capped wave in the great tide rip of the 1953 election campaign; it had emerged from the boil of current and crosscurrent by forces uncharted. Yet being itself a part of the process, it would have its own effect, however dimly traceable, upon the great currents of human affairs.

If a beginning of such process may be found, it would have been located three days before on the fifteenth floor of the Jamieson building in Vancouver in the office of Montgomery Jamieson.

Having made money, a lot of money, a hell of a lot of money, in building bridges, buying mines, kiting checks, flipping real estate, pioneering the production of lint-free barbecue briquets and just plain luck, Montgomery had, in his middle years, taken to politics and, as is not uncommon with converts, become more Catholic than the Pope. He was the '53 campaign manager, a condition which later developed into a *tic douloureux*. But at this moment, three days before the nomination day, he was still almost normal. The process of defeating the party in power, thereby saving the province from itself and for glory, had involved him with a group of party workers whom he found to be inept, careless, foolish, inattentive and bereft of long thoughts. But he had rather suspected this, seeing how the country had been run to date, and had not been unduly shocked.

Thus when his phone gave him the tinkle that well-bred telephones give in executive suites, he did not hold his hair or wipe his face, but answered it firmly, with resonance in his voice. He had a friendly tone, which stopped just short of condescension.

"How goes the battle, Brydon?"

The phone squawked. Montgomery tucked the receiver in his ear, tucked a Sobranie in his mouth, crossed his feet on the desk and listened. Holding a hand over the mouthpiece, he muttered "the usual" to the Senator, and then returned to his listening, which ran to almost three minutes. He then grunted, which was a signal his executives had learned to recognize, and proceeded to make a series of executive decisions.

"Okay, Brydon. I know what you mean. But even an election candidate has to have some passing acquaintanceship with reality and the reality is that the campaign fund is not the federal budget. It is smaller than the federal budget."

The phone squawked again.

"I know. They are all splendid candidates. Even our bad check marvel in the Kootenays. They're all splendid. But there is no money tree. Now listen, you tell West Cates Park in short, simple words that he can understand, that there is no more money from headquarters. From now on, he is on his own. He has got his fair share of the general fund."

When the phone squawked again Montgomery jammed the cigarette into the jade ashtray and broke it off while its life had scantly begun. There was a harder note in the voice. "You're not telling me that he actually thinks he is going to take West Cates Park from the Premier? What kind of an idiot have we got? The Premier has a Chesapeake Bay Retriever that could take the riding. Does he really think he's going to get the money Point Grey gets? . . . Yes . . . I realize that Brydon . . . But Brydon, this is you and me, here on this telephone, and you and I know we don't have thirty-five seats in the bag. We don't even have twenty-seven for certain, and that's a bare majority. . . . Yes, I know you know. . . . Well, be gentle with him. Tell him we're proud of the fight he's making. Optimistic reports. Tell him that, optimistic reports. And greater upsets have occurred. It's not a new line but it's a good one or maybe your fertile brain can conceive a better one. Greater upsets have occurred. But no more goddamed money. OK? OK."

Montgomery replaced the phone and spoke to the Senator. "We have a candidate who thinks he's going to beat the Premier. What happens to people in election campaigns, Senator? Do they give away all their marbles before they start?"

"People in politics are like newspaper columnists," said the Senator. "After a while they start believing themselves." The voice was *basso profondo*, but soft, like thunder on distant hills. He had been known, in the prime of his political life, as Old Thunder.

"Well thank God I've been in the private sector where the reality is."

"What is the reality, Montgomery?"

"You know better than I do, sir. We talk about thirty-five seats, but the truth is we have to fight to get twenty-seven for a majority. And we can't spend the same money on all of them. The hopeless ones nickel-and-dime us to death. We have got to spend on the twenty-seven."

"So we'll get twenty-seven?"

"I think so. But even if it's twenty-three, twenty-four, that makes us the coming party. There'd be a run-off election in a few months."

"I follow your analysis," said the Senator.

"Well, what do you calculate?"

"You are the campaign manager, Montgomery."

As so often in the presence of the Senator, Montgomery felt the slight shiver that goes when you feel a man walking on your grave. He could not say why. Who could, with the Senator?

The Senator, unlike Montgomery, held no position whatever in the present party structure. He had been a campaign chairman, for campaigns numberless to man. He had been elected to three Parliaments. He now held a lifetime appointment to the Senate of Canada where he was irremovable by man, church or state. In the privately held convictions of Montgomery Jamieson, the Senator was a mere tactician and never a strategist. He recognized that the Senator knew politics, that noblest of callings and vilest of trades, but he felt that the Senator remained a man who lacked breadth and vision. The man seemed uninterested, perhaps incapable of understanding the great intellectual adventure of political philosophy. If Montgomery had been obliged to sum up in a few words, he would have said that the Senator had many years, yet lacked seasoning. Nevertheless, he deferred to the Senator. He also feared him, that homely old bastard, feared him almost as much as he hated him and was mystified by him. To Montgomery, as to so many others in the Liberal party, the Senator was like a cross between a parrot and a tiger. He didn't look like much, but when he spoke, everybody listened. "But why in hell *do I* listen?" Montgomery would ask himself, but could provide himself with no rational answer.

Why, for instance, did the Senator insist on sitting at the far corner of the executive suite, thundering faintly and far away, so that Montgomery Jamieson, a man of the world, student of Kafka, disciple of Adam Smith, instant philosopher and recognized cosmopolitan, was obliged to walk across the room and sit on that leather hassock to listen to what he had to say?

Montgomery walked across the room and sat on the hassock beside the Senator.

"Senator, I know it's all nuts and bolts now, but what this party really needs is a new philosophic direction."

The old man lifted his hands, as to ward off a paper dart. "Montgomery, there is nothing I enjoy more than philosophic discussion with you. But shouldn't we stay to the nuts and bolts for a minute or two?"

"As you wish."

"The thought comes to me that there are fifty-two ridings in this province."

"We can't win them all!"

"Possibly not. However, the convention decision was that we should contest every riding."

The incredible old rogue. He had never so much as read all the resolutions passed at a party convention. Why should he remember that one.

"That was the decision," Montgomery agreed.

"But it seems to me that we have only fifty-one candidates for fifty-two ridings."

"Well, that's so. Chilcotin has not been heard from."

"Heard from?"

"Well, I hope there's a candidate before the nominations close."

"You hope?"

"Hope is the best I can offer Senator. The party organization isn't exactly strong there. In point of fact, it does not exist there. Anywhere. There is no party organization alive."

"Correct me if I'm wrong. But if we have fifty-one candidates for fifty-two ridings, we won't be carrying a full slate."

"Senator, there hasn't been a Liberal win Chilcotin since the days of Sir John Oliver."

"Up there, they're still waiting for John to rise from the dead. Why don't we resurrect him? It happened in Jerusalem."

"Senator, there is no living Liberal left there. We can only parachute somebody in there."

"Well, it's not my decision, Montgomery. You are the campaign chairman. I'm only advisory."

*Thank you, you advisory old son of a bitch.* Montgomery smiled. "You're right, Senator. We should try."

He crossed the room and pressed the intercom. "Miss O'Day. Ask Brydon to come down immediately, please." He turned to the old man seated in the shadows. "My most hyperthyroid young executive in the firm. He's seconded to the campaign."

"Who?"

"Brydon. You've probably met him at a campaign dinner. Young Scottish face that will turn into a bowl of oatmeal by the time he's forty."

"Not the faintest recollection. But I find people ever more forgettable. What's his quality?"

"Enthusiasm."

"Use it, Montgomery, use it. Nothing more precious in the stuff of politics."

The Senator was getting to his feet, using two canes. There was no time that he looked more awkward and, Montgomery knew, no time when he was so adept at firing the Parthian shot. "Never underestimate enthusiasm, Montgomery. You know, at times, I think you do."

"Oh?"

"Sometimes that mind of yours is hard as well as clear. Feel the heart pumping sometimes, Montgomery."

The old man was on his four feet now. As ever, Montgomery had been uncertain whether to help him crank up his steel-braced legs

or to ignore the infirmity. In that usual irresolution he had waited
until the question had answered itself.

"You're not going to wait to hear what Brydon has to report?"

"He reports to you, not to me. Mind you . . . " he paused,
leaning on the walking sticks, and half-turned his large, lumpy
body toward the other man, "if you do find a potential candidate,
I'd appreciate being consulted."

"You will be consulted, Senator."

The Senator continued moving across the room and through the
door.

"Fight the good fight, Montgomery," he said, and with a nod of
his head to the desk of Miss O'Day, thumped toward the bronze
doors of the elevators. Stepping silently upon the carpet, Montgomery followed him for a few steps, then stood and watched him
go.

It was another occasion for him to ponder one of the constants of
political life—the unduly high proportion of cripples. A meeting of
movers and shakers of his own or any other party bore a resembl-
ance to a war veterans' congress. The lame, the halt, the physically
deformed were represented out of all proportion to their numbers in
the general population. Something in the art and practice of politics
attracted such people. Montgomery sighed, turned and walked to
the window and tried to see the north shore mountains through the
rain. His mind had already moved across those mountains to
Chilcotin which was, it occurred to him, another haven for the
handicapped.

His knowledge of that particular region was dim. Sufficient, he
felt, but dim, and likely to remain so.

It was what passed for frontier country and the frontier was not
unknown to him. Business ventures had occasionally driven him
for brief periods into those far latitudes of civilization. He had
found in such places neither romance nor inspiration. His private
observation was that the far regions were peopled not by heroes but
by those who were noncompetitive in the highly competitive world
of the cities. People spoke of their strong individualism but, often
as not, the individualism was less than that, nothing more than a
feebleness of intellect or spirit. He found in those desolate places
not men and women who bravely pushed man's frontier backward,

rather he found people who fled from the settled lands in which the burden of their own incompetence would have proven unbearable. He did not anticipate with joy any activity which the party might have to undertake in Chilcotin.

He was not, however, to be left to his own thoughts. The rich voice of Old Thunder floated into his office from the hallway.

"Now there is a face I've seen before."

Brydon's voice was lighter and had a squeak in it.

"Oh, I don't think you'd know me, Senator."

"Didn't I meet you at the campaign dinner?"

"Well, I was there, when you were talking to some other fellows . . . "

"Of course. I knew I'd seen you. You're Brydon, aren't you? That's right. Brydon."

"Yes, sir."

"I understand you're the man who's going to find us a candidate in Chilcotin."

"Well, as a matter of fact, it's a difficult problem, Senator."

"That, Mr. Brydon, is why we've got you working on it. You know, there's a quality about you. I notice these things. You've got a, hmm, call it a seasoning. A seasoning at an early age."

"Well, thank you."

"I'm sorry we didn't have more time to talk at that dinner. It seems to me . . . you're not from UBC are you?"

"No sir. Acadia."

"That's right, Acadia. The mecca of the Baptists. They all go there for total immersion into knowledge. No offense meant. Just an old joke."

"You sound as though you went there yourself, sir."

"No. Never seen the place. But I just had that recollection that you were an eastern university man. Well, must go. Fight the good fight, Brydon."

"Will do, sir."

Brydon floated into Jamieson's office, his feet twelve inches off the carpet and recounted his conversation for Montgomery's benefit.

"Isn't he a remarkable man," he said.

"A remarkable mind, alright."

"But his memory. How would he remember me from that campaign dinner? And knowing that I was from Acadia?"

"He has a very retentive memory and a very quick grasp," said Montgomery.

"He amazes me," said Brydon.

Montgomery Jamieson eyed his young subordinate thoughtfully. A good kid, but needing a lot of seasoning. Perhaps, if the analogy be kept in the kitchen, some more heat.

"Why haven't you got somebody for Chilcotin yet?" he said.

"I'm making some progress MJ."

"Good. Some progress. Now we can get down to work. Exactly what?"

"I've been on the phone for a couple of days."

"That's what you're doing. I didn't ask what you've been doing. I asked what progress you'd made."

"MJ, we haven't won Chilcotin since the days of John Oliver."

The remark irritated the campaign manager. He had obtained that fact only an hour before he used it in conversation with the Senator and had been rather pleased with himself. The junior executive make the knowledge seem common and cheap currency.

"So much for history. Now get back to today. This is your bailiwick, Brydon. All the booneys, and that includes Chilcotin."

"The best I can say . . . there's a storekeeper in a place called Namko. Named MacGregor."

"And what does he do, when he's not weighing potatoes?"

"He's not in politics. But he was, back in a Montreal riding. About ten thousand years ago. About the time of Mackenzie King, I think."

"You're sure it wasn't Laurier?"

Montgomery should have known better. In repartee, Brydon was as thick as two planks. He answered the question as he had made the statement, with the earnestness of the unaware.

"No. It was Mackenzie King's time, I'm sure of that. Anyway, he won't run. Won't even consider it."

"As progress goes, that's not much."

"Well, there's just a bit. He suggested a man named Larsen. He thinks he can get Larsen to run. And since MacGregor is the whole Liberal organization for a hundred thousand square miles, I guess under the policy of riding autonomy, that would mean Larsen's our man.''

''Forget riding autonomy and stick with common sense. Larsen's our man when we say he is. Who is Larsen?''

''That's the trouble. By the time I got that much information the phone connection was so weak I couldn't hear anything anymore. And the whole phone system closes down at six-thirty at night. I guess you know about that country.''

''Yes, I know the country.''

''In a way, MJ, I was depending on your knowledge of that place. MacGregor seemed to be saying that you would probably know Larsen.''

''Larsen? Yes, I think I might.''

Before his involvement with politics, Montgomery would not have answered such questions in that way. He would not have felt impelled to claim, spuriously, that he was familiar with the Chilcotin. Neither would he have allowed the impression to remain that he was acquainted, however vaguely, with somebody up there named Larsen. In both answers, he was being more political than rational for the reason that he had unconsciously learned a politician's basic rule—never admit to total ignorance of anything.

The origin of this folk habit lies deep in the democratic process. Any candidate for public office operates under the universal fiction that he has adequate knowledge of every subject that may be associated with the office to which he aspires. Whether it be the dairy industry, cyclical budgeting, veterans' pensions, the cost of school furniture or freight rates on the transport of yak butter, he is obliged to pretend to some expertise. If he balks at any of these or a hundred other hurdles, the voters tend to be disappointed. Sometimes vocally. Their man has not played by the rules of the political game. He is guilty of refusing to fight. Those who associate with political candidates fall into the same habits of speech and thought.

Had Montgomery not feinted, Ken Larsen might never have become involved in running the country. But Montgomery, boy politician, had learned to feint and, for practice as much as anything else, did so with Brydon.

''Run a check on Larsen. See what he's doing, lately that is. Maybe he's our man.''

"Right. But you know, MJ, we can't be optimistic. Also, is it really wise for us to spend money in the hopeless ridings? Wouldn't it be better to put the money where there's hope?"

Montgomery slapped his open palm on the desk. It made a sharp, flat sound and Brydon's spine stiffened.

"The party policy was that a candidate be running in every riding."

"Right."

"And if we don't have a candidate in Chilcotin, we don't have a candidate in every riding. Is my arithmetic right in that?"

"Right."

"I thought I was right, somehow."

Montgomery did not need to rise for the interview to end. Brydon departed unbidden.

Montgomery thrust on the buzzer of his desk phone and summoned Miss O'Day.

The secretary came into the big office like a wisp of grey cloud drifting down a mountain valley. She was a tiny creature, grey haired, grey eyed and grey suited. Miss O'Day would be difficult to pick out of a crowd of two. To those who knew her, her reputation for faithfulness and accuracy was immense. Beyond that, few people knew anything about Montgomery Jamieson's little mouse. Her private life was so much so that some people suggested she didn't have one and there was a rumor in the Jamieson building that at night Miss O'Day did not have a home to go to, but instead scurried up and down the dark corridors, nibbling bits of cheese left from people's lunches and dodging the janitorial staff.

"Isn't it a beautiful day," she said.

"It's raining, Miss O'Day."

"Yes, but we do need it." The sun had shone for a fortnight. Only by day, true, but it made the city's older natives restless and spiritually unfulfilled.

Montgomery was leafing through memoranda, which descended upon a campaign manager like heavy wet snow. It was too much to shovel after a session with the Senator so he pushed them all to a corner of the wide desk to germinate what answers they might by the morrow.

"Just one memo, Miss O'Day. To Brydon. I forgot to shoot at him when I had him in my sights. He seems to have got the public opinion poll disease." She was already seated, a notepad on her knee, when his tone altered to dictation style. "Brydon. I am not impressed that forty percent of the under-twenty age group of East Indians in Quesnel recognizes the name of our candidate. You are wasting your time and wasting money on surveys. You will cease and desist."

"He seems a very sincere young man," she said.

"Sincerity? A sincere man, Miss O'Day, can be one hundred percent wrong."

She stood up. "That's all the dictation for this afternoon?"

"I see. You think I'm too abrasive. That's what the Senator was telling me. Now you're telling me."

"I wouldn't tell you what to write in a memorandum, Mr. Jamieson."

"No. Of course. Alright, Miss O'Day. Scratch it out. I'll try it again. 'Mr. Brydon. Congratulations on straightening out our Cates Park candidate. It is hard to tell a candidate that he is only worth five hundred dollars. You did it well. Incidentally, I wonder if we are wise to place so much emphasis on public opinion polls in this campaign. They are not entirely reliable. I would be grateful for your opinion on this matter.' . . . That better?"

"It seems more diplomatic."

"Good. Then drive the iron into him now. 'Meanwhile, do not conduct any more surveys without my express permission.' OK?"

She studied her Pitman shorthand. "I think I have it all."

"I have no doubt of that."

She started for the office door as for a mousehole, squeaking as she scuttered away, that he would, of course, want to talk to the Senator again? She had obtained the Senator a taxi. He would be at his office soon. She would put the call straight through?

"Yes. I need to talk to him. I don't want to talk to him, but I need to talk to him. But I don't need to talk to anybody else and that includes my wife. If she calls, tell her I'm dead. Tell her I went to Hawaii. Keep her off my damn back, Miss O'Day."

"Now Mr. Jamieson. Mrs. Jamieson is a very nice person."

He watched as the door genteelly clicked behind her. "I wish I lived in a world full of all the nice people she seems to find.''

What he needed was a shower in water that hissed and steamed, a shirt and flannels that were loose and a drink. All those being at hand, he went so far as to loose his tie and shuck off his jacket, but then he remembered that in the shower he might not hear the phone buzzer. The Senator would not pick up a telephone unit until the answering party was crouched at the other end of the line. ''Damn him anyway,'' said Montgomery, who used such practices himself and was puzzled as well as resentful when he submitted to them. He wished he could understand what made him play this role to Old Thunder. He wished he knew why nothing much ever happened in the Liberal party in British Columbia unless the Senator took part in the process. He wished he knew why politics was so damn silly and why he was part of the process. Aloud, he said ''I wish I was drunk in a non-Caucasian whorehouse.''

He walked to the chair behind the desk and cast himself into it as a stone down a deep well. ''Somebody has been slipping lead into my pockets,'' he said. While waiting for the buzzer to sound, his head dropped forward and he slept.

The phone call was delayed while Muriel, the Senator's secretary, sought to reconcile the old man to his old antagonist, Alexander Graham Bell.

''Shall I get Mr. Jamieson on the line now?'' said Miss O'Day.

''No. Wait until I get the buttons lined up on the Senator's desk. He's got a phone with buttons and he hates them. Yesterday he hit them all at once with his fist and we had to get the repairman.''

Muriel entered the Senator's office which, except for the new console telephone, was fashioned exactly in the style of 1914, the year he moved in. Some of the bookshelves had not been dusted since.

''Senator, can we get these incoming calls straight? When I buzz, you push down the light that's blinking.''

''Who said anything about me taking phone calls this afternoon?''

''You'll want to hear from Mr. Jamieson, won't you? If he calls, that is?''

''If he's on the line, alright. Which one?''

''No. I say if he does call, just remember what button to push.''

"Confounded machine. Why, after one hundred years, can't they make these things work?"

"And why, after one hundred years of trying, haven't you learned?"

The Senator laughed. "Good for you, Muriel. A good debating response."

He liked Muriel. Most people did. Secretaries, like governors general and other participants in the political process, are important. Of all those involved in the great campaign of '53, Muriel could be described as the best adjusted.

In an age when spinsterism was the fate worse than death for most women, Muriel coped. She cast herself into a thousand activities beyond the bedroom. In unseductive middle age, she sailed, climbed mountains, hunted agates, joined book clubs and attended symphonies. She gardened, did volunteer work for crippled children and sat on the neighborhood library board. She would dearly have loved to learn to fly, but could not afford it. The Senator felt for her an affection as deep as he could hold for another human but, unfortunately for her, he had remained unaware of salary changes common in the Canadian nation since the late forties.

"What I said was, if he phones, I'll push the buzzer and you look for the light and punch the right button. We're paying for this machine, we might as well get used to it."

"That's enough bossing for one day, Muriel. Just make sure he's on the line before you buzz. I haven't got time to sit here with that thing sticking in my ear."

"You won't have to sit with anything sticking in your ear, Senator."

"Instrument of the devil anyway. The political life of this country went to hell when we started using it. It's never been the same since the days when you sat across from a man and talked to him face to face. You could see his eyes."

"So you'd know when to shoot?"

"That, and when to feel compassion too, my dear. And believe it or not, onc is just as important as the other in politics."

What followed between the two men was less a conversation than an encounter.

"I think we may have the Chilcotin situation in hand, Senator."

"Oh."

The usual thanks for a job well and quickly done, Montgomery told himself. On impulse he said, "Someone you know, I believe. From long ago."

"I've met a good many men from Chilcotin."

"Well, I think you know this one. The name is Larsen."

There was a silence long enough that Montgomery came to the conclusion that he had set his hook. The Senator would be reluctant to admit he didn't. At the other end of the connection the Senator signalled to Muriel, indicating by gestures that she should listen while he spoke.

"Larsen," he said. "There's something familiar about that name all right. Now, let me see. Larsen."

Muriel scribbled a note and passed it to him.

'Larsen. Timber license. 1947.'

"Yes," said the Senator, "there was a Larsen I knew there. Logger. Got in some difficulties over a timber license on a Crown grant."

Montgomery could not keep all the surprise out of his voice.

"You know him then!"

"I don't know if it's the same Larsen. But it well may be. There aren't many Larsens up there. There aren't many people up there."

The Senator permitted himself some reminiscence.

"He came into the office on Hallowe'en evening, I remember that. He had a tiny little head and when he took his hat off it reminded me of the peak of Garibaldi, white and pointed. I don't believe he often took his hat off except to go to bed. A rather wispy manner. Very deceiving. He proved to be twenty thousand dollars smarter than I was about his problem."

"He was a very smart man then."

"There were complexities. I won't go into them now. It would take too long. It can be summed up by saying that I thought I was being particularly clever and he permitted me to think so if I wished. Yes. Larsen. But isn't he old? Very old?"

It was Montgomery's turn, "I don't have his age in my notes," he said, consulting a note from his wife which said 'Dinner with Trevor Tuesday and no fail.'

"But does he fit the description? Small. Wispy. Scandinavian accent. Logger."

Montgomery wiped his long face with his hand.

"Similar, from my notes, Senator. But of course we'd double-check."

"Of course. I know you would. Well, I leave it to you. But if it's Larsen the old logger, you have a good citizen. Not forceful. Not a platform man. Possibly not even a winner. But not a disgrace to the party either. Not like the candidate we found in Kootenay."

Montgomery hunched over like a dog trying to screw a punch bowl and thought what a savage, a wicked old bastard this man was but his voice did not waver.

"As I say, we'll have to double-check. But you've been a great help, Senator. Thanks."

"Call on me any time, Montgomery. Oh. Just one thing. If it's not the same man, I'd appreciate hearing from you."

"I wouldn't do otherwise."

"And one more thing, Montgomery. Congratulations."

"Congratulations?"

"Yes. You've filled the slate. Fifty-two candidates."

"Thank you, Senator."

"Fight the good fight, Montgomery."

The Senator's button clicked before Montgomery Jamieson's, who, reaching for his own buttons, said again, this time aloud, "You old son of a bitch."

At the other end of the line the Senator turned and looked at Muriel who was listening, as usual. "As if we had any hope of taking Chilcotin," he said.

"You'd fight for every seat wouldn't you, Senator?"

"I'm getting to be a feeble fighter, my girl. As for that man Larsen, a clever man, a good man. But not for politics. The man was born without any fire to him. You could sense it. No warmth. No heat. No heart. The voters will sense that too."

"Oh well, there are others to win."

"But Chilcotin would be such a victory, Muriel. Did you know we haven't won it since John Oliver's time?"

"I wasn't a gleam in my father's eye in John Oliver's time."

"Now, there was a politician. Honest John. Of course, all politicians named John get to be called Honest John. But he was, you know. I remember when he addressed the Legislature one day, the suave and the clever men of the House had been baiting him. John wasn't suave. He said (the Senator's voice became fuller, richer and louder), 'I have dug ditches by the side of Chinamen, when every morsel of food I carried to my mouth bore the imprint of my fingers in the dirt and I was just as good a man then as I am now. And in the opinion of some members of this House, a better man.' "

"You have a great memory."

"Only when prompted, Muriel. And thanks for prompting me on that Larsen name."

"There's nothing more you need now?"

"No thanks."

She left. The Senator looked at his hand, a large one, and once a hard one but now marred with liver marks.

" 'When every morsel of food I carried to my mouth bore the imprint of my fingers in the dirt.' It was more than just political talk. John had heart."

Muriel tucked her large pumpkin face back through the half-open door. "Congratulations, Senator. You finally got the buttons right. Maybe I won't quit after all."

"Go away, presumptuous creature," he said.

In his youth only three types of women dominated the lives of man — a mother, a wife and finally a daughter. Now a fourth had been added, a secretary. Well, the situation had come about naturally and was now universal, so there must be merit in it.

But how can secretaries be so dumb, Brydon was asking himself. Having received Montgomery's memorandum on public opinion polls, he had just dictated a countermemo, rich in classical reference to American sociological studies.

"Gee, I wouldn't say that to Mr. Jamieson," said Brydon's secretary. Her name was Darlene and she had bedroom eyes.

"He asked for my opinion."

"He asked for it, but I don't think he wanted it."

"Of course he wanted it. MJ doesn't want yes men around him."

"I think if he wants something done a special way that's the way you better do it."

"Honeybear, you just don't understand these things."

"Nope. But I sure wouldn't kick Mr. Jamieson in the shins."

"Well, some things are serious matters, that's all."

"Chaz. I like you when you're serious. I really do. But why can't you be sensible too?"

"Honeybear, you are all a-quiver." He put his hand on her back-combed blond hair. "Tonight, I will put on a ten dollar shirt and we will eat hundred-year-old eggs in Chinatown  Eh?"

Before their breathing grew heavy the phone snarled. It was Montgomery, asking for fresh information from Chilcotin. Brydon had done nothing, his hour having been spent in composing a cogent and closely reasoned memo, but he lacked the fortitude to say that. He was a very junior executive. Bereft of any new information on Chilcotin, he winged it, using a bit of old information which he had not used in his earlier conversation.

"All I've been able to do so far, MJ, is check the phone book. It's an old, old book but it lists a Larsen General Store. He's a rancher now but maybe when that phone book came out he was a storekeeper."

"Oh? Might be our man, then."

"You know him!"

"There was a Larsen up there some years ago. Wispy little man, Scandinavian accent. Not too impressive looking, but a sharp businessman. We could do worse."

There were times when Brydon felt he was a boy set among gods and demons. The Senator, who could tell him what university he had attended. MJ, who, presented with an obscure name from the most obscure part of the entire province, could draw a thumbnail character sketch of the man attached to it.

"We should confirm the nomination then?"

"Yes. As soon as you've double-checked that he is that man. He's no winner. I can tell you that. But he's as good as anything we'll get out of Chilcotin. And he can vote for himself. That's one vote. If he's married, we can hope for two votes."

"You are encouraging."

"Just joking . . . Before you go, Charles . . . impress on that riding president, there is no money for him down here."

"Well the connection was bad when I talked, but from what I could make out, he said they didn't want any money."

"What?!"

"He said they couldn't care less about campaign funds."

"Another goddamed nut. This party is full of them. What in hell does he think you run an election campaign with? Cracker Jack coupons?"

"I don't know, sir."

"These are hard days for all of us Charles. Well, I leave it all to you."

"Right."

"Fight the good fight."

"Right."

"What did he say, Chaz?"

"He said 'Who can imagine anything good coming out of Chilcotin?' " Seeing her puzzled, he added, "I think a Roman emperor said it originally, about Nazareth." That didn't help her much.

She put out a forefinger and wiped out the crease that had formed between his eyes.

"Don't do that, somebody might walk in."

She took the finger back.

"I wonder what this election is gonna do to you and me Chaz?"

"What do you mean, do to us?"

"I was warned about a man who had a third finger longer than his middle finger."

"That bloody numerologist again."

"Well, look how often she's right. She told me about a man with a long third finger. You ever notice Mr. Jamieson's hands? The fingernail on the third finger is long, so it's like the middle finger."

"What does she say about how many seats we'll get?"

"I never asked her that. She mostly talks about people, not about elections."

Brydon tried to refresh himself by looking at Darlene's breasts and bum and found they reminded him of some charts he had made of voting patterns in the Okanagan.

"Tell me, Honeybear, how many seats are we going to win this time?"

"Why ask me?" she said. "I don't know anything about politics. You know that."

"Sure you do. You've been part of the campaign. Come on."

"I don't know."

"Nobody *knows*. Make an estimate."

"Well, I guess, two or three."

"*Two* or *three*? For God's sake. Two or three!"

"Now you're mad. I told you. I don't know."

"But you say two or three out of fifty-two!"

Her voice had a squeak. "Maybe you'll get all fifty-two. How should I know? But I don't see that anybody's very mad at the government. Why should they kick it out?"

"For the good of the country, that's why."

"But isn't everything pretty good? For most people?"

"If you don't look ahead any more than six months, yes, I suppose it is."

"Well six months is enough. If things are bad in six months we can have another election and get a different government."

"Forget I asked."

"I didn't want to make you mad. But you asked. Anyhow, I'm gonna vote Liberal this time. And I'll get Mum to vote for them too. Who do we vote for in Kerrisdale?"

"I'll write it down for you, the night before the election."

"See, you are mad."

"Go down to the Yen Lock, Honeybear. I'll go out after you and be down in about twenty minutes."

On that same afternoon a prime bull moose carried away on his antlers fifty feet of Namko's only telephone line. The bull was looking for a cow moose and had no appreciation whatever of questions of national destiny, but in an election campaign, everybody has a part to play. The line was down for two days and, unable to make more checks on either live or dead Larsens, Ken's nomination was approved and his name duly entered on the lists.

On Jamieson's desk at campaign headquarters in Vancouver the memos multiplied like the flies in manure and from his telephone there came the constant keening of frantic Liberal candidates, demanding money he did not have. He remained in reasonable control of his organization and, more importantly, of himself, but was feeling the first stabs of violent pain in his face, the onset of a malady not yet diagnosed, the *tic douloureux*, a nervous affliction similar to migraine. The first full spasm of the pain hit him and twisted his face into wild grimace when he reached for a memo marked DELIVERED BY HAND from the Senator. Darlene, who chanced to deliver it, said "Are you alright, Mr. Jamieson?" He waved her away with his hand and read the memo a second time.

"Have just learned that the Larsen whom we thought we had nominated in Chilcotin has been dead for three years. Can you advise?"

Disdaining to wait for an elevator, Darlene raced down two sets of stairs to Brydon's office, bum, bosom and perfume flying. She found Brydon studying a chart of fifty two voting patterns which he had painstakingly wrought and which now covered an entire wall of his small office.

"Chaz. Something awful."

"Shut up. There's always something awful."

"Chaz. Listen to me."

"Lay off. I'm analyzing these figures."

She stamped a tiny foot and broke off a stiletto heel.

"Listen to me, damit. You have nominated the wrong Larsen in Chilcotin."

"No!"

"Yes."

"No."

"Yes, I said. The Senator has just fired an awful memo to Mr. Jamieson. It's the wrong Larsen."

Brydon sloped over to his desk and threw himself into the chair. "A great day not to have a revolver with me. But they say cyanide is just as quick."

"He's gonna call you, any minute."

"Don't I know."

She limped across to the desk, carrying the broken heel in her hand. "We gotta think of something."

Brydon was trying to remember what he had learned in executive development courses, but the only lines which came to him were a familiar jingle—"When in danger or in doubt, run in panic, scream and shout."

"Blame me for it," she said. "Tell him I put the papers through without telling you."

"Oh for God's sake. Throw a little lamb like you at that wolf. You'd be gone in two bites and he'd still be as hungry as ever."

"I told you this election was trouble for you and me."

Before he could answer the buzzer snarled. "Yes, MJ," he said. "Right away, MJ."

As he walked out she said "I love you Chaz," but he did not seem to hear.

Mr. Jamieson, said Miss O'Day, would be ready to see him in a moment. "He's changing his shirt."

*Why*, thought Brydon, *when he's going to get blood all over the fresh one?*

"Thank you, Miss O'Day."

She looked at him with her head cocked on one side, like a robin listening for a worm.

"You won't mind if I say something, Mr. Brydon?"

"Not at all."

"There's something missing on that suit of yours."

He looked at his pinstripe.

"Oh, not the suit. It's a very nice suit. But it really needs a flower in the buttonhole." She took a fresh rose—Montgomery kept all the offices supplied with roses—and snipped it with her scissors. Walking around the desk, a straight pin in her mouth, she pinned it in the lapel.

"My father, you know, used to say that a man needed a flower in his lapel. He said it used to give him confidence, all through the day. Now, isn't that better?"

He looked down at the flower and then at her gentle little face. "You're an extremely kind person, Miss O'Day."

"Oh no. I'm a very ordinary person."

"I wonder if it's the same thing?"

Montgomery's voice floated out of the office.

"Charles there?"

"Yes sir."

"Come in."

The shades of Montgomery's office had been pulled and the lights turned low and at first he could not locate Montgomery, who had flung himself into a deep leather chair at the room's corner and almost disappeared into its deep embrace. The dim light glinted faintly on a whiskey glass, held in Montgomery's left hand, and on the whites of his eyes.

"Have a drink, Brydon."

The condemned man refused the bandage, but stood straight, facing the rifles. "Oh, no thanks. I never have a drink until the sun is over the yardarm. Thanks anyway."

"The sun is over the yardarm. Have a drink, I said." Brydon went to the bar at the far wall, poured half an ounce into a large glass of good crystal, returned, placed himself in a chair opposite Montgomery and raised the glass in salute. "Cheers," he said.

"Cheers."

The silence, so lightly disturbed, returned and settled itself in the room again. A long minute passed before the older man spoke.

"Charles, I have got myself in a terrible mess."

"*You* have? I mean, you *have*?"

"Yes. I have approved the wrong candidate in Chilcotin."

"That wasn't you. That was me. I made the mistake."

Montgomery lifted a hand to silence him, the hand with the glass. Some whiskey spilled on his shirt cuff.

"Just what I said to myself. I said 'Watch, he'll take the blame.' No Charles. The blame is mine. I made the mistake." He leaned out of the deep crouch of the soft chair and tapped a hand on the young man's knee. "But you, you are maybe the man who can get me out of the hole I dug for myself."

"I'm a little bit taken aback by this MJ."

"I can see that you are."

"I think maybe I could stand another shot," said Brydon. He went back to the well and this time added ice. When he walked back he remained standing, tinkling ice cubes against the edge of the glass. He looked down. Montgomery looked up. The tone of the encounter had changed.

"Let's start by saying that what's happened is the least important thing, because we can't change it."

"I agree," said Montgomery.

"So let's start from where we stand. We can dump him or we can keep him."

"Mhm. Go on."

"Dumping is disaster. So let's look at keeping. First we thought we had a storekeeper who wasn't up to much. Now we've got a rancher who is maybe not up to much. What is better about a storekeeper than a rancher?''

''That is not a bad way to put it to the Senator,'' said Montgomery.

''We can also put it to the Senator that this is the only candidate we have that represents the agricultural community. Almost all the rest of them are in business or they're retired or they're in university. We have filled out with someone from the agricultural sector.''

''Not bad. Not bad. I follow.''

''And he might not be hopeless.''

''True. On the other hand, he might be one of those pinkos that keep getting into the party. Be kind to cats but to hell with the Americans.'' Like most of the Vancouver business community, Montgomery had been rendered perpetually uneasy by Vladimir Lenin and the Bolsheviki.

''More likely to be on the conservative side, MJ.''

''We've got no room for them. Those are the bastards we're throwing out of office.''

Brydon took another sip of whisky. ''Exactly. And since we don't know, the thing to do is for me to go up there personally. Charter a plane. Fly up today. Meet him. Talk to him. Talk to the people who know him. Maybe start off this campaign for him. If he's respectable and has the basic Liberal philosophy, we've got nothing to worry about. Except losing Chilcotin, which we expected to lose anyway.''

''And if he's so far left or right we can't see him, what then?''

''I say we cross that bridge when we come to it. Your glass is empty, MJ.''

Montgomery extended his glass, which was recharged. A little time brushed past between the two of them in the twilight of the big office.

''Charles, you are absolutely right.''

''Well thank you.''

''I don't know how I'd survive this campaign, except for people like you around me. The people who can bail me out.''

''That's putting it too strong.''

''The people who can bail me out, I said.'' He stood and put a hand on Brydon's shoulder. ''When were you planning to go?''

''Today. I'll charter a plane.''

"Decision. That's the answer to most problems. Decision." He was walking Brydon toward the office door, the hand still on the shoulder.

"By the way, Charles, how's your salary?"

"It's all right. . . no. It isn't. It's lousy."

Montgomery laughed. "That's what I like to see. Nobody worth a damn is satisfied with his salary. We'd better take a look at it, Charles. By the way, you're not sleeping with little Miss Bosoms are you?"

Brydon stopped, but his voice didn't break stride. "My old man told me, sir, 'Never dip your pen into the company inkwell.' "

Montgomery laughed again. "A good political response. A reply without an answer in it. Well, fight the good fight, Charles."

"Leave it to me, MJ."

Brydon, young executive, junior fornicator, boy diplomat, strode though the outer office almost forgetting to nod to Miss O'Day. Montgomery, who walked as far as the secretary's desk, joined her in watching the door close behind the young man.

"He's a very bright young man, isn't he?" she said.

"Bright," he said, "and not too bad under pressure. However, at times he verges on idiocy. Can you imagine? He put through the Chilcotin nomination without having the rudimentary intelligence to check it all out? I should have strangled him with his own intestines."

"But you didn't."

"I have to have somebody to clean up the mess. Who better than the one that made it?"

"There are some calls for you here. Mrs. Jamieson . . . "

"Keep her off my damned back."

"Now, Mrs. Jamieson is a very nice lady."

"So they all are, all nice ladies. If she phones again, say that I got into a lukewarm bath and opened my veins, OK?"

"The West Cates Park candidate called."

"Phone. Say I tried to get him back three times and his line was always busy. Tell him I'm at a meeting now that will last until midnight."

"And the Senator phoned."

"I will write him a memo, pointing out that we got exactly the candidate we intended to get in Chilcotin. A representative of the agricultural community. It might hold him."

"And Durksen."

"Oh, my own personnel manager. I'd forgotten I had a business of my own. Yes, get him on the line. I've got a job for him."

In his office, the main crisis of another day behind him, Montgomery tidied up with what he conceived to be a final act of kindness toward Brydon.

"That little Miss Bosoms of a secretary he's got — get rid of her, will you?"

The disembodied voice of the personnel manager floated out of the intercom. "Something wrong?"

"Nothing in particular, except that young Brydon has never heard of the simple rule that you don't screw anything within six blocks of the office. And she's not good enough for him anyway. It's time he had a secretary who can think a little bit, and spell."

"You seem to be high on Brydon."

"In a way I guess. He can think under pressure."

"You want her shifted to another job?"

"I want her the hell out of here, that's what I want."

"MJ. It may have escaped your attention, but we have a little piece of paper called a union contract now. You can't just fire people that way any more except for exempt staff like Brydon."

"She must have taken one of those Briand and Cockfield tests. How did she score?"

"Well, as I recall, not very high."

"What more do you need?"

"Damit, that's the test we used to hire her."

"If we used it to hire, why can't we use it to fire?"

"I take it I'm being tested myself, to see how I think under pressure?"

Montgomery laughed. "It's OK. I have read that contract, you know. And if my memory serves, you can offer her a raise in pay to go to the Hawaii office. And if she turns that down, it's a reason for firing her. So one way or the other, the thing's done."

"I guess you're right, y'know."

"Then it's settled?"

"Settled, M.J."

"He was terribly unsettled and uncertain," Brydon was telling Darlene.

"You mean he wasn't mad?"

"Mad? No, of course not. Just upset and worried. He wanted my advice."

"I just don't understand it."

By silence, he agreed that, true, she had little understanding. He was stuffing a briefcase with campaign literature and devising his strategy for handling the candidate of Chilcotin. If Larsen could memorize six of the twenty-odd planks of the platform it would, he opined, carry for a month of campaigning in the boondocks. Particularly if, as he suspected, the attendance at a typical mass rally came one or two bodies below the number who partook in the Last Supper.

Turning such plans and speculations on the lathe of the mind, he did not hear much that she said, only enough to become irritated.

"Yettetty yettetty yettetty. How can a man think?"

"I'm sorry."

"This is important damit. We've got a loose cannon on the deck. A loose cannon. If it rolls the wrong way it can capsize the whole bloody ship."

"Oh. I see."

"I'll be gone two, maybe three days. He's made it all my personal responsibility. So try to keep things straight here, will you?"

"I still don't think he likes me."

"Liking? What in hell has liking got to do with business or politics?"

"Not much, I guess."

"Give me a bundle of those *Themes for Speeches*. That'd be a help for him."

"You gonna miss me?"

He riffled the files in the briefcase and judged, quickly, as such judgments must be made, that he had enough ammunition for a battle or two. "Some warm clothes from the apartment. Plane's ready in an hour." He started for the door, swinging the briefcase.

"Good luck Chaz."

"Oh. Thanks."

"And goodbye Chaz."

"Oh. Yeah." He gave her a kiss which almost missed, and then was gone.

"Goodbye," she said again to the closing door, softly this time. "Goodbye, John Charles Brydon."


Brydon boarded the single-engine Cessna on Sea Island at Vancouver and enquired cheerfully about weather in the mountain passes.

"Scattered cloud."

"Is that good?"

"Depends on where they're scattered."

The pilot, who was also the owner of the two-plane charter service, did not much like customers. He accepted them because it was the only way he could afford to fly airplanes, something he enjoyed.

After they took off, Brydon offered the information that he was flying north on election business.

"What election?" said the pilot.

They flew in silence through narrow passes, climbed up on the Chilcotin plateau and droned on, a solitary speck in an immense sky over land that looked much as it had on the first day of Creation.

Brydon wondered what reception committee might await him at Namko. Probably, he thought, only two men, MacGregor, the riding president and Larsen, the candidate. He was two over on that estimate. They flew past the Namko Hotel and Store and landed on the slate black ice, newly formed, of a lake beside Larsen's ranch. Larsen wasn't there either, but was, the pilot learned from somebody at the barn, holed up at a line cabin on the Vestpocket Lake winterfeeding some of his cows. They flew there, while the shadows of the day grew long, and found a small cabin of unpeeled logs which had a line of smoke at the chimney.

"If he's not there, he'll be back soon," said the pilot, handing Brydon his briefcase and suitcase through the door while the Cessna's prop muttered impatiently.

"You aren't coming in with me?"

"I got an hour to make Nimpo."

Brydon, wrapped in all the wool he owned, shivered as he stood on the black ice, looking at the black forest, the grassland quivering under light plumes of snow being blown across it, the line of grey fence, the squalid little cabin. ''The land that God forgot,'' he said.

''Eh?'' said the pilot.

Brydon repeated, shouting. He was angry as well as cold now.

The pilot, for the first time, smiled. ''Nope. He didn't forget this country. He remembers it well. He hates it.'' He turned the little plane, blew bitter air over Brydon, and taxied down the lake for takeoff.

Brydon walked off the lake and through a dusting of snow toward the cabin. A swaybacked horse came to meet him, accompanied him a few paces and then, apparently disappointed, shambled off. He pounded vigorously on the plank door with the heel of his hand but, hearing no answer, shoved it open and strode inside. The cabin had but one window and the light inside was dim and smelled of smoke. A thousand years ago, sometime earlier today, he had walked into a place as dimly lit as this. It seemed almost too far for remembering. But here, as earlier, there was a man who waited for him. In this place it was Ol Antoine, dark and curled like a bacon rind, who sat beside the oil drum which served as a cabin heater.

''Oh. Hello. I was told Mr. Larsen would be here.''

Ol Antoine did not answer. There had been no question for him to answer.

''But I don't see him here,'' said Brydon. Again there was no response. ''So I guess he isn't here.''

By silence, Ol Antoine agreed that, true, Ken Larsen wasn't there.

Brydon dumped his two bags and walked to the drum heater, holding his hands above it and rolling them against each other.

''Ah . . . my name is Brydon. Charles Brydon . . . ah . . . how do you do?''

''Not bad, I s'pose,'' said Ol Antoine.

''Would you care for a cigarette?''

''You got some?''

''Ah, yes. Yes, I have some.''

He pulled a packet from his pocket, flipped the lid and extended it. The old man withdrew one, cautiously and examined it.

''A light?''

Ol Antoine considered this offer and nodded his head to acknowledge that this, too, would be acceptable. He held the cigarette between thumb and middle finger, sucked while Brydon held a cigarette lighter for him and then, without inhaling, blew out the smoke from his mouth.

"I came here to see Ken Larsen. The Liberal candidate. I was told he was here."

"I wait for that fella Larsen long time. Loong time. This morning I come here wait for that fella."

"This morning. But it's night. Is he going to get here at all?"

Ol Antoine did not answer and Brydon continued.

"What if he doesn't come?"

"I kess I wait some more," said Ol Antoine.

Ol Antoine looked at Brydon intently. It was the first good look he had spared for the man.

"Peoples say, that Larsen, he's in koferment now."

"Oh, not in government. Not yet, that is. He's a candidate, and if he gets enough votes . . . "

"S'pose he kets that chob, it's lots money, en't it?"

"Well, no. Not really lots. He gets a sessional indemnity. That is he gets a payment every year, and if he got to be a cabinet minister he would get more money. . . ."

"But it's lots money en't it?"

"No. It's not lots."

"Then what for he takes that chob?"

"Well, he'll be one of the men running the country."

"He koes aaall the way down that place and they don't pay him lots money?"

"Well, that's about the size of it, I guess."

Ol Antoine blew out blue smoke and watched the rising air from the stove rip the cloud apart.

"Sure is funny thing. Who you s'pose kets all that money? All the times, peoples gifs money to koferment, gif all the time. Who kets all that money?"

"Those are pretty hard questions to answer."

Ol Antoine nodded. "Koferment, he's kinda like God en't it? He's all around us, every place, but us peoples we don't efer get to see him or talk with him."

He peered intently at Brydon, who did not answer.

"Smith, he says that Larsen's real good man for koferment."

"Oh. That's good."

"Hea. Smith, he says Larsen, he don't think so good, but sure can talk."

There was a thin, whistling sound, as of a musical tea kettle coming to the boil. It came, Brydon discovered, from Ol Antoine. He was laughing. "Shmart man, Smith," he said.

When Larsen came into the cabin a few minutes later he was, despite the advance billing, not at all talkative. He had been in the saddle since morning. A bunch of the cows had gone out through a break in the Russell fence, panicked by a late-roving bear which had not yet denned up for winter, and he had been combing them out of the jack pines since morning. "It's wet, it's cold, it's lonely work but it's like duck shooting or steelhead fishing, somebody has to do it."

He threw the chaps, glazed with ice at their tips, into the corner of the cabin, dragged off his boots and dropped into a bunk.

Brydon's presence had aroused him neither to gratitude, pleasure or mild surprise. "From the Liberal party eh? Charlie? Well, good to see you Charlie. Better get some grub."

He did not say where the grub was, or how it might be cooked, but drew a grey and greasy blanket over himself and slept with peaceful muttering sounds. Brydon, equally weary if from different causes, found another manger stuffed with marsh hay and another blanket and he, too, slept while full night came down upon the cabin and Ol Antoine, patient as the hills, sat beside the drum heater.

Brydon awoke an hour later in the undiluted panic with which his sleep now so often terminated. In the moments before full wakefulness there was the dire thought that he had missed some appointment of towering import, that he had failed to send some telegram, to write some memo, to make some telephone call upon which the entire fate of the nation pivoted. He sweated on these terrible awakenings and his heart pounded for minutes.

Larsen and Ol Antoine were already awake and arguing beside the heater.

"It's fifty tollars you don't pay me on that hay."

"Like hell I owe you fifty dollars. You forget that fence your boys was going to make. That was a hundred, already paid you, and the fence is still down. Bunch of cows went through it today."

"We make that fence real quick."

"That's right. You do it real quick. After you fix that fence, I pay you for the hay. Right?"

"Might be twenty?"

"OK," said Larsen. "Twenty. On account." He opened a .wallet and handed over twenty. "How about some wood for the stove, eh Ol Antoine?"

"Sure. OK." Ol Antoine went to the woodpile. As he went through the door into the cold night, Larsen, who had watched him go, turned toward Brydon and with a forefinger pointed to the empty door.

"Now that," he said, "is a voter. Yes sir. That is a man whose vote I am s'posed to ask for so I can run the country. Got as much idea about government as my ass has about shooting snipe but that don't make no difference. He has got just as much vote as I got."

"I suppose that is so."

"Terrible mistake, Charlie. Terrible mistake, giving the Indians the vote." Brydon rose from the bunk. The waking dream was longer this time. Something terrible, he could not be sure what, had indeed happened. The other man continued. "That was just one of the mistakes. The big mistake, the big mistake of this century, was giving the vote to women. That was when everything started coming apart."

Brydon reached out for the edge of reality and tried to cling to it with numb fingers. "You say . . . the women's vote?"

"Oh, I know. I know. I'm a practical man Charlie. There is no way in God's green world we can take it back now. Hell, it ain't worthwhile even bringing up the subject. But it don't alter the facts. Look at what happened. The two worst wars of all of human history. The worst Depression ever. That's what came with women voting. That and teaching dancing in the schools and rotting the heart out of the country with welfare. That's what we got. Say. I think you've taken a bit of a chill."

Brydon, who was shivering, did not answer. Larsen reached under a bunk and brought forth a bottle.

"Here," he said. "Friend of mine makes it."

He unscrewed the cap and placed the cold bottle in Brydon's hand. "Not the finest liquor in the world, mind you, but at least the bloody government misses out on taxes with every drink I take."

Brydon drank and gagged.

"Yes. A little fierce. But you can drink it without propping up this damned welfare state we got."

Ol Antoine came back and fed the fire. Larsen fed the clear liquid into his throat, whistled through his teeth, stamped one foot and placed the bottle on the table.

"Oh Charlie, it don't take a very smart man to see that things have gone wrong in this country. Awful wrong. You take the kind of men we got in politics now. They can't run the country. They got no bottom. The old days, there was bigger men in politics. Much bigger men. You take John A. Macdonald now. Or Borden."

"What about Mackenzie King?" said Brydon.

"Ah, I always thought he was kind of an old woman. But the guy that was against him, now there by God, was a man." He rolled the name upon his tongue as he spoke it. "R.B. Bennett."

"R.B. Bennett!"

"Oh, I know, I know. They laughed at him, they hated him, they voted him clear out of the country. But he was a man, Charlie."

"He was a Conservative man."

"I know. And I'm a Liberal. Always have been. But Charlie I can tell you this. If R.B. Bennett was to walk in here tonight, right here in this old cabin, and he was to say to me, 'Larsen, pick up your ictus, man, and follow me. I am gonna lead us to the Promised Land,' you know what? I would follow him. Yessir. Barefoot, down the trail, through three feet of snow, I would follow R.B. Bennett. By damn, man. I think you've got a real chill. Here, have another belt."

Sadly, Brydon said, "I might as well."

"You might try hanging on the edge of the bunk. It helps if you're holding onto something solid when you take a pull at that stuff."

Next morning, a cowboy arrived to relieve Larsen of the winterfeeding duties at Vestpocket. "Why don't you wrap your socks around a toothbrush and come campaigning with me for a couple of days?" said Larsen. Brydon answered wanly that he supposed he might as well. He was enfeebled by severe culture shock and had a hangover too. A morning of conversation over boiled coffee had been comfortless. He had, with some pride of associate authorship, produced a document which outlined the Liberal campaign platform for Larsen to read. Larsen had done so, but without much joy. "It's like trying to get drunk by licking the foam on glasses of beer," he said. Brydon decided to leave the other literature in the briefcase. He would, he decided, follow the candidate on the campaign trail but would listen rather than talk. Possibly there would be an opportunity to drown the man.

Pounding the frost deeper into narrow, rutted trails, they visited first the home of Frenchie Bernard where they discussed grazing regulations, beef prices and the latest quotations for prime beaver pelts. They next visited somebody called Old Man Campbell, where the same subjects were discussed in reverse order. They overnighted at the Smiths where there was a full, free and frank examination of the plans for Namko's annual Stampede, which was to be held the following June.

Next morning they passed by the hotel where dwelt the Chilcotin Liberal president. "He talks so much we'd be there all day," said Larsen. He then took an almost indecipherable wagon trail south and found the cabin of a bachelor horsebreaker named Seldom Everson. His proper handle, Brydon was told, was Seldom Swift, but over the years it had been shortened to Seldom.

Seldom was a horsebreaker and former saddle bronc champion, also, clearly, a man for whom Larsen had a large affection. For four hours, scarcely interrupted by the eating of moosemeat and beans, Larsen and Seldom talked about rodeo horses and rodeo men and, in the end, reached consensus—all the best horses, all the best riders, were now dead. "The men I rode against when I was young, why, there ain't a rider today fit to lead one of their horses to water," said Seldom.

A full day of campaigning had now been completed, and so far the fact that an election was being held had scarcely been mentioned and the fact that Larsen was one of the candidates, never.

As they drove out of Seldom's gate, Larsen remarked that this campaigning business was kind of fun. He had not, he said, seen Seldom in almost a year.

Cold, tired and dispirited as he was, Brydon was roused to protest. "We have talked so far to seven voters," he said. "At this rate, the campaign will have to last a year and a half for you to cover this riding. Nobody's thinking about an election as far as I can see.''

''Why should they? They got their own affairs to think about . . . Charlie, you look plumb cold again. Here. Seldom gave me some real whisky as we was leavin'. Take a pull.''

''Why not.'' said Brydon.

''Road straightener, we call it,'' said Larsen. ''Here, I think I could use some myself.''

They drove until midnight, found beds in a dark and silent ranch house and greeted their hosts at breakfast next morning, at which time there was discussion of hay and the probable length of the winter.

A day later, when they reached the valley of the Chilcotin River, the road was better and there were frame ranch houses with shingles, propane stoves, electric light plants and telephone poles. Brydon realized that Namko, whence the party had plucked their candidate, was the outermost fringe of ranch country. It was the desolate high country to which penniless men had been driven, finding land that nobody else had wanted. But even here in the older, richer valley of the Chilcotin the politics he thought he knew were skewed, as at the House of Crazy Mirrors in the circus midway.

They dined one night at a red mahogany table in a rich, old room of brass and silver and cedar. For the first time, Brydon was served beef which had not been fried or roasted until black, but which came to the table rare and red as the mahogany. The candidate for Chilcotin exercised his powers of diplomacy by telling the hostess that he had seen animals hurt worse than this get up and walk away.

Later, when they sipped port wine, their host raised the subject of politics. ''All my life I have had the choice of voting for right-wingers who steal my money and left-wingers who waste it. But I have always been of the opinion that the right can't steal as fast as the left can waste, so I have always voted Tory.''

''I s'pose I shouldn't say this, all things considered, but I figure what you say is plumb true,'' said Larsen.

Brydon dictated a telegram over the federal government phone lines, detailing Larsen's age, marital status, apparent affluence (as measured by Namko standards, which he did not describe), also his

wide acquaintanceships, the positions he had held in various cattlemen's associations, his direct and practical knowledge of agricultural
practices in the B.C. interior and, thinking privily of miles rather than
numbers, commented upon his wide acquaintanceship with the voting
population. He could have telephoned to Montgomery instead of to
the telegraph office but, if the truth is to be told, lacked the moral
fiber. In a direct conversation, Montgomery would extract from him
the precise degree of Larsen's commitment to the Liberal ideology,
and Montgomery Jamieson, he knew, perceived Liberals to be a
group divinely inspired to govern but, unhappily, a group ever in dire
peril of infiltration by Bolsheviki on the left and the Vancouver Club
on the right.

In fact, Montgomery perceived his crusade to be menaced not only
by the iniquitous agents of the left and the right but also by the Senator
who was behind. Sometimes the Senator was in front also. Montgomery pleaded that Miss O'Day should divert the Senator's calls. "Say I
was stolen by the gypsies," he would tell her. She would smile and
put the Senator's calls through anyway. However, as the campaign
organization became ever more convulsive in its movements, she
ceased putting the Senator through by buzzer, but would instead
tippytoe to Montgomery's side and whisper that the Senator was nigh.
Montgomery had never been sure why he feared the Senator, but he
knew his face hurt a lot when he encountered the old man. The
Senator reduced all discussion of politics to matters pettily, dismally
practical. "What is this political mass consciousness of which you
speak Montgomery?" he said one day. "How does it fit with the fact
that our Point Grey candidate did not introduce himself to a cab driver
nor shake his hand?" Montgomery had answered, "Well, the loss of
one vote. Too bad." The old man answered "No, Montgomery. The
loss of two votes. There is the one which the taxi driver did not give us
and the one which he did give to our opponents. That is two votes. Not
one vote. Two votes. Such is the arithmetic."
Montgomery took what comfort he might from the knowledge that
the grand old man would soon be a grand old dead man and that
fresher spirits, such as his own, would revive the soul of the party. But
in the meantime the peculiar essence of party power, the stuff some
called the royal jelly of politics, rested in that twisted and narrow old
man. Montgomery knew power almost as well as he feared it and he

could never face the Senator without sensing that his bowels were about to empty spontaneously.

"It's the Senator," Miss O'Day whispered from the doorway.

Montgomery took three deep breaths, counting to five on each, picked up the phone and spoke in tones that were mellow with confidence.

"Hello Senator. It's nice to hear from you."

"Hello Montgomery. I just wondered if we'd obtained any more information about the Chilcotin candidate. The one we finally did choose, that is."

Montgomery relaxed. He had Brydon's telegram on the desk.

"Not bad, Senator. Not bad. Family man. Well respected. Knows everybody in the country apparently. Former president of the Cariboo Cattlemen's Association. A Justice of the Peace. And, a knowledge of agriculture. Our first candidate with an agricultural background."

"Nothing more?"

"Nothing much that is specific."

"We have, as always, checked the political background?"

A small alarm bell rang in Montgomery's liver.

"Ah, not as well as we might have preferred."

"You know, of course, that his wife is a daughter of Peter Green?"

"Peter Green. I don't think I know the man."

"You probably wouldn't. He was a tailor in Moncton, New Brunswick."

"Oh, well, I wouldn't then."

"No. Green, of course, was not the real name."

There was a trap in the path, but the path was narrow, with sheer cliffs falling away on either side and the grizzly bear behind him. It was now a familiar dream to Montgomery. He walked on.

"Yes?" he said.

"No. The name was Zielenski. Stefan Zielenski. Polish immigrant. Very active politically."

"Yes."

The Senator's voice was clear, even, relentless.

"A candidate for, an executive of and a lifelong member of the Communist Party of Canada. The name was raised recently in the Un-American Activities Committee in the States."

A telephone conversation conveys some of the advantages of

memo writing. There is less time for recovery than in the use of paper, but there remains the distinct advantage that the other party cannot read body language. Thus Montgomery was able to physically expend his anguish and terror in wild contortions of face and frame while the phone lines carried nothing but a silence. There was the time for him to turn his face from the telephone receiver and take two deep breaths to regain voice control. He was still bereft of anything to say, but luck, instinct perhaps, served him as well.

"Yes," he said. "Go on."

"Go on?"

In the instant, Montgomery perceived in the tone what had not been there before. A hesitation. A momentary loss of balance.

"I was waiting for you to go on, Senator."

This time there was puzzlement. "Go on?"

Montgomery smiled and spoke with tongue of angel. "I'm sure you're not suggesting that the Liberal party of British Columbia gives a sweet damn about what somebody's wife's uncle was doing in Sir Robert Borden's time?"

There was a pause of many seconds and Montgomery knew he had him.

When the Senator finally spoke the old voice came strained though gravel. "Congratulations, sir," he said. "Yes. Congratulations. Many a campaign manager would have panicked. Just couldn't resist my little joke, Montgomery. What I really phoned you about was that report on advertising funds you were going to send me."

"Oh yes. That report. I sent it over two days ago."

"Ah, yes. So you did. So you did. I see it's right here on the desk in front of me. Sorry about that."

Montgomery picked up a paper and his grin was now vulpine. "On your desk, Senator? I think you must be mistaken. It seems to be back here, on my desk. With your initials on it. And in fact, you've written a couple of comments in the margin. I'll read them to you . . ."

"It's alright. Alright. I was confused for the moment. I'm sorry to have bothered you about nothing, Montgomery."

"Not at all, Senator, not at all. Call any time."

Montgomery hung up. "And how do you like them apples, you sadistic old bastard."

Muriel came into her Senator's office like hell on a broomstick.

"That cheap little snit," she said. "And I don't mean snit."

"You've been listening on my phone again, Muriel."

"He was putting you down."

"That's the price you pay for getting old and out of touch. He's right, you know. It doesn't matter what somebody's uncle did in politics when the earth was young. I just shouldn't tease tigers."

"Him? A tiger? He's a spoiled kid and always was."

"He's fighting a good campaign."

"He's fighting because he wants to be a senator."

"Is that ignoble?"

She didn't hear. Her quills were up like a porcupine's. "And if he gets to be senator, what's his mum going to buy him next Christmas? The snotty nosed, little son of a bitch."

"Muriel, where do you pick up such language? At that rock-and-gem class of yours?"

"It's not fair, Senator. It's not fair. You held the party together out here all these years. Now when the Liberals are going to win, suddenly it's Jamieson driving the bandwagon."

"Oh. So we're winning?"

"You know we're winning. Everybody knows it. And you are the man who should be getting credit."

The Senator dragged himself up by holding the edges of his desk and reached for the nearby canes. "I think it's time I went home. I'm leaving early today."

She brought him his coat. He leaned the canes against the desk and, tottering gently on the leg braces, put out his arms. One arm caught in the lining. He lurched. She grappled with him. Like a single, misshapen beast, the two bodies lurched in strange embrace in the dusty old office. She caught him before he fell and propped him against the desk. He was breathing heavily. "Age doth surprise us all. Who said that? Walter Raleigh, wasn't it?"

Muriel had difficulty with her voice.

"Senator," she said. "Don't take a taxi. I'll get young Sawchuck to run you home today."

He closed his eyes, sighed, and opened them again.

"No," he said. "Not the taxi. Not Sawchuck either. Phone my son. He'll be down at the club. It's only four o'clock. He won't be drunk yet. Ask him to come up."

"Yes, Senator."

The hulk of the old man who was once called Old Thunder swayed on his aluminum sticks and, this one time, there was self-pity in the deep bass voice. "I don't want to drive home with a stranger tonight, Muriel."

But when the next day came the Senator was again dominant, because that was his nature and Montgomery Jamieson resentful and subordinate, as the nature of political process dictated. And Brydon, with oatmeal for brains, continued to do his best.

Brydon and Larsen had journeyed to Alexis Creek, capital city of the Chilcotin, population one hundred and sixty-five souls, counting dogs and government people. Here in the eastern Chilcotin, the original Chilcotin Country where the big river had carved a wide valley ten thousand years ago, there had been a profound alteration of the economy. The lodgepole pine forest, which ranchers had been cursing and throwing matches at for two generations, had become saleable. By grace of new technology, the thin black sticks could be profitably sawn into two-by-fours or rendered into chips with which, by further process, women's stockings might be built. Almost overnight logging had replaced ranching as the bread and butter of the land.

The Korean war and other natural afflictions, however, had withered the United States' housing industry and, apparently, had had an equally devastating effect upon the nylon stocking trade. The new logging industry was near collapse. Half of the loggers were without jobs. At Alexis Creek, Larsen was run to ground by a reporter of the newly established Williams Lake radio station. There was no time for Brydon to prime Larsen's pump for such an interview, nor could he have done it had time been offered him. The man was unteachable, he had learned.

In gloom, he sat in Alexis Creek's beer parlor, all patrons being silenced for the occasion, and listened while the interview proceeded.

"I hear things are really bad this year out this way," said Larsen.

Brydon experienced hope, the mainspring of the whole machinery of politics. There was a genuine concern in the candidate's voice. Larsen might not know the facts. He might well be immune to any innoculations of knowledge. But the concern was there and it was sincere.

Yes, said the man with the recording microphone, things were not good.

"Tell me about it," said Larsen. "Explain it to me."

Good, thought Brydon. Good and getting better. People don't really expect politicians to know everything any more. It's good enough that they will ask.

The man from the Williams Lake station obliged in gentlemanly fashion. He explained the drop in the market, he told how many mills had gone to short shifts, how many had stopped hauling logs.

Larsen cut him short. "To hell with the goddamed sawmills. I was asking about the grass."

Brydon fled to the nearest airline terminal at Williams Lake and was borne away to Vancouver, a city which frequently mistakes itself for the province of British Columbia, and there reported to Montgomery that, in the broad spectrum of Liberal philosophic thought, their Chilcotin candidate stood somewhat to the right of Attila the Hun. Montgomery in turn reported to the Senator whom he had vanquished a mere twenty-four hours before. As is the nature of politics, that was yesterday's victory. Today, in some manner he could not understand, the Senator had again resumed the command, which was not his in the first place, and he, Montgomery Jamieson, found himself reporting as to a general.

"It's a good thing he can't win. He's clearly an antediluvian Tory."

"The party's arms have always been broad," said the Senator.

"What's more, the man is stupid and I say a stupid man is more dangerous than a crooked man."

The Senator, who had lurched into a chair in Montgomery's office, an untidy heap of blue serge ready for the Salvation Army clothing box, raised his head.

"Stupid. Now that, sir, is an interesting statement."

The windup, Montgomery told himself. Where in hell was the pitch coming this time?

"Tell me Montgomery, how stupid is the man? Would you say that ninety percent of the people of B.C. are smarter than this man?"

"I said stupid. How can I quantify it?"

"Anything can be quantified. Are seventy-five percent of the general population more stupid than our candidate?"

"Well, if you press me, OK then, yes. From what Brydon tells me, three out of any four men on the street are as smart as our Chilcotin candidate."

"I see. Seventy-five percent. Tell me, haven't three quarters of the people of this province a right to have their representative in the Legislature?"

"You're playing word games, Senator."

"I'm not. But let it pass. What are you doing about this riding?"

"I've sent him five hundred dollars, which is two hundred and fifty more than any other of the hopeless candidates are getting. That's so he can cope with the problems he has to face getting around in such a large and sparsely populated area. I told him we wouldn't call on him to help Liberal candidates in the neighboring ridings. Also, he won't be coming to the big rally in Vancouver."

"I see. Running him with a paper bag over his head. It's a technique. It's been used before. How did he react to this idea that he be treated as an idiot in a madhouse?"

"Like an idiot in a madhouse. He said it was a terrible amount of money to spend and that anyway he didn't have any intention of going outside Chilcotin. He said he was enjoying the campaign, right at home."

"I see. Well, you've done well. There was no . . . hesitation?"

"Some, maybe, from his wife. She must have been standing near the telephone when we were talking. I gained the impression that she had some reservations."

"I'll play another word game with you. *Cherchez la femme.*"

"The wife, Senator, is the Communist's daughter. Zielenski. The man whose name appears on Senator Joe McCarthy's lists."

"Yes. Raised in a school of tremendous dedication, immense heart for the business of politics."

The audaciousness of the old man's attack almost overwhelmed Montgomery, as he had been almost overwhelmed the previous day when accused of being an agent of the Kremlin. He smiled, amiably. "Senator, don't you think we should now turn our attention to the thirty-seven seats we could win?"

"As you wish. You lead, we follow, Montgomery. I'm purely advisory."

In the great campaign of that year, Ken Larsen did come to the great final rally of his party in Vancouver. He came with his wife. He wasn't sure why he came, but he came anyway.

As to the great rally, there are two colleges of thought in the great university of politics. One adheres to the theory that by the time an election writ drops, all the voters have already decided how they will vote, and campaigns and rallies serve no purpose except to provide entertainment for what might otherwise be a rather dull performance. No newspapers adhere to this school. If they did, there would be nothing to write about for four to six weeks of any election year. The other school of thought envisages voters as an unusually cretinous assembly of consumers whose appetites must be tastefully aroused and appropriately brought to climax. Books are written and reputations made by people who perceive that a campaign has peaked too soon, or too late. Since no one has ever penetrated each mind in the multitudes of individuals, all different, who comprise the great mass called The Voters, one school of thought has just as much proof of its theory as the other.

Those who dwell within the structures of political parties must adhere to the view that voters are influenced, day by day if not hour by hour, by intricate partisan maneuvers. The 1953 campaign was no exception to that hallowed tradition, sanctified by the men and women who work for television, radio and newspapers.

Montgomery Jamieson and his electoral legions chose Vancouver's Georgia Auditorium for their rally. With a capacity of about two thousand it was the city's second largest meeting hall. Georgia Auditorium was an old structure built of wood, although patrons were prone to the impression that the seats were made of stone.

The goal was to get as many people to the rally as possible, by whatever form of conscription or persuasion was at hand, but always to arrange that there be more people than seats. For the purpose of the priceless and unpurchaseable newspaper headlines the next day, it was necessary that there be an overflow crowd. To campaigners, those were the magic words. To fill the Coliseum was the ultimate, glorious objective. But five thousand in the Coliseum weighted less than two thousand five hundred in the two thousand-seat hall, or for that matter, six hundred in a five hundred seat hall at the Seaforth Armouries. It is all a numbers game. But, then, so is the voting.

To ensure that at least some of the audience would have to stand in the hallways and listen to loudspeakers, the party emptied the last of its treasury and extended the last of its limits of credit on advertising and buses. The buses traveled throughout Greater Vancouver, much of the Fraser Valley and southern Vancouver Island all through that day, coaxing aboard any citizens of voting age and a few who were not. The party would have sent buses to the West Kootenays for rally customers, had there been any expectation of filling them. They would have sent them anywhere, except to pick up Ken Larsen.

Through the fading hours of that grey winter day the trickles of people began moving out of suburbs, out of Fraser Valley towns and on toward the glow of the city. Within Greater Vancouver, the phone batteries were in action, reminding, cajoling and sometimes commanding the presence of supporters and putative supporters at the great rally.

There were the usual failures. Nobody in the town of Haney was collected by the bus because not a single notification about transport had been sent to the party workers. The phone blitz of Kitsilano, South Burnaby and Port Moody collapsed; in each case the party workers with the name lists failed to appear in the campaign offices. Paranoia, the occupational disease of all politicians, had long since seized Montgomery Jamieson. In all these lapses he saw evidence of treason. No doubt in some cases his judgment was correct, the failure to act at critical moments can be more devastating a blow than open hostility. Even when the frightful lapses were no more than ordinary human fecklessness, Montgomery knew the consuming frustration of those who call upon the services of the unpaid. Although in Ontario and Quebec political campaigns had long been conducted on a salaried and businesslike basis, British Columbia parties clung to amateur status. One cannot cut the salary of a volunteer, nor threaten him with demotion or firing. Such a man will resist admonition. He will not tolerate abuse. No man in the nation is more independent than a volunteer worker in a political campaign. Appropriately, it is the same position of total independence that will be achieved by the candidate who is elected to office.

Montgomery wept and, deep within his bowels, raged, but at the witching hour, the theater filled, first slowly, then swiftly. The party leader, keynote speaker of the rally, was relaxed and confident. It did not matter that his relaxation and confidence came from the oh-be-joyful pills which he had been popping for two days. He gave every indication of being able to deal earnestly and well with the fearful banalities of which large rally speeches are constructed.

Even had he known that the Chilcotin candidate was off the reservations, Montgomery might have been calm within reason. Besides the Liberal leader and the party president, who would act as the meeting's chairman, there were fifty-one chairs on the stage which would be filled by fifty-one candidates. If there was need for a fifty-second, he would be little more noticeable than an extra baked bean in the bowl.

Montgomery could have taken further comfort from the fact that nobody in Namko had been on time for any appointment for as many years as the memory of man runs.

Margaret Larsen had insisted on what was known as a Hudson's Bay Start. Fur brigade leaders had long ago found it prudent to move their men and horses two or three hours out of a fort on the first day. Even though that night they camped within sight of the post, their journey had commenced and, on the next morning, they would move out swiftly and efficiently in the early light of dawn.

Larsen did not quite achieve a Hudson's Bay Start. His truck broke again on the afternoon scheduled for their departure. It was almost noon the next day before they left. Margaret resolutely prevented him from campaigning at ranch houses through Chilcotin, recognizing that to him campaigning had become another word for visiting. At Chilliwack, however, two hours before the meeting was to begin, under the pink glow cast by the big city into the western sky, Larsen bought gas from a man with whom he had once cowboyed for Chilco Ranch. Larsen and the garagemen moved into the shop for one quick one and then had another. Margaret's complaints became loud and feverish. Larsen silenced her, speaking in a tone of voice that she could recognize. He had, he said, no intention of going to any political meeting stone-cold sober. So they came late to the rally.

It was five years since either of them had been in Vancouver. This time, as before, they were astounded that so many types of road signs could be posted telling people not to do things.

Having twice risked disfigurement or death by driving the wrong way on one-way streets, they finally located Georgia Auditorium. It was the end of the beginning. The party president was a man who knew very little very earnestly. In his role as the rally's master of ceremonies, he spoke loudly about the few ideas he held firmly. Then, with as much archness as can be found inside a barrel, he had introduced to the audience, one by one, the candidates who were to fill the next provincial House.

When Ken and Margaret Larsen joined the ushers, associated functionaries and a few others standing against the dim back wall of the theatre, the candidate of West Cates Park was being introduced.

"Robert Jordan *TOMLINSON*!!!" There was applause. "Married. Father of *twin boys*." There was more applause. The man who had accomplished the twins bobbed his head in pleased recognition. There was nothing in his appearance to indicate a capacity to sire anything. His head was large, but fixed loosely to the rest of the body by a thin neck. It had been said of him that his father brought about his conception through a silk handkerchief. "And a *daughter* who, I understand, was just elected best Little League Shortstop of West Cates Park. We're *all* getting elected this time." The applause, which had been perfunctory, was now louder, the key word "elected" having been uttered.

"And it is with great pleasure, great pride, that we introduce the last of our long and full list of candidates in this election, the man who is about to take the seat out from under the *present Premier*."

West Cates Park rose and bobbed his oversized head. It did not fall off. His main job of the night was done.

"As you know, we are contesting *every* riding in this election and we intend to *win* every riding."

He waited for applause but it came reluctantly and mixed with whistles and one or two boos from hecklers.

"Unfortunately, our candidate for Chilcotin, Mr. Kenneth Larsen, was not able to be here tonight. He's busy campaigning in the *rugged Chilcotin.*

"Tell him you're here, Ken."

"I don't need to tell him. I'm here. I don't need to go up there."

"Yes, ladies and gentlemen, Mr. Larsen is campaigning in the *real grass roots of British Columbia.*"

"Go on up."

"The hell. We're late. We'll sit back here."

"Tell them you're here."

"No goddamed way."

"Tell them you're here."

"I'm here," said Larsen.

It chanced to fall within a period of silence in the hall.

"What's that?" said the man on stage.

Larsen's voice was quieter, but it carried. "I'm here," he said.

"Mr. Larsen?"

"Yeah. That's me."

The audience applauded, faintly, and it put more strength in his voice. "I'm sorry I'm late. Had some trouble with the truck." There was a murmur of what he took to be friendly laughter. "Had some trouble with a bottle, too," he added.

"Come down, Ken," said the president. "There's a chair here for you. There wasn't but as he spoke it appeared on the stage in position fifty-two, pushed by hands that could not be seen.

"How could this happen?" said Montgomery.

"I'm not surprised," said the Senator. "Any time you tell me what is happening in Chilcotin something else happens."

As befitted their roles in running the country Montgomery and the Senator were seated in an alcove next the main stage. They could see the people on stage well and the audience dimly but were themselves unnoticeable.

They watched Larsen come down the main aisle, through a lane of languid applause. On a horse Larsen sat well; also he could start a horse well, one of the things that distinguishes the good from the adequate in horsemanship. But he had never been a good walker. He moved with a slouch and a slide and generally resembled nothing more closely than a man going late to the toilet.

"Oh boy, is that a winner," said Montgomery.

The president's voice boomed on. "It's no wonder our candidate has trouble with the kind of roads the present government has provided in this province. But when it's a Liberal candidate, *the roads don't matter. He gets here anyway!"*

The president scratched around in the shallow well of his memory for the Larsen biography. "I'll introduce him as he's coming to the platform, ladies and gentlemen. Mr. Larsen is one of the men opening up the great plains of the Chilcotin. The country that has the kind of sturdy, independent men who are the *guts* and the *backbone* of our party."

There was some sympathetic applause.

Larsen's suit did not fit. He had taken his hat off to walk forward, put it on his head again while walking and now, climbing the steps to the platform, removed it once again and held it behind his bum as if trying to hide a treat from some small children.

"Mr. Larsen is a prosperous and successful rancher." The president grabbed his hand and clamped an arm on his shoulder. "He has, I understand, what is called a *big spread.*"

Larsen smiled weakly and scuffed a foot on the floor.

"Oh no, not me. I'm just a small rancher."

"He says he's a small rancher but . . . . "

"No. Really. I'm just a small rancher. Just a few head."

"And he's a *modest man too.*"

"He's got lots to be modest about," came a voice from the audience. This time there was some laughter. It was clear that Larsen heard it but not that the president did.

"So I present to you our *next MLA* from Chilcotin. Mister *Kenneth Larsen!!!"*

Those in the seats who had been resting on the left cheek of the buttocks shifted to the right. The clapping was like falling leaves.

The president, with gentle force, led Ken toward the distant empty chair.

Out of the audience came a voice.

"Speak up, Chilucootin."

Larsen stopped because of the way the word was spoken. The crowd paid attention because of the way it was delivered. Crisp, clear and sharp.

"What's that?"

"Right over here, Ken," said the chairman, pointing to the vacant chair.

"I said speak up, Chilucootin."

Larsen stopped, and because he weighed more than the Liberal party's president, the president was also stopped.

"I've heard that voice," said Larsen.

"You cowboyed for me."

Larsen pushed the president away from his elbow and walked to the edge of the stage. He peered into the darkness of the crowd, shielding his eyes with his hand.

"I can't see you across these lights," he said.

"Do you remember stealing a horse from Hungry Johnny?

"You're Old Man Fitzgibbons. You had the original Elk Park Ranch."

"That's right."

"I haven't seen you for thirty years."

"I've ranched in Chilcotin, I've ranched in Saskatchewan and I've ranched in the Kootenays. And I'm as poor today as the day I started."

"I'll see ya after," said Ken.

"Yes, now Ken, we'll put you in your seat," said the president.

"That's not what I said," came the voice from the dark. Larsen stopped again and his herder, perforce, stopped with him.

"I didn't come here to drink coffee in the lobby. I came here to listen to what you had to say for Chilucootin."

"Well," Larsen turned and, with an arm, waved at the stage full of silent men on chairs.

The president spoke largely. "You may be sure, sir, that British Columbia will be hearing from Mr. Larsen."

"Stop chattering, you pompous ass. I'm talking to Larsen, not you."

Larsen was looking toward the voice from the darkness beyond the stage lights.

"Larsen, damit man. Don't stand there like one more pigeon on a statue. If you've got something to say, spit it out of your teeth."

"By damn," said Larsen, "I think I will. I have never made a political speech before but now I am gonna do it."

There was some laughter. He looked toward the laughs.

"That's right," he said. "I am gonna do it."

"Why the hell can't they steer him into his seat?" said Montgomery.

"I've been hearing for weeks that you need spontaneity at the rally," said the Senator. "Well, you're getting it."

"This isn't what I had in mind."

"Spontaneity seldom is."

For all that he was overweight, that his shirt was wrinkled and his string tie was creeping toward his right ear, Larsen for the moment had the crowd's attention. The hat, which he had not known what to do with, he handed to the president, who, also not knowing, held it like a tray.

Fitzgibbons' voice rang out once more.

"Don't tell us about Germany and Korea. There's any number of idiots can talk about that. Tell us what you're going to do for the ranchers."

"The answer is, not much. But it ain't because I don't want to. It's because I won't get elected."

The few hecklers cheered but the rest of the people, being more claque than crowd, murmured. "No," they said.

"You say no. But most of you people that get close to politics, you get so close you don't know anything that is real any more." He ignored a continued murmur. "Why, when I come in, this gentleman here is introducing the man who is running against the Premier and thought that even he could win a seat."

Larsen turned to face the West Cates Park candidate. "No offense intended, friend. But to beat the Premier? In his hometown? Well, all I can say is, I would be a very surprised man."

The crowd began to listen.

"As for the reason I can't win, it's the same reason that ranchers can't win. There ain't enough of us in this world." His voice had only a trace of slur in it. Larsen held liquor well.

"The truth is, Fitzgibbons, there is very few ranchers or any other kind of producer left in the whole country. It has all been taken over by insurance salesmen and bankers and stockbrokers and a lot of other parasites."

This time the crowd gave voice. Some laughter, some jeers, some groans. Larsen's voice came back louder, stronger.

"Yes, that's what I said. Parasites. Never dug a ditch nor raised a crop nor chopped a tree in all their damned lives. PA-RA-SITES."

"We're going to lose this election, Senator," said Montgomery.

The Senator, gazing intently at Larsen, made no answer.

"We're going to lose the election."

"Yes. Yes, of course."

"You didn't hear me. I said we were going to lose."

"Yes. I heard you." The Senator turned his face from the stage and looked at his companion, struck by a new and interesting thought.

"Montgomery, correct me if I'm wrong. Are you telling me you thought we were going to win?"

"Well, I thought it was a near thing . . . "

"But you thought it was possible to win? To become the government?"

"Yes."

The Senator wagged his big head. "You amaze me, people like you. You're well educated, you're fluent, you're well read. You have every intellectual advantage. And you, Montgomery, you believed?"

"But we've talked about thirty-seven seats. You and I."

The Senator barked at the back of his throat. "Talk. What does talk matter in the middle of a campaign? We all talk of victory. Otherwise we'd be mutes."

Had there been time, had his attention not been on Larsen, the Senator might have explained to the campaign manager that opposition parties do not defeat government parties. When the time for change comes, governments defeat themselves. It is the physiology of political life. The Senator, in years past, had served as an elected member and Montgomery had not; therefore he knew political life was a constant hemorrhage of physical energy. Any government, any government leader, in time became exhausted. This was seldom admitted and not always recognized, but the human body would know and shout "no more, no more." When that time came government parties did foolish things, premiers and prime ministers said arrogant and foolish things, subconsciously appealing to the electorate for the blessed rest and relief of defeat.

The British Columbia government of this year, the Senator knew, was not tired.

"How many seats then?" said Montgomery.

"Listen to this man Larsen," said the Senator.

"How many seats. You've played the numbers game like all the rest of us."

"Yes. I have played the numbers game. I've studied the opinion polls that you do not like. I have talked to a lot of people. I have looked at a voting record of all fifty-two ridings, Montgomery. Yes, I've played the numbers game."

"Then how many, Senator?"

"As closely as I could calculate, I have felt we could take two. Maybe three."

"*Two! Three!*"

There was a roar from the crowd. It was not for the Senator's estimate of two or three seats. It was for Larsen, who was shouting now.

"There is only one thing gonna make this country work again and it is when the belly is up against the backbone."

"You don't really mean two or three, Senator?"

"Shsht. Look at the people out there. Look at them."

Montgomery looked at the people in the hall. Faces appeared. He could see Muriel, who went wherever the Senator went. He could see Miss O'Day. That surprised him because Miss O'Day was not known to leave her West End apartment after sundown. He studied the face of the man Fitzgibbons, who had precipitated this buffoonery with the Chilcotin candidate. Snow-white hair, bold nose and wide mouth, a skin dark as redwood. What kind of life had carved that handsome face? He looked at the other faces, and all of them were different.

"For God's sake Senator. There's that little secretary of Brydon's, who I had fired. What on earth could bring her out to a political meeting?"

"Shsht, listen to this man."

A heckler had caught Larsen in his open sights. The party organization had spotted professional hecklers in the crowd who were charged with firing questions at the Liberal leader, whose spontaneous responses had been long rehearsed. But this was a wild heckler, a real one.

"If you're against welfare, why is your party raising the welfare payments?"

"Aiy?"

"I said it's your party that is promising higher welfare payments."

"Well, I'm against it. Like family allowance. Damndest fool thing the country ever did."

"It was the Liberal party that brought in family allowance."

"The bigger fools then."

The roar from the crowd was like breakers on rocky shoreline.

The chairman plucked at the Chilcotin candidate's sleeve and was flung away by a wide sweep from a heavy arm. "Leave me alone. I'm talking to these people."

There were longer and wilder responses from the crowd. Some were shocked, some were amused, some were frightened and some were angry, but all were responding.

So, Montgomery noted, did the Senator. In the oldest of British parliamentary tradition, he was slamming his hand on the railing of the booth—the parliamentary substitute for clapping or cheering. The thought was born upon Montgomery that perhaps, in addition to all the fool's carnival of a campaign rally, he had, possibly, to contend with the old man's final descent into senile dementia.

"Raise it to four, Montgomery," said the Senator. "We are going to carry Chilcotin, for the first time since the days of Sir John Oliver."

"Have you lost your mind? They're not cheering him, they're laughing at him."

The Senator continued as if the other man had not spoken. "Spend five thousand dollars in Chilcotin in the next seventy-two hours. You can do it. You have learned how to spend money."

"There is no money."

"Spend. I will find the money. Spend five thousand dollars. Fly up a bunch of Vancouver newspapers tomorrow. They'll pick up the word parasite. Marvellous word. It's so true. Chilcotin will like that word. Parasite."

Nothing much mattered any more, thought Montgomery, because all politicians were mad and now he, too, was probably afflicted. He turned to watch the Chilcotin candidate.

"There was five of us in that old bunkhouse and we was fed rice, beans and tripes. We was all lousy. The cooties slipped out of our pantlegs while we worked. Bedbugs, man? Yes. And the crabs. There was a three-holer outhouse. Somebody had wrote on the back wall 'No good to stand up on the seat, the crabs this place jump fifteen feet.' ''

The roar, unintelligible for content, or spirit, rose from the dark area of the hall where the people sat.

''Watch,'' said the Senator. ''He'll drop his voice.''

Whether by instinct or luck, Larsen had learned the old debating trick — for your most telling points, do not shout, but lower the voice so the people lean forward to hear you. He lowered his voice and they leaned forward to hear him. ''But by God, we built seven miles of snake fence, and it still stands to this day, and there ain't a panel out of it. We made a mark on the face of this province.''

''There is one more job for us tonight, Mr. Campaign Manager,'' said the Senator.

''Yes?''

The Senator turned his big head toward the far and darkened edge of the great hall. ''Down there, there is a woman who is crying. That will be his wife.''

''How could you possibly see a woman crying at the back of this hall?''

''I don't have to see very well to see her. She's going through a terrible torment. She probably got him into this, now she wonders what she did to him. We have got to reinforce the woman. She'll be important to him.''

''What am I going to tell that woman?''

Using his arms on the railings, the Senator almost sprang to his feet. He grabbed the canes before the other could reach for them and thumped out through the curtains at the back of the booth. Bumping down the corridor toward the back of the hall, plans tumbling in his mind and spilling out on a tongue of bronze, the Senator had, for the moment, the energy of which political life is built.

''They probably haven't anywhere to stay in town. I'll have them out to my house. Get one of your boys to phone the house-keeper please. Make beds. Lay out some port and crackers. We'll talk and argue politics all the night until dawn.''

''I'll see she's phoned.''

As they neared the back of the hall the Senator stopped and turned to face the younger man.

"I have never laid eyes on this woman. But watch and see if I am not right. When we meet, I will know her. And she will know me. That woman and I, Montgomery, we will know the glory of battle. She and I, we will see the victory."

If Montgomery made a reply it went unheard amid the crashing roar of the crowd in the hall who were listening to the candidate from Chilcotin.

The Senator was a wise man, but not omniscient. Larsen did not win Chilcotin. He did, however, come second in a field of four and missed victory by only a few hundred votes, an accomplishment of note in that riding, particularly in an election which saw the Liberal party take only two seats in British Columbia. The Vancouver papers spoke in awe of Larsen for a long time, some two or three days, before forgetting him and the country from which he sprang.

Two weeks after the election, all the people who had set out to run the country had dispersed. The campaign had been like an electric magnet which drew to itself hard metal of all shapes and sizes. When votes had been cast, the current was switched off and the magnet of government became cold, dead iron. All the pieces fell away from it into other fields of attraction. Almost all of what had seemed unforgettable was soon forgotten.

None of the participants, however, was ever quite the same again. The atoms of their being had been politically polarized. They were unable to think exactly as they had thought before the events of the great campaign.

Brydon was shifted to the Toronto office of Montgomery's company and later married an Oakville girl of grand inheritance.

Darlene, Brydon's first love, disappeared into the nameless, faceless void called The Public and the rest of her story is not known to us.

The other two secretaries, like the Senator, had been tempered by the heat of many political fires and continued their lives apparently unchanged and unchangeable.

For Larsen, there was another crisis of life. Two years after the election, the MLA for Chilcotin died and the Government party, recognizing a bone-and-marrow conservative when they saw one, offered the nomination to him. In a by-election, there was no doubt of the result in that year. Nomination was the same as election. Change had overcome Larsen. More than anything else he could ever remember wanting, Larsen wanted to sit in the Legislature of British Columbia and run the country. When the offer reached him he took a saddle horse and rode, all day, in an agony of indecision which was appreciated only by God and, possibly, his wife. In the end he turned them down. He was, he said, a lifelong Liberal and to turn his coat went against his principles.

The great loser was Montgomery Jamieson, who wanted to sit in the Canadian Senate even more than he wanted to win the election. His great defeat came weeks after the election, when the Prime Minister invited the Senator to drop into his East Block office for a chat. The PM, with the ruthlessness which distinguishes prime ministers from other men, reminded the old Senator that he would be dead one of these days and that he, the Prime Minister, was of a mind to appoint a political understudy to him in the Red Chamber. What, he said, about this fellow Jamieson who ran the provincial campaign?

The Senator spoke movingly about Jamieson, his indefatigable efforts in a hopeless cause, his wit, his grace, his charm, his business acumen, his self-confidence and his high intellect.

"It's a pity we can't find men that good to be prime minister," said the Prime Minister. "Does he have no faults? Possibly a wart on some visible part of the body?"

The Senator was by nature a kind man and now, at the age when personal ambitions fade, he was more kind. So it was with regret that he loaded his pistol, cocked it, pressed it to the nape of Montgomery's neck and fired. He did it for the sake of the party, for the sake of the Senate, for the sake of the country, perhaps for the sake of Montgomery.

"If I have any criticisms, it would be that he lacks breadth. Politically, he needs seasoning. A lot of seasoning."

To be sure, he fired a second shot. "I must also tell you, Mr. Prime Minister, that I'm not sure he has enough heart for it."

The Prime Minister nodded, in understanding, in gratitude, and with his pencil drew a line through the name of Montgomery Jamieson.

# DECEMBER
# NILSEN

ARCH ARRIVED IN Vancouver in late afternoon and found all that
had been familiar to him for thirty years—the brown air, the trash
of traffic on the streets and the murmuring crowds of people,
white-faced by the lack of sun, slightly damp with the constant wet
and anxious by natural habit. They clustered at every street corner
and peered at street lights, waiting for the walk signal with the
apprehension and impatience with which the religiously inclined
await the Last Trump.

"Every time I leave this place I say it's for the last time and
every time I return, like the dog to his vomit," he said.

He reflected that perhaps he was getting cranky in his old age
and, since he was on a mission requiring elements of diplomacy,
tact and wit, he repaired to a hotel room where he washed and
changed his shirt. It had been a long journey south from Williams
Lake on a bus given to many pauses. In the Fraser Canyon, where
part of the road still consisted of wooden shelves built out from the
cliff faces, cruising speeds were fifteen to twenty miles an hour.
Fourteen hours of his life had so sped past. He regretted them all.

His intention was to do business in this city with all possible
haste and then, with luck, depart silently and unnoticed in the
morning. So the calls were made to people whom he dimly remembered as the knowledgeable people of Vancouver—bail-bond
fixers, bootleggers—those of the various trades and avocations of
whom it may be said that they neither work, nor want, nor go to
jail. All the calls were unproductive. Things had changed in the
years since he left. Well-known establishments were not only
gone, but apparently forgotten. Phone numbers were not in service
or were answered by strange people.

Arch considered applying to a taxi driver for knowledge, for
such men are often wise beyond their years. But instead, if for no
reason than to test his personal capacities, he set out alone and
unaided. He took one taxi, which delivered him to the city's newest
and costliest expense-account hotel. He did not enter the establish-

ment but began walking the grid of streets which surrounded it, square by square.

After twenty minutes he found what he sought. It was a large, old house of many rooms and had, in the reign of the seventh Edward, cost a fortune. Now it needed paint and a few more shingles. The iron entrance gates had been torn from the stone walls and taken to the melting pots. In the garden, only the monkey puzzle tree survived. The front door, however, of solid dark red mahogany, was richly varnished and glowed in the light of a street lamp.

He pressed the lighted button and chimes within the old house played a soft melody. The door was opened by a lady expensively dressed wearing pearls. Her lips were thin, her eyes a cold blue and her chin was sharp enough to split hailstones. She looked without enthusiasm at Arch's blue serge suit, which had not been new for fifteen years.

"Yes?"

"I wonder if I could see Lily?"

"There must be some mistake. There is no Lily here."

Arch removed a ten-dollar bill from his hip pocket and peered at the signature of Bank of Canada Governor Graham Towers. "That's funny," he said. "It's the address I have written down here."

"Perhaps you had better come in," she said.

After consultation he considered that the girl named Marie might well do. The negotiations took time, much time. Arch wanted to take Marie downtown to dinner. This was irregular and irregularity was not easily tolerated in that establishment. The pearl lady and Arch, both keen students of the dollar, sparred for almost half an hour before recognizing that neither party to the contract was given to needless generosity. Once this position was established, price came rapidly and clearly into focus and when they sealed the bargain over a drink of Scotch he was served from a Cutty Sark bottle that had Cutty Sark inside it. The lady would have been mortified had she known that he was to casually press a twenty-dollar bill into the palm of the headwaiter at the Vancouver Hotel's main dining room.

"I won't tell her," said Marie in a voice just loud enough to register on his good ear.

"Don't, for God's sake. There are more negotiations likely tonight and they'll be harder."

"Don't forget, you've got to convince me too."

"Of what?"

"How do I know? Whatever it is you want."

"I probably will convince you," he said. "And if I can't, then price wouldn't help anyhow."

If he expected this to arouse her curiosity he was disappointed. She studied the wine list.

"You've got no questions?"

She took a Virginia Oval from a silver cigarette case and inclined her head in thanks when he lit it for her with a candle flame. "You'll tell me in your own good time," she said.

"I like that," he said. "When I have a story to tell it's something like an old Indian we have up our way. Ol Antoine. Ol Antoine says (he dropped into the Indian accent), 'You know the sun. He gets up here. (He pointed an arm at one corner of the dining room.) He comes over here. (The arm made a sweep, slowly, from side to side of the room.) He goes down over there . . . Same like my story.' "

She laughed, something she did well. The hard lines were beginning to settle at Marie's eyes and mouth, too early, for she was yet in her twenties, but when she laughed it was like the sun striking the ripples of clear water.

She was a slim woman, blonde, with amber eyes, and she walked with a limp. She had trained for ballet, but one day, in the exercises, the tendon of one leg snapped and went rippling up the calf of her slender leg while she screamed in agony undreamt of. Thus ended whatever hope she may have had for the stage. She was, at the time, engaging in prostitution to pay both for her dance lessons and an MGTD sports car. The sideline became the profession. She contented herself with the thought that she might one day become a famous author and, in that spirit, she welcomed the unusual johns, such as this one, and encouraged them to be garrulous.

"Tell me about where you live," she said. "If it's boring, I'll stop you."

'Let's talk about hell instead."

She spooned her consomme, leading him on with her silence.

"Everybody has his own idea of hell. My idea of hell is a small room with an orchestra that plays all the time. That orchestra is composed of all the people who live in the Namko Country.

"Being the Namko people, they give it all they've got. They play with lots of energy. But because they are from the Namko Country, every musician plays his own separate tune. That is what hell is gonna be like."

"But if they don't talk about football, it isn't really hell," she said.

"You're interrupting."

"Alright. I'll listen. Honestly."

"A long listen? You know, the sun comes up, he goes across . . ."

"Yes, really. Just one thing first. Tell the waiter the soup is neither hot nor cold."

He summoned the waiter, who went away and brought some hot consomme. "Now," she said, "talk to me."

Arch could speak very well about the Namko Country and its people. He was a dumpy little storekeeper with ill-cut hair, an antique suit and glasses, but, at times such as these, there was a touch of magic in his voice.

He told of winters at sixty below when pink and green northern lights blazed across the wide sky and of gentle summers when he fished the rapids of the Nazidalia with a Doc Spratley fly. He talked about the inhabitants, individually and collectively, their feckless enthusiasms, their loves, their hates, their morose convictions about the state of the nation and the prospects of bitter winters yet to assail them.

Of Morton Dilloughboy, who was in every way a remittance man except that he received no remittances, of Frenchie's Wife and her mysterious strengths and of the ever varying luck of Smith. He talked about great cattle drives. He had not seen them but he spoke of them so well that you could smell the sweat of horses and men and taste the alkali dust in the back of the throat. Reckless of time and place, he revived for her the story of how Norman Lee tried to drive fifteen hundred head from Hanceville to the Yukon gold fields and with her lived again the tales of the Chilcotin War, of Alexander Mackenzie and of old legends half-heard, half-remembered, but nevertheless of epic quality.

When she was finishing the cut off the standing-rib roast he said,

"Now of all of them, who's the one who stands out in your mind?''

"The man called December,'' she said.

"That's because of his name.''

She looked across the candles at him with a light smile and shook her head.

"No,'' she said. "I was listening to what you said, but I was listening to the tone of your voice too. When you mentioned December, the penny dropped.''

"You're ahead of me, like too many women.'' He lit a cigar and watched the blue smoke rise between them.

"As for the name, which you pointedly do not enquire about, it was natural enough. His mother, whoever, wherever she was, had a daughter in June, named June, and a son in August, named August. When December was born she carried on the tradition. Maybe she thought all kids were christened that way. But it made a great name. December Nilsen.''

He had met December almost twenty years ago, when he was so much younger, so much stronger and so wildly foolish that he hunted moose — all this despite the fact that Arch despised horses, both saddle and pack horse varieties. As for the hunting, when the moose was hit and fell he seldom felt anything but deep sorrow. Such were the ways of younger men, however, even of younger men who would some day become wise, like Arch McGregor.

Morton had guided Arch up the Tallywacker, a creek which was born in glacier country and ran pale green through the forests and meadows of the high country. They came at evening upon December's trapping cabin. The month was October and December was preparing for a winter's work.

"It was like finding the gingerbread house. It was, may God strike me dead, exactly twelve feet long and eight feet wide, with the roof overhanging the porch by another five feet to shelter the firewood. There was a cache for his fur, built ten feet off the ground and roofed, like the cabin, with hand-split shakes. There was a feeder creek to the Tallywacker, which splashed down some rocks and made a pool.

"For all the rest there was the country as God had made it, forever and ever. And in the middle of it all, December Nilsen.

"He was an old man even then. Sixty-odd. He didn't stand more than five-feet-four, but he had to stoop every time he went through the door of that doll's cabin. He was slender, bowed a little. His cheeks were pink and his eyes were blue and his hair was white as new snow. All that, and he was shy as a deer. Except for saying hello, he didn't utter a word until we had finished coffee and bannock cakes in the cabin.

"I had the feeling that I'd stepped into Hans Christian Andersen country."

December had come to British Columbia in a method once considered usual. He had jumped ship in Victoria after a season of shooting seals in the Pribilof Islands of Bering Strait and fled to the remotest of the mountain country. He had lost all his teeth to scurvy in one bad winter. He had never voted, nor married, nor driven an automobile and only once, since he deserted the sealer, had he worked for wages. During the war, by some impulse unfathomable to those who knew him, December had gone to Vancouver and worked in a shipyard which made lifeboats for Liberty ships. That had lasted three months.

"He told us about it that night, while we were smoking tailormades by the little bit of light that came from his bug. 'Just think of it,' he said, singsong-like, 'there was all those governments, all over the world, spending millions and millions of dollars to bomb people and drown people and shoot people. And what was I doing? I was building lifeboats to save people. I was ashamed of myself, working against the war that way, so I came home.'

"I s'pose it was humor, It must have been. But with December you could never be really sure."

"How could you doubt that he was kidding?"

"Because," he said, "people like you and me don't understand the December Nilsens of this world."

She heard another penny drop. "Then why?"

"We can't understand true simplicity any more, that's why. I think maybe I do, a little bit. You, my dear, might never have met a simple man."

"Don't bet on it."

He held up one pudgy hand and waved it, so the smoke from the cigar made a figure S between them. "Think about it for a minute. Total simplicity. That is not necessarily stupidity. There may be the usual quota of intelligence to begin with, but it lies unseeded, unploughed, uncultivated. That was December Nilsen. He knew where the animals lived and how they moved. He knew the sky, and its moods. He knew a lot about weather, because it was very important to him. Being able to read a sky was sometimes a life-and-death matter for him. He knew small things and made them large. Discovering that one kind of firewood burned better than another and whether he could grow a cabbage or two beside that little cabin in the mountains in the short summers were things to which he had devoted time, experimentation, thought.

"The printed word? He read little. Practically nothing. By the end of each day he was tired and slept. What little information he had picked up about industry, or government, was incomplete and basically all wrong. The cash economy lay beyond his little world entirely. He shipped his fur out once a year to a buyer. He got a check back. We never knew for how much, nor did anyone know what he did with it. For himself, he paid everything in cash, and that wasn't for much—rice, flour, now and then a pair of boots and a suit of Stanfields. His life was not all that far removed from that of a medieval peasant. He worked. He slept. He kept himself clothed and fed. He had, probably, nothing left beyond those small and grim necessities."

"The persistence of the adult and the mind of the child," she said.

He nodded. "But even December was overtaken by change," he said. "You ask, what changed him?"

"No, I didn't ask. I thought my job was to listen, and later on to agree to something."

"Right enough. Okay, I continue. What changed December was three things—people, money and love."

"And of these, the greatest was love," she said.

"I'll forgive the interruption because you speak so well. But I'll reach love in my own time."

She ate baked alaska and sipped Drambuie. "I feel as though I have known you for a long time, Archibald," she said.

"It's part of the plan," he said. "Now eat that gaudied-up ice cream and listen silently."

The people who changed December, he explained, were those with whom he suddenly found himself surrounded. Rheumatism and age had finally driven December from the mountains and he had settled, not without trepidation, in the community of Namko, one place in this world almost small enough to contain him. Namko was then Arch's store/hotel, Herb's garage and gas station and a couple of sheds, all the rest of the populace being distributed at five- or ten-mile intervals in the ranches. One of the sheds became December's home and he promptly set to work surrounding it with the largest, the neatest stack of firewood the country had yet beheld.

It was at this late date that Arch and the rest of Namko discovered that December didn't get the old-age pension. There was good reason. He had never applied.

There were two parties to convince before the pension could be paid. One was the government whose records were entirely innocent of any proof that a man named December Nilsen had ever lived. December had no birth record nor a relative to testify when and where his birth had taken place. There was no record that he had entered the country. He had never paid taxes nor gone to hospital, jail or church. If such matters were settled by the standards of civil law, in which cases are decided according to balance of probabilities, the probable finding would have been that no such person lived.

''We got around that with affidavits which established his age at well past seventy, but we still had to convince December that he should take the money. For a long time, he was adamant.'But it isn't right, Arch,' he would say to me, 'it isn't *right*. The government don't owe me any money.'

''I would say, 'But December, everybody gets it,' and he would say, in that lovely, simple way of his, 'But what if everybody is wrong?' ''

The other argument advanced by December was that he didn't need money because he already had so much of it. This, to the astonishment of many, proved to be so.

December had twenty thousand dollars' worth of government bonds. As liquid capital, it represented a vast sum in that region. Even Larsen, owner of the most prosperous of the ranches, had probably never had twenty thousand dollars in his possession at any one time.

''I don't know that even then he comprehended that the bonds were paying him interest. Like most people up there, he had loaned and borrowed once or twice but these were transactions made on the basis of need and were repaid without interest. He seemed to perceive, dimly, that he had loaned his money to the government and that the government was keeping it safe for him.''

"My God," said Marie. "How wrongheaded can anybody be about a government?"

"I agree, but that was his thought. The government was keeping the money for him and wouldn't let it spoil and when he wanted it, he could have it back.''

After persuasion, December agreed to take the old-age pension, although some months he couldn't find ways to spend it and left the check uncashed. Arch, for reasons which seemed good to him, also let the word of the twenty thousand dollars in bonds loose where the vagrant winds would carry it around the land.

It was for December's own good.

"As a pauper, he had represented a responsibility to the people. The women would bring homebaked bread and cookies to his cabin and it distressed him like hell — the same way the old-age pension had distressed him. It was charity and it bewildered him and upset him. But as an independently wealthy man, he could be accepted for what he was: December Nilsen, trapper and pioneer. So for the first time in his life, he became a member of a community. People liked him. There wasn't much there to like, but what there was, they liked.

"In fact, he was elected an honorary member of the Cattlemen's Association. If I didn't make it clear before, let me make it clear now. The Cattlemen's Association is more exclusive than the peerage in Britain. It has every bit as much snobbishness.

"There was even a time when December made a speech to the cattlemen. The government men had some plan they wanted to sell to them. Range improvement, I imagine. Any time the government talks about range improvement up our way it results in three more civil servants and one new airplane being hired. December got up and made his speech. 'Now you gentlemen all heard what the gentleman said. He wants you to vote on this. And it is your duty to vote. It don't matter how you vote. You can vote either yes or no. Because he is going to go ahead and do what he wants to do anyway. But it is your duty to vote.' You never saw a bunch of men so proud as those ranchers were proud of December. He had joined the brotherhood.

"I told him that one day afterward. He had come into the store making about as much noise as a wisp of fog coming through the door. 'I hear you made quite a speech at the Cattlemen's Meeting.' He said, 'Oh no. I just said what was true. And it was true. They voted no and the government men are going to do it just the same.' 'It wasn't what you said that mattered, December. That never matters in political speeches. It's the way you said it. You are one of the bunch now.'

"He seemed to be moved by this. So much so that he bought a Hershey bar and ate it, very slowly, one square at a time. 'But I'm not really one of the people, am I Arch?'

" 'And why not?' I said.

"He said, 'Because the other people are all the same.'

"Jesus Castiron Christ. If there was ever a place in the world where the people were not all the same, Namko it is. But you see, to him, they were a herd, a bunch. All acting the same and thinking the same and doing the same things.

"I tried to imagine December working for General Motors but it was too much for my imagination and I gave up. We had a drink of whisky together and he talked about something he liked and understood. Muskrats, I think it was."

Marie and Arch were at the third Drambuie. She was bolder now. That or more curious.

"You haven't come to love, which is supposed to be my department. That's when the bargaining starts, is it?"

He called for another cigar.

"Love came to December not very long after that. It was out of that meeting it came. He had bought a raffle ticket. The entire beef industry of the province was selling raffle tickets that year. They had done it their own peculiar way . . ."

"Let me guess. The first prize was a week in Toronto and the second prize was two weeks in Toronto."

"You're close. The first prize was the pick of any two-year-old stud on seven selected ranches, all of whom had horses which were crossed with cougar, and the second prize was a week in Hawaii. December won second prize and after the usual agonizing—he kept saying it wasn't right that a man should be able to fly halfway around the world for a dollar—he went. We made a cavalcade to

Williams Lake, seven cars and trucks, and put him on the plane. When he came back he was married.''

''I can imagine the effect that news had.''

''The news got to Namko about two days before December did,'' said Arch. ''He had hung up for two days in Williams Lake on the way home. The trip had also introduced him to another new mystery of the age. Television. He couldn't part from the tube easily so he holed up in the Lakeview for two days and lay on his bed, feet on the pillow, face shoved up against a screenful of snow, and soaked up the new culture. He was particularly taken with Tarzan movies and with Tarzan's son, whom he described enthusiastically as a real smart little bugger.''

''You are the damndest man for indirection. You know I don't care about Tarzan shows. What about the marriage? How did the news go down in Namko?''

''It was, I might say, startling. Some prayed, who'd never prayed before, some cried, who'd never cried, some cast themselves upon the ground and some just lay and sighed.''

''I'll bet.''

''But that, you see, was a first reaction. We had two days to digest the news before December got back home. So by the time he got back, everybody had adopted the usual pose with which they prefer to greet wars, earthquakes, the Second Coming or other natural and unnatural phenomena. In short, they were all, outwardly, casual.''

December rode home on the weekly Stage, which brought the mail. More than the usual number of the citizenry were waiting for their mail that day. The Smiths, the Larsens, Morton Dilloughboy.

''Moccasin telegraph says you got married, December,'' said Larsen.

December, who was alone, acknowledged this with the usual bashful smile. ''I thought it was about time,'' he said.

''You might have asked some of us who are experienced in that business first,'' said Smith. ''We might have been able to talk you out of it.''

''Stop trying to be funny, Smith,'' said Norah. As usual, least reserved among the wives, she was the first to ask the question. ''Where is she, December?''

She was not, December said, ready to come yet. "She is study-ing, to be a dancer. I sent her to a college. In Hong Kong. A dance college. When she is through studying, she is going to come here with me."

"Oh," said Norah.

"Because she loves me," said December.

There was, Arch recalled, some shuffling of feet in the store, which had grown quiet. But then the threads of thought were picked up and some strands of conversation woven together.

"He had brought her picture. It was a lady in very few clothes. She had a smile. A professional smile, would be the best way to describe it.

"December said she was twenty-five years old. Maybe she was. From the picture it was hard to tell because it had been heavily retouched. Mary Ann, as he told us her name, seemed to have been photographed through a veil of thin gauze. The general effect was striking. Erotic, I guess you could say. But vague. An outline rather than an explicit statement.

"Right there and then, in my little two-bit store, I watched the battle of the sexes start again in Namko. In the end, it seemed to me that every female in the country ended up on one side and every man on the other. Damit all, you women. A marriage you don't arrange yourselves, your own or somebody else's, will never satisfy you."

"Leave me out, Archibald. I'm not one of the general run."

"I doubt that . . . but anyway, December's bride . . ."

The men, that day, responded to the news, to the picture, to the story, as people should, Arch said. "They admired the girl. They clapped December on the shoulder. They called him you old son-of-a-gun, you. All of them, they picked up where Smith left off and made the usual clumsy, pointless jokes about married life.

"Those two women, both of them stiff as cedar shakes, man-aged to fire off two questions: when was she coming, and what was the cost of Hong Kong dance colleges. After December went off to his cabin to thaw a month's frost out of the logs, both of those women turned on us like a pair of cats, demanding to know what we were going to do about December and his twenty thousand dollars in bonds. As if we could do anything. Or had any business thinking of doing anything.

''Smith said, in his mild way, 'After all, you haven't met the lady yet.' ''

'' 'And we never will,' '' said Norah.

'' 'Why can't we just all mind our own business?' he said.

''From there, all conversation ran steadily downhill and finally both the women were demanding that they be sent to Japan to study flower arranging and the men plaintively demanding to know what in hell they were being tried, found guilty and hanged for.''

Arch sighed. ''It went on for two years. With me, being the resident male at the community post office, taking most of the blows. But I suppose if you're a postmaster, that's part of your job. The government didn't tell me that when I took the job, but I s'pose they just forgot.

''As for December. He went on. Heedless and happy. The way simple people are. As I say, he had become liked and respected in Namko, and that I think he sensed. And he liked it.

''But every now and then he would let slip another piece of news about Mary Ann, who loved him and wanted to be with him soon. She had gone to another college, this one in Australia, and he had sent her a couple of his bonds. Because it was important to her, to be a dancer, and he wanted her to be happy, because he loved her.

''All of us, I suppose, got fidgety about the vanishing bonds. Men and women both. Twenty thousand dollars was a lot of money. But college educations — she was in New Mexico next — plane fares, all those things cost a pile of money. And it was all leaking away, five hundred at a time.

'' 'It's gonna break old December's heart when that last bond is gone,' Norah told me one day. She was almost in tears. The news was out that December had bought his bride a mink coat, something you wouldn't think there would be much need for in New Mexico.

'Does it matter?' I said to her. 'December can hardly find ways to spend the old age pension.'

'' 'Don't act dumb, Arch. You know what will be gone. She'll be gone.' ''

''And what happened when the last bond went?'' asked Marie.

Arch held his cigar upright before her. ''See that?'' he said. ''The rising smoke.''

''Yes.''

"That's another duty of the Namko postmaster. He is the rising-smoke man. My other name. Chief of the Rising Smoke.

"In the cold winter, one of my duties was every morning to check, about eight o'clock, to make sure that smoke was coming out of December's stove pipe. It was just a regular thing I was expected to do.

"One morning there wasn't any smoke so I went over and December had died. He had died just as simply as he had lived. He had gone to sleep and had not woke up."

"You didn't tell me it was a sad story," said Marie.

"It isn't a sad story. He was somewhere up in the high eighties. He had lived doing wrong to no man. And on the table in that cabin there was a bottle of whisky, half full. He had gone before the bottle was empty. Isn't that a description of a good death?"

"I take your meaning," she said.

"So now," said Arch, "you know it all."

"Yes," she said, "including my crummy job. Jeezus, Archibald, you expect me to go to that funeral. And pretend to be the widow?"

"I expect you to charge for it."

She began drawing patterns in the linen tablecloth with the heel of a silver knife.

"Think about it," he said. "You have listened to me. And you're a person who knows how to listen. So you know everybody in the Namko Country now, just as if you'd been learning about them from December's letters."

She kept marking the cloth. "It's easy to make a Star of David, because it's balanced. It has six points. But the five-pointed star is hard because when you start out, how do you keep the proportions for five angles?"

He breathed on his glasses, wiped them on the table napkin and examined the shine against the light of the candle. "I'm not hurrying you," he said.

"What actresses charge nowadays I don't know."

"Check and find out. I'm executor of the estate. It can afford it."

She tapped the heel of the knife on the cloth. "And worker's compensation," she said. "For when all the local yokels try to stone me to death."

"But you know they won't, don't you? After all, you can put together any kind of story you want. In their own funny way, they'll appreciate a proper and formal ending to December."

"You are even crazier than I could have thought."

"We are a long way past simplicity, my dear. You. Me. Even the people of Namko. We lost simplicity a long, long time ago. December was the only man who kept innocence."

"I like you a lot, Archibald," she said.

"And now that I know you, I know you're gonna do it," he said. He reached across the table and shook her small hand in his.

"The one thing you haven't asked me is why," he said.

"I'm ahead of you, Arch. The why is that December would have wanted his widow at his funeral, in black. There doesn't have to be any better reason than that, does there?"

"Not in my book, there doesn't."

He called for the check.

"There's nothing more I need to know?" she said.

He shook his head. She laughed, aloud this time. "Archibald, Archibald, I'm still ahead of you. Miles ahead."

"Go on," he said.

"As the executor," she said, "you had to handle all the estate. And the bonds? They were all still there. With the uncashed coupons on them. And the will said, that except for a good big funeral, the money was all to go to the SPCA, or the Scandinavian Old People's Home, or some midnight radio Bible thumper. He couldn't leave it to the wife. There never was one."

"He didn't have much in this life," said Arch. "In death he should have what he wanted."

# THE EDUCATION
# OF PHYLLISTEEN

OL ANTOINE'S CABIN sits on the highest rise of the Namko Reserve and you would have a nice view of the mountains from it if most of the windows weren't covered in cardboard to replace the glass. When he built it he was middle-aged and strong and he ran as many cattle in this country as whites did. Now, like him, it has gone grey and slouched. So has most of the Reserve. Just gone to ratshit. When the first whites came in here, in the twenties and thirties, the Namko Indians were as good or better than any of us. But then they seemed to just go downhill. Somehow, they couldn't compete. Either that or they didn't want to. I have never had much time for thinking about that kind of question, being kept busy competing with government and all the other bastards of this world. I didn't think about it much that day either.

"I got business to talk to you Ol Antoine," I said.

He was sitting in a pile of rags that might have been blankets one time, on an old brass bed looking out a broken window. He didn't speak and he didn't move and I recognized that I would have to show some manners. I had come into the place kind of fast and I knew better.

"Klahowya, Ol Antoine," I said.

"Klahowya, Larsen," he said.

"Ikta mika tumtum?" I said.

He moved his shoulders a little bit but didn't speak. His heart was not too good, not too bad and not worth discussion. I sat on a box, rolled a smoke and passed it to him. I rolled one for myself. I lit them both. Everything with an Indian takes time, and I didn't have much of it. But sometimes there is no other way to go.

He looked at me after a while and said, "Kah mika chahko?"

"Oh, I been up Basque Meadow country for a while, Ol Antoine. Nice country up there, this time of year."

"Nawhitka," he said. "Nawhitka. Kloshe illahie."

"Ol Antoine," I said. "I hope we don't gotta do all this in Chinook, because I have got business to talk."

There was a pause while he thought this over. "Sometime," he said, "I talk business reaal goot in Chinook."

"That is exactly what I mean."

He smiled some and we got to business.

"Ol Antoine, you know that school we put up this summer. All the whites, you know. We build that school. School for the white kids."

He puffed out some smoke. It made a little cloud in front of his face and then got thin, like the white hair on his head.

"You know that school? You see that new cabin, down by Arch's place . . . ?"

"I don't see so good right now."

"Yes, but you know that new schoolhouse. Well, we build that school. We hire a teacher. The Cattlemen's Association. We hire a teacher. And when we start the school, the government, it gives us a grant, it gives us money, to run that school."

"Aha."

"Now it turns out, we don't get that government money. It turns out we don't have enough kids."

"Then what for you build that school?"

"Well, we figure we need it. But there is only nine white kids school age in this country. Only nine. The government says we got to have ten. We ain't got enough kids."

He looked at me straight and for the first time the old eyes got a pointy look in them.

"Funny thing," he said. "Intian peoples don't got that trouble."

"You're a dry old stick. Anyhow, Ol Antoine. That's our problem. We was gonna borrow a white kid from the Nmiah Valley, and that deal's fell through and now we got to get one right away, tomorrow. We got to have another kid."

He was enjoying himself now. "White man's always hurry, hurry. Now he wants kids tomorrow. Don't got no time to wait the old way. S'pose you want kids, Ken, you got to start looong time ago."

He brought his hand up to his head and tapped his finger on his forehead. Then he shoved his arm out, the finger pointing out front.

"Got to think *ahead*," he said.

"That's right. But now we are between the rock and the hard place. No extra kid, no money, no school for nobody. So we figured maybe you could help us out. See, you got that little girl, stays here with you."

That surprised him. I had tried not to, but it surprised him anyhow. He looked at me, at the wall and at the floor. He didn't look at the girl. She had been in the cabin with us all the time. About ten or twelve I guess, or maybe fourteen, and small for her age. I had never noticed her much, but then I never pay much notice of kids. There's time enough to get to know them when they grow up.

"We figured, just maybe, we could borrow her from you. She would make ten kids, you see. And we would get the government money."

"She's Intian, en't it?"

"Well, yeah, I s'pose. But she ain't off this Reserve. She's from someplace else. What place she comes from, Ol Antoine? How come she helps you out in this place?"

That was the way it was for them. He was almost too old to help himself and she was pretty much too young to help anybody else, but the two of them, somehow, had been limping along together for a couple of months.

"She belongs a man, he's sort of my cousin. But he goes to jail. Long time he goes to jail."

"Well, is she Indian? I mean, is she on the Indian list?"

"She's Intian."

"Well, she ain't officially an Indian unless the government says she is. Might be she's like some Indians you know this country, Ol Antoine, they ain't on the list, so as far as the government is concerned, they ain't Indians at all?"

"When you see her," he said, "you know she's Intian, en't it?"

"Yes, but do you know, do you yourself know that she's on a list?"

"List? Halo kumtux list."

"Anyway, Ol Antoine, it don't matter. She's on a list, she ain't on a list, it don't matter. We work it this way. She comes to my place, lives with me a little time. We put her in the school under my name. The name don't matter. So we call her a Larsen. So far as the government is concerned, she is part of my family. She is white, see?

"Pretty soon, some inspector will come up. He counts heads. There's all ten kids in the school. Then she comes back with you, helps you this place. See? It works good."

"I don't know."

"Sure. It works, Ol Antoine. And you understand, she stays in school all year. Next year too. She stays all the time she wants to stay in school. And we buy her all the books. It don't cost her anything. It don't cost you anything. What can anybody lose?"

"I don't know if it works."

"Sure it will work. And it is all free. Cultus potlach. A real deal."

He looked across the little cabin at the girl. She had never moved nor made a sound all the time we talked. He spoke to her in pure Chilcotin, which I can't follow. I had another scare. Maybe she didn't talk English yet. But in the mood I was in, which was desperate, I would have found some way around that too if I'd had to.

Now and then, in the Chilcotin, English words like "school," "Larsen" and "month" kept popping in and out of his talk. Those were words they'd never needed in their language I guess. She answered two or three times, only a few words. After a while, she looked at me.

"You been to school some I guess?" I said.

She nodded yes.

"Very long?"

She shook her head no.

"Well that don't matter. You want to go to the new school, I guess. Lots of fun, havin' a school to go to. Other kids to play with."

She turned her face from me to the old man. So did I.

"Well, whatya say, old friend?"

He stayed still a long time, as if he hadn't heard, but that time I knew he had. Then he nodded his head, just once.

"Good. Then it's all settled. Can she pack her stuff and come with me now?"

Ol Antoine spoke to her again, in Chilcotin, and she walked out the door toward my truck.

"How about her stuff, Ol Antoine? Her iktus. She gonna pack her iktus?

"She got all her iktus," he said. What she owned was all on her, a ragged shirt, a pair of jeans and moccasins. By God, they do live poor.

I pulled out my wallet and counted out three tens.

"Ol Antoine, guess you will need some help in this cabin for a while s'pose she ain't here. You can maybe pay somebody else on the Reserve to clean up for you, en't it?"

He never looked at me or the money, just stubbed the wilted cigarette in a dirty dish.

"Yeah, and Ol Antoine, you know that old roan I got, the one you wanted to buy. You can have that horse. You know that horse. You just take him. It's potlach."

"Klahowya," he said.

"Ah, yeh. Klahowya, Ol Antoine."

His back was already turned when I went out the door.

Outside, she rassled open the door on the passenger side and got in on the seat. Straight and solemn. If she was scared, she didn't show it.

"By the way, what's your name?"

"Phyllisteen."

"Phyllis?"

She spoke louder, clearer." Phyllis*teen*," she said.

"Oh. Phyllisteen. Well, Phyllisteen, when a girl goes traveling, she needs a bit of money to travel with. So here, you better have this."

I handed her a dollar.

"Thanks," she said.

"And some luggage. Now, just happens I got something here in the glove compartment." I opened it up and pulled out an old school reader. It had a picture of the Fathers of Confederation in the front of it. "That's a school book I found around the place, Phyllisteen.

"It ain't the one you'll be using, you understand. But it'll be a couple of days before we get your books. So here is one. Got some pretty good stories in it, I wouldn't be surprised."

"Thanks," she said. She never opened the book. It lay on her lap.

I shoved down the clutch, which would hardly disengage at all in that transmission, and hammered the gear lever into low with the heel of my hand. It sounded as though all the teeth were coming out of the box and up into our laps.

"Just throw 'em together and let them sort themselves out," I said. But she didn't see the joke. We went back to the ranch in dead silence and I introduced Margaret to the idea. It took longer than explaining things to Ol Antoine for some reason.

She kept saying it wasn't fair.

"Not fair," I said. "Not fair to who? We are being fairer to at least one Indian than the government ever was. What does the government do? Takes them away from their own parents and shoves them in a residential school where they damn near die of homesickness. Is there anything worse than that? Is there anything crueler than kidnapping kids from their parents?"

Phyllisteen had already been taken from her parents, but if you're arguing with a woman, you use everything you got, so I passed that part of it over.

"It comes down to whether you want the Namko School to open or stay closed," I finally told her. She went along with it, ending by saying something a lot like Ol Antoine had said, she wondered if it could possibly work. Being a woman, of course, by the time the head count at the new school was over and we smuggled Phyllisteen back to Ol Antoine's cabin, she didn't want to let her go. I suppose every community has a general doer and fixer who gets abused from everyside and, in Namko, I'm it.

The teacher, now, she was something else again. The original bad-news woman. She had gone to college, where she learned half of a lot of things and now she was being turned loose on a community, totally unfit for anything, even teaching school. Although most said she was pretty, I had an objection to her as a woman, too. Her hair was pretty near short as a boy's and she wore slacks. I know, almost every woman in the country wears pants almost all the time. But they're housewives. They ain't in a public position. My wife never wore slacks when she taught school.

I was for saying something about it, but the rest of the Cattlemen's Association, which for the purpose of some government act was also the school board in Namko, told me to let well enough alone.

I went to the school the day it opened. I figured like everything else in this country it would start Indian time, but no, she had started at nine sharp and, when I got there about the, she had already dismissed them all for the day. They were drifting out through the yard as I drove in.

"Whacha doin', Ken?" said one of them.

"*Mister* Larsen, if you please," she said. She was standing at the doorway watching them go.

"It's okay," I said. "That's one of mine. At least, he looks like me, so I guess he is."

That seemed to set her back some. She was a funny combination, wore slacks to school, but insisted on calling everybody Mr. and Mrs., and me, from time to time, Mr. Chairman. She was never gonna fit into the country, that was clear, but when you're a small outfit you hire what you can get.

When we went into the school — it was just one room with another for her to live in at the back of it — and the first thing I saw was the blackboard propped up against a wall.

"You mean to say Herb ain't got that board up yet? He promised me sure he'd get it up a week ago. I'll do it myself. That is the only way anything gets done around here."

I went out to the truck for a hammer and some nails and when I came back she was talking with Phyllisteen, who she held back when the others were turned loose.

"Now dear," she was saying. "We have to decide what grade you're in. And I guess you're not sure?"

Phyllisteen wasn't sure, that was easy to see. She wasn't even able to answer or shake her head, one way or the other. She was just plain scared, so far as I could see, and the teacher wasn't helping. She was sitting right beside the kid in one of them double desks. Stop crowding her like that, I wanted to say, it's no wonder she's nervous. Don't crowd her. But I didn't say it. What was the use, it was the teacher's nature to push and crowd.

"This about the right place for the board, Miss Melcher?" I said, slapping a piece of the wall. She looked up as though she had forgotten I was there. "Oh, yes, yes, that's fine, Mr. Larsen."

I started pounding. Behind me, I could hear her talking.

"Have you seen this book before, dear? No? How about this one? Have you used this one?"

"How's this for level?" I called out. I asked twice, without an answer, and then I left the board, dangling by one nail, and walked over to them. The teacher was going through schoolbooks, grade by grade, and Phyllisteen was just shaking her head for no.

"Say, Phyllisteen, that's the old book I gave you, ain't it?" I said. "How come you brought it today? Ain't she got her books yet, Miss Melcher? Don't tell me they ain't arrived yet."

"We're just deciding which books she should use."

"Well, don't let me interrupt you if you're busy. Just hang a look over here and tell me about the board's level, OK?"

She gave a little bit of a sigh and granted me a minute's attention. Why that was such a chore I don't know, her work for that day was already over. In the end, after a lot more one-way conversation, she handed Phyllisteen a couple of books from her stack.

"Well, dear, what we'll do, we'll start you with this one. And if that's too easy, well we just go along to the next. Don't you think that would be a good idea?" She stood up and looked down at the silent kid. "Is that all right, dear?" She put her hand over Phyllisteen's.

I could see the kid wanting to pull away. Indians don't like being touched. They can hardly bear to shake hands when they're introduced. But what the hell, Miss Melcher would have to learn. Throw them together and let them sort themselves out.

"You're going to enjoy school, I know that," said Miss Melcher. "It'll be just lots of fun. You wait and see."

Chatter, chatter, chatter. What did she expect the kid to say? You bet? You win? You're right? Something like that?

''So, see you tomorrow, Phyllisteen.''

Phyllisteen got up, silent, picked up the books she was given and the old one I gave her and walked out the door. She had a good walk, very straight, like she was on rails.

After the door closed behind her the teacher said, ''I didn't know there'd be an Indian in the class.''

''Well, now, Miss Melcher, as far as this school is concerned, she ain't exactly Indian.''

''But she must be Indian.''

''Well, there is Indians and there is Indians, if you get what I mean.''

''I don't really, Mr. Larsen. But I'm awfully happy she's here. I've always admired them. They're so, well, so dignified. Such a noble race.''

Something about the way she said it put me off. ''If you want to have a look at dignity and nobility maybe you better take a walk down on the Reserve someday,'' I said. ''Up here, we call it our Eighty Acres of Hell. . . . No, on second thought, maybe you better keep off the Reserve. You might not be welcome.''

She started some yawp about indigenous people and culture shocks, but after a while I got her to turn her mind to the blackboard. We got it nailed up level and I pulled out, just living in the hope that, dumb as she was, she might manage a one-room school.

That, and hoping that Phyllisteen would at least stick it out till the whistle blew. There would be a school inspector around and there was no resting easy, not for me anyhow, until he finally stamped us government-inspected. As far as I could find out, he scared hell out of everybody in the schooling business, although nobody could tell me exactly why.

For that reason, we done our best to keep Phyllisteen at my place until the inspection was done. She had the loan of a horse to take her to school each day. My own two kids, which was how many we had at the time, doubled up on another. That pleased Phyllisteen some, the horse. But more and more she strayed. The horse would be standing outside Ol Antoine's cabin from school-closing until there was just time for her to canter back to our place for supper.

She would take off early in the morning, visiting him before school started. Weekends, often as not, he came up to our place and more or less camped on us. And silent, God, how that kid was silent. Not sullen. Not rude. But silent.

"I cannot reach that child," Margaret said to me. "I've tried, and I can't."

"The truth is," I said, "she is plumb homesick. I kidnapped that kid. I have got to be just as immoral as the government. Let her go back to Ol Antoine on the Reserve. The Inspector don't go around inspecting the houses where the kids come from, does he?"

We did it that way but, just to make sure, the day Moccasin Telegraph told us that the inspector was coming, I drove down to the schoolyard, getting there before the teacher beat on the angle iron, to count heads.

"Where's Phyllisteen?" I said to one of the kids in the yard.

"She ain't here."

"You mean she ain't been comin', for God's sake?"

"No. She's here every day. But sometimes she's late. She'll be here soon. Walks up from the Reserve." Phyllisteen didn't have my horse then. The Reserve was just walking distance from the school.

"Well, that's a relief. Hey, off the Reserve, you say?"

"Sure."

"Listen, today Phyllisteen is not walking up off the Reserve. You go down and meet her, walk around the long way with her."

"My Dad says s'pose I go down on the Reserve he'll warm my bum real good."

"Well, if you don't go down, I will warm your bum real good. And I'm a lot closer to you than your Dad is right now. Go on, get moving."

To help him along, I gave him a bit of a boot in the behind, something I suspected none of them were getting enough of at that school.

Then, having second thoughts, I called him back. I drove down to Ol Antoine's and picked her up in the truck. It's as I say, around here; the only way to make sure a job gets done is to do it yourself. I delivered her at bell time and, still playing it safe, I drove out to the crossroads and caught the inspector's car as he turned in to Namko.

He didn't look like much, that was for sure; old, wrinkled as a raisin, pale as a maggot. He was crowding retirement. He told me that. A year to go. I wouldn't have laid money on him making it. To me, he looked to be good for about one more clean shirt. I never discussed the school. That wouldn't have been the way to do business with this man. He was all business. You could see that. But I did find out he was wild for steelheading and then and there I became a steelhead fisherman too, and promised to take him down the valley right after he finished his inspection. There is times I have a lot of diplomacy in me, I figure, but it is a talent that don't get developed much in cowboying.

We drove down to the school in his car, me driving.

"We'll go, Inspector, just as soon as you're finished the inspection," I said. "Go over to Arch's store, get some tackle. I s'pose an inspection is pretty much a full morning affair?"

"Oh no," he said.

"Well, tell the truth, I'm new at this job of school chairman. So I don't know what an inspection is, exactly."

He half-smiled. "Every school inspection," he said, "begins with two lies. The inspector says 'I'm here to help you' and the teacher says 'I'm very glad you've come.' "

The voice was the strongest part of him. Deep and heavy. A bull's voice. Like a bull, no mannerisms, no looking over the shoulder to see if anybody was following. An old bull now but, like any good bull, knew who he was, didn't have to ask anybody what he was s'posed to do.

He scared Miss Melcher, just by shuffling into the classroom. Her hand went up to her throat, fingers pressed in.

"Good morning, Miss Melcher. Good morning class."

"Good morning Inspector. It's nice to see you. Class this is . . ."

He interrupted her, holding up a bony, blue-veined hand. "No, Miss Melcher. No introductions. You just carry on with your class. Pretend I'm not here."

"Yes sir."

"Perhaps I could have the lesson plans?"

"Yes sir."

She brought him a book full of something and he sat at a desk with it, opened it and began reading. Looking up, seeing her still standing beside him, he said, ''Kindly ignore me. Just go on with your regular work.''

''Yes sir.''

I sneaked down to the back of the room, near Phyllisteen, and sat. Nobody seemed to have any trouble ignoring *me*.

The teacher plugged away and so did the kid who was reading.

''Sally said, 'Oh, Spot. Dick and Jane went to school. They have friends at school. We will go to school, too.' 'Bow wow,' said Spot.''

Well, the inspector had told her to go ahead with whatever she was doing. He couldn't complain because she did it. But I saw his head snap up from the papers when he heard the kid reading. Looked like a man who had just bitten into a chocolate, not knowing it was hard-centered.

'' 'Bow wow,' said Spot. All the children looked up. They saw Sally and Spot.''

The story went on and on. There was a father and mother and a kid and a dog and a milkman and what they had in common was that none of them amounted to much. Alright for school, I s'pose.

You would have thought the inspector would be hardened to this sort of thing, but not enough, I guess. After a few minutes he snapped shut the book and began prowling around in the aisles, looking over the kids' shoulders at their books. Every eye kept pace with him as he moved. Pretend I'm not here, he had said, but it was like asking them to pretend not to notice a black thundercloud in the classroom.

He came up short at Phyllisteen's desk. I could see what he was looking at. It was the old reader I had given her. The one with the picture of the Fathers of Confederation in the front. She was still packing that old thing around, together with her new books.

''Hel-lo!'' he said, ''What have we got here?''

The kid reading stopped dead. The whole room went so quiet you could hear a gnat fart. Of course he never noticed. Like I say, he was an old bull and acted like a bull.

He picked up the book, let it fall open in his hand and riffled a few pages. ''Fancy that. I thought these had all been burned by the cultural police. Is it yours?''

She nodded.

He gave it back to her.

''Like it?''

''Yis,'' she said.

''Better than that one?'' He pointed at the 'Spot and Jane' book.

''Yis.''

''So do I,'' he said. ''Everybody else seems to be interested in dog and milkman stories. Must be something funny about you and me, I guess.''

I could see Phyllisteen's face from where I sat. She came close to a smile.

The inspector sat down in a seat across the aisle from her. ''May I look at it again?''

She handed it to him.

He looked at it while he talked to her.

''What's your name?''

''Phyll'steen.''

''You read all these stories, Phyllisteen?''

''Yis.''

''You like them all?''

''I lek most of them.''

''How about this one? 'Lars Porsena of Clusium, by the Nine Gods he swore . . .' '' He waited. She spoke. '' 'That the great house of . . .' '' ''Tarquin, yes,'' he said. '' 'Tar-quin, should suffer wrong no more,' '' she said.

''Yes,'' he said, ''you do know it, don't you? Now, just tell us the story, Phyllisteen. What happens in this story? Lars Porsena, raises an army to conquer Rome. . . .''

''He comes to the river?''

''Yes. What's the name of the river?''

''Tiber?''

''Yes. The Tiber. The Tiber that flows past the Seven Hills of Rome. And what happens there?''

''Horayteus . . .''

"That's right. Horatius."

"He goes to the bridge. With two men."

"Yes. He goes with Lartius and Herminius. That's it." He turned to the rest of the class. As I said, he had a great big voice for such a little man and it filled the whole room. He was all excited. "Just think of that, class. Here's the Tiber River, and just one bridge across it. And all the Tuscan army on one side. And on that bridge, just three men, that's all, three men, against the whole army. They had little short swords, only about so long . . . Phyllisteen . . . can you remember what Horatius says before they go on the bridge to face the army? What does he say?"

There was a bit of pause, but then she spoke. She was faint at first.

"Then out spoke brave Horayteus.

The kepten of the kate, . . ."

Like almost all Indian females, she had that toneless way of talking to strangers, her voice with no ring in it, flat as a stove lid, but she had every word perfect. I know, I read it over myself later.

"To efry man upon this earth

Death cometh, soon or let

And how can man die petter

Than fessing fearful otts

For the eshes of his fathers

And the timples of his Kots."

"Ah, Phyllisteen," said the inspector, "you and I, we still believe in heroes, don't we?" I saw then how he was different from that teacher. He didn't talk down to a kid.

"Now," he turned around to the rest of the bunch, "do you want to know what happened next?"

Yes, they did.

"Well, Phyllisteen and I are going to tell you the rest. You and I, Phyllisteen."

In fact, he did all the rest of it. She had used up all the nerve she had, getting that one verse of the poem out. But he was able to act like it was both of them talking. He told some of the story straight, then every now and then he would read some of the poetry. It was a performance, I tell you. None of them kids, nor me either, had any idea whether this here Horatius was somebody who was crucified or went down on the *Titanic*. The littlest ones, I don't s'pose they could really understand much of it, but even them, the little ones, got it into their heads that they were chewing on some good red meat instead of Juicy Fruit gum. And it was good stuff, the way he said it, the kind of story that stays with you. I can still remember the last lines. "How well Horatius kept the bridge, in the brave days of old."

He had all of them eating out of his hand by that time. For the next fifteen minutes the kids were all talking, telling him about their horses, talking about fishing, asking him about trains and other stuff they had heard of, but never saw. He showed them tricks with arithmetic and stunts with spelling. He even introduced them to the subject of logic, which, he said, schools used to teach.

"If you call a tail a leg, how many legs has a horse?" he said. He started with the teacher and she said five. Most of them said five. Asked me, too. I said five. But there was three of them, including Phyllisteen, who said four. "Alright," he said. "Those of you who said four have the beginnings of being students of logic. Because you can't make a tail into a leg just by calling it a leg. It's still a tail, and the horse still has only four legs."

It was great stuff but it was taking a lot out of him. His face was getting greyer than his suit. He was spent. So, all of a sudden, he just got up and everybody knew the inspection of the Namko School was over. "Well, on with the work, class." He walked out. When the teacher and him and me were out the door, he was just in a mood for ordinary formalities.

"You're well up on marking, Miss Melcher. The lesson plans might be a little more detailed."

"I was told that all inspectors say that."

"All inspectors do, I imagine."

"I'll put in more time on them sir." She was glad to have it over. I could see she had been worrying about him coming even more than me.

"One thing," he said.

"Yes sir."

"What grade is that little Phyllisteen in?"

"Well, frankly, it's been a problem to know where to put her. Normally she just doesn't participate. I've tried, but there is no responsiveness. Frankly, sir, you've had much more success with her than I've had."

"So she's left in primary?"

"I haven't known what else to do. If I could only get some response. She's perfectly well behaved. Never troublesome. But . . ."

"Passive," he said.

"Yes. Passive."

"But she's not stupid, is she?"

The teacher got stiff-legged at that. "We don't have testing capacity, Inspector. But I'm sure she's not slow-learner category."

He stiffened just as much. "Don't use slow-learner words please, Miss Melcher. Stupid is good, plain English. Generations of teachers have understood it."

"I'm sure her intelligence is at the norm, possibly better."

"I'm inclined to agree. But, you do have a problem. Unresisting but unresponsive. It's hard to combat."

"Yes sir, it is."

"Miss Melcher," he said. "It's your class and your school and I wouldn't presume to interfere." *You old son of a bitch*, I thought, *that's the first dishonest thing I've heard you say.* He went on. "But as a suggestion, why don't you jump her ahead two grades? No, not two. Jump her three. Throw the work at her. Mark her hard."

"Do you think that might work?"

"Probably not. But it's better to fail Grade Four than fail Grade One."

"That seems to me a very negative attitude, Inspector." There was something basically cranky in that woman. God help the man who is probably married to her by now.

"Negative, perhaps. Another word is realistic. After all, she's Indian."

"That is a very racist remark."

"What's this word racist? Is it like culture and the other German words we've started using?"

Her voice got squeaky. "There is nothing wrong with being an Indian," she said.

"Not for us, perhaps. But for her, it's tragic."

"I don't understand you."

"No," he said, "no, I suppose you don't. You don't see any

tragedy." He shook his head slowly. He looked older, frailer, sicker. "Oh my dear Miss Melcher. To be an Indian child, in a world that only has white heroes left in it."

"And what have you done about it, Inspector?"

"I am a year from the pension," he said. "And what I am doing about it is going steelhead fishing with Ken Larsen. Do you understand that?"

"No," she said.

"I thought not. But that is the way the world wags, Miss Melcher. Good day. Good luck to you."

When we got in the car I asked him a couple of questions. I wasn't sure we was out of the woods yet.

"How'd the school strike you, Inspector?"

"Not bad."

"And the teacher?"

"Not bad."

"The kids seem OK?"

"As I say, not bad."

"Well, we do our best," I said.

"Why is that little Indian in a white school?" he said.

"Indian?"

"Phyllisteen."

"Oh, Phyllisteen."

"Kindly don't play cute. We're both too old for that."

"Inspector," I said. "She ain't exactly Indian. Not exactly. As you know, there is Indian and then there is Indians that don't have Indian status. Her last name, as it is on the books you see, is Larsen."

"She's no catch-colt of yours," he said. "It's my guess that she is on the Indian list. And in any case, calling a tail a leg doesn't make it a leg. And the law says that she should be in a residential school, provided by the Federal Indian Affairs Department, and that she should not be a charge against the provincial taxpayer."

I felt all the wind go out of me. But then I looked across at him and there was more than half a smile on his face.

"I can't help teasing a bit," he said.

I still didn't know what to say.

"Listen, Ken Larsen. I have been traveling around little schools like this all my life. It's hard to get a new school started. It's hard to find teachers. It's hard to find children, sometimes. And it's hard to fight your own government to give you back some of the money you give it. Don't you think I know that?''

"Thank you, sir,'' I said.

"In fact, in spite of what we've been telling the children in the schools for a long time, life is hard, Mr. Larsen.''

"Inspector,'' I said, "I had told you I was gonna try to find you a steelhead. Now I am telling you I am gonna get you a steelhead. No matter what, you are gonna get a steelhead. We will get one if we gotta get us a CIL Wobbler for it.''

"Dynamite is a trifle illegal,'' he said.

"Yes, and some people say not fair to the fish.''

"Illegal and unfair,'' he said. "But most things are illegal now, and it's always been an unfair world.''

We never used the dynamite. Nor did he ever wet a line in the river. He had a long nap at my place and decided to start back for Williams Lake. I guess he had never really intended to go fishing, he just liked talking about it.

What a great big man he was. I will never forget him.


I would have forgot the school, after that day, if I could have. It was running. It had the Government Grade A stamp on it. There shouldn't have been any more for me to do. But I reckoned without Miss Melcher, who could leave nothing alone that was working well. Every time she saw me she would run up barking. Her talk was all about motivation, peer groups and, from time to time, Phyllisteen. I would nod my head to whatever she yapped about and say, "Miss Melcher, you may well be right." That would satisfy her for a while, although not long.

From a distance, I could see that things weren't going too bad. From time to time, I would ask my own kids, "What were you taught today?" They would say, "Nothing." That is exactly the answer I remember giving when I went to school. It's the very nature of kids and schooling.

One day my oldest, Mollie, came home all in a snit. Phyllisteen had won some contest put on by the Kinsmen Club at Williams Lake and they had all been given copies of her story, by the

teacher, as a guide to good writing. This was bound to upset
Mollie. She is one of them kids that has to be the center of
everything that goes on. Unless she has some kind of a hand in it,
the stars don't shine at night, nor the sun come out by day. It's a
quirk. Some people are that way. A lot of them get to be politicians.

I read this thing that Phyllisteen had wrote and thought it pretty
good, particularly for a kid that didn't have that good a handle on
the English language. Phyllisteen could write English better than
she could talk it. The story was called *Fleet*.

'Fleet was a deer. He was born in a cave. The cave was a small
one, but it was a good home for him. When Fleet was small,
his mother was shot by a hunter. The shot did not hit her heart
and it made her bleed slow. His mother ran to a cliff and up on
a rock. Then she went to a little creek that ran between two
rocks. They went down the creek to a small place. Fleet saw
his mother drink the water and he drank the water. The water
was cool and the water was sweet. While Fleet was drinking,
he saw his mother lie down. She seemed to be sleeping. Fleet
walked and stood beside her. He heard a sound. He didn't
know what to do. Then he ran out of the cave. When Fleet was
three years old he fought another deer and won. From that
time he always won when he fought another deer. He was a
very strong big deer. One day, when he got old, he was not so
careful. He was pushed off a cliff by another deer. He did not
die right away. He went to the place where his mother died and
he drank the water in the pool again. The water was sweet to
him again. Then he died.'

"Strikes me as pretty good," I said.
"Ol Antoine was there," said Mollie.
"Oh. Ol Antoine. He goes to the school?"
"Sure. He comes and he just sits."
"He has been just sitting for a long time. It might as well be in
the school as anyplace else."
"Miss Melcher made a big fuss about Phyllisteen's story and
then Ol Antoine said he wanted to ask about the deer."
"Oh yeah."

"All the kids laughed. Ol Antoine said you were s'posed to shoot a deer for him and you didn't do it."

"You kids shouldn't laugh at Ol Antoine. He's old and you will be old yourself some day."

"But he said you were s'posed to get him a mowitch."

"Never mind, Mollie. I will look after the deer situation. You get an education. Is that okay?"

She wouldn't leave it alone.

"After that, he starts talkin' in Indian to Phyllisteen. So the teacher, she wanted Phyllisteen to translate. Phyllisteen, she didn't want to, but the teacher kept pluggin' at her so she did. She talks that Indian way, you know. She says, 'Ol Antoine, he says all this talk about deer is thin gravy.' We really laughed."

"You better stop laughing and start working," I said.

I didn't think much more of it at the time, but the deer and Ol Antoine came back to me a week or so later.

That day started with a paint we called Steamboat. He was a cross, half-stupid and half-alligator and mostly I used him for packing, but this day I saddled him, figuring to ride down to Arch's and he pulled his usual stunt of trying to buck you off when you're five miles from home. He was a mesachie horse and I'm too old for them, but I stuck him while he went through every trick there was. He spun and he sunfished, he bolted and he hit trees. I was surprised at myself, that I could stay aboard him. Like the Indians say, my coat went off both sides of the road, I was a one-man crowd. But finally he surrendered and we come down into Namko past the teacher's place with lots of lather on his shoulders but in general agreement as to which one of us was in charge. It just happened, she came out the door at that minute to shake the crumbs off her tablecloth. She was that kind of woman. Tablecloths and washing ashtrays with soap and water. The tablecloth flapped in front of his face and he cut loose again. I figured he had used up every trick there was in the book, but he had one more he had been holding back. He reared up straight and fell over backward.

I got a foot out of the stirrup as he went back and it happened he rolled right and I rolled left. Otherwise I wouldn't be here to describe what was troubling him.

When I got up she was just looking at me, surprised in a mild sort of way.

"I never saw a horse do that before," she said.

"I am training him, for the circus," I said.

"Really?"

"Yes, really, you can be part of the act if you will bring that there bedsheet with you."

I did not mention that I had been trying to get past the school without her seeing or talking to me. That would have been true, but unmannerly. She would almost always nail me if she could see me over the horizon and talk about the dominant forces of modern society and I would sit there, wishing I knew as little about the subject as she did. Well, we went into her section of the schoolhouse and drank some poor coffee while she yipped and snapped at my heels.

"Ol Antoine," she said, "has been at the school asking about some deer meat you promised him."

"Miss Melcher, if I hear any more about that damn deer . . . Listen . . . Henry James shot a deer weeks ago. He took it down to Ol Antoine's cabin. But Ol Antoine had a bunch of relatives come to visit and in about one and a half days, the entire deer was eaten up. He forgets that. He can't remember that we got him that deer."

"Well, actually," she said, "it's not the deer. What I'm concerned about is a larger matter."

I stirred the coffee with my finger. It was half-cold anyhow.

"I'm concerned about Ol Antoine's visits to the school," she said.

I didn't say anything. I waited for her to rattle on.

"I think he has a disturbing effect upon that child."

"What child?"

"Well, Phyllisteen, of course. He comes and sits beside her. Which is very nice. But I don't think the effect is good. She withdraws from the class."

"Walks out, you mean. You shouldn't let her do that."

"No, Mr. Larsen, she doesn't walk out. She becomes withdrawn. She stops participating."

"They are usually withdrawn," I said. "As for participation, either she does the work she's told to do or she doesn't. Why do you figure Ol Antoine is to blame for that?"

"I am not blaming him. He is a splendid old man, I'm sure of that. But he cannot understand what happens in a school."

"Can't, eh."

"No. He simply doesn't. It's not his fault. He's been culturally deprived. But he can't."

"Well, I think you have described it pretty well. I don't think he does understand."

"It would be just fine if he would participate, but he doesn't. At first, I used to ask him to tell us about Indian culture, to share folk stories with us. But I could never seem to make contact. He's very deaf, you know."

"Yes, he is, from time to time."

".'And if I ask him, he just withdraws, like Phyllisteen."

"Well, then, why not just leave him alone? They want to withdraw, I guess they got a right to do that."

"But he could be a cultural resource person and for some reason he just won't. The other day, I was telling him how well Phyllisteen has been doing. I talked to him very slowly, about what a marvelous opportunity it could be for her. She could be a nurse. Or a teacher maybe. A professional person. Somebody who could come back and help her own people."

"Oh yes? What did Ol Antoine say?"

"All of a sudden he stood up. He said, 'Chilcotin peoples last Intians to fight the white man. Wildest peoples in all the country.' And then he walked out. It had nothing to do with what we were talking about."

"Well, Miss Melcher, probably to him it did, somehow. Don't worry yourself about it."

She went on. It was important that the child be brought into the mainstream. Educated, integrated, emotionally supported. she could use words almost endlessly.

"I like Ol Antoine," she said, "and sometimes he can be very charming. But if there's anything of importance that I want to discuss with him, all of a sudden he's all Indian and doesn't understand anything."

"Just possibly, you rub him the wrong way, Miss Melcher."

"On the contrary, I have been extremely diplomatic."

"Oh," I said.

"You don't seem to understand," she said.

"You may well be right," I said.

It was almost a relief to get away from her and back to that rank paint. He didn't know I was chairman of the school board, but our cultural relationship was, somehow, simpler and easier to live with and I didn't mind so much that he bucked all the way home.

The next time she caught me was down at the store.

"I just happened to notice your truck was here so I came over," she said.

"Well, here is where I am, Miss Melcher."

"Actually, I've been trying to reach you for a week. But I just haven't been able to keep up with you. Mrs. Larsen said you were out riding when I went up to the ranch."

"Oh, yes. Yes. That was too bad."

"Then I came here one day just when you were driving away. I shouted, but I guess you didn't hear me."

"That was too bad."

"And I sent a message up to you two days ago, with Henry James, but I guess you never got the message."

"Cowboys, Miss Melcher, are very unreliable."

"But anyway, I have found you at last."

"Yes, Miss Melcher. Is there something you want?"

"Yes. It's very important. We have got to do something."

"We? Have got to do something about what?"

"About Phyllisteen."

"What about Phyllisteen?"

"She has left school. It was the day or two after I had that peculiar conversation with Ol Antoine and he talked about the Chilcotin War or whatever it was. She just disappeared."

"Out of school, eh? Well, that's the way it goes. Too bad, ain't it?"

"Ol Antoine had no right to take that child out of school."

"Nothin' much you can do. He's her parent, so to speak."

"Parents can't take their children out of schools."

"But she's Indian, remember?"

"That doesn't make any difference."

"Maybe it does. Anyhow, how do you know Ol Antoine took her out? Might be she just left. Just pulled the pin."

"She would not leave. The child was doing very well. She was taking part more and more. She was working well. She was joining in group activities. It was when we were making arrangements for the graduation party, . . . all the children were fully engaged in the planning, and suddenly she stopped coming. Two of the children saw her going down the road with Ol Antoine, in a wagon.''

"Well, then, she went away with him in the wagon. Your question is answered. You know where she went. She went away with him in the wagon. Don't he have no rights to take her?''

"Nobody, Mr. Larsen, had a right to take a child out of school.''

"Are you going to make a fuss like this any time I want to take my kids out of school and go fishin' for a few days?''

"Then you know where she is. They're at a fish camp.''

"I never said no such thing. She might be anywhere. Fish camp. Visiting relatives. Digging wild potatoes. You can see, Miss Melcher, that half the time the Reserve is half-empty. They take it in their heads to go somewhere, they go.''

"They can't go. There are times a child can't go.''

"It's a free country, ain't it?''

"No, it's not. Not the way you mean it.''

"I see. It ain't free. Well, I thought you might take that side of the argument.''

"You're the school board chairman, Mr. Larsen, and you are being no help whatsoever.''

"I am being no help because there is nothing I can do.''

"Well, if you won't help, I will find someone who will. I am going to talk to the chief.''

"Now just a minute. You leave Macdonald Lasheway out of this. All this has nothing to do with him. Phyllisteen's schooling is a special deal and Lasheway has got no place in that deal.''

"I have met the chief and he strikes me as an extremely progressive man.''

"Anyhow,'' I said, "Macdonald is hell-and-gone from here, building irrigation ditches over around Chezacut some place. He has been gone over a month. Miss Melcher, why can't you leave well enough alone? Things have a way of solving themselves, you know.''

"The chief has had to educate himself, just as she's trying to do,'' she said. "That child has a right to the same things. I'm going to see him. Perhaps I should have gone to him in the first place. White people around here just don't seem to be concerned. Perhaps he will be.''

I never thought she would carry through but she did. Borrowed a car some place. Booted it over a lot of rocks and potholes. Ran poor Macdonald to ground someplace in the Chezacut. I got a report on it after.

"It en't easy for me, Miss Melcher," he said. He was leaning on his shovel, two hands over the top of it and his chin on his hands. Quiet sort of man, the chief. Works better than he talks. He was bound to have hard going with a woman like that.

"But you're the chief."

"I'm 'lected the chief," he said. " 'Lected chief."

"Well what difference does that make? You're chief."

He didn't answer.

"Is it because of this business of pretending that Phyllisteen is a white, so they could get enough school children? Is that it?"

"She's a little bit white now, I guess."

"But you'd agree, that child deserves to be educated. It doesn't matter how, she deserves an education."

"Sure. That's right."

"Are the people on the Reserve resentful because she's in the white school? Is that the opposition?"

"Old peoples always the same, I guess. Don't like changes."

"But they have to change. Mr. Lasheway. The world changes. They have to change. You see that, don't you?"

"I try to help them change, Miss Melcher. Kind of hard job." He smiled. "Don't pay so good, neither."

"Most of the children on your Reserve don't even get to the residential school. They don't even go there."

"We're a long way back in the sticks, Miss Melcher. It's hard."

"Well, I don't see why you can't quietly and firmly order Ol Antoine to send that child back to school."

"I don't think Ol Antoine he minds her in that school. I don't think he takes her away."

"Of course he took her away. He was seen taking her away."

"I don't think he minds, Ol Antoine."

"Well, she would not leave willingly. Take my word for it."

"I don't think Ol Antoine takes her, Miss Melcher."

"He did take her."

"Might be, Miss Melcher, s'pose you just don't do anything, after little time, she comes back OK."

"And I know that that won't happen."

She waited some for him to answer, but he had gave all the answers he had.

"Then you will not use your authority?" she said.

He was finally exasperated, trying to show her what she would not see. His calm voice rose a little bit.

"Miss Melcher, *I don't got 'thority*. I'm 'lected the chief, every two years. I just lead the people so far as they want to come after me."

She could have got the same answers from any politician, Indian or white. But maybe she had never talked to any politicians. I don't know who she had talked to in the world she came from. Maybe she had been brought up in a barrel and they shoved books at her to read through the bunghole.

Then it was my turn for another go-around with her.

I wasn't riding the mesachie paint that day, but I might as well have been. I had the old truck, one of them old army trucks which make you wonder how in hell the Germans could ever have lost the war. I had a flat. The jack was broke. I had pried up the front end with poles, kicked sticks under the axle while I lifted, and was finally trying to get five bolts through five holes on a slipping drum. That is a job which will get you thrown out of the Holy Name Society. It was hot enough for the sagebrush to sweat and my back hurt. I never saw her until she was right beside me.

"Well, Mr. Larsen, I've found you. I am in luck."

I let the wheel thump down on my instep and sat in the dust, looking up at her.

"That's the way luck runs, Miss Melcher, sometimes good, sometimes bad."

"Are you having trouble?" she said.

"I wonder if you would mind getting into the cab, easy please, and put a foot on the brake to stop this wheel turning."

"I went to see Chief Lasheway," she said.

"That's nice," I said, lifting the wheel up again. It weighed more every time I lifted. Somebody had been putting sand in it while I wasn't watching.

"We had a nice long talk."

"Glad to hear it."

The drum still turned on me. I let the tire flop over and got up to look inside the cab.

"The *brake* pedal, Miss Melcher, the *brake*, not the clutch."

"Oh, I was thinking of something else, I guess."

I went at it again.

"*He* was extremely helpful," she said.

That was a lie and I knew it, as it happened, but it didn't matter much at the time. The wheel was finally hung.

"Would you mind now stepping out and handing me them nuts?" I said.

She stepped out on the edge of the hub cap and the nuts was scattered from hell to breakfast time. "Oh dear," she said, "I've spilled them, haven't I?"

"Yes, I guess you could say that."

"Never mind. I'll find them."

While I hung onto the wheel she hunted, talking at the same time. "Ol Antoine and Phyllisteen are at a fish camp down at Scairt Woman Crossing. They say I couldn't get that car down there, but this big truck of yours would make it."

"Oh," I said.

"So when we get this wheel on, we can both go down right now. You will take me, won't you?"

I sighed. "Be glad to, Miss Melcher." They wear you down. Somehow they wear you down.

When we got to Scairt Woman Crossing and found their camp I thought once again that maybe the Indians are the only people who really know how to live in this country. They had an old canvas tent, set back from the water a couple of hundred feet. A small, simple, but clean camp, with whisky-jacks and squirrels for company. An Indian ain't much for keeping house, but he sure keeps a clean tent camp. There was a salmon run. You could see them finning in the pool at the bottom of the fast water. The air was warm, the sky was clear and the fast water made music. I imagine the Garden of Eden was something like this before we got drove out. I thought of the teacher and the rest of us whites at Namko, worrying, arguing, fighting, chasing the almighty dollar night and day, and maybe, s'pose we survive long enough, at the end, we might go camping like this by a river like this. Ol Antoine and Phyllisteen, they took that prize, right here and now. The rest of us was too stupid to take what was free for our taking. There was nothing in this world I wanted more, right then, than to just stay in this place with them. Stay until I lost count of the days and the weeks.

But not that woman. She just stomped in, heading for the tent, going so fast she pretty near never noticed Phyllisteen, who was slicing fish. There was a lot of fish guts around and she had fish blood on her face and in her hair and the flies had found them.

"Hello, Phyllisteen," said the teacher.

" 'Lo."

"We've missed you at school, Phyllisteen."

The kid didn't answer. She went back to cutting fish.

Me, I liked watching her do it. You talk about surgeon's hands. It was so clean, so perfect, the red meat of the salmon opening up behind the moving knife. It just seemed like two, three passes of her hands and there was the fish, spread open for the sun-drying rack, every bone out of it and not a nick, not a tear, in the meat. I guess the teacher was in no mood to think about surgeons.

"Where is Ol Antoine, Phyllisteen?"

She pointed with the bloody knife. "He's over there," she said. If I had known how the teacher was going to behave, I might have arranged things better. But I probably couldn't have stopped that wilful woman anyhow. She just planted herself in front of him, where he was admiring the same country I had been admiring, and yelped at him.

"Ol Antoine. Phyllisteen must come back to school."

He never looked at her. He was doing his best not to hear her.

"You should not have taken her out of school, Ol Antoine."

He muttered something.

I had been scuffling around in the dirt with my toe and there was a broken stone knife there. The kind they used before the whites came out here. I was flipping it around in the palm of my hand while she kept going at Ol Antoine.

"You must understand. It's the law. The law says that Phyllisteen must come to school. She can stay with me for a few days, or she can stay with Mr. Larsen. But she has to come back."

This time he spoke loud and clear.

"Will you translate for me, Mr. Larsen?"

"I couldn't Miss Melcher. He's talking pure Chilcotin. All I know is a little bit of Chinook."

"Anyway," she said, "he speaks English."

"Maybe he don't want to talk English. It's a free country."

I had to do something, before things got worse, because she was a woman with a low boiling point.

I handed him the chipped stone knife. "Your peoples fish this country a long time, Ol Antoine."

He looked at the rock, but not at me. Then he threw it away.

"I think he would like to be alone, Miss Melcher. Why don't you and me go down and sit by the river for a spell. Watch the fish coming up."

"This is going to be settled here and now," she said. "If you can't translate for me somebody else will have to." She called out. "Phyllisteen. Will you come over here, please. I want you to translate for me."

"Now just a minute," I said. "You leave that kid alone. You have got no business getting her mixed up in a fight with Ol Antoine." I waved my hand over the fish racks. "It's all right, Phyllisteen. You go ahead with that fish."

"And you listen to me, Ken Larsen. You may be a big pooh-bah in the Namko Cattlemen's Association. But that doesn't fizz on me one bit. That child deserves an education and I'm going to see that she gets an education. As for you, you are an extremely stupid man."

My father taught me I was never to hit a woman and I never did, after age ten. But I was close. If there was one thing she needed it was to have a few teeth loosened. I guess she could see that because she went a little bit white and stepped back a foot. But that was all. I will say that, she had some sand in her, that woman. She wasn't gonna take a second step back from me.

Ol Antoine got up and walked between us, seeing neither of us. We watched him. He went down to the fish racks and spoke to Phyllisteen a little while. After a bit they came back to the tent together.

"Ol Antoine says I come back to school now," said Phyllisteen.

The teacher put an arm around her. "Well, that's fine, dear. That's just fine, isn't it? Splendid. Now, you get your things together and we'll go, right now."

"She's got all her things," I said.

"Oh. Well, let's go, dear."

She herded the kid away from camp, up to the truck, all the time telling her how happy she was s'posed to be about what was being done to her.

Ol Antoine gave a bit of a sigh. "Lots she don't know," he said.

"Who," I said. "Phyllisteen or the teacher?" He didn't answer.

We left him there alone. A couple of days later, he was back at the Reserve. Both of them run out of paradise, not by God, but by their fellow man.

The last day of school that year we all had to attend. Most of the men had other things to do, things they would rather be doing. But it is the nature of a woman to stop a man doing what he wants to do and to make him do something he don't want to do. All our wives said we had to be there and most of us went along with the idea, but sourly. There was a rebellion of sorts among the men. Not one of us changed out of our working clothes and there wasn't a man took off his hat inside the schoolhouse.

Smith, who had been castrating, had blood caked on his hands and his shirt was black with sweat.

"What is this big deal about the last day of school?" he asked me. "You turn 'em loose and you let 'em drift. What else is there to it?"

"I don't know," I said, "But there's been a half-stampede in our house all week."

The schoolhouse was all dressed up, even to flowers.

"That's nice," I said to the teacher, "having flowers even when nobody is dead."

She wasn't sure how to take that. She often wasn't sure about me. She herself, for once, looked pretty and was wearing a dress.

She began explaining the first go-around to me.

"We're going to have presentations first, Mr. Larsen. I'll read them out and you give them when the childen walk up. Every child gets a presentation."

"That's a new one," I said. "What kind of a race is it where everybody wins?"

"Well," she said, "they're little presentations, most of them. One for the boy that always lit the fire. One for the best finger painting."

"What does little Phyllisteen get?" I asked.

It tickled her to tell me. "Phyllisteen won in a big race," she said. "One you'd recognize, Mr. Larsen. She gets the Williams Lake Kinsmen Award for the best Grade Four essay in the whole school district. The whole district."

"Well, I'll be a go-to-hell," I said. "Good for her. Good for Phyllisteen. The little Siwash kid beat them all. That will teach the rest of them something."

She didn't seem to take that right but I meant it, every word. I was proud of that kid.

"Afterward," she said, "it's party time." She walked me over to a table which was covered with a big white cloth. She lifted a corner of it. She could see I was startled some and she lifted more.

It was some sight. Eggs with red and yellow stuffing. White bread sandwiches, cut in stars. Cakes with icing and jelly beans around the sides. Cookies covered in chocolate and stuff that glittered.

"What is all that?" I said.

"The children made it all," she said. "After the presentations, all the adults are the guests and the children are the hosts."

"They made it all?"

"All of it. The boys and the girls. Back at their homes. You haven't noticed, have you?"

"No, I haven't."

"Also the children all give each other presents."

"Presents!"

"Oh, just little things. Nothing over a dollar was the rule. Things they bought at Arch's store."

I just stood there.

"Is there something wrong, Mr. Larsen?"

"I feel sorry, I guess."

"Sorry?"

"Yes. I'm sorry for Phyllisteen."

"What do you mean?"

"I mean Phyllistine ain't gonna be here."

"Of course she'll be here."

"Show me what she made, that's on the table."

"She's probably bringing it with her. She's a secretive child, you know."

"Cakes with icing. Candy. Presents. Presents for God's sake. Miss Melcher, have you ever been in that cabin of Ol Antoine's?"

"No, I didn't feel that I should . . ."

"Well, it's kinda too bad that you didn't. Miss Melcher, get this into your head, if you can get anything into your head. There is no cake flour in that cabin. There never has been. There never will be. There is no icing sugar. There is no cookies and no marshmallows and no jelly beans. There is no one dollar presents.

"Say, did she know about this party when she took off with Ol Antoine for that fish camp?"

"Well. Yes. I suppose she did."

"Judas Priest," I said. "And there are people who call me stupid."

My wife had come up by now and, in her usual way, said there wasn't any problem that couldn't be fixed.

"We'll just cut up everything that's here and put different pieces on a whole lot of plates. That way, no one child can claim anything as his own work. It will be all put in together and anonymous. And you, Ken, you go down on the Reserve and bring up Phyllisteen."

"O yes, Mr. Larsen, please do it."

"There's no please about it," said my wife, "just do it, Ken."

"Talking to Ol Antoine about this will be about as easy as floating a crowbar in a slow cleek," I said.

"Ken," said my wife. "Go. Now." I went.

Three of us came back. Ol Antoine. Me. And Phyllisteen, with her hair in two thick braids and a fancy white dress that she had somehow got real clean. She must have been on the edge of comin' after all. Getting that dress so clean had to be something she'd put in time on.

There was a beautiful pair of moccasins in the cabin. Someone on the Reserve had made them for her. Lovely work, all in the old original Indian colors, orange and black. But she wouldn't wear them. She wore a pair of dirty old canvas running shoes with a hole in the toe. I suppose that's what the white kids were wearing. I didn't argue. My job was to get her there.

The teacher had started proceedings without us. I guess the herd was getting restless. When we come in the door she had just handed out some kind of prize to some kid for not falling in the creek, or whatever it was she had dreamed up, but when she looked up and saw Phyllisteen, her eyes lit up like candles in the dark. Then her tongue started to run. As usual, hinged at the middle and loose at both ends.

"Finally," she said, "finally it is an honor, a great honor, to present the Kinsmen Club Award for the finest, most beautiful essay . . ."

Goddam, I said to myself, if only she could stop talking. But she had to. It was her nature to flannelmouth and neither God nor man could stop her.

"Come forward, Phyllisteen," she said.

Phyllisteen started down the aisle. The kids were sitting either side of it, in the seats they had been in all the year. All the adults were around in the back of the hall.

"How nice you look, Phyllisteen. And what a lovely dress."

One of the kids spoke in a loud whisper, that everybody in the little room could hear. It was, God forgive me, my Mollie. Who else? Mollie, who had to be the center of everything.

"That's my old dress," she said. "My mum gave it to her."

Phyllisteen stopped in her tracks, right beside Mollie's seat.

I thought at her as hard as I could drive thoughts. There wasn't anything else to do. Thinking was all that was left. Don't cry, Phyllisteen. For God's sake, don't cry. Stand your ground, kid. You are as good and better than any of them. Don't let them run you off.

Well, she didn't cry. But then, the Indians so seldom do after childhood. But she didn't hold her ground neither. She looked at Mollie, a minute or two minutes, it seemed, and then she turned and started walking out. Still straight, her feet moving like on rails.

If there was any single thing that was half-decent at that moment it was done by old Morton Dilloughboy. I have been critical of Morton from time to time, but there are moments when his instincts are faster than the rest of us. He took off his hat as she came near. Of course, then all the rest of the men took off their hats. Not that it meant anything to her. Not that it could. I don't s'pose she even saw. Her eyes were dry, but they were eyes that weren't seeing anything.

The teacher flapped down on me like a bat after Phyllisteen went out the door.

"Stop her, Mr. Larsen. Go get her."

"Miss Melcher," I said. "Once again is one time too many. You cannot keep doubling up on your losses forever."

She turned to Ol Antoine, saying nothing and Ol Antoine, answering nothing, obeyed her. He went out the door on his creaky old legs and at the steps he called her name. Once. She stopped. He went down beside her, put a hand on her shoulder and spoke to her low.

When she answered him, she answered in English. I guess she had got more used to it than her own language.

"Leave go me," she said. "You en't nothin but cultus Siwash Sem lek me."

His hand dropped and she walked away, over the hill and into our Eighty Acres of Hell.

That was the end of the education of Phyllisteen.

There were those who said, well, wasn't it something great that she stuck it as long as she did and done so good as she did. Me, I felt sick about the whole damned business.

The school stayed shut the next fall. Not just because there was no Phyllisteen for it. There was a big family of whites pulled out of the country and we was way too short of kids. The little cabin stood empty and a family of bushtailed rats took it over. What they learned there I wouldn't know.

# CABIN FEVER

ON A DAY as cold as a witch's tits, Smith booted open the door of the Namko Beer Parlor and stood, stomping snow from his boots and brushing more of it from his hat and shoulders, while he adapted his eyes to the dim light which late winter afternoon sun was shoving through one dirty window. "Bloody dump of a place," he said. It was not a dump but, for a beer parlor, it was unusual. For one thing it was the smallest beer parlor west of the Atlantic Ocean and north of the Mexican border. It had once been a three-table dining room of the little old log hotel building. By an unusual combination of several miracles, the ingenious Arch MacGregor had induced the authorities of the Liquor Control Board in faraway Victoria to license it instead as a beer parlor. Possibly the authorities were misled by the Namko Chamber of Commerce, of which MacGregor was the entire executive and membership. By consulting a school globe, Arch had determined remarkable features of Namko's geography. Namko, he found, was almost exactly the halfway point between Hawaii and Iceland, Manila and Madrid and Kamchatka and Cuba. This enabled the Chamber of Commerce to rank Namko with other famous places as The Hub City. Whether or not the expensive Chamber notepaper had any effect, it is clear that the bureaucrats eventually learned that they had erred about the nature of Namko and its hotelkeeper, and traveling liquor inspectors had visited many regulations upon Arch. The law of the time required a separation of all beer parlors into men's and women's sections. There being no room for a partition in the Namko establishment, Arch made do with a line of white paint which came down one wall, crossed the floor and climbed the other.

It was not sufficient, however, that he divide the outdoor toilet into two sections. He was ordered in uncompromising terms to install flush toilets. He had ordered two of these devices from Eaton's mail-order house, but had wisely taken the precaution of obtaining several blank shipping labels. The toilets stood, still cased in wooden slats, in a corner of the room, unconnected to any septic tank. There was no septic tank. Arch did, however, renew the shipping labels twice a year and, until the day that the same LCB inspector came twice to Namko, he was able to fend them off by showing that the toilets had been but newly shipped and that time was needed before he could effect connections. On this day, the room being not only cold but also dark, Smith tripped over one of the packing cases as he made his way to the bar. He snarled and kicked again, breaking one of the packing-case slats.

That the beer parlor was innocent of customers, waiter, light and heat was not unusual of a winter's day. Arch frequently left it untended, hour after hour. Customers helped themselves to the bottled beer which was stacked behind the tiny bar and rang up their money into the cash register. On this day Smith found something else missing. There was no beer. He cursed in masterful fashion. There were probably no new words in his cursing, but he had new and interesting arrangements of the old ones. It had been done before, by others. In Namko, it was not possible to be a customer of Arch MacGregor's and serve God also.

He went to the Namko General Store, Arch's other enterprise, prepared to reproach him with the same vigor and in the same terms. To his surprise, he found three other Namko residents had anticipated him. Ken Larsen, his cowboy Henry James and Morton Dilloughboy had corralled Arch in the small office at the back of the store. Larsen, the spokesman, dealt at length with the various laws and regulations as he conceived them to be: that a beer parlor was supposed to have a waiter in it to serve the beer and collect the money, that a beer parlor should be heated and provided with light during business hours and that, above all, a beer parlor was supposed to have beer in it. Arch responded in tones firm and even. "Half the last batch I ordered froze and broke in the Stage coming in from the Lake. Half of the rest of them froze in the back room of the beer parlor while the whole bunch of you never set foot in the place for damn near three weeks."

"I was busy winter feeding," said Larsen. Morton said he had been hunting horses. Young Henry said he would have come but was unavoidably detained. Henry's excuse was particularly sound. He was of the type described as good man in the bush, poor man in town. At New Year's, being in the town of Williams Lake and well-lubricated, he had been arrested and charged with borrowing a citizen's truck with intentions of keeping it. The penalty was thirty dollars or thirty days and Henry, being by that time out of cash, took second prize and had spent a month at the coast as a guest of King George VI.

"I do not give one sweet damn why none of you patronized my establishment," said Arch. "What I understand is profit and loss and until this last cold spell quits, all of Namko is teetotal. Why don't you all bugger off and form a local chapter of the Band of Hope?"

"That means there is no beer coming on the Stage today either," said Smith.

"Right," said Arch. "No beer popsicles. Those of you who don't like it, patronize the next place. It's right over there. Over that way. In Tokyo."

They had to forgive the man. Other people with whom they did business, the suppliers of binder twine, groceries, boots, axle grease and lumbago liniment, these were never so forthright when they failed to deliver. When other suppliers failed they offered long and unverifiable excuses. They spoke about back-ordering, of the failure of jobbers, the carelessness of wholesale shipping clerks and of wrecks on the railroad. Arch, when he didn't want to do business with you, told you plainly so you could understand. As philosophers have noted, a 'no' from the mouth of a firm man can be more pleasing than a promise of 'yes' from a weak one.

Arch's view was understandable; he was a man whose instinct for commerce, everfitful, fell to near absolute zero in winter. Winter was his time of hibernation. He wished to read books, to rest and, from time to time, by day or night, to sleep softly. In those long, dark months he preferred that there be no guests sleeping in the six bedrooms of Namko Hotel, no patrons in the beer parlor and, to the greatest extent possible, few customers at the store. This is what made him so different from others in that land. He never suffered cabin fever. Either that or he got his own strain and actually enjoyed it.

They left Arch in the thick, blue tobacco smoke of his office where he promptly resumed reading his book. They did not, however, leave the store. Where was there to go, except home? What was there to do, except wait for spring?

They looted a shelf of coffee and canned cow and brewed it on the drum heater in a bucket and moped about, disconsolate as birds in the rain. They discussed politics. That didn't take long. The country was going to hell in a handbasket. Larsen and Morton dickered halfheartedly about a horse trade. It was a mare that neither man loved nor respected. Larsen had sold her to Morton three months before. Morton now wished to sell her back. "It's only fair, it's your turn," he insisted. The trading petered out with neither man quite sure whether a deal had been made or not.

Smith fidgeted. He read the labels on soup cans. Tried on chaps. Fingered spurs and coils of rope. It took him about twenty minutes to make a complete circuit of the shelves, at the end of which time he began again. Henry undertook to sweep the floor and raised such clouds of dust that Arch emerged from his office to complain that he was in danger of an asthma attack. "If I didn't want that dust there it wouldn't be there. Leave it lay. Don't stir it around."

"You know what's wrong with us?" said Morton. "We got cabin fever. The whole bunch of us."

"You want to know about cabin fever, you should spend some time in Hotel Crowbar," said Henry.

"Well maybe you had it there. But you still got it here," said Smith.

Cabin fever was endemic in the Namko Country in late winters. Most ranchers, who had wives to fight with, had lighter attacks. Among trappers and similar hermits the attacks were often severe and sometimes tragic.

They discussed one such case which had involved Alabam, an American from the Deep South who had tried to winter in an eight-by-ten pole cabin in the high country some years before. One day in February, overwhelmed, Alabam was apparently left capable of only one clear thought—that home lay south. Without pausing to pick up a rifle or a pack, he simply started walking south. It chanced that his absence was discovered within a day or two and a search party went after him. His performance had been awesome. Mile after mile, the tracks bore due south. Rather than deviate from the course set by the lodestone in his head, Alabam had crossed high ridges rather than detour a mile, or less, to cross at a saddle. A half-day out, when they were within sight of icefields, a wind covered Alabam's tracks and all that is known of him is that the mountains took him, with his dream of the warm savannah country, and kept him forever. Somberly, this day, they remembered Alabam's cabin fever. Without being able to put words to it, they longed for some such release for themselves. Not the fatal kind of solution. Some other kind. Some release, some escape from what had become a terrible sameness. Such a release came with the supply truck from Williams Lake, although it was Arch, not they, who first recognized the fact.

"Turnaround is five minutes," announced the driver. "She's drifting in on Scatterass Flats. I'm lucky I got through."

"Give me the mail and go," said Arch. "And take this bunch with you. There ain't one of them can think but they all can shovel for you."

"Sure," said Henry. "We'll make sure you get through it."

"Not a bad idea," said Morton. "We might just ride on into Williams Lake with you. In case it's drifting on Sheep Creek too."

"Couldn't possibly go to the Lake now, all the work I got waiting at my place," said Larsen. "But I'm going, anyhow."

They asked Smith what he thought. He nodded, once.

Both Larsen and Smith, family men that they were, thought of their wives, left alone on the windy meadows in the houses with the iced windows and the hoarfrost caked on the nails of the doors. They left Arch elaborate explanations for him to pass along to the women, should he see them before their return. Arch listened to these stories solemnly, attentively, and swore faithfully to deliver them truly. As soon as the stage rolled down the road he dismissed them from his mind and returned his attention to literature. He was, that winter, reading his way through *Encyclopedia Americana* and, so far, had reached only "Birds of Paradise Bullfinch."

The wind had died on Scatterass Flats and the truck stormed the few drifts easily. Eastward it sped through the gathering dusk and the enveloping chill of the night. Each turn of the big wheels left Namko a little farther behind, a most satisfying experience for people who felt they knew their home country far too well.

Larsen and Morton had ridden in the cab as befitted their rank in the Namko Country hierarchy — Larsen was the best rancher in the country and Morton the worst. Smith and Henry James rode in the box beside a drum of gas with a loose cap, too scared to smoke, too cold to care.

They bunked down one night at a ranch house about mid-point in the long trail east. It was empty and cold, their unwitting host and his entire family having shifted to a cabin on a meadow ten miles distant to winter feed. They ate sparingly of his food, of which there wasn't much anyway, and left him a note of thanks. Hoping to cheer him up some, Morton added a few lines of poetry:

> I've drunk to your health on roundup
> I've drunk to your health when alone
> I've drunk to your health so damn many times
> That I've pretty near ruined my own.

The wind had drifted Becher's Prairie shut next day and they shoveled the truck out three times. By the time they came over the hill and down into Williams Lake, they needed that town a lot more than it needed them.

On the steps of the Lakeview Hotel, for the first time, they considered the question of what they were going to do and how they might do it. Researching their pockets, it turned out they had practically no money. Larsen had twenty, Smith about ten and Morton three dollars and seventy-three cents. Henry James had a pocket knife and a deck of tailor-made cigarettes, but nobody expected more of Henry.

Clearly, they could not afford both whisky and rooms. It would be necessary to get the rooms on credit.

Normally, this would present no problems. Many ranchers did all their Williams Lake business on jawbone, paying once a year when they sold their crops of beef. The Lakeview had just changed hands, however, and the new management, it was felt, might be unfamiliar with the institution of jawbone.

The new manager, who shared ownership of the Lakeview with two banks and his mother-in-law, had been instructed in jawbone, although obliquely. Ranchers are hopeless, he was told by the previous owner, but also honest and, anyway, who had built the goddamed country if it wasn't those people?

He was less than sunny when Larsen approached him. He had just undergone a trying experience with a bull cook from the Alkali Lake Ranch. The old bull cook had locked himself in room fifteen with whisky and an old dog. Neither had left the room for days. The meals, which the staff slipped through the door now and then, proved not to have been for the cook but for the dog, and the animal's digestive processes had not improved anything in room fifteen. The bull cook had been threatened with eviction and had won reprieve only by paying an extra fifteen dollars for cleaning up the room, such payment being, of course, on jawbone.

The bull cook himself had a somewhat different version of the same events. The new management at the Lakeview, he reported, had a lot to learn about customer service. He had found it necessary to summon the manager before him and warn him that unless a complete change of attitude became apparent, he might find himself obliged to take his custom elsewhere. This had smartened up the new bunch somewhat, the bull cook reported.

Where, between the two versions of the event, truth may lie is really not of much importance. It is mentioned only to demonstrate once again that doing business in the Cariboo is an art and not a science.

The manager permitted himself to be persuaded to invest in the future conduct of Ken Larsen, but not joyously. Neither was he reassured later when the room clerk told him that the four new guests had arrived without luggage.

Henry James having hired out at Larsen's for that winter, being also the youngest of the party, became the step-and-fetch-it. He was delegated to take almost all the pooled money and walk the several blocks to the Liquor Commission store.

"Go to His Majesty's Happy House and nowhere else," said Larsen. "We will be spinning out two dollars in the beer parlor."

"Don't be overcome if you pass a Salvation Army kettle," said Smith. "This is no time for philanthropy."

"No," said Larsen, "nor for giving away any money either."

Morton suggested that the decent thing would be for Henry to call at the Stage Lines office en route and invite the truck driver who had brought them to town to drop down for a drink. They could not foresee that the truck driver was already engaged with four others in the back shop, studying the combinations and permutations of straight-draw poker. It they had, they would never have entrusted the job to Henry, a merry but simple lad who, at the best of times, handled money the way a rabbit handles lettuce.

Henry called at the Stage Lines garage before visiting the liquor store and was quick to perceive a solution for all the difficulties to

which his party had so unjustly fallen heir. He sat in on the game.
He was welcomed as a jolly companion, but warned strictly in
advance that no checks or IOUs were in play. "If the last of your
money goes, you are only welcome to stand around with a sad,
sweet smile on your face, Henry," as one man expressed it.

Twenty-five minutes later Henry thrust his way into the office of
the manager of the local Royal Bank branch, a man who, until that
moment, had been innocent of any knowledge of this weedy
cowboy who would not, apparently could not, cease talking long
enough to take a good breath. In minute detail, Henry poured forth
to him the story of the most recent hand of the poker game: who
opened, who drew how many cards, who dropped out and who
raised. Rather than summon a policeman or a doctor, the manager
attempted a shock treatment. He slammed the palm of his hand flat
and hard upon his desk. At the noise, Henry stopped.

"Now," said the banker, "may I ask what all this has to do with
me?"

"I was just getting to that when you stopped me."

The manager shook his head. "Proceed," he said, "since you
will anyway."

"What has happened," said Henry, "is they pushed me out.
They bid me out of the game."

"Yes?"

"So, you see, I need you."

"You need me. I see."

"Yes. They agreed to give me twenty minutes to raise the money
to call them. We all turned our hands down on the table and they're
counting the twenty minutes."

"During which time they can, of course, turn your hand over
and look at it."

"Oh, don't get them wrong. They're perfectly honest. Mean,
dirty players, yes, but there's nothing dishonest about them."

There is, thought the banker, sometimes something new under
the sun. He was being asked to lend the Royal's money for poker
play.

In that era, banks were sterner places than most jails and the
Royal at Williams Lake was no exception. It was said that the
bank's main fear was not armed robbery but the prospect that some
citizen might want to borrow some of its money. On this day,

Henry, by some curious instinct, proved to be far in advance of his times in economic thought. Banks, he told the manager, were in the business of lending money, weren't they? Well, he was offering this bank an opportunity to do business. Even though he had no account here, or in any other bank, nevertheless he was willing to cut them in on a highly profitable deal.

"That's not bad economic theory," said the banker. "However, there are also rules about lending money. And the main rule is that we don't lend unless there is security."

"Security?"

"Yes, Mr. James. Security."

Henry gave a slight sigh. "I knew you would ask me that," he said.

The manager tapped his fingertips on the desk. A sign of impatience, an indication that the conversation, interesting as he had found it, was now just about over.

"However, that's all right," said Henry. "Security I have got."

"Oh?"

Henry reached into his shirt pocket, drew out a piece of paper, twice folded, and pushed it across the desk.

The manager unfolded it and read. On the paper was written: "FOUR QUEENS. Signed, Henry James."

The manager refolded the paper and walked to a teller's cage, Henry in close pursuit. "Give this gentleman seventy-three dollars," he said.

"What sort of paper do I make out?" asked the teller.

"Just put this one in the drawer," said the banker, handing her Henry's note.

"Is this a joke?" she asked.

"No. It happens to be the best security anybody out of Chilcotin has offered me in more than a year. Give him the money."

"I knew you'd see it my way," said Henry.

"Take it and run," said the manager, "and be back twenty minutes from now with seventy-five dollars. That's two dollars interest. I plan to use the two dollars to make a frame for your paper."

At the Lakeview beer parlor it had taken Larsen, Smith and Morton Dilloughboy less than a minute to perceive that the place was full of loggers, railwaymen and similar lesser breeds. There wasn't a man there to whom they could talk about anything in this world that mattered.

"There is a different element in this town now," said Larsen.

"Sit down, we will start with one small glass apiece," said Smith.

"Think of it," said Larsen, "you can come in here and not see a single face you know."

"It's terrible," said Morton.

"Three small," said Smith to the waitress.

"I used to be able to talk to every man I met on the street," said Morton. "Every single one. I did, too. Sometimes by the hour."

"Billy Pinchbeck was saying that ten years after he founded this town," said Smith. "The country is always changing. Why be surprised? You sound like a couple of old hens."

"Speaking of old hens," said Morton, "we are being looked over by one in the women's section right now. She makes me wonder if I've washed my face today."

They were being examined not sternly but diffidently by Daphne Fitzhugh, residence: Kitsilano, age: fifty-nine, occupation: schoolteacher, specialty: history, appearance: homely as a hedge fence. She had bought a ticket on a Cariboo bus tour and had come, eager as a spaniel, to see real cowboys, but the bus had visited towns which looked pretty much like small versions of those in the Fraser Valley.

"She looks kind of lonely to me," said Larsen.

"She looks like she feels just the way we do," said Morton. "A town full of people and nobody to talk to."

"You're right. We'll invite her over for a beer. You invite, Morton. You're the oily one."

Thus the party grew, as parties do, a body at a time. They had not suspected Daphne's greatest talent, which was to listen. She showed an interest in them which was as open as it was sincere. Nagged as they had been by the suspicion that nobody in the country gave a sweet damn about ranchers anymore, they opened up to her like morning glories to the sun. They competed with one another to tell her stories. They delighted to find that even old, old, oft told stories, stories that were mere bare-bones truth with no embroidery at all, were to her delightful. They forgot that Henry was more than half an hour late in returning and when he did they insisted that Daphne should join them upstairs. She demurred, but Morton won her over with a variation on the theme of the late Sir John A. Macdonald, that a drink without a lady was like springtime without flowers.

As they made their way upstairs they scarcely noticed that Henry was like a young setter on point. Only when they opened the door on the largest of the adjoining rooms they had rented did they realize that they stood in the presence of magnificence and that Henry, somehow, was the cause of it.

There was not a bottle of whisky, but a case, a full twelve. There were six dozen beer and four bottles of champagne. In addition to these were canned prepared ham, canned prepared chicken, tinned oyster soup, bacon, eggs, bread, butter and a new Coleman two-burner gas stove on which to cook them. Plugged into another wall outlet was an electric popcorn popper and, beside it, twenty-five pounds of popping corn. Popcorn was Henry's favorite food, but one in which, up to this moment, he had never been able to fully indulge himself. The popcorn machine was already in operation. Unlidded, it threw a great white blizzard across the floor and upon the nearest bed.

There were other items, still bagged and boxed, in this room of sudden wealth. Morton, opening one box, found a bottle of Napoleon brandy mounted on a finely wrought mahogany gun carriage with wheels that turned.

"Forty-three dollars," he read, aloud, from the label.

"He has robbed a bank," said Smith. "We will spend the next five years in jail."

"In the name of God, what happened, Henry?" said Morton, caught by the same spasm of fear.

Only Larsen, who also suspected that Henry had robbed the bank, kept his head. He was one of those fortunate mortals whose thoughts become clearer as the confusion surrounding them increases.

"I have learned never to question miracles," he said.

He unscrewed the cap of one whisky bottle, threw it to one side and held the liquor up to the ceiling light.

"Let us proceed with my favorite recipe. First, extract the contents of one bottle of whisky." He drank, and passed it to the next man.

In a very short time it seemed the most natural thing in the world that they should be sniffing brandy while wading through drifts of popcorn.

By midnight fresh troops had arrived. The driver of the stage was there, frying bacon on the camp stove next to an open window. He was urging all to lay a base, as he put it, for serious drinking. A cowboy from the Burnt Lake Ranch had joined them. Nobody knew his name or could remember it when he told them, so he was referred to as Burnt Lake. The Alkali Lake Ranch bull cook was there. So was his dog, which was reveling in a meal of canned Westphalia ham and canned peaches. The dog got sick later, but you could see that it had no regrets.

Henry had put a tin of chicken on the stove to heat, but had forgotten to punch a hole in it first to release the steam. There was a lot of chicken on the ceiling. The explosion had also cracked a window.

By the time the desk clerk made his third visit of protest, three more had attached themselves to the party. One was an official of the local Agriculture Department who was one of the few government men ever to be liked, another was a semi-professional juggler who could spin four bottles in the air at a time and the third, a man with orange hair who weighed three hundred pounds, was unknown to all. He attended, drinking and not speaking, throughout that entire spasm of Chilcotin hospitality.

In later years, the desk clerk claimed to have seen him, sitting on Larsen, who was sleeping, and eating popcorn. All other participants deny to this day that he ever existed.

Daphne Fitzhugh, who was drinking nothing but atmosphere, remained on the fringes of the gathering, but never alone. At one time or another during that evening, everybody except the orange-haired man had enquired earnestly about the strange and unnatural life of a schoolteacher in Kitsilano and had listened to what she had to say with profound attention. She had been invited to ride, to fish, to hunt agates, and to visit ranches in places distant as the moon, to attend a roundup or a stampede. With it all she was totally inebriated.

The desk clerk's first visit had been gently remonstrative and he was met with a friendly offer of hospitality. On his second visit he was firmer. Somebody told him he worried too much, a bad trait.

On the third visit, when he protested strongly, the atmosphere turned plainly hostile.

The desk clerk, too, was new to this hotel and this town. He should have known that parties of this nature can be killed only by exhaustion and that the prudent course was to remove the other guests, who were complaining, to quieter sections of the hotel. Instead, he considered calling the police. However, he checked first with the manager, who had a suite in the far corner of the building, and at one o'clock in the morning the manager pulled on a shirt, pants and shoes and went to the second floor.

All was quiet as death. He had, for the moment, the happy thought that all had left or quietly slain one another with long knives.

These thoughts cheered him as he neared the open door from which spilled yellow light and blue cigar smoke. They had long since ceased closing their door. Left open, it had ensured a continuous supply of personnel for partying.

Within a foot or two of the door he was stopped by Morton who came to him pressing a long, nicotine-stained finger to his leathery mouth.

"Don't make a sound," he whispered. "He's about to start."

"Who?" asked the manager. He, too, whispered. He didn't know why.

"Smith," said Morton. "You have to get him at just the right state or he'll never do it. You can come in," he added graciously, "but be very quiet."

Smith began just as the pair entered. Morton sat on his heels at the doorway and pressed the manager into the same position beside him. Larsen, refreshed by his nap beneath the man with the orange hair, squatted on the other side of him.

The room was a rare spectacle. The manager considered that he had never expected to see quite so odd a collection of human beings outside the British Columbia Legislature.

Smith stood on a coffee table with a bedsheet tucked under his chin. The performance was *Largo al Factotum* from *Barber of Seville*.

Two things had impressed Smith during his war service in Italy. One was the Italian women. He maintained that if the Italian women had fought the war, the Allies could never have won. The other was the Rome Opera Company. By some chance, he attended a performance of *Barber of Seville* while on a leave and had been overwhelmed. He went to every performance for a week, and when shipped back to his unit, had found a libretto from which he had memorized, word for word and gesture for gesture, the whole of *Largo al Factotum*. This he now delivered with an enthusiasm fully the equal of the original, more highly-paid performer whom he had once seen do it.

"Isn't he magnificent," breathed Morton.

The manager was awestruck. "Doesn't he *know* that he's a monotone?" he asked.

"We have never been able to find out if he knows or not," said Larsen.

"That is what is so magnificent," said Morton.

When the performance ended, to cascades of applause, the manager accepted a drink. An hour later, when the desk clerk made his fourth sally from the lobby, he was met by the manager at the door of the room. "Complaints?" said the manager. "Complaints! Tell the sons of bitches they've got a simple choice. They can come join the party or they can get the hell out of my hotel."

At four o'clock two of them carried the manager back to his suite and tucked him into bed, head first, with his feet on the pillow. An hour later somebody remembered this and suggested he might smother. That would be a hell of a thing to do to a man in his own hotel, and there was probably a law against it besides. Returning to his suite and finding him alive, they discussed his character and decided he was a genuine man. They made a stretcher of a closet door that needed new hinges anyhow and carried him back to the party room, startling a few of the early rising hotel guests as they plodded down the hallway with his body.

While the rescue party had been absent, the others had cooked twenty of the twenty-five pounds of popping corn and carpeted the hallway with the stuff. The stretcher bearers had to pause while Burnt Lake gave a snowshoeing demonstration on the popcorn, using shoes which had, until then, decorated the wall of the lobby.

The innkeeper was aroused by this event and proved to be recovered enough to drink some champagne, which made him ill again. Beer somewhat calmed his gullet.

Soon morning came, as mornings must, and the hotel and the

rest of the town was launched into another working day. Among the celebrants there were those who slept. Others, having slept earlier, were awakening, refreshed, prepared to grasp life with both hands and drink it. Daphne, who had sipped champagne judiciously and listened splendidly through all those long hours, was moved to take center stage. Being possessed of an almost encyclopedic memory, she proved able to sing every word of every verse of "Strawberry Roan," accompanied by Smith rattling two spoons on his knee and somebody else who had a mouth organ.

The significance of this performance was climactic, although she may not have known why. By local legend, the original strawberry roan was a wild horse, captured by Joe Bulmer in the Stump Lake Country near Kamloops and later sold after a Madison Square Garden rodeo for the unheard of price of $10,000. Whether this was truth or legend didn't matter. The song itself was classic. Whoever wrote it — nobody knew his name — had said in that song everything that needed to be said about a great saddle bronc, but he had stopped short of saying too much so that you lost your belief. In a world full of second-rate things, this was the exception — a single, absolutely perfect song. Not only that, the tune wasn't bad either.

As wise people do, as politicians usually fail to do, she left while she was winning, insisting that her bus left in half an hour and that neither God nor man could keep her from her schoolroom in Kitsilano the next day. When pleading failed, Morton and young Henry escorted her to her bus. In the lobby, Henry snatched the Japanese paper flowers from the vase on the clerk's desk. At the bus, Morton pinned a paper rose to her dress.

There is no joy without sorrow in this world and Daphne's was the one sad story. She left the town happy, but within a couple of days in familiar surroundings in Vancouver, she came to the conclusion that she had been included in the great winter party only because the rest of them were all drunk. Her parents and her sisters and brother had all impressed upon her, as a child, that she lacked all the graces which make a person attractive, and it was a lesson she had learned too well. She could not know that all the invitations extended to her were genuine and that months and even years later people speculated as to why she had not come to visit them, as promised, to admire their horses and their lands. They remembered her as someone who was a lady and smart besides, a truly rare combination.

By midafternoon the hotel manager had a Presbyterian hangover and was wanly tending desk in the lobby, his clerk having quit, when he was confronted once again by the Namko gang. The Stage, panting on the street outside, was about to make another run across the cold, white plains of Chilcotin. Morton slumbered in the back between two drums of stove oil, and Henry James lay across him. But Larsen and Smith, still more or less vertical and possessed of some of the powers of reason, left the front cab and came into the hotel.

With them was the government man.

In a final act of grace and contrition, these three had gone to the government offices, broken out some official papers, sneaked the government agent's seal and mailed an imposing document to Ottawa to be entered in the Canadian livestock records. They now presented the manager with his copy. To this day, he remains the only hotel manager in Canada who is also a certified Black Angus bull.

"You don't know what this means to me," he said. It was true. He was still trying to sort it out.

But for the men of Namko, there were no doubts as they rolled west toward Sheep Creek Bridge on cold snow that screeched at the touch of the big wheels. They had, said Smith, broke the back of that winter. From now into the new grass of spring they had it by the tail on the downhill drag.

# FRENCHIE'S WIFE

BEFORE FRENCHIE'S WIFE, there was Frenchie. Their story begins with him. He was there first. We know more about him. Also, ranch families have been, pretty well since Genesis was written, patriarchal, for which reason the woman was usually called Frenchie's Wife. In cattle country, Helen of Troy would have probably been known as Menelaus's Wife.

Frenchie came to the Namko Country in the thirties. There was no road then, just a trail for pack horses. He had walked, all the way. A familiar enough sight for those times, one of a generation which traveled but not for pleasure. The Prairies, the Coast, knew them in the tens and hundreds of thousands. Most of them moved only where the rails ran but now and then one such as Frenchie strayed from the cold lines of steel which carried the national message of fear and frustration.

He was a weedy little man and had a face almost all nose. There wasn't room enough left on his face for the other features. If he laughed, which he was known to do at one time or another, his eyes closed. If he opened his eyes wide, his mouth would purse. He was short. He might have been normal height if so much of him hadn't been turned up for feet. They were huge, size fourteens. He walked across Chilcotin in dress shoes which he had probably picked up at a charity depot in a prairie tank town and over them rubber buckled overshoes which, by the time he reached Namko, were worn through the soles.

Frenchie found Ken Larsen pitching firewood on a wagon. Larsen was a survivor in those days—no mean accomplishment.

Frenchie did not introduce himself. He started pitching wood on the wagon. He and Ken worked together twenty minutes, half an hour, before they took a breather and introduced themselves. Then they went back to heaping jack pine on the wagon and, as the day was leaning out, they rode back to Larsen's place behind an old horse that looked as if it had never known an act of human kindness in its life. In the house, curling his hands around the hot cup of tea which Margaret Larsen produced, Frenchie came to the point.

"I don't suppose you have work for a man," he said.

"I have work for ten men," said Larsen, "but I'm all of them."

"You must be hungry," said Margaret.

"Some," said Frenchie.

"In our house," said Larsen, "it's like the story of the old Indian chief who tells the tribe the bad news and the good news. The bad news is that there ain't enough food for the winter, and the people will have to eat moose turds. The good news is, there is plenty of moose turds."

"Such language," said his wife.

There wasn't much in the Larsen house except moosemeat, rice and turnips, but as he had said, there was plenty of moosemeat, rice and turnips. Frenchie ate until they worried he might founder himself. There wasn't much conversation.

Margaret, trying to make some, said at one point, "Where is your home, Mr. Bernard?"

"Under my hat," said Frenchie.

They did not pursue the matter. It was not polite.

That night Frenchie slept in the barn on the hay, using a spare blanket roll. The next morning he went out with Larsen again and they cut and hauled more wood. The third day they built fence.

It was the third day that Larsen said, "This can't go on, Frenchie."

"I'll go if you like."

"Your going is as bad as your staying. There is nowhere to go after here. The mountains start here."

"Then maybe we can leave things as they are."

"No. I will not use you. The truth of the matter is, I cannot pay you a dime. Not a five-cent piece. Not one five-cent piece. I cannot pay you."

"I'm not complaining."

"I am complaining. I was hungry and cold in the big crash of 'twenty-two and men took advantage of me. I swore there would never be a day when I would use another man that way."

"I ain't complaining."

"I keep telling you, it is me that is complaining. I can't take it. I won't have it."

They sat on the first log of the snake fence panel and talked in the quiet, desperate way that men did in those days, and out of it came a deal. Frenchie would have bed and board, the use of two horses, the loan of a saddle, mail-order boots, and once in the year, his pick of twelve calves. Twelve calves wasn't much. If he could have got them two hundred miles out to the Williams Lake stockyards, Frenchie might have got five dollars apiece for them. But for those times, for Larsen in his condition, it was fair and they knew it. What Larsen, or what nobody could then see, was that those calves, to Frenchie, were the sure and sound foundation for becoming a cattle baron. The dreams of youth. It's something produced in the glands of the young, pumped into the system to carry us into the middle years when we live upon what is left of the dreams.

In a year or two, times were a little better. Frenchie had the beginnings of a herd and he still had his health, which is maybe the greatest thing any man can have in any time. And he could work. That he knew. As to play, to this day, he has never quite seen the trick of it. But work he understands.

To that was added luck. It was the third year, or the fourth, that a mining promotion outfit in Vancouver found they needed a hole in which to bury some stockholders' money. It was on the West Road River. They needed somebody to run supplies to the camp on a Hudson's Bay-style riverboat, and they hired Frenchie for it. They may have remembered a Hudson's Bay saying, that a Spaniard or an Indian can pack a horse but only a Frenchman can handle a canoe. They paid him fifty cents an hour, ten hours a day, including stops for mealtimes. At the end of half a year he had a stake, almost five hundred dollars. That was enough for a mowing machine with iron wheels, a wagon, a few horses, a set of tools, some rope and land. He took up the Dancy Meadow, one hundred and eighty acres at a dollar an acre.

A dollar an acre. Not everything about those times was bad. Those were still the years when the people of British Columbia thought the Queen's land was their own land. When they wanted some of it, they got it pretty much for the price of the paperwork.

It's all very different now. Now the bureaucrats keep the Queen's land and tell us that it is far too good for the common people. They say they are holding it in trust for the next generation. The next generation, we must suppose, is obliged to hold it in trust for the generation after that one and that one has to hold it for the next. Who eventually gets to own the land we don't know. They do not trust us to handle that kind of information. It is a matter of policy, which we could not hope to understand.

Back then, it was different. In the thirties, it was thought quite proper for a private citizen to lay claim to some of his own country and to improve it, and the government went so far as to help people do it. Settlement, it was called. It was considered not only decent but even faintly honorable. We were a different kind of country in so many ways, those days.

So, almost single-handed, Frenchie began to make the old Dancy Meadow a ranch. In most of this country, that takes at least two generations, but he was determined to do it in one.

Water was his problem. It usually is. Too much or too little. He had too much. Most of the Dancy Meadow was swamp. Frenchie had a drag-behind bucket-rig, a scoop affair. He cut himself two oxen, which he yoked Lunenberg-Dutch style, by the horns. He cut channels through the swamp to drain it. It didn't work. There was too much water coming out of the springs. Did he cry? Who would listen? Frenchie abandoned the entire ditch system. He cut new ditches around the edges of that meadow to carry off the spring water before it got there. He drained the swamp. Mussolini tried to do it on the Pontine Meadows beside Rome and never made it. Little Frenchie, there in Namko, he did it.

He still had nothing, of course, except that he had an accomplishment. But accomplishments should count for something in this world.

He shot his own meat and he bought as little food as he could. Every morning a mountain of plain oatmeal mush. Sundays, they say, he would add six raisins to it.

He did not have a wife, nor much prospect of getting one. He paid court, a year or two, to a girl two valleys over but she chose a visiting bulk gas salesman. It couldn't have been too hard a choice.

There was not much joy in Frenchie.

Arch MacGregor, storekeeper and poor man's philosopher, bears testimony to that flaw in Frenchie, if flaw it be.

"Maybe life had been too hard for him. But poorer, hungrier men could laugh. To me, it is the French character.

"People talk about the gay Frenchman. Who is he, except for Maurice Chevalier? I knew the French in the Pas de Calais in the First World War. I have known them in Quebec and in the

Maritimes. They have great qualities, but gaiety is not one of them. Their quality is more that of the North American Indian. At heart, withdrawn, inwardly turned. By and large, morose. You can find gaiety in the Danes, the Dutch and even in the English. Even us in Scotland, who are probably closer to the French temperamentally than any other nation in Europe, even us, we have a laugh in us. So often, your Frenchman doesn't. He has charm, which he turns off and on with a spigot, but most of the time the spigot's turned off tight so there won't be any waste."

Arch may be prejudiced, of course. Yet it is true, as he says, that there was a bond between him, the Scot, out of the Highlands and through old Montreal and the Frenchman, out of the Bay of Biscay Country, through old Acadia and modern New Brunswick. No man, not even Ken Larsen, was closer to Frenchie than Arch.

Frenchie was a man who might never have got married but for Morton Dilloughboy. Hands idle, as usual, Morton found mischief to do with them. Morton, and two or three others. They were drinking at the time, and it was one of those ideas that liquor improves. They got a few bucks together and decided to advertise for a wife for Frenchie Bernard. They arranged for a postal box in Williams Lake and every few months they would collect some mail and pictures and then write interesting letters back to unattached females. A silly, childish sort of game. The rest soon tired of it, but Morton, who was drunker oftener, kept it up for some time.

The upshot of it came one day in the Lake when Morton, Smith and Frenchie were all there together. Morton dragged Smith off to one side. One of those goddamed women, taking them at their word, had jumped the fence and was on her way to Williams Lake. Given the delay in their pickup at the Williams Lake post box, she was damn near already there. And what were they going to do about it?

The foolish thing they did about it was admit all to Frenchie. They learned something more about him that day. Or saw something they should have observed before. He was a man of extremely rigid ideas. Women, children, men, had particular and unique places in his world, and men did not play jokes on women. He wasn't angry. He was enraged. Livid. Beside himself.

He should have whipped Morton, who was the author and main actor in the whole farce. But Frenchie had a rule about that too.

Young men did not beat up old men. So he thrashed Smith for a substitute. That seems to be one of Smith's roles in this world. After a while Smith and Frenchie wiped the blood off themselves and it was tacitly agreed that honor, somebody's honor about something, was satisfied.

Morton, of course, was like any other child who cannot believe that his willfulness has caused tragedy. He was tearful, remorseful, and frightened that perhaps, this one time, there might not be forgiveness and an erasure of all that had gone before. Casting about for something, anything that would meet the demands of a child—that clocks turn backward and that something not happen which had already happened—he offered to meet the woman, ask her forgiveness and give her a ship ticket home.

"You will shut up and get out of town," said Frenchie.

"There is an obligation for us to do something, we made the trouble," said Smith.

"And you shut up and get out of town," said Frenchie. "What was done in my name will be undone in my name. I will meet her at the station.

"One thing," he added. "How will I know her?"

They couldn't help him. She had sent a photograph, but it was back at Morton's ranch.

"Just bugger off," said Frenchie. "Don't look back. Bugger off."

Smith did get out of town, chastened and badly marked about the face. Morton, again the child, hid in the Lakeview and watched the Pacific Great platform the morning that the woman finally came. It is from him that we know what happened.

There came the PGE, only a few hours late that day. On the platform, Frenchie, a new hat, new shirt, new jeans and, because the money had run out, worn moccasins on his feet. Stiff and uncomfortable as a kid at confirmation. And the woman. Dark. Slender. Age uncertain. The PGE conductor carried her tin suitcase off the train for her.

She stood, suitcase at her feet, and looked at the dusty platform of that dusty station of that dusty little town. Frenchie walked forward, toe and heeling like an Indian in his moccasins. He took off the new hat and made a slight bow. "I am Jean Bernard," he said.

She said, "How do you do?" She did not offer her hand.

Frenchie said, "You are more lovely than your photograph could tell me."

He picked up the tin suitcase. He crooked his arm. She put her arm in his.

They walked to a borrowed old Chevy pickup, a six-banger with four cylinders firing and two going around for the ride. Three quarters of the way home he returned the truck and picked up his two saddle horses, on which they rode to the Dancy Meadow and began married life, made formal a few months later by a visiting Oblate missionary when she was in her first of several pregnancies.

There it is. Meeting. Courtship. Marriage. Just as it happened. Inexplicable. But, then, most marriages are, for one reason or another. Why do a particular man and a particular woman marry? Why do they remain married? Is it love, and, if so, what is that?

On the marriage certificate her name is given as Mary Schmidt, a name one might claim the privilege of doubting. She was from somewhere in Mitteleuropa, or perhaps it was the Balkans that could be heard in the voice. But to say that is to say nothing. What place? What family? Morton's ersatz communications had gone to Berlin. A Berliner she was not. Berliners are like New Yorkers, brittle, slightly demented, but distinctive. Berlin had been no more than what such large cities often are, a catch pond of people, fed by small streams originating in places of the purple far. Hungarian? Slovenian? Crna Gora? The official record says German, Berlin. There is no record except that official record. Some time before she boarded the PGE for Williams Lake, Frenchie's Wife had cut every thread that connected her with family or with home. Arch, who candled her mail for many years, confident that this was a right vested in him by the Post Office Act, could report that there was never a letter to her or from her outside the usual range of Namko correspondence within the province of British Columbia.

Arch was, of course, in love with her. Most men were. That is to suggest that she was a beauty. Another unanswerable question, for it asks "what is beauty?" and no man really knows.

There are many photographs of Frenchie's Wife. They are taken at stampedes, Cattlemen's meetings, at her home. In each of them, she registers as a platter of mud. The features are heavy and the skin is without glow. Who knows, Helen of Troy might have photographed in the same way. Perhaps it was not beauty, but the thing called presence. Or, possibly, the analysis of MacGregor can be accepted.

"In my short and unsuccessful career as a seducer of women, I made two findings. One was that when a woman is of a mood to yield, the first thing she does is remove her shoes. The further advance comes with the dilation of the eye pupil.

"Women have known that for thousands of years. It is the reason Italian women used belladonna to widen the eye pupils. It is why the most important part of a whore's clothing is her shoes. Frenchie's Wife had eyes which were almost all pupil. And her feet were small and delicate and she accented that by wearing moccasins.

"But what doesn't, what cannot fit is that it was all without calculation. Her eyes were that way because she was so shortsighted she could hardly hit the floor with her hat unless she wore glasses. And her feet, well, she liked moccasins.

"Yet she did not, for all I know she could not, do anything purposely to attract a man. She was not hostile to men, nor cold. But even the milder forms of flirtation were things that she had either never learned or, having learned, had found trivial and boring.

"College educated. You could hear that in the voice too — the way she could use a language that was not her own, so that it always expressed exactly what she wanted to say, yet never more. Language that was correct, always, and like the woman, graceful, always.

"Above all, the most private person I ever met in this country except perhaps for Stettler. But Stettler was different, for he had ashes and dust for a soul."

When questioned, she answered, easily it seemed, but from the answers nothing could be learned. The narrower the question the broader the answer. She had been born in a small place. As small as Namko? Well, in Europe of course small had a different meaning. Her family were professional people, but not exactly professional in the normal sense, you understand? Questioners were left to understand nothing except that she had an ability common to some wild birds which can estimate precisely their shotgun distance from a man and, so protected, can go placidly about their feeding while never being startled into sudden and awkward flight.

Did Frenchie know more of her? Who knows?

She was aided in this gentle evasion by the curious arrogance of the people in that land, since they believed that nothing of real importance ever occurred outside of the Chilcotin. Nowhere is this better shown than in the case of Morton Dilloughboy who had, in youth, captained an Arab *dhow* in the Red Sea, helped run a Ceylon tea plantation and served on a square rigger named the *Herzogen Cecilie* on the grain run to Australia. Stories about Morton were many and all were fondly and often told, but all began the day he came west across the Fraser River to the Chilcotin plateau. All other events of his life had happened back East, or as it was also called, Somewhere Else, and were thus of scant interest or importance. In time, Morton, too, came to agree with this assessment and tacitly agreed that his life had commenced on the west bank of the Fraser.

It was Morton who once obtained from her a response to a highly personal question. He had, by this time, conveniently erased from memory the fact that he was the man who made the marriage. "Mary, how come you married an old mossyhorn like Frenchie?" It was at a party. They were dancing. She laughed.

"He's younger than you, Morton."

"Frenchie was born old," said Morton.

She smiled and nodded. It was at the Stampede Hall. They were waltzing, which they both did well. "Probably," she said, "I decided when we first rode into the Dancy Meadow and I realized that Jean was so rich he owned his own sunset."

The term passed into legend. To this day, you may meet in Chilcotin a man with a hundred-dollar saddle on a twenty-dollar horse, moosehide chaps, a spur missing on one boot and two bits in his pocket. "Mister," he will say, "where I live, I personally own all the dawns and the sunsets." He won't know where the expression came from. It came from Frenchie's Wife.

Morton, talking later with Smith about that conversation, was still intrigued by it. "Maybe it was the Meadow, Smith," he said. "It was in good shape by that year and Frenchie had just hayed and the smell of the hay must have been there when they rode in. It was around sunset. Lascar Mountain would have been purple, and standing closer to the meadow than in daylight. I have rode across there, Smith, on the end of a day, you know, and there is even music in the air. Just about at the limit of human hearing, there is a sound of music.''

''It's horse bells in the jack pines,'' said Smith.

''No,'' said Morton. ''Elfin bugles, faintly blowing.''

''If bullshit was music, Morton, you would be a full regimental brass band.''

''Then what else did she see?'' said Morton.

Indeed, what else?

Long before they reached Namko, the bride must have known that scarcely anything in the letters Morton had written was true. What was in the letters is not known. Morton had the wit to burn them all. But Morton was known and he was a man who, if he could stand flat-footed on the ground and tell you the truth would instead climb a tree so he could tell you a lie.

She had to see, on that first day, the cabin. Frenchie was no more given to personal daintiness than most bachelors. He had skinned beaver on the porch all winter and the rancid fat blackened it. There were no cabinets in the kitchen. He used pack boxes, rawhide, with the hair shedding. The living room section was home to dirty socks and mounds of saddles.

When she saw this did she weep, rage, storm, laugh? Probably she made supper. We do not know. The country only knows that within a couple of months she had built her own kitchen shelves — there were never to be true cabinets — that she got the saddles into an outbuilding and the beaver grease out of the porch planks. She gentled a couple of the half-wild horses and did it well. Whether by training or instinct, she could handle horses. In that, she was at odds with Frenchie, who could not. Frenchie made his living in the saddle but, MacGregor excepted, was the worst horseman in Chilcotin. When he rode, he rode all over the horse. Smith, watching him on somebody else's sleek little Arab at a Stampede, observed, ''Things would go a lot better if either one of them had any idea of what the other wanted to do.'' But the wife could make a poor horse look good. On the good horse, the wind and sun stopped to watch her go by.

Morton, Smith and Norah watched her go by one night by moonlight. The three of them had ridden out from Smith's place in the morning, inspired by Morton to make a ride to somewhere, to anywhere, for no purpose, cultus coollee. When darkness caught them they were to their surprise halfway up Sheba Mountain at the timberline. There are two Shebas, two round mountains like a woman's breasts. The name came from the Bible, which says that the Queen of Sheba had a perfect pair. The moon was late in rising that summer night, so the darkness was heavy and thick. They decided to wait for the rise of the moon. They built a fire beside the trail. The twisted pines at timberline, old and crooked as sin, were stiff with pitch and burned in a rage. Over the snap and the snarl of the pitchpine, Norah said, "There's something moving. Maybe it's a cow moose." She had been chased by a cow with a calf not long before and it had spooked her.

One of the saddle horses, tethered to a pine nearby, whinnied. There was no answer.

Smith listened.

"A horse, I'd say."

They stepped away from that small and noisy fire and the two men, who had listened so often for important sounds faintly heard, held their mouths open so that the eardrum might register better.

"Maybe wild horses," said Norah.

"No," said Smith. "One horse."

Morton whispered. "Saddle horse. You can hear leather creak."

"And no bridle, no jingle," said Smith. "Hackamore. Probably a young horse. Singlefooting. Hear it? TaKAHta, taKAHta."

"Trotting a horse? On that trail? When it's black as the Earl of Hell's waistcoat?"

"Comin' this way," said Smith.

They watched the trail, looking across the dance of yellow flames and the gusts of a thousand red sparks which flew upward from it, as horse and rider came into that small theater of light and warmth. It was Frenchie's Wife, riding a broom-tailed buckskin mare. The saddle was one of Frenchie's antiques, an A-frame roping saddle, blackened by the sweat of man and horse over twenty years. Her long black hair, unbound this night, fell in a shower almost touching the cantle. Her eyes, in the firelight, were dark and her teeth were white as she smiled. The horse did not break stride as they went past. She raised a hand in casual salute, said "hi" and rode on. The night drew a curtain upon her and the horse. In a few minutes, the soft air of summer night soaked up the thunk of the horse's unshod feet on that trail of the meadow in the mountains. She was four, perhaps five, hours' riding from her house.

It was as casual as the encounter of acquaintances on a busy city street, but this was on the rim of the alpine meadowlands of Sheba and by night when the loom of the moon was faint against the arched horizon of the peaks. Also the encounter occurred in the society in which friendships were strained if a man who could visit for four days stayed only one. Time was one thing they all possessed in abundance and no man or woman was so poor that he could not spend some of it with a neighbor. But this was Frenchie's Wife and her manners went unnoticed. Instead each of them was impelled to a different and personal response.

Morton, oblivious to the impulses which had brought him up that mountain, said "What in hell is that woman doing on Sheba tonight?"

Smith said that he recognized the horse. It was a spoiled barrel racer who bucked when you reined her sharp left.

"I've seen the occasional gelding cured of it but I never saw a mare turned around before."

Norah, in a faint cry from the heart for what she could never be, just said "She's glamorous."

Norah always spoke well of her but, then, Norah spoke well of everyone. There was a streak of the Mormon in Norah and she abided by the tenet of that religion, that before you spoke of another person you asked yourself was it true, was it kind, was it helpful and unless you could answer yes to all three questions, you did not speak. True, she did not apply that rule to her husband, but there is a limit to what you can expect of a woman.

Among the women of Namko the more cogent opinion may have come from Margaret Larsen. Being married to the one man in the country with more than three hundred head of breeding stock had given Margaret a social position of sorts. She had not sought it. It had sought her. But there was, now, this dark and strange woman out of nowhere who, by the very act of disdaining attention, had become the focus of it. It was more than a year before Margaret was heard to pronounce upon her but when she did, it was praise such as few men or women ever know. "I have never known Frenchie's Wife to do anything or to say anything for the purpose of impressing somebody else."

Yet, whether or not she sought to impress, she did. Her judgments, when uttered, became memorable and because her words were few, they were all easily remembered. There was, for instance, the period when Chilcotin was host to a traveling evangelist of unusual talent for persuasion, one of the great captains which emerge from time to time among the many freebooter sects of Christianity with which the west coast of North America abounds. When he preached to men of communists, Satan, range rights, taxes and perverts they could not, afterward, remember exactly what he had said, but they knew they liked his saying of it. And matronly women in his audiences, beholding a man whose clear and original destiny was stud horse for a nation, were moved to strange fancies which they thought to have put behind them. Only Frenchie's Wife was out of step. Sitting among a group who were, one night, discussing that muscular Christian, she was asked for an opinion.

"Do not ask me, because I am prejudiced. I have never been able to trust a man who squats to pee."

It was outrageous, unbelievable, an atrocity, but two years later, when the newest of new churches dissolved in gross indecency charges at the Assizes, who could forget the instant judgment of that woman? Who could understand it? It verged upon witchcraft.

By pretty theory and conventional wisdom, by which the witless gain enough nourishment to make their passage through life, the woman should have vastly changed Frenchie Bernard. Much as theorists may explain, or despair, this did not happen. He had pride in her, no doubt of that, for the aura which she bore about her reflected on him. He was flattered by the attention given her by other men and sometimes jealous to a high pitch of emotion we may not measure. But to suggest that this woman, or any woman, could alter the course of Jean Bernard, yea, by so much as the breadth of one hair, was absurd beyond laughter. He was Frenchie. He remained what he had always been, the cattle king without the cattle empire. In that grand design, a woman, like a horse or tractor, had her function to fulfill. It did not include writing the checks.

One of her functions was the production of children. She had a slight bulge and a flat-footed walk carrying their first when they were married. Five months later, she was vast, awkward with the weight and appetite of the fetus, when she and Frenchie were caught, over the mountain in the Long Jim Meadow, by her labor. He had been combing the jack pine for one last lost steer and came back to their line cabin to find her grunting and waxy in the face, the sudden snow drifting on the edge of her bedroll through the unchinked walls. All the horses were gone and uncatchable. He had no more talent for horses than for women. He rigged a sled of sheet metal roofing and dragged her through the storm twelve miles to Larsen's where the child was born on the kitchen floor with Margaret for midwife.

It did much for Frenchie's reputation. All the country agreed that he was one hell of a man, dragging a toboggan with a hundred-odd pounds of deadweight all the way from the Long Jim to Larsen's place through heavy, wet snow. Frenchie and his wife proceeded to have more, two of which were stillborn. Only on the fifth occasion did she breath the ether in Williams Lake Memorial Hospital, Frenchie having, by this time, learned of hospital insurance.

Part of Frenchie's trouble was that he coveted, but not well. He wanted land, as birds want air. But as with so many men, the Great Depression gelded him. He could not understand credit. To ordinary men, as well as quite a few fools, there is honor in borrowing. It is testimony that other men are confident that you can make their money grow faster than they can. To him, credit was dishonor, debt was proof of failure. The meadows he might have bought went to other men, who used borrowed money. Frenchie used stoneboats, which he owned, while others used tractors to the joy and ease of both themselves and their bankers. Frenchie was the last to buy a good stud, a good bull, a Woolworth dress for his daughter or a good wood stove for his wife.

"My husband has his own ways," his wife would say.

"What the hell kind of man is he, leaving a wife and kids in conditions like that," said Leo Dupres. Leo, the game warden, had driven by truck to Frenchie's Meadow on meadows hardened by frosts but not yet burdened in snowdrifts. He had intended to buy a colt. By evening, he had returned to Namko Hotel, rigid with either anger or cold, and was reporting to Arch. "We sat down for lunch. Macaroni. Macaroni with about one tablespoon of grated cheese on it. I could hardly eat for lookin' at those kids. They were hungry, Arch. Plain damned hungry. There is nothing in that house, I tell you. Macaroni, some rice, some oatmeal, maybe a few cans of fish she put up last summer. How can he leave them like that?"

"He took the beef drive out to Williams Lake this year," said Arch. "Then he got the chance of a contract to freight into Likely and he's been freighting for more'n a month. He did leave them a quarter of meat hanging on the rack but we got that Indian Summer in mid-October and I guess it spoiled on her."

"He might figure that out, mightn't he, wherever he is?"

"He figures there's a profit in the freight job. And when Frenchie gets an idea, he doesn't let go of it easy. If you understand that kind of thinking, Leo."

Leo never heard the shot going past his ears. He grunted, and drank deeply of dark coffee. Or, perhaps, like many men, he could never recognize that he occasionally met himself in this world. In all of Chilcotin, only Leo Dupres was as inflexible, as uncompromising, as blindly obtuse as Frenchie. Born in the Lorraine in France, Leo had left home to join the Foreign Legion and, his father lacking the money for his train fare, had walked almost the entire length of France to the recruiting office in Marseilles, where he was turned down for flat feet.

This so enraged him that he left behind him not only France but the entire continent of Europe. Landing at Montreal, he made his way west, that he might further distance himself from his birthplace. Had he been able to swim, he might have gone on to Japan, but as it was he fetched up on the western ridges and became a game warden of fearsome probity. He was not a swift thinker. Men said of him that he began each day by counting the fingers of each hand, and if they came out to ten, this completed his intellectual exercise of the day. He then released his formidable instinct. "Twenty-three miles northwest of here, on a horse trail that hasn't been used for three months, there is a guy who has just shot a grouse out of season. I am going to go up and arrest him and take his gun away." He would then do exactly that, or perform similar miracles of detection. He always prosecuted. "I'm a warden of the game, not a warden of the people.'' There was, at one time, a movement to put a bounty on the game warden's head. However, when Dupres arrested a minister of the Crown for being one jacksnipe over legal limit and went ramrod straight to court to press the case, the country came to the realization that here was a man peculiar but also unbreakable. Lest his career be damaged by the court case, depraved poachers as all of them were, they tendered him a testimonial dinner and invited the press.

''I tell you she was barefoot. Barefoot and pregnant.''

''Pregnant quite possibly,'' said Arch. ''Not barefoot. She was in moccasins, I'll bet.''

''The same thing,'' said Leo.

''And calm, wasn't she? Unruffled. Amost placid?''

''It's bloody awful.''

''Well, don't worry. If things are that bad, we'll get some meat up there to her.''

''She's got some now.''

''You killed one of the calves?''

Leo grunted.

''A new experience for the Bernard kids. Something they have never tasted before. Their own beef.''

Leo smacked his cup on the table. ''Changed my mind. Startin' back for the Alexis Creek tonight.'' He left, not saying thank you for the coffee.

He had borrowed a saddle horse that afternoon at Frenchie's to look over colts on the range but instead of hunting horses he had hunted moose and shot one. It could be reported to the Bernards as an illegal kill and given to them. Having the time anyway, he gutted and quartered the moose. Then, thinking of the woman and perhaps one or two of the children wrestling with two hundred pound moose quarters, he had instead returned to the ranch, taken out two pack horses, loaded them and brought all the meat into the yard where he hoisted it on the meat rack behind the tool shed. He was rehearsing some kind of a lie when he realized that she had come into the yard and was standing behind him. There was a sweater across her shoulders. The cold, uncaring wind of November had thrown a swatch of her heavy dark hair across her thin face.

"You are a very considerate man, Mr. Dupres," she said.

All the high-class lying he had planned went out of his head. He wiped his bloody hands on the khaki uniform which the King had given him and spoke the only thoughts he had. "It's a hard winter, Mrs. Bernard."

She smiled. "In the spring, flowers will bloom and the grass will come green again."

He shook her hand and left, taking the broken bits of a lifetime of integrity with him.

Two months later, that all accounts of honor be squared to the uttermost farthing, Frenchie drove, wordless, into Dupres' yard at Alexis Creek and hung, behind the house, four quarters of one of his prime steers. His own family continued to live on fish and moosemeat and, just now and then, an old or injured Hereford that could not be sold. And on the table, for the bread she made, there was margarine one night and molasses another night but never, on the same night, both molasses and margarine.

Then came the day when she was gone. Gone as suddenly, as silently, as she had come. There were a couple of children by that time, but they were walking. She deposited them with Margaret Larsen. Ranch kids trade around easily. They are the most adaptable species of life in Western Canada, next to the Norway rat.

Frenchie was away at the time, driving cows to summer range. She rode down to Arch's place, turned her horse loose to find its own way home and got on the stage with a small cardboard suitcase. As ever, calm. As ever, communicating not one scintilla of thought more than she wished to him or to anybody else.

"I didn't think much of it at the time. But when Frenchie came down to the store, a few days later, and asked if I'd seen her, then I did. I did, but I didn't know what to say, so I said as little as possible and stretched the telling as long as I could. He grunted, and went away. Two weeks dragged to three, then a month and then a month and a half. Nobody dared talk to Frenchie, not even Margaret, who had the kids. Margaret did come to me.

" 'I think Frenchie needs your advice,' she said.

" 'Frenchie is a grown man,' I said. 'What kind of advice can he get from me?'

" 'He needs advice,' she said.

''She wore me down. I agreed to take a ride on the tiger. But I only went so far. Frenchie and I were alone in the store one afternoon.

'' 'Frenchie,' I said.

''He grunted.

'' 'Frenchie, if you was to want advice, would you feel you could come to me?'

''He considered this. 'Yes,' he said.

'' 'That's all I have to say,' I said. And that is all that was said that day.

''I next spoke to him when the Moccasin telegraph brought in the word that Frenchie's Wife was headed home, on the stage. He came down to the store to wait, his face like a scorpion's vulva. There was the feel of violence around him. Everything was stretched far too tight for any man to want to stand close. But there is a sort of duty on friends at a time like this. That's the way I felt, anyhow. So I took it on myself to speak a second time.

'' 'Frenchie, this is no business of mine.'

''He didn't look at me, but the set of his shoulders showed that he agreed that yes, it was no damn business of mine.

'' 'But I am gonna say something to you whether it's my business or not.'

''Again, he did not speak.

'' 'At this moment, Frenchie, that woman is free to go any place in the world. Vancouver. New York. London. But she is coming back here, to you. I ask you to think about that, Frenchie.'

''He looked at me, but he did not speak.

''When the truck came in, I made it my business to sort mail, immediately. And the few other people that were around made it their business to collect it. Silently, Frenchie and his wife rode away on two ponies.

''What passed between them nobody except themselves knows. But my suspicion is that it was nothing. My hunch is, has always been, that she had never talked about herself or her life to her husband. The day that they met on the PGE platform at Williams Lake was the first day of their calendar and before that, for her, nothing, a nullity, a nonexistence. And now, in a curious way, she repeated the process. Coming to him, who knows from where. Having been what? Having done what? All silence. She had said something to me once which seemed to confirm that, however obliquely. 'A wise man,' she said, 'knows that every day is the first day of Creation. Unfortunately, the Europeans have never learned that. It is a continent of fools'.

"If that was wisdom, I don't know why she wasn't wise enough to see that everybody does that, and few more than Frenchie Bernard.

"In his own way, Frenchie was an extremely strong family man. In his own way, I say. He treated his wife and his kids no better than his horses. But written somewhere in that hard head of his were rules about the place of a husband, a wife, their children, in family. The rules were chiseled in stone. The stone of his head. You could not change them without breaking the stone. So in this matter I suppose his head almost broke, but not his heart. The heart wouldn't matter so much. He was a head man.

"Then she left again. The kids were older the second time and the older ones could care for the younger, more or less. After a few days I took the fly rod and walked to their place to take Dolly Varden from Frenchie's creek. A silly sort of excuse, but the only excuse I had.

"I couldn't have arrived at a worse or a better time. He was throwing her stuff out the door into the yard and the children were crying. The uncalloused mind of the child perceives tension and tragedy so much faster than the adult's.

"Once or twice in my life, I have been faced with the need for instant action and not the faintest idea of what that action should be. At these times, you can only rely upon instinct. You've got to trust that your ancestors faced such crisis and that somehow the decision they made was printed in the genes that passed into your father's balls. I acted on instinct. I don't know if the instinct exists. But as I say, I acted on it. I did not say a word. Not to Frenchie. Not to the children. I just started carrying her stuff back into the cabin. He would throw out her jeans, her dress, her shoes to the dust of the yard. At the same time I was collecting a book, a frypan, a hank of yarn, walking into the house and laying them, side by side, on the kitchen counter. It was Mack Sennett comedy. Silent comedy. Badly done, amateurish, absurd comedy. But comedy. Nothing as absurd as that which was happening anywhere in this nation on that day, except maybe in Parliament.

"Finally, we both tried to get through the door at the same time. He was carrying her Singer foot treadle sewing machine and I was trying to come in with her framed Russell print, 'Trail Boss.' There wasn't room for us both to get through.

"He stepped back and waited for me.

"I stepped back and said, 'After you, m'sew Bernard.'

"He said, 'Oh, for Christ's sake,' and sat down and began to cry.

"We made coffee and began to talk. I asked the questions and Frenchie, for once in his life, let down some gates. He had always had the gates up before when people asked him personal questions. It's a family matter, he would say, and that would end all discussion.

"Was she a good wife, I asked? Yes, she was. A good mother? Yes. Didn't they laugh together? That puzzled him. Laughter, he said, what did laughter have to do with anything? Well, I passed that over and kept talking. I asked him did he ever, truly, expect anything or anybody in this world to be perfect and he said no. That was a lie, of course. He expected his own family to be perfect. But he had the grace to lie.

"That's what I mean, Frenchie. All things in this world are balances. I know. I keep a store. You add up all the credits and you add up all the debits and there is either a profit or a loss. For you, isn't it profit? Good mother. Good wife. Good worker. So what if she is shacked up with six rodeo cowboys in Williams Lake. Where is the balance?'

"The wrong thing to say. His face went the color of the inside of a mallard's wing. I had touched on the point that had been pulling the guts out of him, a yard at a time. I talked faster, giving him no time to answer, the words coming out the mouth and in the mind, my arms fanning the air, trying to grab a thought. Get yourself a detective, I told him. It wasn't the solution I would have preferred, mostly because I had the idea that maybe she was shacked up with six cowboys at the Lakeview. But you grab what you can get in a conversation like that one. We made a deal, the best that could be arranged, given the time, the place, and the kids who were crying. He hired a detective.

"That was, I suppose, the one occasion when I might have asked him, and been told, whether he himself knew who she was or where she came from. I didn't ask. That is how a man passes up the great opportunities of a lifetime. On the other hand, if I had taken the opportunity, I would have been ashamed of myself afterwards.''

It took the detective only a week to get the answer for Frenchie, which must have astonished him. Frenchie could spend that long trying to find City Hall in Vancouver.

Norah Smith picked up the kids. Frenchie picked up some money from Arch and went to Galiano Island, off Nanaimo.

She was shacked up on a little split cedar shanty which slouched on the edge of some clam flats. It leaned over the water and the waves slapped at its ankles. She was away, walking on the flats, when he got there.

''Hello, Jean,'' she said when she came back and found him with his face screwed up like a pine knot.

He did not answer.

''I'm sorry you found me. Next time I'll have to go somewhere else.''

She began to make water for coffee, her back to the dark face.

''Are you disappointed that there is no sign of a man around?'' she said. ''No cigar butts? No socks? No boots under the bed?''

''God damn,'' he said.

''I've had plenty of men in my life. After a while, one is enough.''

''God damn,'' he said.

''There'll be coffee soon.'' She stoked the wood stove. ''I can fry you a piece of fish if you like.''

''I don't want fish.''

''Then there will just be coffee.''

''God damn,'' he said. ''How can you do this to me? Make me ashamed in my own house.''

''Shame comes from within yourself. Nobody can put it on you.''

He reached for his hat, so he could have something to throw, and he threw it on the floor. ''Goddamit all, you make me a fool for the whole country to laugh at, and it's only a holiday. A goddamed holiday.''

''You may call it that, if you choose.''

''I call it that.''

''Then it is as you wish.''

"All you're doing, all you're doing is getting away from me."

"You have said it. Should I argue the point?"

He pounded his knee with his fist. "To act this way," he said.

The long silence fell and she watched him, unmoving while the rage and shame tore through him.

"Don't look for me here again," she said. "In fact, next time, don't look at all. You might never find me."

"In the name of God!"

"Here. The coffee isn't ready, but here's a drink of whisky."

He took it and looked at it.

"Am I such a bad man?"

She looked at him, dispassionately, rationally, the way she might have looked at him the first day on the PGE platform at Williams Lake. The answer was without warmth. It was clinical.

"No," she said. "As a matter of fact, you are, I suppose, a good man." She thought about this for a time and then repeated, "Yes, you are. You are a good man. What a pity that you are also a fool. If it weren't for that, you might also have been a great man."

"I cannot understand you."

"That is true."

"Am I a bad husband then?" he said.

She said, "You are as God made you, as He made me."

He drank some whisky and, going down for the third time, was so bold as to introduce the word love. It angered her, and her voice showed it in the accent she gave to the English words.

"Lawv, lawv, what is this lawv business?"

She filled a second shot glass from the whisky bottle, sat on a stool beside the old black stove and knocked it back. After that, her voice came cooler, calmer.

"Ask Henry James, ask the young people about love, Frenchie. The young, they understand everything. I am not as wise as the young. I am too old to know about love."

"What in hell are you saying?"

"I am saying that you are my husband, I am your wife, and that is enough."

"What would you say if I shot myself?"

"I would say what I say to you now. That you are a good man but unfortunately, you are also a fool. But then, I suppose most men are fools. There is no reason for me to be disappointed that you are too.''

So there he was. He had found all and he had discovered nothing. In the end, he still had only one oar in the water, one chopstick in the chow mein. He sat there silent for a minute or two, aged a couple more years, stood up and put on his hat.

''I am going now.''

''Goodbye,'' she said.

He pulled the door open, turned and looked at her. ''You will be home soon?''

''A little while,'' she said.

He started up the crooked path which wound among the arbutus trees that clustered on that rocky shore. What may have been in his mind we cannot know. There may have been some peace. His pride had been bent, but it had not been broken. But then she spoke again, standing at the limping door of the old shack.

''One thing, Jean,'' she said. ''This is a family matter.''

A family matter.

There was, after all, the deviousness, the touch of malice, in this woman that some men thought perfect. She could have released him with his pride, to explain, as he cared, that his wife holidayed, that she was here, was there, that it was all with his husbandly approval and consent. But that release she would not give him. She knew him. She knew the words that would stitch shut his mouth no matter how vast the impulse for him to cry out. A family matter.

He did tell Arch, but that was a debt to be discharged for it was Arch who had preserved the marriage, such marriage as it was. To all others, he never spoke of her absence, never explained, never apologized. Nor did his suffering cease, for she continued to run away.

She was gone once for more than a year. There were always rumors. Somebody thought they had seen her waiting table at a resort hotel in Puget Sound. She had been seen clerking in a cigar store in Edmonton. Working in the Boeing plant in Seattle.

Rumors. Whispers. Silence.

Frenchie aged and more hair grew from his ears than from the top of his head. He became almost a hunchback. People said it was because he was dragged in his rigging by a half-broke horse, but more probably it was just too much heavy lifting on a spine that was never fed enough calcium when he was a boy. He acquired much land. He remained, as ever, in the grip of his original obsession to live poor and die rich.

And the woman? The suet collected at her slender hips. The long black mane of hair became silver tipped, like a grizzly's, and lines collected at her mouth and eyes. But her charm remained, and when home, she was, as always, uncomplaining, gracious, hardworking—the perfect ranch wife. And there was never running hot water in that house.

Once, in the later years, Arch told much of the story to a visiting Oblate priest. He did it not to amuse or to instruct but to tease, because the missionary was new to the country and properly subject to such treatment. The pair of them had a bottle of Scotch on the table between them and were testing to see if the flavor at the bottom was the same as the flavor on top. They were about three-quarters through the job.

"So, Father, you can tell me. Why do any two people get married? And what is love? And is there such a thing?"

The priest was silent, so he prodded him some more.

"Of course, it's no problem for you Christians. It's God's will. Marriages are made in Heaven. God understands and He will tell us some day. I suppose that's what you will say."

"Oh no. The Church's explanation would be no good to you Arch. We are not expected to conquer invincible ignorance."

Arch complained that such was the usual evasion, designed by Jesuits to be sold by Oblates, but the priest just smiled and said, oh no, there was no evasion, none whatever. There was, he said, a good pagan explanation, suitable for men such as Arch. It just so happens that Frenchie Bernard of the Namko Country got married to Persephone.

And Arch was silent, as men so often were when they thought about Frenchie's Wife.

# SALE OF
# ONE SMALL RANCH

WHEN NORAH CAME downstairs, Smith was leaning with folded arms on the kitchen counter, looking out the window whose panes were rimmed with heavy frost. He had not set the coffee on to boil nor lit the fire.

"What are you doing, Smith?"

"Nothing."

"I can see that."

She waited for him to say more, but he didn't. She shaved three feathersticks, there being no newspaper with which to fire kindling. She lit these, crammed some split jack pine into the stove, filled the coffee kettle, and shouted upstairs to wake the boys. She brought pancake batter down from the cupboard and beat it in a pan, whittled some rashers off a slab of bacon and cut up meat for frying, sometimes working on one side of Smith and sometimes on the other at the linoleum-topped counter. He never moved. The two older boys came down, fetched wood and water and lit the oil drum heater in the living room. He ignored them, too.

"What are you doing, Smith?" she asked.

His answer, as usual, was mild." I am just looking at the mountain," he said.

"Exactly how long do you plan to spend looking at the mountain?"

"Well, it ain't much of a mountain, not really. I would say that another five to ten minutes would take care of it pretty well."

Norah and the boys had almost finished breakfast when he joined them at the table.

"She's gonna be a bad winter," said Smith.

"Can you tell that by looking at the mountain, Smith?" said Sherwood.

"No, it's a combination of a lot of things. How the leaves blow off, when the first frost bites in, fur on the horses. You can feel it. Can't you feel it?"

"No," said Sherwood, "I don't feel anything."

Smith looked at him in some surprise. Now and then he encountered evidence that not everybody in the world thought exactly as he did and it invariably surprised him. "You'll pick up the idea as you go along," he said.

"What are we gonna do today, Smith?" asked Roosevelt.

"We'll pull the shoes off all the horses we can catch. You guys run in the bunch from the horse pasture."

"Pull the shoes," said Norah. "What for?"

"Don't I usually pull the shoes off all the horses before the snow hits?"

"But what do you want to do now for? Today, I mean."

"Because it might snow tomorrow. And stop looking at me that way, the light hurts my eyes."

"You two boys get out quick and do what your father says," said Norah. She walked over to the stove and found something unnecessary and noisy to do until Sherwood and Roosevelt were gone. At the slam of the door she came back to the table, hooked her elbows into the linoleum and stared at Smith, who continued chewing his bacon, slowly. He was a slow feeder.

"I never told the boys about us selling."

"Uhuh."

"Did you?"

"Me? No. Why should I? There is no sense getting them upset; I am upset enough myself."

"Then what is all this business about taking shoes off the horses? The horses will go with the ranch, won't they?"

"Could be."

"Goddam it, Smith, why can't you ever give a straight answer to anything? It's always maybe, could be, might be. I get goddam sick of it."

"Nothing is certain in this world, Norah, except death and taxes. God and the government have decided they should be permanent. Coffee?"

She brought him more coffee.

"You said you was gonna sell, you know."

"If I get my price."

"And the price was thirty thousand."

"Well, I don't remember saying exactly the price. But if the price is good enough, we will sell her out."

"Well, you will never get more than thirty."

"No, I s'pose not. Mind you, a man could say that thirty thousand is not much to show for most of my working life. But then no doubt I am prejudiced."

"What have we got to show now, for God's sake? An old log cabin and no running water. A lot of fence around swamp meadow that nothing ever wants to get into in the first place. A bunch of cayuses that nobody in his right mind wants to buy and some beef for a falling market."

"And a discontented woman," said Smith. "Don't forget to add that." He went to the peg on the wall, took his hat, held it at arm's length above his head, placed himself under it, dropped it on his head and went out to where the wind was talking about the dreadful things it planned for the winter ahead.

Twenty minutes later, when he drew the leg of the first horse between his knees and grabbed the worn, silver-bright shoe with the tongs, Sherwood said, "You ain't gonna sell out, are you, Smith?"

"No," said Roosevelt. "He ain't gonna sell. If we was gonna sell out, we wouldn't be getting the horses ready for winter."

Smith pulled off the shoe, examined it and threw it to the ground six feet away. "That pile will be for ones too much worn to be put on again. I will make another pile to the right of ones we keep."

"And we put them on again next spring," said Roosevelt.

"No, stupid," said Sherwood. "When we get spring ice, we put ice shoes on them."

"All depends on whether there is ice," said Smith.

"Then you ain't gonna sell, are you?"

Smith said, "You boys have been listening to conversations that don't concern you."

"Sure as hell does concern me," said Sherwood.

Smith, about to start on the second foot, let the horse's leg back on the ground and looked at the boy. "You are right, Sherwood. It does concern you. I apologize about that."

He addressed them both. "I been planning to say something to you for a while," he said.

"Mum wants you to sell, but you don't want to," said Roosevelt.

"You boys should know that your mother is right about some things," said Smith. "Sometimes a woman sees what a man won't let himself see."

"Then what does she see?"

"What she sees is that this ranch is on the fiftieth parallel north latitude and thirty-five hundred feet elevation. Do you know what that means? No, I s'pose not. Well, what it means is that nobody should have started trying to make a ranch out of this country in the first place."

"We done alright," said Sherwood.

"Lots of horses," said Roosevelt.

"And beef is going up next spring," said Sherwood. "I heard a guy on the radio say it."

"I admire your style," said Smith, "but there comes a time to look at facts. The facts are, the winters are too long and my life is too short."

He looked the two boys over. "So that's the way it is," he said. He returned his attention to the horse with some sense of satisfaction. Normally, he didn't talk to his kids much, any more than his father had talked to him; but now and then, he knew, a good, long, heart-to-heart talk was a big help to a boy. He felt a certain gratification at having contributed so much of his morning to them.

"He still hasn't said he is goin' to sell out," said Roosevelt to Sherwood.

"Is my mare among the bunch?" asked Smith.

"Bringing her in is like herding a cougar," said Sherwood.

Smith gave a short laugh. "Yeah, she is difficult."

"Are you gonna sell out or not?" asked Roosevelt.

"We have talked that subject out," said Smith. His voice was sharp; they knew the tone. The matter was not raised again and they spun out the morning pulling shoes, filing hoofs and stacking usable shoes in the barn.

Norah spent the morning shining tables, counters, windows and the floor. For all the good it will do, she said. The buyer would be interested in the grass and how it grew and the water and how it flowed. The condition of the house would mean nothing to him. The living room might as well be strewn with saddles and horse buns. They were all the same, the men of this country, the dull sons of bitches. She had both barrels loaded and cocked by the time

Smith and the boys came in to dinner; to placate her he went upstairs and put on his best pants, his ten-dollar shirt and his Llama boots. The boots were the most expensive articles of personal adornment he had ever bought and were known to the household as the Bull-Buying Boots. They were too fine to work in, but he always put them on when going to a bull sale.

"Is he buying me, is he buying my clothes, or does he have some idea of buying the place?" he said to her in the bedroom.

"I'm going to get the boys clean, too," she said. "I'm going to wear a dress, too. We may be poor whites but there's no sense in giving him the advantage of seeing it. He'll talk more money the better we look."

"I rather doubt that," he said.

"Don't be so down in the mouth. We'll have money to buy a house, a real house in Prince George. And a guy that can do anything, like you ... do you know what cat operators are getting at Prince?"

"More than I am, I'm sure of that."

"Right. A lot more. You will get real money."

"And I will be working for somebody else."

"And there's the boys. They'll go to school. They'll be in hockey clubs and stuff."

"And they will grow up to work for somebody else."

"Smith, almost everybody in the country works for somebody else now."

"Just because you see a lot of guys jumping into the river, it don't mean you got to jump in, too."

"Hey. There's somebody coming in."

They stood and heard heavy steps at the doorway. "Oh, my God," she said, "and my hair isn't done."

Smith walked to the top of the stairs, steep as a ship's ladder, which connected the upstairs loft with the ground floor. "It's Larsen," he said. "Hello Ken."

"You got a hand pump, Smith?"

"I guess. You got troubles?"

"Truck stalled about half a mile past your gate. I figure I got a blockage in the gas line. Maybe I can blow it through with a pump."

"Wait a minute; I'll give you a hand."

He stepped up the ladder stairs and spoke to Norah. "I'm gonna give Ken a hand," he said. "He is no good with machinery anytime."

This was a slander they all passed upon one another in the Namko Country. Oddly enough, each man believed it when he said it and had a curious faith in his own exemption from the general rules of carelessness and neglect with trucks, tractors, diesel power plants or any other manifestation of the internal combustion engine. If Canadian law provided fines or jail terms for wanton cruelty to mechanical equipment, most men in Namko would have been hanged. They were adept at fixing equipment after it broke, but they would seldom avert breakdown by so much as regular oiling and greasing, or the checking of antifreeze. They could understand that horses, even the poorest of them, responded well to attentiveness, care, even a bit of affection, but they had never been able to transfer this thinking to machinery or, often as not, to their wives.

"Ken has no feel for equipment." Feeling that something more was expected of him, he went on, "If the buyer shows up, he can't miss us."

"Not unless he comes in the other road."

"In that case, won't take ten minutes to get us. Or he won't mind waiting. If he's come this far by a car, be must be a man with time for spending."

When he was about to leave, she came over and stood in front of him. There were shadows in her eyes.

"There's something I haven't told you . . ." she said.

"Tell me after."

"No. I am telling you now, Smith. I want you to get this through your head, all the way through it."

"What is it, Norah?"

"Maybe you don't really plan to sell this place for any price. I don't know. I can't read you. But whether you do or whether you don't, I am going to Prince George, Smith."

He looked at her a long time. Then he dropped his head and looked at the floor. He scratched his ear.

"I'll take the baby with me. As for the boys, we can figure out about them later. But by this week's end, I am gone from this place. You can sell and come or keep it and stay.''

He shook his head, twice, up and down. ''I hear you, Norah,'' he said.

''Smith,'' came Ken's voice from the kitchen. ''Just tell me where to find the pump. No need for you to come out.''

''No, I'll give ya a hand,'' said Smith. ''Might as well be doing something useless this afternoon.''

He left before Norah realized that he was in his best clothes, his only good clothes, and it occurred to her that engine oil would never come out of the Bull-Buying Boots.

After a time she relented. She took off the print dress, got into slacks, her second-best outfit, threw Smith's old clothes and boots into a gunny sack and went down the road to find the truck. She rode a Tennessee Walking Horse named The Colonel. He paced instead of trotting and although she was only average as a rider, he made her look good because of the side-to-side gait. His long legs were driving as they came down the road, the thin, cold dust rising behind them. Norah's hair, freshly curled, blew in the breeze of their passage and there was a delicate flush on her cheeks. On The Colonel, drudgery, children, husband, money, all the several woes of womankind fell away from her and she was again young, warm as the breath of spring, even lovely.

''Pretty,'' said Larsen as she came up. ''Pretty. Pretty.''

''He's showy,'' said Smith, ''but he ain't much for working cows. Won't lift his feet enough.''

Norah hit him with the bundle of clothing. ''For God's sake, get out of your good clothes,'' she shouted.

''In a minute,'' he said, throwing them to the side of the road.

Norah might have persisted but at that moment she saw Margaret Larsen in the cab of the truck. She stepped lightly off The Colonel and let his lines drop to the ground, so that he stood. She ran across to the other woman. Months sometimes passed between their meetings.

''You're all dressed up, Norah,'' said Margaret.

Norah was startled by the reminder of the larger affairs of that day, but recovered. ''We're expecting someone from town.''

"Anyone we know?"

"Prob'ly not. It's a Mr. MacKenzie."

"No. I guess not."

The matter was dropped. Selling out was like divorce; you did not discuss it with neighbors until the hard part was over.

"Come up to the house. You can't sit here. You'll catch your death."

"They say it'll be fixed in a few minutes."

"Like hell it will," said Smith. He and Larsen expressed the wish that the women would leave them to their unique and powerful sorrows and, with the usual yeaing and naying with which such simple requests are commonly surrounded, Norah and Margaret finally left, The Colonel stepping sedately behind them on the lead.

Within an hour the two women were joined at the ranch house by Morton Dilloughboy who was hunting for his horses. Since most of his horses were lost most of the time, Morton had an ever-available excuse for visiting most of his neighbors most of the time.

In late afternoon, Frenchie Bernard, accompanied by his wife, towed Larsen's truck into the Smith yard behind his own. He had come to return some borrowed wrenches and accept the loan of others.

As darkness was rushing down on the ranch from the grey hills of the west, Henry James rode in on a buckskin mare, loaded with half of a deer which he had shot the day before and the freight of loneliness earned by five unbroken weeks of riding the Ildash Meadows.

Thus did a small back-eddy of the great river of time catch up these human morsels in the great emptiness of the range country. None were surprised nor questioned the process. It was the way life flowed in that land, particularly in the winter, whose breath they now felt for the first time in that year.

Similarly, without comment or question, the women collectively prepared dinner. Frenchie's Wife made a mountain of golden-yellow potato salad. Margaret cut meat from Henry's haunch of mowitch, doing it Chilcotin style — no chops, no steaks, no roasts of any name, but chunks which would become the staple fare of the country — fried meat.

Finding her regular cooking duties relieved by two other women, Norah found time to make two dozen baking powder biscuits and two pies filled with raisin and canned peaches. From the porch she brought four quart sealers of canned, smoked trout which she had prepared the previous summer. They were a dusky rose in color, firm and well chilled.

The liquor was not in good supply. Morton, who seldom traveled without the necessities of life, had half a bottle of rye left when he reached the ranch and Ken had a mickey of rum under the seat of his truck. The Smiths had one bottle of Liquor Control Board rye, the seal of which they had planned to break when the buyer arrived. Smith, who foresaw a long night, poured it all into a large bowl and added three quarts of grape drink, mixed from powder, and the juice from the pie peaches.

On the top he floated slices of lemon. They were old and evil lemons, dark, small and hardened by months of neglect. But the brew seemed to revive their spirits and the lemon slices made a handsome garnish. The taste of the punch was dreary, but the older men spoke well of it, comparing it with the home brew they made during the Depression, the drink of youth, Peaches Wine.

The party, for such it had become, burned brighter as the cold October wind beat stronger against the little log house, the flame of it fed by the sums of all their individual loneliness. The process resembled that of the fire which had burned that summer on a corner of the Long Jim Meadow. For weeks that fire had smoldered in the peat, revealed only here and there by a thin strand of blue smoke. A sudden chill wind came down from the snow mountains one afternoon and the whole upper end of the meadow burst into a yellow flame which swept grandly, wildly, across the grass, caring not where it was taken or what was in its path.

When MacKenzie, the buyer, drove into the ranch yard, none noticed his car lights and when he knocked on the door no one answered. He stepped inside, as he should have done after the first knock anyway. He found them dancing while the dinner steamed on the old McClary range. Larsen was playing his push-button accordion which, by chance, had been in his truck; Morton blew his mouth organ and Margaret Larsen was beating time with two spoons. Smith was dancing with Frenchie's Wife and Norah with Frenchie. Frenchie had in his big feet all the grace which God had failed to put into his face and the pair spun about the crowded little room as lightly as soap bubbles. When she saw MacKenzie, Norah broke away from Frenchie and stood a moment, unable to move toward the man at the door. The color went down from her red cheeks and a crease appeared on the top of her nose. MacKenzie could not be sure if she was frightened or angry, but he knew that in that split second he had seen the face of a woman dreadfully dismayed. Damn, he said to himself, Smith wants to sell and the wife doesn't, I'm into the middle of a family fight.

"You're Mrs. Smith? I'm Aaron MacKenzie." He held out his hand. Damn, he thought, and pretty too. Worn, but pretty still. The kind who makes the family decisions.

Before he retired and became a part-time real-estate salesman, MacKenzie had been a B.C. provincial policeman and he had a reputation of being a good judge of men. He was not, however, a good judge of women; police work, during his active years, hadn't much involved women.

She poured apologies all over him. They hadn't seen his lights. They thought maybe he wasn't coming until tomorrow. Had he been knocking on the door? Was he cold? Was he tired? Smith, who had joined them, was introduced by Norah. "We're dancing away a hard winter," Smith said. "It's an old tribal custom in these parts."

The buyer was introduced as "Aaron MacKenzie from Town" and no one asked more about him. The occasional stray from Williams Lake drifted through the country from time to time. They were acceptable, sometimes interesting. The music started again. MacKenzie went back to his car and brought, as his contribution, a bottle of Glenfiddich single-malt Scotch. "Much too fine to mix with anything," said Smith, holding the pale, straw-colored fluid up to the light of the hissing gas lantern. "But," he added, "this is a communist society." He poured the Scotch into the punch bowl. MacKenzie burst into tears, but not so that it could be noticed.

"You'll be staying the night, of course," said Smith.

"Well, thanks, yes. I guess we can talk business tomorrow morning."

"Oh, I don't doubt we'll talk over our business tonight. It won't take long. I'm a very simple man. Maybe the simplest man you ever did business with."

"You want to talk right now?"

"Sure. Why not?"

"Smith," shouted Morton from across the room, "I was telling Ken . . . what was the year you and I had the Great Goose Hunt?"

" 'Forty-nine," said Smith, "God, what a shoot." He smiled at the memory, collected himself for a moment, long enough to dip MacKenzie a drink from the punch bowl and addressed the room at large about that memorable occasion. "It was right this time of year, but even colder. The country was almost seized up. There was only open water left on the Big Slough and not much of that."

"And you froze a finger," said Morton.

"Froze *two* fingers."

Morton held two arms aloft. "We never got a single bird." he cried.

"Not a one," said Smith. "They were coming down out of the north like fleets of bombers and we were right where they wanted to sit."

"Every time they came in I'd say, 'Morton, be calm. Don't get excited.' All of a sudden my gun would be empty and I couldn't remember firing a shot."

"We were too cold and stiff to swing the gun," said Morton.

"*Of course* we were. And too dumb to know it. I think myself our brains had curdled that day. You were firing that old Damascus twist . . ."

" . . . with light shot, so it wouldn't bust its gut . . ."

"That's right. Light shot." Smith turned to MacKenzie. "I asked Morton how he could expect to reach out for a goose. Morton says, 'When I pull the trigger, I give just a little push, with my shoulder.' "

"Oh God, we're into hunting stories," said Norah. She took MacKenzie's arm. "Come and eat," she said. "Those stories are never exactly the same twice, but when you've heard them fifty or so times they seem to be all the same. I have heard all fifty varieties of the Big Goose Hunt."

In line for the buffet, which had been laid out on the counter in the kitchen, MacKenzie found himself flanked by the two Smith boys. He introduced himself, but they admitted nothing except that he was probably who he claimed to be. This bothered MacKenzie, who prided himself on understanding kids almost as well as he understood men. When he dipped the ladle in the gravy bowl and found a spoon had dropped into it, he offered it up as a small joke.

"I don't know if that spoon is cooked enough." He laid it on Sherwood's plate. "What do you say? Is it tender? A spoon takes a lot of cooking."

Sherwood did not look at the spoon. He stared directly at MacKenzie. "It's cooked all you can cook a goddamed spoon," he said.

"Sherwood!" said Norah.

"That's alright; he's exactly right in what he says," said MacKenzie.

"That was rude, Sherwood."

"Rude but right, you know," said Smith. "It won't improve with any more cooking, Norah. Help yourself to them biscuits, Aaron; they're homemade, but they're good."

MacKenzie found himself surrounded by Smiths as he ate. Smith himself sat beside him on the sagging sofa while Norah ate nearby, standing, there being no chairs, stools or other places for sitting left in the living room. The two Smith boys sat nearby on the floor, cross-legged, watching him as they ate. If I make a sudden move, thought MacKenzie, one of those little buggers is going to bite my ankle.

"You'll be wanting a horse to ride around and look the place over tomorrow," Norah suggested.

"There is no place on this ranch his people ain't ridden over," said Smith shortly.

"That's right," said MacKenzie, "we know about as much about this place as you do."

"Not quite as much. If you knew as much, you wouldn't be willing to buy it."

"Don't sell yourself short. You've done a lot of work on these meadows."

"That is true," said Norah.

"Who is buying, anyhow?" said Smith.

"The name you'll see on the papers is just a holding company and doesn't mean a damn thing."

"In other words, a big outfit."

"Yes. They want it for summer range. They have the idea they can truck cattle here for summer feeding and take them out in the fall.''

''Then the house will be empty all winter?'' said Norah.

''It'll be empty all summer, too,'' said MacKenzie. ''There'll be a couple of cowboys under canvas on the range. That's all.''

''You mean, there won't be anybody living in this place?''

''They've got no use for the house. They'd pay you as much if it wasn't here. It's the grass they want. I suppose they might use it for an equipment shed.''

''A toolshed!''

MacKenzie saw in her face the same wan terror that had showed, briefly, when he first came to the ranch-house door.

Smart man, MacKenzie, he told himself. To this woman and the kids, you're a son of a bitch who's coming to throw them out, and you help it all along by telling her the house is only good for a toolshed.

''Not that it matters,'' Norah said. ''It's just, gosh, I think of the work that went into varnishing these logs.''

''It's a shame, Mrs. Smith,'' said MacKenzie. ''This is a handsome little place. But it's a small rancher's house and the small rancher is going out in this country. We might as well all be honest about this. Only the big outfits can make a go of it at today's beef prices.''

''That is absolutely true,'' said Smith.

''And it's better that way, really,'' said MacKenzie. ''The little man is going to earn a far better living at something else.''

''Earn a lot more money,'' said Smith. ''There is not a doubt in God's green world about that.''

''So I'm told to bid twenty thousand,'' said MacKenzie.

''Smith,'' called Morton from across the room, ''I'm right, ain't I? It was Jerome and Thaddeus Eriksen who homesteaded on Big Creek.''

''Jerome and Thaddeus? No, that was the names of the brothers that started the Gang Ranch.''

''Mind you, twenty thousand is our starting figure,'' said MacKenzie.

"Jerome and Thaddeus Harper," said Smith, "they must have been big men. Drove cattle all the way from the Gang to Ogden, Utah, one time. Fifteen hundred miles. A fifteen-hundred mile drive." He turned back to MacKenzie. "Excuse me, you were saying something?"

"I said twenty-five," said MacKenzie.

"What about Norman Lee's drive from the Chilcotin to the Klondike?" said Larsen.

"He never got them to the Klondike," said Smith. "They had to butcher them on Lake Bennett and try floating the meat down on rafts."

MacKenzie smiled and kept eating. He had seen these men do business before.

Early in his acquaintance with them he had attended a sheriff's auction and joined a knot of ranchers who were surrounding two cases of beer with conversation. They drank it all and told wonderful stories and the last cow in the auction had been sold before he realized that his companions had been bidding and buying at the same time they were drinking and telling stories. Their ways were their own, private and personal possessions which he had no license to disturb. He sat back and watched the many conversations run. The ghosts of old ranchers whose bones were now mixing with the pale, yellow earth of these hills were brought into the room and vastly admired. There were stories about old practical jokes, about rank horses and cold winter camps. Smith's favorite saddle horse was compared with a camel, unfavorably, but all insults appeared to translate into praise within the mind of Smith. They played penny stook, they danced some more. The boys were herded to their tiny upstairs bedroom, stacked together in one narrow cot so that the other bed should be left for MacKenzie. When MacKenzie himself made his slow passage to the bedroom, Morton, who had been most often to the well, was asleep on the sofa, but all the others remained in full cry; Norah was making yet more coffee and Frenchie and Larsen were shouting at one another in an argument about the merits of the McClellan cavalry saddle.

MacKenzie had, as far as he knew, done no business. But then you could never be sure. There was the problem of the woman.

Always the woman, irrational, illogical and, for all their winsome ways, inflexible in purpose.

It was, as it turned out, a woman who interrupted the negotiations next morning, but she was not human but horse: Smith's old mare. The mare had immense stamina, but not much else. She was an ugly animal with a matching temperament. Smith's pride in her was, typically, perverse. "She has never let me lose my respect for her," he would tell people. "Even after fourteen years together, I cannot approach her without whistling or talking first or she will nail me with her feet or her teeth."

She was not in evidence when MacKenzie came downstairs for breakfast in the middle of a grey and shabby morning. Nothing much moved outside the cabin. It had rained during the night, freezing as it fell. All the land was sheathed in pewter. Larsen's truck was in the yard. "Leave her lay where fate has flang her," he had said, while he and his wife rode home with the Bernards. Young Henry James was beside the drum stove, preparing reluctantly for a slow and hard ride back to the Ildash.

Old Morton had a hangover and said his hair ached. Norah had taken pity on him and poured him a shot of brandy from the medicine chest stock; this revived him sufficiently to take coffee, provided it was uncontaminated with cream or sugar. The boys had been herded to a corner of the living room with their correspondence school textbooks. The baby slept in his crib. Smith was looking at his mountain. Norah was busy.

When the men sat for breakfast, Morton went outside, revolted by the smell of food. He would saddle up, he said; when the ice softened he would pick his own way home.

Henry brought forth grizzly bears, the previous year's stampede and next year's stampede as openers for the kind of long, pointless and thoroughly enjoyable conversations which had filled all the previous night. But there were no takers for conversational games and Henry faded to silence. Then Smith casually picked up the thread of old conversation.

"You said twenty-five," he said to MacKenzie.

"Actually, there was something I wanted to say," said Norah.

"You?" said Smith.

"It's kinda dumb, maybe . . . Mr. MacKenzie, you said they wouldn't be using this house?"

"No, they don't care about the house."

"Then do you s'pose they'd mind if, before we moved away, we burned the old place down?"

"There is a woman for you," said Smith. "Always complicate the simple. That way, nobody can ever be sure exactly what is going on."

"I would have to ask them, Mrs. Smith."

"Let's talk in numbers," said Smith.

Every figure at the table was stiff. MacKenzie, for the moment, considered that each of them were encased in the ice of the storm. He also had the sensation of smothering.

Henry James, who couldn't have been more embarrassed if found in a strange bedroom, walked stiffly into the kitchen section to pour coffee for himself and remained there by the window, looking at the mountain and humming loudly and without tune.

"How does twenty-eight sound," said MacKenzie.

"I can hear it plain," said Smith.

"We figured on thirty," said Norah.

Smith said, "There isn't much difference, really, between twenty-eight and thirty."

"Then if there isn't much difference, they can pay the extra two," said Norah.

Smith spoke sharply. "Am I talking, or are you?"

"Last and final, thirty," said MacKenzie.

"Smith," said Norah.

"Smith," said Morton, standing at the open door, "give me your gun."

"No hangover is that bad, Morton; I know. I have had some bad ones, but it is not that bad."

"Shut up," said Norah. "He isn't joking. Look at his face."

"I'm sorry, Smith," said Morton, "your mare has had it. There isn't any easy way to tell you that."

"Had it how?"

"The ice, I s'pose. Foreleg snapped right through."

"I will take a look at her."

"There is nothing to look at that you want to see, Smith. The bone is out through the skin. She's down by the gate."

"Well," said Smith. "Well, well, well, well, well." He walked across to the gun rack and pulled down the 30-30. "In this country it's like the nightly screw. Everything comes at once."

"I'll take the gun," said Morton, holding out his hand.

Smith ignored him. "Hell of a thing, she had to go with all that pain. I would think God could arrange things better if He would only put his mind to it."

"Give me the gun," said Morton. "You don't want to see her this way."

Smith placed his hand on Morton's chest and gently pushed him away. "I have always shot my own horses," he said.

"Let him go, Morton," said Norah.

"He was always proud of that," she told MacKenzie after Smith walked out. "Everybody usually has to shoot an old horse or two just before winter, the ones that aren't gonna make it. A lot of the ranchers would trade the job so's they shot each other's and not their own, but Smith always done it himself. I think he figures it's a sort of self-discipline."

"I don't think that mare fell at the gate," said Morton. "I think she got to the gate somehow on three legs. I never heard of a horse doing that, but I think it happened."

"Your coffee is cold, Mr. MacKenzie," said Norah. She brought the pot to the table.

After they heard the shot she excused herself and went out into the yard, a heavy sweater flung over her shoulders. He came across the yard with his eyes on the ice. She stood and waited for him. He did not look at her until he was beside her.

"Smith," she said, "there's something I want you to know. I know how you felt about that mare, and I'm sorry she's gone."

"It probably doesn't matter much really," he said. "I was gonna shoot her when we left the place. There was nobody would have taken her; there wasn't another man in the country would have put up with her biting. And I wasn't going to see her neglected or abused."

He took a step toward the house. She stopped him with a hand on his arm.

"Smith, what I really wanted to say . . . I ain't found life too bad on this place . . ."

He looked at her with half a smile. "When you growl and snap at me, I don't mind, not really. But when you wag your tail, you make me nervous.'' He slapped her behind, lightly, and walked into the house. There were tears in her eyes as she followed him.

''I'm sorry if you've lost a great horse,'' said MacKenzie. ''They don't come our way very often.''

''No. Fact is, she was not a great horse. I got along with her. But she was not great. Not great in any way.'' He poured coffee and, standing, sipped at it. ''You know, Mac, if you wanted a reason to pull out of this country, you had it seeing that old mare.

''Born to a hard life, lived a hard life, died hard. Never praised. Never thanked. And hardly noticed when she went by anybody except me.

''I was thinking that when I stood over her with the gun. And a funny thing happened. You know what happened, Mac?''

MacKenzie did not interrupt.

''I was just bringing the gun down on her and she looked me straight in the eye. As straight as she could look, that is. She was walleyed, you know. 'Smith,' she says to me, 'Smith, goddam it all, don't sell.' ''

''And you are going to take her advice?''

''She was older than me, as horses' ages go. Years count.''

''I can't tell if you are fooling or not,'' said MacKenzie.

''I couldn't tell with her either.'' said Smith. ''She was a deep one in some ways.''

''I'll go back to them and see if they'll go to thirty-five,'' said MacKenzie.

Smith waved an arm in dismissal. He did not bother to answer.

''I can tell when a man's mind is made up,'' said MacKenzie. ''When this coffee is done, I'm on my way. Since we can't shake on a deal, let's shake anyway.'' He shook Smith's hand, and then Norah's. To her he said, ''I tell you this sincerely, Mrs. Smith. I hope you winter well. I wish you both the best of luck.''

''We'll winter alright,'' she said.

But Smith, at the counter, looking again at his mountain, was somber when he spoke. For the first time in their marriage, his wife could hear all the years of Smith's life in his voice. ''We are gonna need all the luck there is to winter this year,'' he said. ''She is gonna be a bad one. You can feel it, comin' at you.''